ALSO BY REGINA BLACK

The Art of Scandal

A novel

REGINA BLACK

GRAND CENTRAL

New York   Boston

This book is a work of fiction. Names, characters, places, and incidents are the product of the author's imagination or are used fictitiously. Any resemblance to actual events, locales, or persons, living or dead, is coincidental.

Copyright © 2025 by Regina Black

Cover design by Lila Selle
Cover images by Shutterstock
Cover copyright © 2025 by Hachette Book Group, Inc.

Hachette Book Group supports the right to free expression and the value of copyright. The purpose of copyright is to encourage writers and artists to produce the creative works that enrich our culture.

The scanning, uploading, and distribution of this book without permission is a theft of the author's intellectual property. If you would like permission to use material from the book (other than for review purposes), please contact permissions@hbgusa.com. Thank you for your support of the author's rights.

Grand Central Publishing
Hachette Book Group
1290 Avenue of the Americas, New York, NY 10104
grandcentralpublishing.com
@grandcentralpub

First Edition: July 2025

Grand Central Publishing is a division of Hachette Book Group, Inc. The Grand Central Publishing name and logo is a registered trademark of Hachette Book Group, Inc.

The publisher is not responsible for websites (or their content) that are not owned by the publisher.

The Hachette Speakers Bureau provides a wide range of authors for speaking events. To find out more, go to hachettespeakersbureau.com or email HachetteSpeakers@hbgusa.com.

Grand Central Publishing books may be purchased in bulk for business, educational, or promotional use. For information, please contact your local bookseller or the Hachette Book Group Special Markets Department at special.markets@hbgusa.com.

Print book interior design by Marie Mundaca

Library of Congress Cataloging-in-Publication Data

Names: Black, Regina, author.
Title: August Lane : a novel / Regina Black.
Description: First edition | New York : Grand Central Publishing, 2025.
Identifiers: LCCN 2025003303 | ISBN 9781538767528 (hardcover) | ISBN 9781538767542 (ebook)
Subjects: LCGFT: Romance fiction. | Novels.
Classification: LCC PS3602.L3252413 A96 2025 | DDC 813/.6—dc23/eng/20250220
LC record available at https://lccn.loc.gov/2025003303

ISBN: 9781538767528 (hardcover), 9781538767542 (ebook)

Printed in the United States of America

LSC-C

Printing 1, 2025

For James

AUTHOR'S NOTE

This book contains discussions of domestic abuse, addiction, mental illness, a past (off-page) sexual assault, reproductive rights, grief, and dementia. A complete content list can be found at reginablack.com.

PART ONE
THE INTRO

This Is Our Country: Podcast Transcript

Episode 12—"Jojo Lane"
August 21, 2024
Host: Emma Fisher, Senior Writer,
The Breakdown Magazine

[*Theme music*]

Emma: Welcome to *This Is Our Country*, a country music podcast for *all* of us. I'm your host, Emma Fisher, and when I say *all*, I mean *all*, regardless of who you are, who you love, or what town you grew up in. If you love country, you belong here. Today, I'm thrilled and a little nervous to introduce my guest for this special, supersize episode. I've been a huge Jojo Lane fan all my life—

Jojo: [*laughter*] How old are you? Wait, never mind. I don't want to know.

Emma: [*laughs*] Sorry, sorry, but it's true. I listened to "Broken Dreams" on repeat when my ex-boyfriend dumped me.

Jojo: You and everyone else. There's a meme floating around about people breaking up to that song. It's about my first hairdresser, though.

Emma: Is it really?

Jojo: That's your first exclusive. "Broken Dreams" is about me mourning the best roller set I ever had. Jamal hated being on the road. Those backwater dive bars made him nervous.

Emma: Okay, wow. Thank you for the exclusive. [*laughter*] See, this is why I'm nervous. You don't do many interviews, do you?

Jojo: No, I stopped talking about myself a long time ago. Twenty-five years and twelve albums into it, people still ask me the same questions. What's it like being a Black country

Emma: singer? Tell us about the Delta Teen Pageant and losing your crown. That was thirty years ago! Plus, it's all online. They can look it up.

Emma: So, you don't want to talk about those things today?

Jojo: No, I will. It's just that those questions don't feel genuine. That's the sum of me to some people: country music's Black fallen beauty queen. It's never a conversation. But after everything that's happened, I figured it's time I had one.

Emma: Well, I'm honored that you chose this show to do that. Out of curiosity, what's your least favorite question, one you wish people would stop asking in interviews?

Jojo: You may not want to know.

Emma: Why not?

Jojo: Because you've asked it before. I've listened to you interview other Black country singers, and you do it every time.

Emma: Okay, well then, yes, I'd *really* like to know.

Jojo: You're embarrassed already. Your face is red.

Emma: [*laughs*] It's okay, it's okay. It's good medicine, isn't it? I'll never get the stories right if I keep asking the wrong questions.

Jojo: True. That is true. Okay, well, I hate when people ask me why I picked country.

Emma: You're right, I do ask that.

Jojo: Uh-huh. Well, how 'bout I ask you the same thing? You're a British girl who's what? Twenty-four? Twenty-five?

Emma: Twenty-seven.

Jojo: Why do a podcast about country music? Why not soul or R&B or blues? Those are just as good. Some would say better.

Emma: I love country music. I grew up listening to it. My dad was a huge fan of Hank Williams and Johnny Cash. It's my childhood soundtrack.

Jojo: See, I hear that in your voice. The passion.

Emma: Yes. Gosh, you have to be passionate, don't you? To make it your whole career?

Jojo: That's right. So, tell me something. Why is it when someone who looks like me is sitting across from you, that's not the immediate answer? They must have chosen it because they love it.

Emma: It's a bit more complicated, isn't it?

Jojo: Not at all. My mama loved Dolly and Reba. It's my childhood soundtrack, too.

Emma: Okay, well. I don't want to push back too much because this is your experience we're talking about today. But country music has a massive problem with race.

Jojo: But like you said, this is about my experience, right? My choices. I chose it for the same reason anyone chooses anything: out of love.

Emma: Right. I think I understand. When I ask that question, it's a form of othering, isn't it? Like, the goal of this podcast is to normalize diversity in country music, prove it's always been more than conservative white men, but I'm treating you like something different.

Jojo: Oh, I am different. Ain't nobody out here doing what I'm doing, that's for damn sure.

Emma: [*laughs*] Noted, yes. Absolutely.

Jojo: I don't know about othering. But it's a wasted question. The answer's sitting right there in my work. All you have to do is listen.

CHAPTER ONE

2023

The last guitar chord hung in the frigid air that pumped relentlessly from the air vents of the Memphis Best Value Bar and Lounge, while the customers stared blankly at Luke Randall like they were still waiting for things to get interesting. Someone cleared their throat, and the sound startled them out of a trance. Their applause was slow and drenched in pity. But, hell, he'd take it. These days, he'd take anything that wasn't ambivalence.

Luke leaned forward and drawled "Thank you" in a deep, smoky tone he'd been told gave his voice more swagger. "That was 'I Fall to Pieces' by *the* Patsy Cline, one of my favorites." He flashed a smile. "Not a big fan of sad songs before dinner, huh? I don't blame you. But that's country for you, right? Everybody's leaving. No one's gettin' laid."

Someone snorted and chuckled. Even when the music was shit, he could still work a crowd. "Always wondered about that song," he said. "Like, there's got to be a story there. There's always a story." He ran his hand along the guitar frets. "Maybe they were married. Whoever Patsy was singing about, I mean. Feels like the bad side of a divorce—"

"Just play the fucking song!"

The heckler slurred the words from the back. The audience re-animated as if the guy had tossed raw meat into a herd of zombies. Someone shouted in agreement, and they started clapping, for real this time, staring up at him with feral eyes. "Do it," their glares told him. "I paid five bucks to hear the one song that makes you worth a shit, and if you don't play it in the next five seconds, no one will ever find the body."

Luke didn't acknowledge the man, who'd yanked off his John Deere cap and started pumping his arms like they were at a football game.

Arguing was pointless. As the lone Black man in a sea of drunken white faces, it was also potentially dangerous. Instead, he retreated into himself, as he usually did when this happened. And it always happened. Like clockwork, every Thursday around eight, before the kitchen started serving entrées and the bar started watering down the whiskey, someone's patience would snap, and the vitriol would spread like a virus.

Luke took a long drink of water, leaned into the mic, and sang the first lines of the song he hated with every fiber of his being. *"I'm frozen in place / My heart's gone numb / But you keep breaking the part that still feels something."*

He locked eyes with a cute Black woman with waist-length Sisterlocks in the front row. She was perched on the edge of her chair, fully aware of the figure she struck in a hostile room filled with camo and denim. She smiled without murder in her eyes, and he smiled back out of habit. That's how he usually got through this. Focusing on a friendly face who got a kick out of being serenaded made the hardest parts go down easier. Because every song did have a story.

This one haunted him like a ghost.

Even now, thirteen years after "Another Love Song" hit the top of the country charts, Luke couldn't play the first chords without fumbling. His fingers wanted to strum the original arrangement, a blues ballad the people in this room would barely recognize. But no one really likes sad music. That had been drilled into him on the soundstage of *Country Star*. At seventeen, he'd been coached through the reality show that started his career by a fast-talking, sloe-eyed man who claimed to have discovered every mid-list country singer on the verge of hitting big. Luke couldn't remember his name anymore, but he'd never forget the thick line of gold rings that squeezed the man's knuckles as if they had been purchased during younger, leaner times. Luke had watched them as the guy fingerstyled a faster, twangier version of "Another Love Song" he claimed would impress the judges instead of sedating them. "Or make 'em cry, which they'll pretend to like but never forgive you for. No one wants a snotty nose on national television."

Golden Rings was right. When Luke had sung the song that wasn't his song, the crowd screamed and hollered, like he'd been changed into someone else, too. Instead of a clueless country boy fresh off a Greyhound, he became a charming bro who understood what they were here for—good times, cheap beer, and southern nostalgia. The song had propelled him to the semifinals and a few months later, his first record deal. But deep down, he'd always figured he'd change back to that guy from the bus. That one lie was okay if whatever came next was true.

But big lies don't work that way. Not when millions of people fall for it. Hand yourself to the world wrapped in a shiny, whitewashed package, and it's the only way they'll ever accept you. They wanted Luke, the pop star who made you want to grab your girl and dance, not Lucas, the crooner who made you want to burrow with her under the covers and trace her skin until it didn't feel like skin anymore.

The friendly woman's smile pulled Luke back to the present as he slid into the bridge. He almost winked but stopped himself. She'd get the wrong idea, which was the last thing he needed. She wasn't flirting with him. She was making eyes at some poster she used to have on her wall.

His voice went up an octave too high on a key change because it was a hopeful chorus he could never quite sell. *"But if I wrote a different love song / took your hand in mine / threw out all the lines."* He belted out the rest so they wouldn't notice how much the song messed with his head. Just once, he'd like to get through it without thinking about her.

Just once.

The room exploded with applause before he finished. He nodded thanks and told them he was taking a break. Most would be gone when he returned for a round of Tim McGraw covers. They had gotten what they came for—a dose of late 2000s nostalgia and a 25 percent discount coupon for the buffet next door.

The woman from the audience headed his way, so he pivoted toward the bar. A middle-aged white man with dark hair cut him off before he could reach it.

"Buy you a drink?" The man didn't smile, but there was no hostility there, either. It hadn't been Luke's best performance. Some people took that personally. The man tapped the drink menu. "What's your poison?"

All of it. "I can get my own. Thanks." Luke crooked his finger toward the bartender, who nodded and pulled out a bottle of tonic water with his name scrawled across the label.

"How the hell did you manage that? Boylan Heritage?" The man leaned against the counter. "I thought this place only mixed with Canada Dry."

Looking more closely, Luke noted that the man didn't fit the room at all. His black oxfords gleamed with a shine you could only get from an airport terminal. His hair was freshly cut. His aftershave smelled like wood sap drizzled over money.

"David Henry," the man said, extending his hand.

"Luke Randall." They shook, and Luke added, "Most people call me Lucas."

David squinted. "Do they really?"

"Nope." Luke grabbed his tonic water and took a swig. "But whenever I meet someone new, I figure it's worth a shot."

The corner of David's mouth lifted slightly. The guy had a resting no-bullshit face. It was probably as close to a smile as he would get.

"Dodging nicknames is a waste of time around here. I flew in last week." He stuffed a twenty in the tip jar. "Never been called Dave a day in my life but watch this." He caught the bartender's eye. "Another."

The bartender nodded. "Sure thing, Dave."

David rolled his eyes, grabbed a table, and indicated that Luke should join him. Luke hesitated. He tried to avoid the bar when he wasn't onstage. But this guy had a business edge that reminded Luke of industry types from LA. He was probably recruiting for some D-list reality series starring former pop stars willing to trade their dignity for clout and views. Listening to the pitch would be more interesting than watching HGTV in the dank closet the bar called a dressing room, so Luke went to the table.

David picked up the tonic water as soon as Luke sat down. "How long have you been sober?"

"Five years." Luke was too startled by the question to lie. Was it that obvious he was in recovery? He'd had nightmares about his old benders being seared to his body like a brand.

"Impressive." David returned the drink to Luke and scanned the room. "Not the best workplace for you, though."

Luke drummed his fingers on the table. Five years may sound like a long time to most people, but Luke measured his sobriety in hours. He could identify every cocktail in close proximity by color and smell. "Not the best place" was putting it mildly. But there weren't a lot of dry music venues clamoring to put him on the schedule.

"I'm sorry, who are you?" Luke asked, because there was no way in hell he was going to discuss the weekly mind fuck of being a sober drunk in a bar with a stranger.

"David Henry," he repeated, as if the words were a business card. "You've never heard of me?"

"No."

David looked annoyed. He jabbed a finger at the empty stage. "How many times have you performed that song?"

Luke had been eighteen when "Another Love Song" was released as a single. Between opening for bigger acts, performing at award shows, and recording gimmicky remixes, he'd probably sung it a million times. "Not sure," he answered, then grabbed a napkin from a holder. He made a triple fold, the way his mother had taught him back when she had it together enough to care about that sort of thing. "Every time I sing, it feels like the first."

"Bullshit. You were struggling up there."

Luke tossed the napkin on the table. "Sorry you were disappointed."

"Me?" A deep, bully chuckle burst from David's chest. "Oh, I'm not a fan. My buddies and I used to make fun of that song when it was popular. Sweet'N Low country is what we used to call it. For people who don't really like the music."

Luke glanced over his shoulder at the clock. The conversation was getting meaner, and the smell of David's martini was bothering him. "To each his own," he mumbled, instead of telling the guy to fuck off, that the song hadn't been like that when it was written, and *let's see you get your heart ripped out onstage every night.* "It's getting late—"

"Like I said, I'm not a fan." David drained his drink and shoved the glass to one side, far away from Luke. "I'm a manager. For Jojo Lane."

Luke didn't believe him at first. Jojo Lane's manager randomly showing up at a Memphis bar sounded like the sort of delusional scenario he used to conjure up when he still had the hope of being rescued from career purgatory. But nothing on David's face revealed anything but impatience. He was waiting for Luke to acknowledge his status as music royalty. The way Jojo's career was skyrocketing these days, he'd probably earned it.

Luke had been five years old when Jojo Lane released her first record, a six-song EP of acoustic country covers. He got the album for his seventh birthday and had it on repeat for weeks. His life was a cage back then. Jojo escaping Arcadia to follow her dream felt like a message she'd bottled up and sent directly to him. It said keep playing that old guitar. Keep dreaming, even on the days it feels like this might kill you.

Everyone in his hometown knew Jojo's story. She was a former beauty queen, the first Black Miss Arkansas Delta Teen in the region's history. In 1994, a sixteen-year-old Jojo made national headlines for being a sign of racial progress in the Deep South. People started calling her "little Lencola," after the first Black Miss Arkansas. But then word got out that Jojo had a one-year-old daughter. While not technically against the rules, the scandal was enough to force her to relinquish her crown.

But she didn't disappear for long. At nineteen, she moved to Nashville to pursue a music career. The novelty of her race, paired with the local beauty queen scandal, gave her album more traction than it would have gotten otherwise. One journalist called her an "obstinate rebel, determined to make room in industries that are clearly hostile to her presence."

Jojo recorded more albums, earning her a small, devoted fan base but no radio play. Her music was mainstream enough to be dismissed as pop and, sometimes, mislabeled as R&B. But last year, Charlotte Turner covered Jojo's song "Invisible" on her album. A scathing op-ed about the optics of a white millennial superstar singing a song about being a Black woman who had been overlooked by Nashville sparked enough controversy to make Jojo's original version go viral.

Suddenly she was everywhere. At the CMAs. The Grammys. Jojo was officially dubbed a Black country pioneer. Her new single, "Rewrite the Story," had spent the last two months in the top five on the Hot Country Songs chart.

"You really work for Jojo?"

David nodded. "For over twenty years now." He gave Luke an assessing look. "You're from the same hometown, right? Went to school with her daughter?"

"Yeah. Au— S-She and I were...friends." He flattened the end of the sentence, hoping David wouldn't notice how badly he fumbled it. "Does Jojo have a show nearby?" he asked, eager to change the subject. "Is that why you're here?"

"No, she's in the studio. Working on the new album." David reclined in his unreclinable chair and propped his ankle on one knee. This was a guy who'd never had an awkward conversation in his life. Which meant he was either brilliant or a psychopath. "It's been a while since you've been home, hasn't it? To Arcadia?"

Luke ran a hand over his hair and tried to focus through the fog that had settled over his thoughts. That's what happened whenever someone brought up his hometown. His brain would try to protect him from the shit he used to drown in gin. "Yeah," Luke said. "There's not much to the place, is there?"

"That's true. It's definitely existential crisis country. Jojo hates going back but feels obligated because of family. You've got family there, too, right? Friends?"

The last time Luke spoke to his mother, she'd been so high that it took her half an hour to realize that it wasn't his little brother on the phone. "We're more of a Facebook only family."

"You don't have a Facebook. Or Instagram. Or fans with Facebooks or Instagrams."

"You stalking me?" Luke scanned the room. The crowd was thinning, and the manager was giving him impatient looks. He still owed another set. "Look, tell Jojo I said congratulations on her success. Glad they're finally giving her the attention she deserves."

Luke pushed back his chair and stood. David cocked a brow and said, "Sit," in the low octave people usually reserved for kids and animals.

"No," Luke said, matching his tone. "You've got five seconds to say something to change my mind."

There was a familiar shift in David's demeanor. It happened when someone stopped seeing the kid on those old album covers and realized there was a tattooed, six-foot-two former football player standing in front of them. Not fear. Just a heightened awareness.

"I'm not stalking you. I'm vetting you. Making sure you're not a tabloid nightmare before I offer to change your life."

Luke didn't sit down right away even though hope surged through him hard and fast. He couldn't do that. He couldn't hitch his dead dreams to Jojo's big moment because odds were this conversation wasn't what it looked like. Last week, he'd watched a newscast where the Tennessee lottery announcer read winning ticket numbers next to a cage of Ping-Pong balls. The first few matched Luke's birthday, and even though he hadn't bought a ticket, his heart skipped a few beats anyway. Now, it did that same pointless jig. Jojo's manager offering to work with him was a long shot in a game he'd stopped playing.

Luke folded his arms and schooled his face into unreadable stone. "I'm listening."

David smirked. "Well, this is different. Until now you've had the get-up-and-go of a surly Muppet. Is this broody thing the real you?"

"Still not hearing anything that makes me want to grab that chair."

"Fine, fine." David motioned to the bartender, pointed to Luke's tonic water, and showed the man two fingers. "I'll need a clear head for this. Still trying to accept that I'm actually here, trying to convince you of all people to perform at one of the biggest events of Jojo's life." He sighed. "It's the Hall of Fame. She's the first Black woman to be inducted. Only a few people know it yet, but the news will break tomorrow."

Luke sat down again. The club manager jabbed at his watch, but Luke ignored him. Nothing could distract him from the man sitting across from him, claiming history was going to be made and that Luke was about to be a part of it. "The Country Music Hall of Fame?"

"That's the one."

Luke turned it over in his mind. Not Linda Martell. Or Sister Rosetta

Tharpe, the woman who'd inspired Elvis's career. Even though Jojo had been in the industry for twenty-five years, she was a bold and probably controversial choice. It acknowledged that all those albums country radio had ignored for decades were real country.

They weren't honoring history. They were rewriting it.

"Holy shit."

"Yeah." David looked earnest for the first time that night. "I don't have to tell you how big this is. They're pulling out all the stops for Jojo. International press, a streaming concert, and a new album release after her induction." David leaned forward. "This is legacy making. I need you to understand that."

"I get it," Luke said. "I won't tell a soul until it's out there."

David leaned back, reclining again. "Good. Because Jojo wants to sing 'Another Love Song,' with you at her concert if you're interested…" David looked around. "Who am I kidding? Of course you are."

A sound burst from Luke's throat, half shout and half "goddamn" that he muffled quickly behind his hand. He still didn't quite believe what the man was telling him. "Why me?"

"Are there any other Black semi-famous country stars from her tiny speck of a hometown that I don't know about? If so, I'd love more options." David sighed. "She likes the song. It was one of the first covers she mentioned adding to the set list." He paused. "You haven't said yes."

"I'll do it. I'll do whatever she wants."

"I bet you will." David studied him for a moment. "But like I said, I've been looking into you. Probably closer than anyone else has in years. I know about the drinking. And the rumors about your marriage."

Luke's excitement faded. He hadn't thought about his marriage to Charlotte Turner before accepting the offer because those rumors were true: They *had* been separated for years. The lack of an official divorce was their attempt to avoid an even bigger scandal than her covering Jojo's song. Charlotte had cheated on him with the woman she was currently engaged to. If her conservative fan base found out that not only had she been unfaithful but she was also secretly queer, it might ruin Charlotte's career.

Luke briefly wondered if this man knew that his entire life was one lie toppling over the next. But David had made it clear he wasn't a fan. If he knew the truth, he wouldn't be there. "All that stuff about Charlotte and me is old news."

"Agreed. But I just want to make sure that's all there is. You've been off the radar for a long time. Any other skeletons I should know about before we put your name in micro font beneath the headliner?"

Luke's thoughts turned to "Another Love Song," but like always, he wrestled them back down a different road that wasn't littered with potholes. "No," he said. "What you see is what you get."

"Well, that's probably true." He gave Luke a long look. "You really haven't been home in thirteen years?"

Luke was thrown by the sudden change in topic. "No. Why?"

David shrugged. "Just seems odd. I imagine it'll be strange going back next month."

"Going back?"

"The concert's in Arcadia. During that music festival that they hold every year." He pulled out his business card and scribbled something on the back. "Think you can sing that song one more time?"

Luke nodded, even though his heart was trying to strangle the life out of him. "Does um..." He cleared his throat. "Does August Lane still live there?"

―•―०―•―

August didn't realize how drunk she was until she laughed when Shirley Dixon called her a backstabbing cunt. She'd convinced herself that the faint buzz in her ears was nerves. Or, more accurately, guilt. Ringing the doorbell of your married ex-lover at one in the morning was bound to be hazardous to your health. Staring into the angry abyss of Shirley's blue eyes confirmed it. That kind of venom left a mark on everything in its path.

August tried to explain that, despite appearances, she wasn't there to cause a scene. But what came out was a slurred "This isn't what you think," coupled with a desperate "I don't want trouble."

The irony of her sad little protests made her want to laugh again. The windows of the shotgun houses lining the gravel road were lit up like spotlights for the show on Shirley's porch. The neighbors were watching. Charlie Leppo peered through the curtains. Alice Magee took out a drooping trash bag that could have waited another day.

"First you steal my husband," Shirley said, her high-pitched voice sharpening the words into needles. "Now you embarrass me in public?" Her eyes shifted sideways to the small crowd of Black faces watching the drama unfold. She was one of two white people currently living in the Eastside neighborhood, and both of them had married in. Shirley's parents owned the local newspaper and drove the only Tesla August had seen up close. They'd disowned their daughter when she got engaged to a Black UPS driver but had paid for her wedding anyway, because that's what people with money did: freeze you out politely.

That had to be something. Going from country club receptions to this.

"I didn't think you'd be here," August said, which was true. Head spinning aside, she remembered Terrance saying that his soon-to-be ex-wife usually worked the late shift at Kroger, which seemed like the perfect time to talk to him alone. Only August hadn't factored in her detour to the county line liquor store. Or that her inebriated brain would decide that inching down a country road at five miles an hour was the best way to avoid slamming her Nissan into a tree.

"I need to drop this off." August shoved her hand inside her pocket and fingered the velour jewelry box she'd stashed there. It sobered her slightly and reminded her of the reason she'd come. Some things were more important than her pride or Shirley's feelings.

"Why are you like this?" Shirley looked her over like a bruised apple marring an otherwise perfect produce section. "Greedy. Like everyone owes you something 'cause of your mama."

August didn't want to talk about Jojo. But Shirley probably knew that. They'd gone to high school together. While August wouldn't call her a bully, Shirley used to laugh loud and long whenever someone insulted August with comparisons to her mother. But August never held that against her. Shirley was just trying to survive the ruthless hierarchies of Arcadia High. August had done the same, even though it hadn't done her much good. Despite spending most of the last decade single and caring for her sick grandmother, the fast reputation she'd earned as a teenager was etched in stone.

"I'm sorry," August said, because she knew it was all anyone wanted to hear from her. Sorry I broke that thing you loved. Your marriage. Your heart. Sorry that I'm broken, too. "I don't know what Terrance told you, but I didn't know you two were—"

Shirley's hand whipped out so fast August barely saw the motion. The slap was force and a loud *pop* followed by a numb burn along the left side of her face. August staggered back as the air filled with shocked hisses and chatter from the people around them.

She would've rather been punched. A punch was the beginning and end of a fight. It said I respect you enough to win this now because I don't know what will happen if you punch me back. Slaps were reminders not to step out of line. To know your place. The surprise had curved August into a slight crouch, and Shirley sneered down at her in triumph.

That look did it—the sneer. It reminded August of who she was, but more importantly, who she wasn't and would never be again: weak. Anyone's victim. The low voices around them had taken on an indignant tone because, while Shirley lived there, she wasn't Eastside. August had been born in this neighborhood, and in a town of four thousand people, street addresses weren't something you ever shook off.

August lunged and grabbed Shirley's hair, weaving it between her fingers, and pulled so hard the woman nearly fell on top of her. She kicked out and hit Shirley's shin before a strong arm wrapped around her waist and pulled her back.

"Enough! That's enough!"

For a moment, August tried to fight both people at once. She still had a handful of hair, and she knew the man who had lifted her like she weighed nothing had always been terrified that he'd accidentally hurt her with his bulk. Terrance was twice her size and thick all over, and even now, with August's hand clawing at his wife's scalp, his grip was slack and careful, like she was made of glass instead of bone.

"August, please," he said, mouth to her ear. "Let her go."

The surrounding voices had become shouts and whistles. She finally let go of Shirley's hair.

Charlie Leppo yelled, "Get your house in order, Terry!"

Alice Magee laughed so hard she doubled over.

Shirley was hysterical, screaming that August was a "crazy bitch who was going to regret this." Terrance stepped between them and blocked Shirley's view with his Superman shoulders.

August watched him convince his wife to go back inside the house and let him handle things. He had a voice like Teddy Pendergrass. It was hypnotic. She'd told him that once when they were listening to music after dinner. It had been a nice, normal date, which she now knew neither of them deserved.

The first time August had slept with Terry was the day of her grandmother's funeral. Although she'd managed to face the burial dry-eyed and upright, she had to skip the repast with its tear-soaked casseroles. Instead, she'd driven to McDonald's and ordered half the menu because she didn't want to eat anything without knowing exactly what it would taste like.

Terry had found her an hour later, sitting in a park, staring at a mountain of cold sandwiches and fries. He didn't mention the funeral. He sat across from her, claimed he was starving, and asked if she'd like to share. August laughed. And the fact that he could do that, make her laugh on that day of all days, made her trust everything else he said.

Her willful ignorance had been a relapse, the resurgence of an old addiction to unsolicited kindness she should have outgrown years ago. It always felt like love. Not the real kind, but close enough.

Terry told her repeatedly that she could cry on his shoulder if she wanted to. She didn't. She would never. But she did ignore the knot in her stomach that told her his frenzied touch couldn't be trusted. Now, as they faced each other on a bald strip of grass between his house and its bright yellow twin, he was giving her that same look—soft and hopeful, like this was going to end any way but badly.

"You left something at my house," she grumbled, so he'd know this wasn't some big romantic moment. Terrance made everything into a sappy movie, as if bumping into each other at the park had been fate instead of a side effect of living in a small town.

She pulled out the jewelry box. His face crumbled when he saw it, and the rawness of it made her head spin faster. Her stomach whirled, too. She was a home-wrecking tornado. "You never should have given this to me."

"Mom would have wanted you to have it." He opened the box and pulled out a rose-shaped ruby pendant. "She said give it to a girl you love, and that's you."

"No, it's not." If she let Terry love her, she might love him back. That would mean convincing herself that being the latest pit stop for his wandering eyes was enough to build a life on. She'd leave that misery to Shirley, who was still wailing in the distance. "I only took that necklace because you wanted me to. That's all we ever did. Say yes to each other when we should have been saying no. That's not love. It's just lazy."

His lip curled. "So, you used me."

Again, she thought of Birdie, who'd been buried three months ago today. This was how she'd chosen to mark the occasion, with a busted lip and a stomach full of whiskey, anything to dull the image of that open casket.

August sat on the ground, lowered her face to her palms, and muttered, "I don't know. Probably."

Terrance cursed beneath his breath. August looked up and spotted a police car easing along the curb. The lights were off, but Shirley rushed out of the house and pointed in August's direction.

"Goddammit, girl!" Terrance yelled. "Why'd you call Bill?"

Shirley covered her face and started sobbing again.

"Midnight brawl," a familiar voice drawled. "Ain't you too old for this, August?"

August took her time meeting Bill Parnell's eyes. As always, his deputy sheriff's uniform was wrinkled and two unfastened buttons away from respectability. His cattleman hat, however, was pristine, blinding white against his ebony skin. At some point, he'd probably told her a story about where it came from—some backwoods fairy tale that was completely unverifiable.

He extended his hand, beckoning her forward with a finger quirk. She had the urge to defend herself, remind all these people that she was just a thirty-one-year-old woman having a bad night. This was not a new chapter in that same old pitiful August Lane story they'd been telling themselves for years.

"I'm drunk," she mumbled, then managed to stand on her own. But she stumbled, and he had to prop her up, anyway.

"Don't say that too loud." He guided her toward his cruiser. "Then I'll have to take you to the station instead of dropping you off at Birdie's." His eyes widened as soon as he finished his sentence. "Her old house. I mean... Shit, I'm sorry." He snatched the hat from his head and looked down as if they'd been transported to her grandmother's graveside. Birdie had been gone long enough for people to say her name in hushed tones, but also recently enough that no one could believe she wasn't still rattling around the house where she'd lived for decades.

"Don't take me there." August kept her eyes averted so he wouldn't see how panicked she was at the thought of sleeping in her old bedroom. She hadn't been back since the funeral. Birdie's extended family had been in and out of the house—picking over her things, cleaning, crying. And all of them had a bone to pick with August, the person they'd entrusted to take care of her. August couldn't deal with their questions. She couldn't handle their bitter comfort, like they resented being forced to offer any. They hadn't been brave enough to face Birdie's mental decline and hated being around the person who had.

August slid into the back seat, slumped low, and closed her eyes. Bill slammed the car door closed, and the jolt made her stomach roll again. "Can we hurry up?" she grumbled.

"Yes, Your Majesty. But I need a destination first."

She told him her address, an apartment complex on the opposite side of Arcadia. He gave her a disapproving look. "How long have you been staying over there?"

August stifled a groan. This was the worst part about this place. You couldn't even get arrested without people sticking their noses in business that wasn't real business. "A few months," she said. "It's not as bad as people say."

He sucked his teeth and turned on the ignition. August looked out the window, but the motion made her nausea worse. She closed her eyes again and listened to the radio. She wished it were louder. Sometimes she'd put on headphones and turn up the volume until her jaw ached from the vibrations.

"So, uh... Terrance has always been a little misguided when it comes to women. Should probably leave him alone until that divorce is final."

"Done," August said without opening her eyes. She fell silent, praying Bill would stop talking so she could focus on holding back her bile. But the next song ripped through her concentration like razor blades.

Bill shouted, "Oh ho!" and turned the volume up to a window-rattling level. "Arcadia's finest. One of ours plays on the radio, you gotta sing it. That's the rule. You know the words, right?" He didn't wait for her answer and started belting a strained, keyless soprano that made the agony of listening to Luke Randall sing "Another Love Song" infinitely worse.

She used to think this would get better. Eventually, she'd hear that song and listen to it like Bill did, as a familiar piece of fluffy nothing that drifted in and out of her life on the whims of a DJ. But now she knew it would never feel that way. Each time would be a new haunting.

You know the words, right? Of course she did. They were hers. At seventeen, she'd written one of the biggest country hits in the world. Then she'd given it away.

"You know..." Bill shook his head. "I love this kid, but I always figured he was a gridiron dummy back in the day. Just goes to show, you never know some folks."

Bill pulled into the apartment complex and turned to face her. "Heard he's coming to town for your mama's concert. How cool will that be? Two local legends at once." He frowned, studying her face. "You okay, August?"

The music was louder now that they had parked. Luke whined "*I just want to write a love song,*" just as August shoved the door open, pitched forward, and vomited.

CHAPTER TWO

2009

Anyone who passed through the center of Arcadia might assume the town was dead or dying. The houses were old. The buildings were the color of prisons. After a hundred years of hemorrhaging citizens, the people still living there were dismissed as aberrations. Dead bodies twitched as the life drained out of them, didn't they? Nothing to write home about or stop the car for.

Only those people were wrong. The old, ugly buildings had been built by Black hands for Black businesses back when all-Black towns were havens. That legacy made Arcadia immortal. While poverty kept some tied to the dwindling community, most stayed out of love, for each other and occasionally something else. For August Lane, it was the town's biggest export, something you could hear, but unless you stopped the car to catch a show, would never see.

Arcadia was an incubator for Delta music—gospel, blues, and soul—all brushed with the South in a way that shouldered up to country but was rarely identified as such. Which was fine for the long timers, who preferred to be left alone. But for young people like August, convinced she'd built her seventeen-year-old passions from the ground up, choosing safety had started to feel dangerous, like the quickest way to disappear.

Arcadia had two major events: the Delta Music Festival, which was coming in a few months, and the county fair, which was happening now. August loved the fair. She loved the rides, the long lines, and the sickly sweet smell of funnel cakes layered over earth and sweat. She loved the sudden drops from big heights and spinning in spirals that rearranged her insides. She also loved the concerts, which, despite the flat, treeless land surrounding the stages, still felt intimate with their acoustic instruments and rowdy stomps. All that love made August reckless, convinced her that going out on a school night to see a blues band was worth the risk of running into people she was trying to avoid.

Being ignored was a privilege most people didn't appreciate. August was the only child of Jojo Lane, the town's most famous citizen, and lived under watchful eyes that had witnessed every mistake she'd made since birth. Since the event drew fairgoers from three neighboring cities, she'd assumed she wouldn't be recognized. So far, she was right. Any waves or smiles had been the polite greetings of strangers.

August had taken extra care with her appearance. Her hair was pressed into a silky black sheet that hung to the small of her back. Her shirt was formfitting, with a lower neckline than she was brave enough to wear to school. Her ears sparkled with tiny diamonds that glittered like stars against her skin. She felt shamelessly pretty. Free to bask in attention without being judged for it. She'd nearly reached the concert venue with all that confidence intact when a familiar voice shouted her name.

Richard Green (or Dicky, as he harassed girls into calling him just so he could leer when they said it) stood in the center of a group of football players waiting in line for the Ferris wheel. He wore a white Arcadia High T-shirt, and his dark hair was damp beneath a backward baseball cap. He poked out his bottom lip and mouthed, "*I miss you*," while his teammates laughed.

August had only been a student at Arcadia High for two weeks. She'd attended Eastside High until the state decided two public high schools were unnecessary for such a small town and closed it before her senior year. Arcadia High was newer, bigger, and whiter, since it pulled from expensive subdivisions in the unincorporated areas of the county. That summer, the school had paired the majority Black Eastside transfers with Arcadia High peer mentors hoping to, as they stated in the official welcome letter, "smooth the transition."

August had been paired with Richard Green. He was cute in a way only rich boys could be: carelessly confident, with an infectious playfulness that seduced you into adopting his optimistic view of the world. From June through July, she'd been someone else, a girl who was taken on picnics and had long make-out sessions pressed against leather BMW seats. But on the first day of school, when someone wrote *slut* in permanent marker on her new locker, all those romantic moments were revealed for what they were. August had been the poorly hidden secret of a guy cheating on his girlfriend. In twenty-four hours her loose reputation was cemented, and now Richard only looked her in the eye while making jokes about fucking a local celebrity.

Guys like Richard were the reason August never dated. No one saw her. They saw Jojo Lane's daughter: Jojo the Oreo, as everyone liked to joke. Richard had tricked her into thinking he was different and didn't consider a Black woman singing country weird at all. "Jojo's cool," he'd claimed in that flippant way that made you feel silly for worrying about it. "Good music doesn't have a color."

August spotted the funhouse and shoved her ticket into the hand of the guy watching the door. Once inside, she stumbled when the floor started scissoring back and forth. Her heart was pounding. The memory of what she'd done with Richard was a bomb in her chest.

She took careful steps until the floor gave way to colorful platforms that were supposed to move up and down but were suspended in the air, probably broken, which explained the lack of people waiting in line. Two pimply boys jumped on one, shaking it while they screamed like monkeys. The hall of mirrors was next. She caught a glimpse of her reflection. The clothes and makeup that had made her feel confident five minutes ago seemed desperate now. She ducked into the next room and was doused in darkness.

After a bit of grasping, she found a patch of wall and leaned against it. The speakers played music from a local country station, and August tried to focus on the lyrics. It was the last verse of "Travelin' Soldier," a song she loved. She sang softly at first but was lulled into something louder by the good acoustics. Soon she was belting the chorus with vocal runs that made her throat hurt but also kept her from crying over Richard, which so far, she'd managed not to do.

The song ended, and she heard labored breathing. Someone stood a few feet away, but it was too dark to make them out. August pushed away from the wall and widened her eyes, as if that would infuse light into the pitch-black room. "Is someone there?"

A low voice answered "Yes," then added "Me" between rapid huffs of too little air. She waited for his name, but he asked, "Are you okay?"

The question stumped her. He was the one who sounded like someone had a pillow pressed against his face. Then she realized he'd been there the whole time, listening to her whine about never holding another guy's hand. "I'm fine," she reassured him. "It's a sad song."

"Yeah, it is."

She sensed him moving closer, so she folded her arms so they wouldn't accidentally touch. They stood silently in the dark, listening to the opening lyrics of "Islands in the Stream."

"The Bee Gees wrote this song," she said, then instantly regretted tossing out *that* particular fact. No one knew how much she loved country music. It always led to more comparisons to her mother. More bullying. But the guy couldn't see her. There was no way for him to know she was a Black girl with an encyclopedic knowledge of eighties country pop.

"The Bee Gees?" Disgust strengthened his voice. She could almost hear his mind rebelling against the thought of disco royalty having anything to do with the iconic duet. "Are you serious?"

His voice was deep and winding, the way cowboys spoke in the Westerns her uncle Silas watched. That man would put up with almost anything except her talking through an episode of *Bonanza*.

"Gross, right," she said flatly. "Wasn't disco just cocaine and the Hustle?"

He made a sound, an amused snort smothered by a grunt. "You makin' fun of me?"

"Yes." She listened for a moment. "It's a good song."

"One of the best songs," he corrected. "Underrated. The whole thing is this big romantic gesture—"

"Like Dolly and Kenny were musical soulmates singing about finding your soulmate."

"Exactly." His voice echoed in the empty room, and he immediately fell silent. When he spoke again, it was quieter. "You have a nice voice."

"I know."

"Better than Natalie Maines."

"Don't get blasphemous."

He laughed. She smiled, thrilled at prompting the sound. It was a small thing that felt big, making someone laugh.

"Do you ever sing in front of people?" he asked.

"In the choir at church."

"Everyone sings there. I mean, do you perform?"

August pictured her mother bouncing across the stage in rhinestones and heeled boots. The word *perform* always made her think of something from the circus. "If you mean, do I stand onstage alone with a microphone, no." She paused, then admitted, "But I want to. I will one day."

"You should," he declared, and it warmed her insides. She liked how he'd recklessly tossed it in the air like truth. A silent beat fell between them, then he cleared his throat and said, "You haven't asked why I'm here. Lurking in the dark."

"Do I want to? Is it gross?"

"No."

"You have pants on, right?"

"Yes."

"I should have asked you that sooner."

"I'm cool, I swear."

"Okay. I believe you," she said. "So, why are you here?"

"My friends tried to make me ride the roller coaster. I hate it. Makes me nauseous." He took a deep breath, and she was relieved to hear it. Earlier, he'd seemed seconds from passing out. "They were assholes about it, and I . . . I don't know, I had to get away from them."

"They don't sound like very good friends."

He paused, then said, "They're my teammates," as if that explained everything. And to an extent, it did. Friends should be chosen, but sports in Arcadia made a lot of those choices for you: who you hung out with, how you dressed, what weird rituals you followed that no one else understood. Her cousin Mavis, the middle hitter for the volleyball team, choked down cheese grits every Friday even though she hated them because her coach claimed they brought good luck before a game.

"Are you at least good at whatever you play?" August purposely kept the question vague so the conversation wouldn't devolve into a ball player sob fest. She'd never cared for sports and would probably say the wrong thing.

"I don't know." He paused. "I think I hate it." He sounded unsure of himself, like it was the first time he'd said the words out loud.

"You should quit," August advised, probably with too much glee. "Do something you enjoy."

"I've got a scholarship to LSU." He announced it like a prison sentence instead of a free ride to the largest university in Louisiana. She understood. Most people in town couldn't afford to turn down free money. "I play guitar, though. I enjoy it."

"Well, are you good at *that*?"

"Yeah." She heard him shift against the wall. "I mean, I think so."

"You said yes really fast. Don't get modest now."

He laughed again. The sound was just as good as his voice—warm and contagious, the kind that invited you in. "I'm kind of like you. I only play at church. They give me a solo sometimes, but that's it."

"Wow, you get solos? I've been banned from solos."

"Banned?"

"By my grandmother. She's the choir director. And before you ask, no, I didn't deserve it. She thinks it builds character to deprive children of things they want."

"Wow." He paused. "She sounds—"

"Like Ebeneezer Scrooge? There's a resemblance." She pictured Birdie in her Sunday best, all big brown eyes and deep dimples, swathed in pastel florals. "I'm kidding. She's only fifty-eight and immortally gorgeous." So was Jojo. Kingdoms were known to fall when her mother and grandmother stood in the same room. They looked like the former beauty queens they were. August, in contrast, had strong, unforgiving features that would frighten small children if she wore too much eyeliner.

"Do you write music?" she asked, trying to move the subject away from her family. She didn't want him thinking about the fact that they hadn't exchanged names.

"No. I mean, yeah, but not for real. Just a hobby. Do you?"

"Yes," August admitted, even though she'd probably regret it later.

But she never talked about songwriting with anyone. Secrets were lonely. "I'm moving to Nashville after graduation."

"To be a singer? That's so cool." She could hear the smile in his voice. "Is that why you're here? Rehearsing in the dark?"

He'd been honest with her about what brought him there, so she felt obligated to do the same. "I was hiding from someone. A guy from school."

"Oh. Ex-boyfriend? I'm not asking to hit on you. I have a girlfriend."

"So did he. Only I didn't know until it was too late." That they were talking like this, trading secrets, felt too intimate for someone she hadn't technically met. But she didn't want to stop. Telling him made the shame feel like something she could eventually peel off.

"We had sex," she said. "It's all over school. People hate me."

He grabbed her hand. She stiffened, then wove her fingers through his. His hand was much bigger and calloused, probably from playing his guitar.

"I'm sorry that happened to you," he said. "No one should treat you that way."

August didn't want to be pitied, but this might be worse. It was genuine kindness—easier to trust and fall for. The enormity of what she'd confessed to this stranger was starting to frighten her. "I should probably go," she said.

"Oh? Right, yeah." He sounded disappointed. She tried to pull her hand back, but he gripped it tighter. "Let's walk out together."

August moved slowly as he shuffled behind her. The darkness lifted as they got closer to the exit, and the funhouse music was drowned out by the metal grind of carnival rides and screaming voices. His hand loosened and fell away. She turned around, but a wall of bodies obscured her vision. She tried to look through the crowd and spot the guy she was eager to meet properly, but no one met her eyes. She spun around, searching, but only spotted Richard and his friends holding cozy-covered beer cans.

"There she is!" Richard grinned and slung his arm over his friend's shoulders. The guy was Black and wore a ball cap jammed over his short, curly afro.

"Come here, August," Richard slurred. "My boy's a virgin, and his girl won't put out. He's never even had his dick sucked. Told him you'd do him a solid." Richard pointed to a porta-potty. "Even found y'all the perfect spot."

August tried to ignore him and walk away, but Richard kept talking, yelling her name along with more lies about the amazing things she could do with her mouth. He'd said the same thing when he kissed her: that her lips were amazing, and he'd never felt that way when he kissed a girl before. *Like I'm floating.*

August stalked to where they were standing. She ignored everyone else, including the mute virgin buddy he was using as an armrest. "I don't do pity fucks anymore," she said. "Sixty seconds of heaven isn't worth it."

Richard's face iced over. Someone behind him coughed a laugh into their hand, and soon they were surrounded by snickering. He glanced at his friends and sneered, "Slut."

August laughed. It felt good. Or at least better than crying. She looked to his right, to the supposed friend he'd made the butt of his joke, prepared to tell him that the company he kept was the real reason his girlfriend wouldn't sleep with him. But the guy wasn't laughing like the others. He was staring at her like he'd seen a ghost.

"Come on, Luke." Richard slapped his back. "This bitch is boring."

They drifted away. Luke didn't move. He opened his mouth but closed it quickly, like he'd forgotten how it worked. When he finally spoke, his voice was deep and winding, the same one she'd stupidly handed all her secrets to.

"August Lane?"

In third grade, kids had called him Cowboy Luke. He couldn't remember the name of the boy who started it, only that he was thin and white, with a face full of so many freckles, they looked like brown splotches on his cheeks from a distance. The boy had leaned over, took a dramatic sniff, and loudly declared that Luke Randall smelled like horse shit. "You tryin' to be a cowboy?" he'd asked, with a sneer that implied it was an unforgivable sin.

The freckled kid moved away, but the nickname stuck, even after Luke's mother sold off all their livestock and started using the barn for storage. At his predominately white school, Black boys were supposed to be cool and urban like the rappers everyone listened to, not country and dusty from working on two hundred acres of farmland surrounded by dirt roads. It took a while, but after a few years of excelling in every sport the school district offered, coupled with a meticulous hygiene routine, Luke left the cowboy behind him. He had better nicknames now: Lightning, because he was the fastest running back in the district. Ups, because he could jump higher than a basketball center who was half a foot taller. Sometimes he overheard girls calling him Funshine, like the yellow Care Bear from the eighties. He still hadn't quite figured out why, but their tone made it clear it was a compliment, which was the most important thing.

Luke was well liked. People laughed with him instead of at him. So once word spread around school that he was a virgin, he felt he had to remedy that condition immediately.

His girlfriend agreed, which wasn't surprising, because as last year's MVP on their district champion volleyball team, Jessica Ryder valued winning above everything. She would have done something drastic if he hadn't suggested having sex. Like dump him. Or make up a different rumor to counter the first because, as she put it, "I won't be the loser who can't get a virgin to fuck me."

They'd been dating for only three months. Jessica's family had moved to Arcadia during his freshman year when her father, a burly man with a Lionel Richie mustache, started working with the county sheriff's department. Her mother, a Mariah Carey look-alike, was a homemaker who sold Mary Kay products for spending money. Jessica was a mixture of the two: stunning, tall, and slender, with loose curls that had all the boys mesmerized. She played volleyball and basketball, and quickly joined Luke's group of friends, a cluster of Black athletes who'd played in the same sports programs since kindergarten. For years, she'd dated blond, blue-eyed Wesley Harris, the star pitcher of their baseball team, until their senior year when he dumped her for a freshman at Rhodes College. Jessica had pivoted to Luke almost instantly. Later, she told him her friends had hassled her about dating him forever. "They said we'd look cute," she said while gesturing to their similar golden-brown skin tones. "A perfect match."

Luke had always figured his first time would be momentous, ideally with someone he cared about who also cared about him. But Jessica had said I love you so early in their relationship that it hit his ears with high-pitched feedback. He'd gone rigid, with all the right responses bricked inside his mouth. Her face had reddened and she looked close to tears, so he'd said the first thing that sprang to his mind.

"I've never had sex," he confessed, which only made her flush more. So he added, "I've been waiting for the right person," because it implied he'd been waiting for her.

Jessica liked to believe she was special. Unique but not different. If someone served her chocolate cake with sprinkles, she'd say, "I haven't eaten sprinkles since third grade," not, "No thanks, I like vanilla," because not liking chocolate made you weird. It was the same with Luke. She enjoyed having a boyfriend who was saving himself just for her, but he had to be someone everyone else wanted—her big, strong football player. And Luke went along with it because she was fun and beautiful, and he'd chosen to be that guy. But it also meant that the girl who claimed to love him couldn't possibly love all of him.

Jessica must have been bragging about his celibate status to one of her friends because the rumor spread like wildfire. That's when she realized that something that felt romantic in private could seem odd and pathetic to everyone else. The entire football team started giving him repulsed "Who the hell doesn't want to fuck?" looks, so Luke let go of romantic notions about his first time being special. They were probably a side effect of cramming his brain with too many love songs anyway.

That Sunday after the fair, they had sex in her bedroom. It was too slow, then too fast, and then so intense it was humiliating. When it was over, they lay together in a loud silence that seemed to press against his skin. He said I love you because it felt like he should, and her answering smile convinced him he was right. But Monday morning, when he picked her up for school, she barely made eye contact as she slid into his truck.

By that afternoon, everyone knew he and Jessica were having sex, often and everywhere, in positions he had to look up online. Three days later, the gossip mill decided he'd been cheating on her with three other girls, former friends who'd exacted their revenge by sucking him off behind the bleachers. He got backslaps that made him feel like shit. No one wanted to hear his denials. *Luke's a nice guy, of course he wouldn't admit it.* It was like they looked at him and saw someone else, the version of nice that ruined people's lives behind closed doors. It made him think of Richard Green bragging he'd bagged "celebrity pussy" in their locker room.

But lately, everything reminded him of August.

He saw her everywhere now: at lunch, in the hallway, at the back of his English class, sullen and silent as she gazed out the window. The morning after the fair, he sat at a slight angle at his desk to keep her in his line of sight. The next day, he'd sat in the back of the room, convinced it would help him focus, but all it did was give him a better view of her. He was supposed to be learning about sonnets, but by the end of class, he hadn't taken a single note on iambic pentameter. Instead, he'd memorized the constellation of freckles behind her knee.

When the state shut down Eastside High, it had tripled the Black student population at AHS. Although Luke was excited to feel a little less alone in the locker room this year, he hadn't been brave enough to approach the daughter of his favorite country singer. He'd been intimidated by how she carried herself, like she was seconds from whipping out a knife. But that night at the fair had changed his perspective. August didn't barrel through the hallway looking for a fight. She was bracing for an attack while covered in armor.

After four days of staring, the perfect opportunity to speak to her again finally presented itself. They were the last two in the classroom, finishing a quiz that would have taken him half the time if he'd actually studied. August always finished her work last, which was probably intentional. She wanted to avoid her classmates. The bell rang, and they stood in unison, on a collision course for the pile of completed tests.

August eyed him like an unexpected traffic jam while Luke tried to think of something clever to say. He looked at his paper, staring blindly at the wall of multiple-choice questions. "What did you put for number six?"

Her annoyed expression didn't change. "C."

Luke nodded like he remembered which question that was. "C's always good. Reliable. Good odds of being right. 'None of the above' fucks things up though."

She looked at the stack of quizzes. Then at his test. "Are you trying to cheat off me? I have a D in this class."

"No!" He threw his paper down like it had caught fire. "I don't cheat."

Her expression shifted to pity. "Was that flirting?" Her tone made it clear she hoped it wasn't.

"No," he repeated, and then immediately broke out in a bold-faced-liar sweat. "I was just making conversation. Being nice."

August glanced at the hallway, which was filled with slow walkers who stared at them as they passed. "Don't let anyone else hear that."

"Hear what?"

"You being nice to me." She put her test down and neatened the stack.

"Why not?" Luke asked, even though he already knew. People talked about her like they were posting comments on some message board: Passionate hate because she stole someone's boyfriend. Vicious ridicule because her mother sang country, which meant the whole family was ashamed of being Black. Sleazy fawning that sounded vaguely threatening, like the way Richard crowed about how much he'd love to get his hands on her again.

Luke had never joined the supportive leers and fist bumps, but he never pushed back, either. He'd stood still and silent, blending with the walls while his teammates reduced her to horny shower fantasies. Looking back on those moments made him hate himself. He might not have been able to stop it, but he could have done something.

"They'll think I'm fucking you," she said, with little emotion.

Luke was embarrassed and irritated because she was right. "They're saying stuff about me too," he pointed out. "That it's all I'm after."

"It's not the same."

He couldn't argue with her. Stories about him sleeping around only made people like him more. They avoided August like a new strain of the flu.

"None of it's true," he said, because he needed her to set him apart. *Those guys are assholes, but then there's Luke.*

August shrugged. "Even if it was, you'd still be fine. They all think you're a good person."

"That's 'cause I am," Luke said, and gave her a half smile that had always worked for him in the past. "Or at least, I'd like to be if you let me."

Something flashed across her face before she smothered it, a look he only caught because it was so familiar. Sometimes when Luke was alone and forgot to dodge the mirror, he'd see his hunger, the parasitic need that only grew bigger the more he fed it friends, trophies, and Facebook likes. Maybe she was starving, too. Maybe they were both just ants addicted to sugar.

August studied him and he did the same to her, since it was the first conversation they'd had with the lights on. Her eyes were large and heavy-lidded, like she'd just stumbled out of bed. She had a wide nose and lips that were almost too perfect, a hard cupid's bow painted with cartoonish precision. It was jarring how pretty she was. With her standoffish attitude, her beauty was easy to overlook, but once it gripped you, it held you by the neck.

"You're cute," she whispered, almost like she was talking to herself. Then she dismissed him with a tiny head shake. "Save it for your girlfriend."

August picked up her books and left. He watched her, so lost in his own thoughts that he nearly overlooked the small black Moleskine she'd dropped on the floor.

Luke only noticed that August carried a notebook everywhere because he did the same thing. His was a black-and-white composition book he'd picked up at Walmart last year, now creased and curled from his constant handling. Inside was an incoherent cloud of lyrics and music notes he was starting to think would never be more than that. He guarded that book like it held the keys to the universe, or his universe at least.

August was protective of her notes, too. She would dump her books so carelessly on a desk that half the stack would slide to the floor, but the black Moleskine was always gripped in her hand or pressed to her chest. Seeing it on the floor triggered something tight and impatient inside him, like she was offering another secret and daring him to take it. Because he already knew what it was. Keys to *her* universe. But that seemed like a dangerous thing to want from August Lane.

High school was made of boxes. And so far, Luke had done a good job of figuring out which ones he fit inside and which ones he should avoid. Football was a gilded box. It was a social lubricant and a wide-open path to being every teacher's pet. It was guaranteed girlfriends and a place on the homecoming court. It was knowing that every day he walked these halls, anyone who made eye contact with him would do it with a smile. And he needed that in his life. People who were genuinely happy to see him.

But it came with other boxes that he didn't like as much. He was lumped in with the rich kids, even though his family didn't have much. His position in that group was tenuous. If he admitted that he'd never left Arkansas or had only recently learned that Pabst Blue Ribbon was a cheap beer, they'd toss him aside. Which might not be a bad thing, but he wasn't sure what would happen next. Maybe all the other boxes would collapse like dominoes, and he'd be left on some island on the outskirts of a high school maze.

He couldn't survive that. Luke was soft in all the wrong places. He knew perfectly well the world could eat him alive, so it was better to bow to the natural order it imposed. And most days, he was fine with that. On others, he'd end up suffocating slowly in the dark.

August was the first person who'd ever seen him at his worst. Meeting her made him realize how lonely he was. There'd been an instantaneous shift—one minute, his body was being twisted and stretched to the brink of cracking, and the next, she was holding his hand. It was the best feeling. A balm over everything. But it was also like putting on a strong pair of glasses after a lifetime of eye strain. You couldn't know how bad your vision was until someone showed you a clearer world.

August leaving her notebook behind had to be a sign. He'd always believed in things like karma and destiny, so that's what he told himself as he stuffed it into the bottom of his backpack, that everything happened for a reason.

Her handwriting was neat and elegant, with artistic swoops that reminded him of calligraphy. He'd expected something more like his blotted mess of emotions, but August didn't have the same problem he did. She knew exactly how to put her feelings into words.

How do you tell a beautiful boy that you're wasting away in front of him / He could never understand / He could never love a girl who's always waiting for something better.

She hadn't written the songs for him. But it didn't matter. Luke saw his own hunger on the page, and at that moment, he knew he couldn't keep going on the way he had. And it felt good to accept that, let it settle over him while he read and reread those words until they felt like his.

He thought back to her voice at the fair, the way it had trembled as she'd squeezed his hand. Years later, he'd wonder if that was when it happened. That maybe he fell in love with her that night. Just a little.

CHAPTER THREE

2023

In ten years of marriage, Luke had never argued with Charlotte Turner. She'd never yelled at him, either, not even when he deserved it. He'd once gotten so drunk that he'd broken an angel figurine her mother had bought her a year before she died. Even though it hadn't been an intentional provocation, he was relieved when Charlotte discovered what he did. Finally, he would see her fury and learn how to manage it. But she hadn't mentioned the glass angel. She'd lumped that mistake in with the others and locked it away in a mental vault she kept of things about him that didn't matter.

Today, the tight smile she gave him as they sat across from each other in the living room of her Nashville mansion might as well have been a shout. Charlotte wanted him to speak first. But Luke never spoke first. Ever. Waiting for an angry person to take the first shot was written into his DNA.

"You could have called," she said finally. "I heard the news from my publicist."

"Didn't think we still did that," Luke said carefully. "Called with news. I'm sorry."

"Don't—" She bit her lip and dulled her voice. "Don't do that. It's my least favorite thing about you."

He wasn't sure what she meant but resisted the urge to apologize again. "How's Darla?"

Charlotte tensed, then said, "Fine," while her hand tightened on a folded document he hadn't noticed until now.

"That what I think it is?" he asked, even though he knew the answer. It was the reason he was there. After David's warning about avoiding a scandal, he'd texted Charlotte to ask if she'd signed the divorce papers. She'd left him on read for days, as she often did when he broached the subject, and had only reached out when the news about Jojo became public.

"Yes." She placed the papers on the coffee table next to a pen, stroking them flat like that would give her the courage to pick it up and sign this time. "Darla said you never answered her last email about the revised settlement."

"Don't need it," he said automatically, but it was such a big lie he quickly added, "I don't want your money, Charlie."

"Not even for 'Nice Guy'?" She was going for sarcasm, but that was never her strong suit, so it came out petulant. They'd always pretended that the popular breakup song was an inside joke. But when a woman told the world you were "the worst good time I've ever had," part of you would always take it personally.

Luke met Charlotte when he was nineteen years old and the shine on his career was so bright it felt like it would last forever. She'd just stunned the industry with her debut album, a pop twist on honky-tonk with enough drums and bass to spark the same old debates about what was and wasn't real country. Her girl-next-door image had fit perfectly with the party bro schtick that had propelled Luke to TV stardom. A joint tour was inevitable. They'd both been lonely and horny enough to blow past friendship and dive straight into each other's beds.

Sometimes those months on tour felt like the closest he'd ever get to a happy ending. But Luke had been wasted for most of it, so he could never be sure if it was love or the endless supply of weed. Charlotte used to party with him but wasn't chained to being high like he was. Her ability to handle the strain of touring sober made him jealous. He could only face the pressure while floating on a boozy cloud.

Getting married was more about public relations than romance. Luke's team thought it would be a good distraction from the nosedive of his career. His debut album had been a disappointment and the second was bad enough to cancel the tour. Charlotte's team had pitched *Bride* magazine profiles that would expand her fan base into a more adult category.

The media attention was so intense that Luke went on a bender the night before their wedding and nearly drunk dialed August to tell her he still loved her. He pressed all the numbers except the last one, hung up, and did it again, over and over, sending an SOS she'd never hear. *I'm tired of dreaming, August. You're the only one who can wake me.*

It went on that way for the next two years: Luke would buckle under some pressure and self-medicate to take the edge off. Then he'd wake up somewhere he didn't recognize after doing things he didn't remember that were inevitably photographed. He'd feel bad, start drinking again, rinse and repeat. Meanwhile, he and Charlotte saw each other less and less, until he came home one day and walked in on her making out with her attorney.

Luke hadn't been angry. Sometimes he wondered if that was really what ended their brief marriage—that he didn't react the way Charlotte wanted after discovering her affair. But Luke had always believed that loving someone meant loving all of them, even the parts that were better off without you. Before she realized he'd walked in on them, Charlotte looked happier than she'd been since they met.

Luke couldn't give Charlotte the stability she wanted. Still, he could step aside quietly, without filing for divorce, because her fans weren't ready for their favorite girl next door to be an out-and-proud bisexual woman. So for the last ten years, Luke had played the dutiful husband while Darla pretended to be the celebrity attorney who'd become a devoted friend.

Guilt about the lie usually brought them here, hovering over divorce papers, on the edge of abandoning the entire performance. But today had been prompted by his fear and her anger. And, knowing Charlotte's stubborn need to pretend they were still close friends, maybe a bit of hurt.

"I hate that song," Charlotte said. "Even the title is terrible. 'Nice Guy'?" She shuddered. "But people are obsessed with it. Singing it's like..."

"Going back in time," he finished. "Or being stuck there."

Her face creased with sympathy. He'd confessed to not writing "Another Love Song" during the peak of their relationship, when handing over the secret felt like an act of love and not a selfish grab for absolution. But Charlotte wasn't August. She didn't take his ugly confession, put it on paper, and transform it into something beautiful. She'd recoiled, avoided his eyes, and told him never to repeat it if he wanted to make it in Nashville.

Luke stared at the divorce papers. He'd added his notarized signature months ago and had waited in vain for her to do the same. Staying married to him made her feel safe. Until today, he didn't feel right pressuring her to sign after everything he'd put her through. But that was before David Henry offered to rescue his career.

"So, you heard about Jojo Lane," he said.

She flipped her hair back and said, "I'm happy for you," in a tone that implied the opposite. The scathing reviews of her "Invisible" cover had only recently subsided. She probably thought Jojo singing a duet with her husband would cause another round of criticism. "But the news was surprising. I didn't know you were being considered for her concert."

Charlotte had always resented his secrets. But she had never been completely comfortable with the reality of the man she'd married. The few stories he'd shared about his messed-up childhood had made her inconsolable. And he'd never even revealed the worst of it.

Luke rubbed his forearm out of habit, tracing the raised ridges of an old scar he'd covered with tattoos. "I didn't know, either," he reassured her. "Her manager approached me after a show."

"This sounds like a..." Charlotte seemed to be struggling to think of a softer word than scam. "I mean, are you sure this isn't some publicity stunt? To bring all that 'Invisible' stuff up again?"

Luke noticed how carefully she avoided saying what had happened: that she had been accused of cultural appropriation for covering a song about a Black woman's experience. Luke knew she'd added the song to her album because it was one of her mother's favorites. Natalie Turner had died from heart disease while Charlotte recorded the album, and the optics of her choice hadn't penetrated her grief.

Luke found out about it when everyone else did, and the slick, country-pop production had bothered him the same way it ultimately bothered every other critic who knew the soulful original. He didn't say that to Charlotte, though. She wouldn't have listened. They didn't talk about race, not like that. Not in ways that implied being married to him made her more or less culpable.

"The show is in Arcadia, during the music festival," Luke said. "That's why Jojo thought of me."

A new concern creased Charlotte's face. "I guess that makes sense." She paused. "Do you think that's wise?"

"Getting paid? Yeah, I do."

"You haven't been back there in years. With good reason." She picked up one of the water glasses her assistant had placed in front of them and took a large gulp, as if the conversation had a taste she was eager to wash away. "Are you sure you can deal with it without—I mean, you know what happens when you drink."

She fell silent, probably waiting for him to echo her concerns. Charlotte controlled her life through avoidance. If she'd had her way, he would have spent the last decade hidden in one of her luxury guest suites so no one could speculate about the status of their marriage. She knew that if Luke returned to Arcadia, he'd be walking through an emotional minefield. She probably had nightmares about him relapsing and drunkenly outing her before she was ready.

"That won't happen," he said, because he knew his triggers. He'd also developed coping strategies that came in handy when he couldn't avoid them. One was listening to the will of the universe, the way it held up a mirror and forced him to face his mistakes. He couldn't work the steps without truly working them. He couldn't accept another windfall that fell into his lap without trying to become a man who deserved it.

"Stay away from your mother," Charlotte advised. She'd met Ava only twice, but the few stories he'd shared had been enough to convince her he should block the woman's number.

"I'll get a motel room," Luke said. His bank account disagreed, but he'd deal with that later. "It's just a few rehearsals, then the show."

Charlotte didn't seem convinced, but she sighed in defeat. She looked down at the divorce papers. "All this stuff is scary, right?"

He knew she wasn't just talking about him anymore. They'd both seen the punishment for making waves in country. Radio stopped playing you. Your singles vanished from the charts. If Charlotte came out, it would be inspiring to the fans who'd already sensed the sapphic tone of her recent releases, but it would feel like a slap in the face to others, the fans who looked to her music for nostalgia about an ignorant way of life.

She'd also have to face the same questions he did from people who were confused by her refusal to switch genres. Luke had once performed at an HBCU that asked him to sit on a panel to discuss lynching imagery in country music. He'd stumbled through three different explanations about why he'd chosen to sing country before he finally heard the real question they were asking: How could you love this thing that hates you?

It made him think of August: *Because that's what I do.*

He envied Charlotte despite her current misery. There was an obvious light at the end of her tunnel. She could wake up beside the woman she loved, decide she'd had enough, and choose the happy ending right in front of her. "You've got Darla," he reminded her. "Whatever happens, you'll be okay."

"And what about you?" She leaned in and met his eyes. "Are you going to be okay?"

He was slow to answer. For him, okay was survival: a roof over his head, another show lined up, enough money for food and clothes. But now, sitting next to Charlotte, a woman with more to lose than he'd ever have in his lifetime, it felt like a cowardly way to live. "Maybe. All I can do is try."

The show was in two months, enough time to make things right with August. He'd been eager to believe that David Henry's offer was some reward for years of toiling at the bottom, when it was really this. A reckoning.

◆─◇─◆

August woke up hungover and queasy, with Birdie's ghost chasing her out of bed. It was Sunday morning, and her grandmother had never let her skip church. "Saturday sins won't seek their own forgiveness," she used to say, before yanking the bed covers away. August could never argue with that, even though today it felt like making empty promises to Santa for a bicycle. No amount of praying would erase the fact that she'd wrestled in the dirt with Shirley Dixon. The scratches on her face were begging to be used as an excuse to hide in her apartment. But again, Birdie's voice clattered in her ear. "That's coward's thinking. You've been a lot of things, August, but never that."

Her grandmother had been the only person who considered August's special brand of bravery a virtue. Everyone else thought she was just stubborn. Or worse, ornery, like a wild horse too stupid to know it should break. "Comes from her father" they would say, as though August's mother hadn't devoted twenty-five years to a genre that had to be publicly shamed into claiming her. But Jojo was famous. A homegrown success story that lifted all their ships. Everything people didn't like about August was blamed on her father, Theo King—a man so despised she heard the church threw a celebratory BBQ when he disappeared.

The list of things August knew about her father wasn't very long. Theo was the youngest of the five King boys, one of two who were still alive. His father had run numbers. His mother had disappeared so suddenly that it made the town uneasy, constantly on the lookout for a hasty burial ground. During his brief relationship with her mother, he taught Jojo how to play piano, even though she refused to do it, even to this day.

The list of things August didn't know about Theo was too long to care about. But there was one thing in the middle, a truth everyone avoided, reflected in how people looked at her and, more often, in how they didn't. It said she shouldn't be here. Theo King had done a bad thing, one of the worst they could imagine, and it had robbed them of their beauty queen. If Jojo had never had August, she wouldn't have lost that historic crown and embarked on a singing career they initially found confusing and still occasionally considered embarrassing.

Birdie told August that Theo was the coldest man she'd ever met. "He had eyes that would make you shiver in July" was how her grandmother put it. "Nothing ever got to him." It was the only trait of his that August had tried to emulate. Emotional control. Immunity from the elements. August had divided her life into two lists: things that needed immediate attention and things that didn't matter. For the last decade, the first list had a single item: Birdie's welfare. The other list held everything else: Her lack of a career. Other people's opinions. Anything resembling a love life. The mental wall she'd erected between them was a dam that occasionally leaked. That's what happened when Birdie died. The only item on her list that mattered had vanished and left a space she didn't know how to fill. Terry was the closest thing within reach, a warm body to grind herself numb against. It didn't work. Instead of shoring up the dam, more of the other list leaked through. Like how long it had been since she'd laughed at anything. Or how horrible it felt to hear I love you from a man you didn't trust.

Luke's imminent return would cause a flood.

Birdie had called her brave, but that man made her the biggest coward. There was no way she could face him, not when her life was a desolate canyon. The only music she still made was as a back row alto in the First Baptist choir, because it was a Lane family tradition. Birdie was the first to sing at the church, sending her elegant soprano to the rafters in a way that caught the eye of a deacon almost twice her age. Caroline, Birdie's oldest daughter, led the praise and worship team despite having an average voice, something appropriate for lullabies and starting happy birthday songs. Then came Jojo, the star, hitting those impossibly high notes that made the congregation thank almighty God for such a blessing.

August didn't sing like Jojo or Birdie. She didn't even have her aunt Caroline's lifeless tone. Her voice was throaty chaos that insisted on getting louder instead of higher, with a vocal fry that her grandmother had given up trying to train out of her years ago. It was a voice people called interesting but never beautiful, the kind you couldn't comfortably sink into. Every choir director had buried it beneath more polished singers to tame its impact, which had bothered her when she was younger and desperate to be on someone's stage. These days, she was grateful to have a small sliver of something that used to be her world.

But Luke wouldn't see it that way. "What sliver?" is what he'd say, if he bothered to speak to her at all. "Your mouth was moving, but I couldn't hear a thing."

August's hopes of slipping into the church unnoticed evaporated as soon as she entered the sanctuary. A line of heads whipped around to stare. Shirley sat in the front pew, proudly displaying a large bruise on her chin. To her left was Terry, a lifelong apostate, stuffed like a sausage into a dark suit he'd pulled from the back of his closet. His eyes were fixed firmly on the floor.

A rough hand jerked her backward until she stood behind a tall, skinny body encased in a jarring floral print that reminded her of Birdie's bedsheets. Mavis Reed's wide-brimmed hat was supposed to be pinned at a jaunty angle but had skewed sideways into an imperfect lurch, a flaw that was completely out of character. Her cousin kept an iron grip on her pastor's wife image, which included being photo ready at all times in outfits she copied from Pinterest and *Greenleaf* episodes.

Still facing the congregation with a fake smile, Mavis hissed, "What are you doing here?" Her chignon was an oil slick, the relaxed hair slathered with a pound of Eco Styler and pulled tight enough to make her skin pucker at the edges. Paired with her bared teeth, the effect was slightly ghoulish.

"It's Sunday," August said. "Where else would I be?"

Mavis shot her murder eyes and then dragged her to the pastor's study. She rounded on August the moment the door closed. "Are you trying to start another fight? Or finish the last one?"

"I didn't start anything." The image of Shirley's flailing arms flashed in her mind. "I defended myself when she slapped me."

"You slept with her husband and showed up at her house."

"Terry slept with *me*," August snapped. "He told me they had filed for divorce. And I was only at the house to return a gift he should have given Shirley, not to rub it in her face. I was doing him a favor."

"Of course you were," Mavis said, with a sigh of weariness that made August feel like she'd failed some test. "Why did you trust him? He can't be the first man who ever lied to you."

August immediately thought of Luke. Mavis didn't know what he'd done, but she knew enough about August's history to recognize a pattern. Mavis had witnessed the high school Richard Green debacle. She'd watched August unravel when Luke disappeared. Now she had a front seat to this latest dumpster fire and probably thought she'd earned the right to wear that "I told you so" grimace on her face.

August loved her, but they had become friends the same way most cousins in small towns did: by default. They had nothing in common. Mavis was soft-spoken and well behaved, while August never saw the point of being either. There was always a hint of judgment on Mavis's part, starting when she'd been plopped into August's childhood bedroom and forced to share her dolls. They were never clean enough or cute enough for Mavis to sink comfortably into make believe. August could sense her cousin's snobbery and would punish Mavis by putting the dolls' clothes on backward or giving them ridiculous names that made her cousin tongue-tied when she tried to say them.

That was most of their shared childhood, a discordant dance of mutual antagonism. But sometimes fun would find them unexpectedly. One of August's jokes would land, Mavis would start laughing, and her cousin would transform into a regular girl, one who found terrible puns funny and was secretly afraid she would never be as perfect as their family needed her to be.

That was who August tried to reach now. The insecure little girl who snort-laughed when she learned Russian dolls were full of themselves. "I don't want to talk about this anymore. I just want to sing."

Mavis shook her head with an exasperated sigh August had heard a million times. It said: Why are you like this? Why are we related? And why can't I bring myself not to care? "If Birdie were still here, she would—"

"She'd want me to sing," August interrupted. "She always wanted that, even when she couldn't..." Her words trailed off as the memory took hold. On Birdie's worst days, music could sometimes bring her back to herself. August would sing "A Song for You" and Birdie's eyes would uncloud, her lips curved into the coy smile of a woman with secrets. But Mavis wouldn't know that. She'd cared for their grandmother from a distance: dropping off meals, researching clinical trials, and harassing the nurses Jojo hired into quitting out of frustration. Micromanaging Birdie's care had been her only coping strategy. She couldn't sit still with the pain of losing someone slowly.

Mavis looked away, blinking rapidly. "Phillip doesn't want you at the service. It's too distracting."

"Oh. That's who this is about." August had never liked Mavis's husband. She blamed him for Mavis's decision to abandon her career and become a full-time first lady. He and Mavis went to law school together at Emory, and he'd opened a small practice in his wife's hometown instead of joining the big private firm in Atlanta where he'd clerked. Phillip was young, devout, and charismatic, which thrilled their aging congregation, but made August uneasy. For someone so ambitious, he'd slid eagerly into Mavis's small-town life as if he'd wanted something easier to conquer. That included her cousin, who he constantly browbeat with Ephesians 5:23 if Mavis said anything about going back to work.

"What am I supposed to do?" August stared at the closed door. "I can't change what happened. And you know how stuff like this goes. Everyone's excited, but it'll die down, eventually."

Mavis said, "I'm sure you're right." But she didn't sound convinced. "Still, it's probably best to skip Sunday service for now. At least until Terry stops coming."

It took a moment for Mavis's words to sink in. "You're banning me?"

"No, you are not being banned. Take a break. Go to Zion Temple across town."

"It's in the old Dollar Tree. They wear jeans to service." They also played music on a boom box from a CD collection they hadn't updated since the nineties. The service was an endless loop of God's Property and Kirk Franklin. "They don't have a choir."

"I'm sure they have a microphone and a stage."

A small one. She'd be up there alone, staring at a sea of fidgeting congregants who wondered why they were being subjected to her failed dreams. "It's not about that," August said, tempted to admit the truth. Luke was coming. She couldn't face him empty-handed.

Mavis gripped her shoulders and leaned down to look August in the eye. "Take a break. Breathe. Have you cried once since we lost Grandma?"

"There's no point," August said, because she hadn't. Not since they really lost her, which was long before Birdie stopped breathing. Now her grief would only sting and prickle, like a limb that had fallen asleep.

Luke was relieved to discover that King's Kitchen smelled the same as when he'd left Arcadia, like burned coffee and bacon grease. It never mattered what time of day it was or which meal the kitchen was churning out at a rapid pace. Those two scents would prevail, seeping into the wood-paneled walls and parquet floors from open to close. Luke had assumed, at a minimum, the quality of the appliances would have improved over the years. The coffee maker was famous for scorching and underheating its contents simultaneously. He remembered stumbling inside, exhausted and starving after a long night dealing with his mother and being offered a tepid mug along with a Sundown over-easy breakfast on the house. August would ignore his promise to pay the bill, grumbling about overinflated prices while sneaking extra bacon onto his plate.

For the first time since Luke reached the city limits, his stomach wasn't filled with dread. He'd driven into town with a lead foot, praying no one would recognize him, but his mood improved at the sight of the old restaurant. He knew he'd have to face people eventually. But he needed something to make it all go down easier, and the familiar walls of one of his favorite places seemed like a smart way to ease back into his hometown.

"You waitin' on a hostess or something?"

A grizzly, gray-haired Black man sat at a nearby table, a fork raised halfway to his mouth. Luke froze for a second, as he always did when a stranger recognized him, but the man looked idly curious at most, like his open newspaper wasn't interesting enough to keep his attention.

Luke smiled. "No, sir. It's been a while since I've been here. Got lost in the moment."

The man huffed, bored by Luke's answer. "Well, you're blocking the door." He refocused on his meal, dumping maple syrup over his already soaked plate.

Luke grabbed a menu even though he didn't need one. If the smell was the same, the food probably was, too. The left side of the dining room was dotted with customers, but the right was empty. He strolled to the right, not looking to get drawn into another conversation, but then heard another grumpy huff that stopped him midstride.

"Where do you think you're going, son?" the old man chided.

"Leave him alone, Clyde."

Luke's defender was a young, blue-haired white woman wiping down tables.

"You know who's working those tables. I'm trying to help the man, Gemma." Clyde gestured toward the empty tables. "You plan on eating something?" Luke nodded. Clyde lifted his coffee mug and took a dramatic, leisurely slurp before answering. "That girl is in a mood. I wouldn't sit over there if I was you."

A different customer snorted, which set off a ripple of muffled laughter. Gemma sighed and waved at a table to Luke's right. "Go on and sit down. She'll be with you in a second."

He didn't slide into the booth with the ease he would have five seconds ago. A quick menu scan confirmed they still had the same numbers assigned to the same dishes. "Sundown with bacon," he whispered.

"Just use the numbers," someone mumbled.

It was exactly what August would have said. She'd given him so much grief about not using the menu's shorthand that he came up with fifty different ways of ordering, just to watch her blood boil. He grinned up at his server, the story on the tip of his tongue, when a familiar gaze met his, and the world tilted.

"August?"

He stared, not quite believing his eyes. After a decade of pining over her memory, he could still see that version of her clearly—the large eyes, the cupid's bow mouth, umber skin inviting as velvet. But now her hair was a cloud of curls instead of pressed straight. Her body was fuller, jarringly lush under her minidress. That beautiful girl had become a woman. The kind that made you crave things.

Luke moved to touch her arm, but she jerked back with a horrified expression that made him feel like shit. Of course she wouldn't want him to touch her. All he could do was say her name again, like that would fix something, but it only seemed to make things worse. Her face shuttered, and she mumbled words he couldn't make out. "What'd you say?"

She pulled her lips into what she probably thought was a smile. The process looked painful and made him want to slide all the sharp objects out of her reach. "I said," she gritted out, "Order. Something."

"August. I wasn't expecting—"

"Stop saying my name." She grabbed the upside-down coffee mug and set it right side up with so much force he was surprised it didn't crack. "Order so I can leave."

"I didn't know you still worked here. Au— Wait, why can't I say your name?"

"I hate the way you say it. Overly familiar. Like it's yours."

He went still and tucked his hands beneath the table like she'd caught him stealing something. He'd forgotten how good she was at parsing people's bullshit.

She tucked a curl behind her ear, impatient with his silence. "You want the Sundown, right?"

Luke watched her scribble on her notepad and caught her gaze when she looked up again. "You remember that?"

She rubbed her arm like the question made her itch. "Could you just place an order like a normal customer?" She propped up her pen and schooled her face into something politely bland. "Bacon?"

Her name nearly slipped out again. But a quick glance over her shoulder confirmed that half the restaurant was watching their exchange like a tennis match. He stared blindly at the menu and muttered, "Yeah, with bacon."

She pivoted and practically sprinted away. Luke watched her slap the order down at the kitchen window and then reach for an ancient coffee carafe. He shouldn't stare. People would notice, and once someone figured out who he was, Luke Randall's leery eyes would be the topic of conversation in every corner of town.

Still, he couldn't look away. It had been years since he had the luxury of staring at August Lane. She still had that constellation of freckles on her calf. He'd traced it in his mind a thousand times.

"They're working on it," she said when she returned to fill his coffee cup. "That'll be $893.67."

Luke blinked. "Excuse me?"

"For all the free food you ate here. It's time to settle up, don't you think?"

He watched her grab three sugar packets and rip the tops away. "That's a really specific number," he said slowly. "Did you keep track?" The thought of her petty bookkeeping shouldn't please him as much as it did.

She dumped the sugar into his cup. "Don't you think a guy who runs off and gets famous should at least send a check for all his unpaid orders? Plus twenty percent for the poor person who had to wait on him for nothing?"

"How do you know I didn't send a check?" Luke leaned into the table and tried to make eye contact. He was slipping into something, falling through the blurred gaps between then and now. August met his eyes, and he grinned. "You been keeping tabs on me?"

"Why would I bother?" She grabbed a jar of creamer. "You haven't been interesting in years."

The insult was a face full of cold water. Luke sat back and tried to anchor himself to the present. "I need to talk to you."

"We just talked." She set the creamer down. "Now we're done." She pointed to his mug. "Coffee's getting cold."

Luke glanced down at the cup. "I take it black these days."

August stared at the mug, confused, before her expression darkened to fury. "Well, that happens when you disappear for thirteen years. No one knows what the hell you drink anymore."

"August—"

"Stop saying my fucking name!" Her voice ricocheted throughout the room, and she glanced at the startled customers. "Why are you here?"

Luke started to speak but faltered. The words wouldn't come. Not good ones, anyway. It didn't matter whether he'd intended to run into her or not. She felt ambushed. Unlike him, she hadn't been picturing different versions of this day every time she sang their song. She'd probably been grateful for his absence. Hell, she might have been pretending they'd never met.

"I'm—" He moved to stand because it felt appropriate to give the moment its due respect. The contempt that flashed in her eyes kept him pinned to his seat. "I need to apologize for...what I did."

She went still for a moment and then laughed—a sharp, high-pitched burst that made him flinch. He was so startled that he didn't notice the mug sliding across the table until it was too late. She nudged it over the edge, and a wave of sugary coffee doused his crotch in heat. He shot up and yelped. Maybe screamed a little. Not in pain, but with the mental torture of what-if. What if that goddamn coffeepot had worked the way it should?

Luke grabbed a handful of napkins and started wiping his jeans. When he looked up, she was on her way to the door. "August! Wait!"

She jerked her apron off and threw it at Gemma, who caught it with one hand. The door swung open with a loud creak and slammed shut behind her. Clyde stood and stared at Luke with wide eyes.

"Damn, boy. What the hell did you order?"

PART TWO

THE FIRST VERSE

This Is Our Country: Podcast Transcript

Episode 12—"Jojo Lane"
August 21, 2024

[*cont.*]

Emma: There's a rumor that "Sundown" is your least favorite song. Is that true?

Jojo: [*laughs*] I heard that one, too. "Sundown" is complicated. It's a dark song, and I don't do dark. I don't do pain. But that's how it came out. David wanted me to write a song about home—

Emma: David Henry, your manager.

Jojo: Yes. He's been with me since the beginning. We were trying to decide on a demo, and he wanted me to write about home because that's country, right? Leaving it or going back to it or missing it. He thought it would help me be seen in Nashville, and I didn't have the heart to tell him it wouldn't matter. I'm always gonna be this color. Eyes'll skate right on past me. But he was adamant, so I said I'd try.

Emma: Could you talk a little about your process?

Jojo: Every song tells a story. So I tried to think about the good things I missed about Arcadia. Memories I might want to share. But I didn't miss anything. Still don't miss those skinny little streets with no traffic lines. Don't miss being bored out of my mind because there ain't shit to do. I used to walk outside and scream to hear something other than the same sounds I heard every day of my life. That's how bored I was. The only thing I missed was this little restaurant called King's Kitchen. One of those hole-in-the-wall places that makes the whole menu all day. Meatloaf for breakfast, pancakes for dinner. It's been there as long as I can remember. I think it still is. Or at least, I hope so. I hope it's not all Sonics and Pizza Hut now.

Emma: You haven't been back?

Jojo: Not much. My mom's gone so...no, I don't go often.

Emma: But you miss the food.

Jojo: I do. All the dishes have numbers and most people use those. But us regulars didn't even have to use them because the servers already knew what we wanted. I used to hate it when I was young. Too claustrophobic. I wanted to be a stranger somewhere because that seemed more sophisticated. But now I appreciate being known that way. The intimacy of it. I would love to walk into a dining room and have the server say Sundown, instead of asking for my order. That was my dish. A breakfast platter with over-easy eggs. The eggs are face down—well, you get it. That meal has always tasted like home to me. So I wrote a song about it—how much I missed that feeling of being known so well. But it came out sad because it made me feel lonely. And then critics decided it was about lynching and that was it. I stopped singing it.

CHAPTER FOUR

2009

Luke woke to a note in his mother's loopy handwriting that told him she'd be home to make dinner for her boys. The word *boys* was framed with hearts. She was always overly affectionate after a rough night. Instead of apologizing for her bad behavior, she'd pretend it never happened, daring her sons to mention it. If one of them did, she'd cry and yell, call them every foul version of ungrateful. Ava's shout had the force of an earthquake. She'd scream until the whole house shook.

Luke eyed the bruises along his forearm, and the previous night rushed back. Ava had been drunk when he got home. She'd gone out with friends after work and had an argument with one of the other bank tellers about whether her drawer had been short all week.

"She called me a thief. Can you believe that?"

Luke wasn't paying close enough attention. He didn't notice the gleam in her eyes that signaled she was too far gone for an honest answer. "I don't think that's what she meant," he said absently. He was thinking about August and how risky it was to hold on to her journal. He'd been plotting ways to return it without her noticing while the real threat was brewing in front of him.

Ava said, "You asshole." Then she laughed. That's when Luke started paying attention. His beautiful mother, with her amber eyes and tawny skin, had transformed into something ugly, her features contorted with the pain she usually smothered with pills. Doctors couldn't explain her condition. A few accused her of faking. Her prescriptions had run out years ago, so Luke didn't know where she got the Vicodin she stowed in her purse. A few days ago, she'd said she was quitting and made a big show of flushing a bottle down the toilet in front of him. Luke hadn't believed her, but now he realized she'd been serious. After seventy-two hours of suffering, she was tired of hurting alone.

Ava leaned forward and spit in his face. Luke jerked back, rubbing away her saliva, but she followed him, asking who the fuck he thought he was. Her arms went up, and he grabbed them instinctively, trying to stop whatever came next. But he couldn't. He never could. He could hold her down, pin her arms to her sides, or walk away and lock himself in his bedroom, but he could never make her calm or remorseful. Rage spread inside her like an infection. The feverish, killing kind.

Once Ava got tired of wailing on him, she left the house. Luke grabbed two six-packs of beer from the fridge and drank them all. When his little brother returned from junior high band practice, Luke was lounging on the couch, surrounded by crushed silver cans.

"I'll clean this up," he promised, gathering a few in a tiny heap.

"What did she do?" Ethan asked, retrieving a trash bag.

Luke told him the truth because they didn't keep secrets from each other. It was their primary survival tactic, trading information about their mother's moods. The lesson Luke passed on to Ethan, who was thirteen and struggling with hormonal changes that made it increasingly difficult to bite his tongue, was to avoid talking to their mother about work for a while. "She might get fired," Luke had said. "That'll make things worse, so be prepared."

Luke shook off the memory of last night, crumpled Ava's non-apology note, and made his way to the kitchen. It smelled like bacon left in the pan too long. Ethan was at the stove wearing one of Luke's old T-shirts. His brother was tall for a thirteen-year-old, with the bony frame of a kid forced to skip meals when his mother forgot to feed him. The fabric billowed around his narrow shoulders while he poked at scrambled eggs.

"This is burning," Luke said, turning off the heat under the bacon pan. Ethan's face flushed red. Despite inheriting Ava's light brown complexion, Ethan had inherited his Irish father's tendency to turn the color of beets at the slightest provocation.

"I like it crispy," Ethan protested, ever the perfectionist. He'd been that way since birth. Ava said Ethan had refused to cry, even when the doctor slapped him. "They thought he was dead at first," she would say with a laugh. "But knowing Ethan, he probably didn't want to admit being confused in front of strangers."

Luke cleared the table, which was covered with crumbled fast-food wrappers and half-empty wineglasses. "Is she with Don?"

Ethan loaded up two plates with bacon and eggs. "He picked her up this morning."

Don was the latest man Ava had decided would make a good role model for her sons. He was blond and toothy, always grinning even when it made the situation awkward. He worked at a chicken plant and lived in a trailer near the county line, which he thought entitled him to rant about Luke's poor career prospects, even though he seemed to spend more time praying about lottery tickets at New Life Church than murdering poultry at his day job.

Luke knew that with his poor grades and low ACT scores, a football scholarship was his only path to college. He agreed with Don's favorite insult ("A snowball's gonna survive hellfire before you get to the NFL") but going to LSU wasn't about playing in the pros. Baton Rouge was his mother's hometown. If Luke moved there, she might follow him and bring Ethan with her.

"Don told her to kick you out," Ethan said. "That it would teach you a lesson."

Luke shoved down more food and tried to look unbothered. It wouldn't do Ethan any good to see him panic. "She'd never do that."

"How do you know?"

"I just do." Luke fixed his brother with a hard stare. "Don't argue with her about it. I can take care of myself."

"You let her spit on you."

Luke's skin flashed hot. He didn't regret being honest with Ethan, but his brother's black-and-white way of viewing things didn't make it easy. "I didn't *let* her do anything."

"You didn't fight back."

"How? By spittin' back? You want me to hit her?"

Ethan fell silent, and Luke instantly regretted his sharp tone. Although Ethan had seen the worst sides of Ava, her fury had never been pointed in his direction. His little brother didn't understand why they were treated differently and often blamed Luke for not standing up for himself.

Luke knew exactly why the sight of her youngest son was a sigh of relief, while the sight of her oldest sent Ava into a rage. At nineteen, she'd gotten pregnant by Jason Randall, a pitch-black cattle farmer, which had infuriated her rich Creole parents. They'd cut her off and refused to acknowledge their grandson. When Jason died unexpectedly, Ava had packed their things and driven to Baton Rouge, ready to be welcomed back with open arms. But according to his mother, they took one look at Luke and slammed the door in her face. "My people are weird about some things" was her only explanation.

Luke became a reminder of her loss. He represented a choice she regretted and the man who convinced her to make it. Ethan, the unexpected child of a roaming white folk musician she met at the Delta Music Festival, became her humanity. Loving him was the only reason she hadn't given up on life completely.

"How's school?" Luke asked. He wanted to rescue the morning since they rarely had much time alone during the school year. "Did you ace that chemistry quiz you were stressed about?"

"That was last week, and yes." Ethan tried to look grumpy but failed because he loved bragging about being an eighth grader earning perfect scores in senior level classes. "It was multiple choice, so I memorized a lot of that stuff for nothing."

"Not for nothing, Dr. Randall," Luke said. "You'll use it in college or medical school."

"Pretty sure those will be a lot harder."

Luke grinned. "For you? Nah. You'll be whining about it being too easy on the first day."

Ethan smiled down at his food, moving it around his plate. He'd barely touched it. Luke tapped the table and motioned for him to tuck in. "Don't want to be late."

"Because you want to see August Lane?"

Luke frowned. "How do you know August?"

Ethan turned red again. "Don't be mad. I borrowed your iPod without asking and was trying to sneak it back into your room when I saw her notebook open on your bed." He bit into a piece of bacon and spoke while chewing. "Y'all would make a cute couple. Have you met her mother yet? You should play her your music."

"Hold on. One, don't steal my shit. Two, I'm still with Jessica. August and I are just friends."

"August doesn't have friends."

Luke started to argue but couldn't think of a shred of evidence to the contrary. "I thought *you* didn't have friends," Luke said instead. "Who's telling you all this stuff?"

"I have friends, jerk. Ever heard of study dates?"

"You're dating now?" Luke leaned back and tried to look at his brother with clearer eyes. A dark smudge dotted his cheek, threatening stubble. How had he missed it? "What's his name?"

Ethan's eyes shot to the door out of habit. No one else knew he was gay. Their mother, a lapsed Catholic, had become a lot more devout since she'd started dating Don, a Southern Baptist who wouldn't hesitate to send Ethan to some "pray the gay away" church camp.

"I'm not—he isn't—it's new, so I don't want to talk about it yet." Ethan's face was the color of ripe cherries. "Anyway, you'll get tired of Jessica. She never talks about anything interesting. Plus, you don't play guitar for her. You play for everyone you love."

Jessica cringed and shuddered whenever country played on the radio. She called it redneck music. Anytime he thought about her stumbling over his copy of *Learn to Live*, his stomach sank at the prospect of her ridicule. "How could anyone actually like Darius Rucker?" she'd probably ask. Meanwhile, the thought of playing "It Won't Be Like This for Long" for August made him light enough to float.

"It isn't fair to compare them," Luke said, for his own benefit as much as his brother's. "Jess isn't a music person. Plus, I'm pretty sure I'm not August's type." He pictured Richard, who looked and smelled like a men's magazine ad.

"Well, if she's your friend, ask her about *Country Star*. I heard they're doing auditions in Nashville next month. She might know something."

Luke took both their plates to the sink. "What's *Country Star*?"

"A talent competition. *American Idol* for country singers."

"Sounds corny."

"It probably is. But people love shows like that. You should audition."

Luke scrubbed the dishes to give him time to think of a gentle way to remind his brother that he was Black. Those producers would laugh him out of the building. And even if they didn't, filming would probably take months. He felt guilty whenever he left Ethan alone with Ava for twenty-four hours.

"I'm not built for TV," Luke said, which was true. All those cameras pointed at you. All those lights. "I can play around here."

"Where? Delta Blue?" Ethan's voice hardened when he mentioned the local bar. "You should stay away from that place."

"Because of Silas King?" Luke heard stories about August's uncle but had always questioned whether they were true. He couldn't believe some big-time criminal would settle in a town with a single gas station. "I've never met him."

"Not because of him. Because of the drinking," Ethan said. "You don't know how to stop."

Luke said, "Yes, I do." But it didn't sound as convincing as he would have liked. He glanced at the clock, grateful to see the late hour. "Go get dressed for school."

Ethan rolled his eyes, slid from the chair, and shuffled to his room. Luke busied himself emptying the trash, which had been neglected for days. The top was covered with his empty beer cans. This must have been what Ethan had seen when he walked into the kitchen that morning. Luke usually counted, sometimes with little tally marks on napkins, to make it easier to keep track of how many he'd had. Last night had been different. It got away from him.

It had been three days since August lost her notebook of song lyrics. Three days of retracing her steps in an escalating panic, bracing for the public humiliation that whoever found it would unleash at any moment. The worry had worn on her so much that she could barely hide her misery from her grandmother.

"You study for that test?" Birdie asked while adding five lumps of sugar and half a pint of cream to her coffee. She studied August with concern, somehow frowning without creasing her preternaturally smooth skin. She was terrified of getting wrinkles and being identified as the grandmother she was.

"Of course." August watched Birdie slurp down what she'd effectively turned into dessert.

"Well?"

"Well, what?"

"Are you ready?"

To fail? Absolutely. She'd been too distracted by her notebook to memorize any chemistry formulas besides water. "As ready as I can be."

Birdie motioned for August to stand. "Let me look at you."

August took her time standing, a silent protest of the daily ritual. Birdie refused to let her leave the house without inspection. August wore jeans and a striped top, but something about it made Birdie pause.

"That shirt's a little tight."

August rounded her shoulders and folded her arms over her stomach. "It's fine."

"Is it the right size?" Birdie walked around the table to look at the tag. It was a large, the size she'd insisted August buy, even though they were too big for her. The shirt wasn't the problem. It was how her body looked in the shirt, particularly her breasts, which had only recently stopped growing. Bands of thick black stripes made them more noticeable.

"Go change."

August didn't move. "I'll be late."

"Excuse me?" Birdie raised her eyebrows and pointed to the bedroom. "Pick a different top."

And that was that. August changed into the baggiest T-shirt she could find because arguing with her grandmother was like being sucked into a black hole. Boundless and soul crushing, circular in ways that made you lose any hope of escape.

She returned to the kitchen and did a slow, mocking turn for Birdie's benefit. "Do I look respectable now?"

Birdie smoothed August's hair behind her shoulders and kissed her forehead. "Don't be smart."

August made it to school with only a few minutes to spare. People stared at her as she climbed the front steps, but she was used to it now. The key was to avoid eye contact while glaring at the walls like someone had already pissed you off.

She was relieved to see Mavis near her locker. But then her cousin was joined by a group of her volleyball teammates, one of whom was Richard's ex-girlfriend. Mari Stanfield glared at August and whispered something to her friends before bursting into tears. They all converged, rubbing her back while shooting August dirty looks.

The bell rang. August tried to duck into her classroom but slammed into the tall wall of Luke Randall instead.

"Whoa!" He grabbed her waist to steady her and flashed that crooked smile she hated. It looked like flirting. It felt like a finger sliding down her back. August tried to right herself and stumbled, which only made him tighten his grip. The smile became a furrow of concern. "I got you."

"You're in my way," she said, but it didn't come out nearly as rude as she wanted. Too breathless instead of the stone-cold bitchiness she'd been going for. Luke stepped aside but kept his eyes on her longer than he should have, probably staring at her ass the way his friends did. Shane Adams, one of the least annoying members of that group, made a wounded noise when she walked past and gestured at her oversized shirt.

"I liked Friday's outfit better," he said, and cracked up laughing.

August had made the mistake of wearing a dress last week, something Birdie preferred to jeans. By lunch, she'd wanted to rip it off. The sight of her bare skin had kicked the harassment into overdrive. The girls were nastier. The boys were hornier. August had vowed never to wear it again.

Luke said nothing about her outfit. He'd been respectful so far, but so had Richard at first, who'd opened her car door and asked permission before kissing her. She could picture Luke doing that. She could picture him being so sweet and gentle on a first date that she'd immediately crack herself open again and offer up the pieces.

All the seats in the back of the classroom were taken. August sat near the window to have something to focus on besides the people around her. The sun was blazing, the summer heat relentless. She hated sharing a name with this month. The stubbornness of it. The way it refused to let the season fade gracefully.

She didn't realize Luke was sitting so close until he was assigned as her partner to think/pair/share the poem they'd been reading. August had spent the five minutes allotted to think about her assignment watching squirrels brawl over an acorn. She quickly skimmed the Langston Hughes poem so she wouldn't embarrass herself.

Luke had scribbled something on his worksheet. Upon closer inspection, she realized it was music notes. He covered it with one hand and nodded at her blank paper. "Let's use yours."

"You read music," she said, abandoning her plan to stay cool and aloof so he'd stop looking at her the way he was now: hopeful and cautious, as if she wielded power she wasn't aware of. "When you said you wrote it, I didn't think you meant literally writing it down, instead of just playing it."

"Yeah," Luke said, with a slight head dip like there was something to be embarrassed about. God, to be so lucky. She'd love to read music, but everyone in her family played by ear. "This poem, the rhythm of it... I can hear the melody." He shook his head. "That sounds so fucking stupid."

"No, it doesn't." She snatched the sheet from under his hand, then stared at what he'd written. It was like trying to decipher hieroglyphics. "What does it sound like?"

He looked over her shoulder. August turned around and saw Shane eyeing them with wide eyes and a giddy smile. He mouthed *"Bad girl"* to August. She flipped him off.

"None of that!" Their teacher, Mr. Ferris, glared at August. "Turn around and do your work."

Luke leaned against his desk and lowered his voice. "Ignore that dude," he said, nodding at Shane. "He's messy but harmless."

"He's never harmed *you*," she said, shoving Luke's paper onto his desk.

He straightened quickly and glared at Shane. "Did he hurt you?" His voice was low and tight. Heat flowed through her, and she lowered her eyes, staring at her paper until it passed.

He had to know what he was doing. Guys like him always did. The way everyone fawned over him—he'd have to be oblivious not to notice his effect on people. Three weeks into the school year, she'd realized that half the girls were in love with him, probably because he didn't seem to notice or care. Despite his flirtatious demeanor, August had seen no evidence Luke was unfaithful to his girlfriend, something few of her classmates could hide. Their hands always wandered. Their eyes revealed secrets. Luke seemed impenetrable, except apparently, while talking to strangers in the dark.

He cleared his throat. "What did you think of the poem?"

August looked down at the handout titled "Harlem." A list of discussion questions followed the text. *What dream is Hughes referring to? What do you think happens to a dream deferred?*

She tapped her pencil against her desk. "We don't have to talk about it. No one else is." She looked pointedly at the bored expressions of their classmates. "I could write the answers and put our names at the top." Luke looked disappointed. He glanced down at his paper with its mysterious music notes, and August realized she'd just screwed up her best chance to satisfy her curiosity.

"Sure, okay. This is more your thing anyway. Poems." Luke leaned back in his chair, adopting a careless pose. "I might actually get an A because of you."

"These questions are easy." She wrote *RACISM* in capital letters. "That's all he wants us to say."

He glanced at their teacher. Mr. Ferris stared at the clock, picking his nails into angry red nubs. "Do you always mess with that man this way?"

"He only assigns Black writers because he's forced to. He doesn't want to talk to us about them."

"I mean, do you blame him?" Luke looked pointedly at the person beside them, whose worksheet was covered with Biggie Smalls lyrics.

August sighed and erased her answer. "Fine."

"You're welcome." Luke straightened the line of brand-new pencils on his desk. There were four, way more than he needed. August had only one, which was covered in tooth marks and hadn't been sharpened since the first day of class.

"What do you think it means?"

He shook his head. "I asked you first."

She read the poem again, slower this time. "*Does it dry up / like a raisin in the sun? / Or fester like a sore / And then run?*" She read to the end silently. "I vote explosion."

"Unsurprising."

She stared at him. "Why do you do that?"

"What?"

"Talk like you know me." She thought about her journal, but then immediately put it out of her head. If he'd found it, he would have told someone or returned it by now. Keeping it for three days without saying a word made no sense. "We only had one conversation."

"Oh, so you do remember. I thought you got amnesia the minute you saw my face."

The hurt in his voice surprised her. It had never occurred to her that their conversation at the fair had been as meaningful to him as it had been to her. For August, it had been a brief, unguarded exhale that made her realize how long she'd been holding her breath. But she didn't want to talk about it in front of their classmates.

Luke flattened his hand over his pencil collection and rolled them under his palm. August watched the movement, her eyes drawn to a bruise on his wrist. "What happened?"

He slid his hand under his desk and glanced at the clock. "We should probably finish working on this."

August gestured at his pencils. "Why do you have so many of those?"

"So I always have a sharp one." He shot a quick, judgmental look at her pencil, with its tip blunted into the wood, barely usable. August picked it up and waggled it between her fingers.

"Does this bother you?"

He frowned and folded his arms. "No."

"You look stressed."

"I have a sharpener if you want to use it."

"Why would I do that when there are four perfectly good pencils right here?" She reached for one of his. He grabbed her hand to stop her. August laughed and said, "Why are you so possessive?"

"I'm not," he replied, his firm grip softening into a cradle before slipping away. "Maybe you just have that effect on me."

She pressed the hand he'd held against the desk, using its cool temperature to erase any lingering warmth. Then she leaned in and asked in a lowered voice, "Did you take my notebook?"

CHAPTER FIVE

2023

August left King's Kitchen to find a place where Luke wasn't sitting inches away from a steak knife. She couldn't shake the way he'd looked at her. Like he'd finally found her after years of searching. Like *she* was the one who had disappeared.

She drove east until she reached the gravel road that ended at Delta Blue's driveway. The club was built like an old juke joint, with new additions that had been haphazardly attached over the decades. One of them had been a one-bedroom apartment where Silas King lived but refused to call home. According to her uncle, "That word means more than a bathroom and a bed."

Inside, Delta Blue was cold and dark. The heat index was over a hundred degrees, and Silas had the air cranked to arctic levels. The temperature shift made it feel like stepping into another world, which was fitting since she'd always considered the bar a sanctuary. It was a place for customers to commune in a shared love of roots music, songs that reminded them of making out with their childhood sweetheart or the sting of their first shot of whiskey.

As a child, August would pretend to sing for sold-out crowds on the Delta Blue stage. She grew up listening to a diverse roster of local musicians while sweeping floors and washing dishes for spending money. For the past few years, on the nights Birdie's nurse would sleep over, August would come here to drink and pretend to be someone else. That woman was giggly and unencumbered, always looking for a good time.

Sometimes she found it. Sometimes she'd end the night in strange arms, sweating out demons with some musician she refused to tell her name. She'd say call me Songbird and sing a little if he wanted, then revel in how his eyes would ignite at her high notes. She never let on that they were anything special, but she'd smolder under that gaze. Remember how to burn.

August headed straight to Silas's office. The door was open and, like always, she was struck by how much older her uncle looked. Her mental picture of Silas was born in his favorite Westerns, the mythical man in black. He used to wear dark clothes and have a thick beard that obscured most of his face. These days, his beard was streaked with gray and his clothes were a clash of bright prints in breathable fabrics. He even wore reading glasses. They were perched at the end of his nose while he glared at spreadsheets covered with red notations.

Silas hated computers, so he printed everything, even emails. He also hated the business part of owning a business, like managing finances and keeping track of inventory. Delta Blue was his baby, so he forced himself to do what was needed to keep it open. He also owned King's Kitchen, which would have closed years ago if it hadn't been for August. She helped him manage it but refused to accept a formal title. It felt too permanent. An official acknowledgment that she'd never work anywhere else.

August sat in a wobbly leather chair she considered hers. She was one of the few people willing to sit in his presence long enough to hold a conversation. Half the town was convinced he was a criminal kingpin who ran drugs out of Delta Blue and used King's Kitchen to launder money. When August asked why he never corrected them, he'd said he was providing a public service. "People need a bogeyman to feel safe. Evil they can see."

Silas didn't seem surprised by her sudden appearance. He moved to the window, cracked it open, and tapped a pack of Marlboros against his palm. It was his patiently impatient way of asking whether the conversation was worth his one smoke a day.

"That asshole," she hissed, and motioned for him to share.

"Which one?" Silas ignored her request for a cigarette. He flipped open a lighter and cupped the small flame in his hand. "Terry Dixon? That dude owes me a hundred dollars. Or are you talking about his wife?"

"Luke." She hated how his name felt in her mouth. Saying it felt like forfeiting something.

Silas exhaled a cloud of smoke. "Luke, who?"

"*Luke*," August repeated, with emphasis that jarred recognition in his eyes.

"Luke Randall finally called you?"

"He's here. He showed up at King's. Sat in the same booth and ordered the same food as if he'd walked through a fucking time machine."

Silas studied her face. "How'd he look?"

If someone had told August she wouldn't recognize Luke Randall when he walked through the door, she would have called them a liar. She'd memorized that man through the lens of teenage obsession. He was her baseline. She'd rejected dates that looked too similar to him and recoiled from touches that weren't similar enough. That she'd know Luke if she ever saw him again was such a given that it didn't merit thinking about; it was as pointless as worrying about her next heartbeat.

The stranger she'd seen today had been bearded and broad, with sinister-looking tattoos that made her hesitate before approaching him. King's was close enough to the state highway to attract men who'd lost their good judgment years ago—roaming insomniacs looking to ride someone with one foot out the door. Luke had been hunched over the laminated menu with a stiff set to his shoulders, as if he were resigned to being jumped from behind.

"He looked..." August faltered as she remembered how it had felt when Luke said her name. Like a delicious jolt of energy. An illicit charge. She used to crave that feeling. Each day, she'd find those molten eyes and let that energy stoke her desire. For him. For their music. She'd go home high on their stolen glances.

That's what seeing him again was—a new hit of an old narcotic. It had made her panic when he'd tried to touch her. She didn't know what would happen if he did. What she'd do.

"Different," she told Silas. "He looks older, like we all do."

"I mean, how was he? Did he speak to you?"

They weren't having the same conversation. She'd come there looking for commiseration while Silas seemed thrilled at the prospect of Luke's return. She should have known. The two had bonded from the moment she'd introduced them, with Silas eventually becoming a father figure when Luke needed it most. But as far as she knew, Luke had ghosted Silas for more than a decade, too. That her uncle seemed unbothered by it made her even angrier.

"That man had a multiplatinum hit single and is married to the biggest country music star in the world. He's doing fine." August folded her arms. "Even had the nerve to apologize."

Silas paused. "Good."

"No, not good. I don't want an apology. I want—" The memory of his near touch rose again, taunting her. "I want him to leave me alone." August rubbed her face, trying to scrub away anything that might betray her thoughts. *You shouldn't want someone you hate.* It said something bad about her. That there was a wire loose somewhere.

"You sure all this is about Luke?" Silas tossed his cigarette out the window. He grabbed a chair and sat across from her. "You're out here drunk and getting into fights. That's not like you." He sagged in his seat. "Did you go to that meeting I recommended?"

August had attended one of the grief support group meetings Silas referred her to. She'd sat in a room surrounded by people who had experienced more loss in a single day than she may ever see in a lifetime: wives who'd lost husbands, twins who'd lost siblings. One woman had left her four-year-old alone in the bathtub to get a towel and came back to find the girl unconscious. "She had a seizure," the woman had said, devoid of emotion, like there was nothing left to feel.

The idea of processing her grief through their suffering felt cannibalistic. Her loss was so small in comparison. Everyone had been waiting for Birdie to pass since her diagnosis. She hadn't recognized August in a year.

"I *went*," August told Silas. He looked annoyed, so she added, "And I'll go back. Things are just really busy at King's."

"That's a lie, but you can keep it 'cause you clearly need it. Promise me you'll talk to someone about what you're dealing with. That includes Luke."

"I dealt with Luke already."

"Burning his CD in a trash can doesn't count. You ain't a goddamn witch."

She shrugged. "The Chicks say it's okay to hate a man forever. It's very healthy."

Silas frowned. "What chicks?"

"Dixie Chicks."

"Oh. Why'd they change it?"

"Because Black lives matter now."

"Ah." He returned to his desk and stared at the spreadsheets without reading them. "Maybe you should listen to him. I know he hurt you, but it sounds like he's trying to make things right."

August remembered how surprised Luke had been to see her. He'd claimed not to know she still worked at King's, which meant his apology hadn't been a priority. His first trip home in thirteen years, and she came second to eggs and bacon.

"You don't know him like I do," she said. "Luke's only here because he didn't have a choice."

Silas frowned at something to her right. Mavis glided into the room dressed in a formfitting red power suit that probably cost more than August paid for her apartment.

"What's the point of having a phone if you never answer it?" She dropped festival flyers on Silas's desk. "When was the last time you spoke to August? We need to figure out how to tell her that Luke—" Mavis straightened and spun around, finally sensing another person in the room. "Oh. Hi."

August stood. "You're too late. He showed up at King's earlier and made me take his order."

Her face hardened. "Asshole."

"Right?"

"Hold up now," Silas said, lifting a hand. "He tried to apologize."

"There's a sell-by date on those things." Mavis looked at August. "I hope you told him where to go."

"Poured hot coffee on his dick."

Mavis's mouth fell open. "How hot?"

"It was at King's."

Her shoulders relaxed. "Oh. Okay."

"Ain't nothing wrong with that coffeepot," Silas grumbled. He glanced at the flyers. "And I'm not putting those in my window until you put that money back into the showcase budget. If not, thanks for stopping by."

August looked at Mavis. "What money? What's he talking about?"

Mavis glared at Silas and then forced a smile for August's benefit. "Your mother's concert is a huge opportunity for the city, so we revised the festival budget to capitalize on it." Her voice had a CEO edge to it, which always happened when her cousin was in charge of something. Her competitive nature hadn't subsided once she stopped playing volleyball. If there was a brass ring to win, Mavis wanted it. Now she'd decided that Jojo's concert was the key.

"Revised meaning gutted," Silas said. "I've got no support for the showcase. No ads. No signage. Word of mouth won't work, either. All anyone's talking about is Jojo." He waved Mavis away. "Cancel it."

"No!" August moved to block Mavis from his view. "Your showcase is the festival. Everyone knows it. The other shows are just cash grabs and publicity. The real music gets played here." August thought about the previous showcases she'd attended. The event had a reputation that bordered on myth. People used to say that performing there brought good luck, as evidenced by the number of people who'd signed with publishers and producers after the show.

That ended with the pandemic, when the festival was canceled and later downsized out of caution. This year was supposed to be their big comeback, a return to how things were before. But the showcase wasn't on people's radar anymore. After the Black Lives Matter protests, larger festivals committed to being more inclusive. The musicians that would have normally flocked to Delta Blue were booking gigs at higher-profile events instead.

"I think your mother would take issue with you calling her Hall of Fame celebration a cash grab." Mavis gave August the same concerned look she did yesterday while banning her from church. "When was the last time you spoke to her?"

August ignored the question. If she admitted that she and Jojo weren't speaking, they would want to know why, and she wasn't ready to discuss that with anyone. "He's right." She grabbed a flyer advertising Jojo's show and waved it around. "You need to focus on the showcase instead of—" Her eyes caught on a list of names beneath Jojo's photo. "What the hell is this?"

Silas grabbed a copy. He read it, then gave August a warning look that told her to calm down. She swallowed hard and did her best to comply. "Is Luke opening for my mother?"

Mavis looked like she'd been asked to swallow a frog. "This is what I was trying to figure out how to tell you. He's not just opening. They're performing a song together."

August kept her eyes on the flyer. She had to ask. But she didn't want them to see her face when she heard the answer. "Which song?"

Hey, it's Ethan. Leave me a message, and I'll get back to you. Promise.

Luke listened to his brother's voicemail with the weight of ten bricks on his chest. He tried to focus on the road, keep both hands on the wheel until the feeling subsided. It always did once he accepted that Ethan's promise applied to everyone but him.

"It's me," Luke said, elevating his voice for the speakerphone. "You won't believe where I am right now." He scanned his surroundings, taking in the sprawl of his family's land on either side of his truck. "You've probably already seen the news. Or maybe not. Big-time doctors don't have much time to waste scrolling online. I'm back in Arcadia. Doing a concert with Jojo Lane."

He tried to gather his thoughts. If he wasn't careful, the message would devolve into a messy stream of consciousness, things he wanted to tell his brother in person instead of through a recording. But it had been six years since Ethan returned his calls. Six years since his brother said he was done watching Luke kill himself slowly.

Luke had been in denial at first. He would send unanswered texts and tell himself that while Ethan was angry now, he'd eventually relent the way he always did. Then a year went by, and Luke panicked. He showed up unannounced at Ethan's house and was met by his apologetic husband, who gently suggested he wait to be invited before showing up for a visit.

When Luke finished rehab, he'd immediately called Ethan and left a message announcing his sobriety with the smugness of someone who had no idea what it meant. He received no congratulations. No acknowledgment that he'd slain the dragon that had destroyed their relationship. But Ethan hadn't blocked or changed his number, either, so Luke became caught in a painful loop. Something good would happen and he'd immediately think this was it. This was the thing that would make a difference. Today, it was the concert. He thought Ethan might be proud of him for coming home.

"On my way out to the farm right now. Wish you were here," Luke said. "You're still better at handling Mom than me."

He cleared his throat. "I'll have some tickets on hold for you if you want to come down to the festival." He glanced at the clock and realized how long he'd been talking. "Love you," he mumbled, then disconnected.

Luke slowed to a stop when he reached a metal sign with RANDALL written on it in peeling vinyl letters. The farm was emptier than it should be this time of year. The ranchers Ava leased the land to would typically be preparing for calving season and relocating livestock to give the pastures a rest. Now there were new fences and keep-out signs from a large oil and gas company, which meant she'd sold off more of the mineral rights to pay her bills.

When the house came into view, Luke barely recognized it. The bones were there, but the bottom half of the brick split-level was being devoured by neglected landscaping. Deep cracks lined the concrete steps that led up to the front door, and one of the living room shutters had nearly fallen off its hinges. He stared at that window a while before pressing the doorbell, which didn't make a sound. It was a sign, right? He'd played the dutiful son and could leave. Wasn't this bare minimum of effort all he owed her?

His answer was footfalls on the other side of the door. Ava smiled broadly when she saw him, her golden irises swallowed by blown, glistening pupils. Whatever painkiller she'd taken was doing its job, numbing her giddy.

"You're here!" She kissed his cheek and waved him in.

The house smelled like Lysol and lemon Pledge, which meant she'd just finished cleaning. Only, it wasn't clean. A few surfaces gleamed from her efforts, but the furniture was stained and sagging, the carpet in similar shape. A musty smell undermined her attempts to control the odor. The windows were covered with the same heavy curtains he grew up with, which turned the house into a dingy cave.

As a child, Luke was so used to existing in darkness that he found it comforting. That's what he'd been doing when August found him that night at the county fair, using the dark to calm his fears. Part of his recovery had been turning to the light. At home, his shades were always open. He exercised outside. He did yard work for a local shelter so he could spend hours with the sun on his skin.

"Let me look at you." Ava's eyes swept over him. "You cut your hair off."

"I do that every summer."

She nodded, twisting her hands. "Makes sense. It's so hot out there, isn't it? Like we're being punished for something." She grabbed the small dime on a chain around her neck. The charm was supposed to protect her from demons. "That beard makes you look even more like him."

Luke was tempted to feign ignorance so that she'd be forced to say his father's name. They both knew how much he favored Jason Randall. Luke was only four when his father died, but he had seen enough photos to know they could be mistaken for brothers now.

"Where's your suitcase? I can take it to your room." Ava spun around, searching.

"In the truck." Luke eyed the foot and leg massagers on her couch. "Do those help?"

Ava glanced at them and said, "A little," while rubbing her arms like she'd caught a chill. Luke was sweating. She always kept the house uncomfortably warm because the cold worsened her condition. Luke and Ethan used to accuse her of being cheap. Years later, after her fibromyalgia diagnosis, they realized it was just another way of coping with her chronic pain.

"Are you excited to be home?" She rushed past him and picked up a copy of *People* magazine with Jojo Lane on the cover. "I bought this at Kroger yesterday. Thought they'd have a picture of you, but..." She flipped it open and pointed to his name in a small text box. "There you are!"

Luke took the magazine and turned it over in his hands. "I didn't know they still sold these in print."

"Me neither. But I'm glad they do. Charlotte must be so proud of you. How is she? Is she coming to the concert?"

Luke put the magazine on the table. "We're getting divorced."

Ava sucked in a breath. "What?" She looked at his hand and saw the missing wedding band. "When did this happen?"

"A decade ago," he said, which felt good to admit. He wanted to shed his lies. Peel himself down to the core. But he had to keep some of them. The big ones had become scaffolding, holding up all the rest. "She's in love with someone else. I'm happy for her."

"Well, I'm not!" Ava cried. "You two were so good together."

Luke wiped sweat from his brow and started walking toward the kitchen. "I need some water."

"I can get it." Ava moved quickly, trying to cut him off. "How about a real drink? You like old-fashioneds? I know how to make those now."

"I don't drink anymore," Luke said. He'd never considered telling her he was an alcoholic because he knew what she would say. *Well, you came by it honestly.*

Luke could recall the few times Ava had been sober with perfect clarity: Three Christmas mornings. One of Ethan's birthdays. Two trips to Branson. There was one Wednesday game night when he was ten years old that had been nearly perfect. He'd convinced himself that three uneventful hours of Uno and pizza meant things would get better, that they'd reached a level of normal that made him cry himself to sleep. But two days later, when Ava became so flustered by her new coffee maker's instructions that she shattered the pot against the wall, he'd cleaned the mess with tiny glass shards in his hand and hadn't shed a tear.

"You shouldn't be drinking, either," he told her. "It doesn't mix well with your medication."

Ava touched her dime again and wound the chain around her finger. "Fix that droopy face of yours. We should celebrate! How about pizza?"

"I'm not staying," Luke said. He was broke enough to convince himself that he could stomach sleeping in his old room until the performance fee hit his account. But he knew what would happen if he stayed in this house. Five years of sobriety wasted on grocery store chardonnay. "I just stopped by on the way to the motel. Jojo's manager is paying for it."

"For two months? That's a lot of money."

"Not for them."

"Well. That's disappointing." Her voice had risen slightly with the effort to hide her distress. He was doing the same thing. Being there took him to dangerous places. Holding her hair back while she leaned over the toilet. Him blacking out after a game. Now they eyed each other, forcing small talk while their inner drunks tore up their insides.

His phone vibrated. A text from David Henry flashed across the screen. What the hell are you doing in Arcadia? And why the hell did you think I'd pay for it?

"I've got to deal with this." Luke gestured to his phone. "Call you later."

He walked out the door before she could protest. The hot air was brutal, but he took in a lungful, grateful to escape the rankness of that house. But based on David's text, he had nowhere to go.

Maybe it was time to admit his half-assed forgiveness tour had flopped and cut his losses. He could hide in Memphis until it was time to return for the show.

"I know that look. Already plotting your escape?"

Luke looked to his right and there was August, standing next to his truck with a mean smirk on those perfect lips. She'd also pinned her hair into a messy Victorian pile on top of her head, and goddamn if the combination didn't steal his breath.

She looked at the house and her expression softened to concern. "You shouldn't be here."

Luke's eyes never left her. "I know."

―•―○―•―

The silver touches at Luke's temples made him look older than thirty-one. Or maybe it was the look in his eyes, like he was standing in some deep hole and was resigned to being buried in it. August hated knowing that about him, how complacent he could be about things that were objectively unbearable. The thought of him staying here, with the woman who'd made him that way, was more infuriating than the flyer folded in her hand.

"How'd you find me?" he asked.

"I checked the motel and didn't see any unfamiliar cars," she said. There were two motels in town, and only one that regularly changed the bedsheets. "I checked King's, too. This was my third stop."

His eyes shifted to his truck, and a smile crept over his lips. Crooked and flirty. That same damn finger sliding down her back. "So you were driving around town, searching for my truck?"

The picture he painted was embarrassing. Like she'd been squinting through the windshield at random parking lots, frantically searching for signs of him. "It wasn't like that."

"What was it like?" Luke folded his arms over his chest. Those were different, too. Teenage Luke had been tall enough to have an awkward, stringy quality to his limbs. Now he was broader, with the solid trunk of a guy who flipped tractor tires for fun. "A few hours ago, you threw hot coffee in my lap."

She folded her arms, mirroring his stance. "It was lukewarm."

"Did you know that?"

"Yes." He raised a brow. She rolled her eyes. "I suspected. Either way, you deserved it."

"I did." He moved closer with slow, cautious steps, like she was a skittish fawn he'd cornered. "I do," he continued. "Which is why I'm surprised to see you. Figured I'd be the one chasing you around town."

"I'm not chasing you."

"You could have called."

"I don't have your number."

"Hasn't changed."

She pictured his first cell phone—a cheap Samsung he'd purchased before he left town. "Did you really think I'd keep it this long?"

"I kept yours."

Surprise stole her ability to speak. She could still picture the wrinkled scrap of paper she'd shoved into his hand when he'd asked for it. It was the first one he'd added to his contacts, which felt like some grand gesture, effortlessly romantic.

"Why?" she finally managed.

"Because it's yours," he said, with a dismissive shrug that tried to pretend those were just words. His eyes said don't pry if you know what's good for you. That door might be better off closed.

August showed him the flyer. "What the hell is this?"

He was slow to look at it, reluctant to change the subject. When he finally did, horror creased his face. "Shit."

"Yeah. *Shit*." She was spiraling back to rage, which was good. Easier to understand than the dance they'd just been doing. "So much for that apology."

"I would have told you before if you had listened to me."

"Why would I do that?" She shoved the flyer at his chest. "Why would I listen to anything you had to say? You had my number for thirteen years and never bothered to use it."

Luke worked his jaw in a way she'd seen countless times before. He was searching for words that might calm her, rejecting anything that might create more conflict. "You wouldn't have wanted to hear from me," he said. "I wasn't ready for this. For you."

August wasn't ready for him, either. She'd realized it the minute Bill said Luke was coming back. She was right where he left her all those years ago—hurt, angry, and humiliated by what he'd done. It was easier to think of him as a list of offenses instead of a man. Luke lied. Luke left. Luke was selfish. It was a simple and uncluttered hate that only worked in the absence of contradictions. But that's what he was, a bundle of things at war with each other. Luke lied but also looked lost. Luke left but had returned to the sight of his worst nightmares. Luke was selfish but wore regret like a penitent King Midas desperate to touch something real.

Birdie used to say that love wasn't feeling. It was doing. Despite how August felt, she couldn't act on it, no matter how much she wanted to.

She couldn't love him anymore. She *couldn't*. The shame would eat her alive.

"Congratulations on your growth," August said. "But I won't forgive you, so don't bother asking."

Luke's expression sharpened, like she'd cut somewhere deep. "I don't want your forgiveness, August."

It shouldn't have hurt after what she'd just said. She had no right to care. But that was her way, wasn't it? How did Birdie put it? Contrary, just to be contrary? That was her curse. "Then what do you want?"

Luke balled his hands into fists. The word *peace* was drawn across his knuckles in black ink. "I owe you. Everything I have, which hasn't been much lately, but that's about to change because of your mother."

Her face warmed. "Are you offering me money?"

"Only if you need it," Luke said. "Only if you could stomach taking it from me."

August saw herself through his eyes. A small-town lifer who couldn't get it together enough to leave this place. "But not credit."

Luke stared at her for a long moment. "I'd lose everything if I did that."

August felt herself hardening. Any lingering sympathy she had toward him drained away. "Like that money."

"No. I mean, yes, but it's not just that. It's complicated—"

"Well, I'll make it simple." August moved closer. "You're not singing 'Another Love Song.'"

"Yes, I am. I hate it as much as you—"

"No, you don't. I swear you don't."

"Okay." He lifted his hands. "You're right. I can't imagine what you're feeling. But it's what she hired me to do. I don't have a choice."

"This is your choice. Sing one line of that song, and I'll tell everyone you lied about writing it to win that dumb reality show."

Luke looked horrified, staring blankly like she'd transformed into someone else. Maybe she had. Offering money was like baring his neck to a bloodthirsty vampire. He'd made her his monster.

"You want me to quit? Walk away from the last chance to do anything with my life? Music is all I'm good for. I fuck this up, they won't touch me again."

His voice was tight, hinting at the first genuine anger she'd seen since he returned. She wanted more of it. She wanted him to feel what she'd been carrying inside for years.

"I didn't tell you to quit," she said. "Sing something else."

"That song is all anyone wants from me."

"Because you never gave them anything else! Just country-bro bullshit that only works for white boys. You hid more than a songwriting credit, Luke. You hid yourself. You hid your voice."

"You think I don't know that?" He was yelling now, matching her fury. "I am very much aware that I fucked my career before it started. But I can't change it. I tried and failed repeatedly. And we both know it's 'cause I can't write shit without you!"

The solution came to her with such clarity she struggled to put it into words. "You're right" was all she said as a plan tumbled into place.

Luke had everything to lose, but since Birdie died, August had nothing worth protecting. She hated her job. Her family barely tolerated her. She'd spent most of her adult life caring for Birdie because that's what you did when you loved someone. You stayed.

Meanwhile, Luke had done the opposite, putting his ambition over everything. Now here they were, standing at two life-altering precipices with completely different trajectories. Luke's was pointed skyward, with unlimited potential, while hers was a slow disintegration, like an old tree no one knew was dying.

Her salvation was obvious. Music was all she was good for, too. She'd steal his last chance for herself. And was it really stealing when the victim was a thief?

"We'll write something new," she said. "Something better. And you'll sing it at the concert."

"You want to write a song with me?" Luke looked seconds away from laughing but was too furious to let it escape. "After everything that's happened?"

"You'll give me credit this time." Which would require trusting him, which she absolutely wasn't prepared to do. "During the concert."

"August, this is…" He slowly shook his head. "You're not thinking clearly. There's no way Jojo will let me sing something she hasn't approved. The concert is only two months away."

"Then we should get started. Or should I call my mother and put you out of your misery now?"

She pulled out her phone and waited for his answer. Luke's eyes were blazing, shifting between the phone and her face. August smiled, and he stared at her mouth. She had a brief image of them grappling—settling the standoff with tongues and heat.

"Fine," he said, practically growling. "I'll do it. Just put the damn phone away."

"One more thing."

His chin jerked up, a muscle ticking in his jaw. "What?"

She hesitated, but then spoke in the firm, decisive tone she was determined to feel. "Once the show is over? I never want to see you again."

PART THREE

THE LIFT

This Is Our Country: Podcast Transcript

Episode 12—"Jojo Lane"
August 21, 2024

[*cont.*]

Jojo: I had my daughter at fifteen years old. There wasn't any sex education at Eastside High. It was a small-town southern school. They didn't do stuff like that. We watched a video in health class, but it was all birthing videos designed to scare us. I fell asleep.

Emma: [*groans*]

Jojo: I know, right? Should have been paying closer attention.

Emma: What was it like, being pregnant at fifteen?

Jojo: Everybody knew, but they would pretend not to see it. I was this little slip of nothing waddling around with a big belly and they'd only meet my eyes. "Look at those eyes!" they'd say, 'cause light eyes on a Black girl gets everyone excited. For months, I was just a pair of pretty eyes to them because they didn't want to deal with it. This was mainly church folks. They like to pray with their eyes closed.

Emma: Do you still go to church?

Jojo: Not anymore. But I believe in God. You have to. This business is hell.

Emma: [*laughs*] That is true.

Jojo: Amen.

Emma: Your daughter's name is August, right?

Jojo: Augustina Rose.

Emma: Sounds like a country song.

Jojo: Oh no, don't say that. [*laughs*] I never wanted her to follow in my footsteps.

Emma: What does her father do?

Jojo: No idea. He's gone.
Emma: Gone. Like, dead?
Jojo: Maybe. He was the type.
Emma: I'm not sure what you mean.
Jojo: Not a good man.
Emma: Okay. Was that hard? Being a single mother?
Jojo: It's all hard. That's what no one tells you. Motherhood is jail. People will hate me for saying that, but it'll break you. Do you have kids?
Emma: No.
Jojo: Don't. It's the scariest thing. Every nightmare is something bad happening to her.
Emma: Is that why you left her with your mother in Arcadia? To keep her safe?
Jojo: [*no response*]
Emma: It's fine if you'd rather not say.
Jojo: I was just thinking, is all. Maybe? I'm not sure. I traveled a lot after I had her. Did the bar circuit while I was underage. It wasn't dangerous. Or maybe it didn't feel that way because most of us were carrying.
Emma: Carrying? You mean guns?
Jojo: Don't look so shocked. My band was all country kids who grew up with hunting rifles. Mom gave me my first pistol.
Emma: I can see why you wouldn't want your daughter around that.
Jojo: I didn't. But I also don't want to pretend that's why I left her with Birdie. Mom wanted August. I wanted to sing.

CHAPTER SIX

2009

Luke had never been good with words. He was a late talker who'd preferred to communicate with gestures until his fourth birthday. That was the year his father died, and he wondered if, even at that age, he knew that meant his childhood was over. Ava started calling him the man of the house when she tucked him into bed.

His pediatrician considered Luke's sudden willingness to talk evidence that his prior reluctance was obstinance instead of a developmental issue. Ava thought that meant Luke was being difficult and made it her mission to make him easy. Any time he slipped into his old habit of gestures instead of speaking, she'd grab his hand and squeeze until he flinched.

Luke learned to use his words strategically, like tools. He knew which jokes would make his teammates laugh or what kind of greeting would prompt a smile from a stranger. He knew what not to say around his mother when she was hurting. He knew what his girlfriend wanted to hear when he called her each night, even though she hated talking on the phone. "Just needed to hear your voice."

But tools were only useful when you could anticipate the problem. It was like driving around with a tire iron in the trunk. Wheels went flat sometimes, which made it easy to be prepared. Only that didn't work with August. His usual tools were useless because he couldn't predict what she would say. So, when she leaned over, gave him a face full of pretty, and asked about her notebook, he'd nearly choked on his saliva and sprinted from the room when the second-period bell rang.

Now that he'd had a few hours to gather his thoughts, he planned to return it that afternoon along with a note explaining why he'd kept it so long. He was currently on his third draft because he wasn't sure how honest to be. If he wrote the whole truth, that her songs reminded him of his father, it would be weird without elaboration. *He was a farmer, but also a poet. I only have one of his books, which I hide, so my mother won't throw it away.*

He flipped through the journal, looking for the song he loved. "My Jagged Pieces" was about living with a broken heart. *Sometimes it's bitter / Sometimes it's sweet / But I think / since you left / it's forgotten how to beat.* He added a chord progression in pencil just in case she was so mad that he'd taken the notebook, she wanted to erase the music he'd written. But if she wasn't too angry, he would retrieve his guitar from the truck and play it for her.

Eventually, he gave up on the letter, which had taken on a begging quality he wasn't comfortable with. Instead, he planned to give her the notebook in class tomorrow along with the simplest lie he could think of. "It must have gotten mixed up with my stuff. I didn't realize it until you said something. But I wrote some music for you. Keep it. Erase it. Whatever."

Luke walked out of the gym feeling pleased with himself for coming up with a solution. But then he saw August sitting on a bench near his truck. It had to be his punishment for coming up with such a dumb-ass plan. He couldn't walk past her like nothing happened. He had to tell the truth.

Luke approached her from behind and said, "Hey."

August looked startled. She tugged at that ugly, baggy T-shirt she'd worn for some reason and said, "Hey," with more impatience than he expected. It made him wish he'd walked home.

"I'm sorry," he said. She frowned, and he realized that he'd done things out of order, apologized for an offense he hadn't admitted to. He reached into his gym bag and pulled out her notebook. "I found it on the floor a few days ago."

She didn't take it. "Did you read it?"

Luke's arm slacked. "Yes."

"Did you show it to anyone else?"

"No. I swear, I would never do that."

She finally grabbed it and flipped it open. He winced when she spotted his notes. "That's music."

"I can see that." She glanced up at him. "But I can't read it, remember?"

Luke rubbed his neck. "Right. I thought maybe I could..." He gestured at the pages instead of finishing. If there were a trophy for being the biggest idiot around a beautiful girl, he'd win it by the time the conversation ended.

August turned the page and stared at his notes on another song. "Why did you do this?"

Luke sat beside her. She immediately shifted to keep him directly in her line of sight. "I should have asked first."

"Asked?" She slid her hand over the pages. "This is the nicest thing anyone's ever done for me."

Luke couldn't contain the smile that spread over his face, showing all his teeth. He probably looked goofy, but he didn't care. "For real?"

"Yes. But you didn't answer my question. Why? This looks like a lot of work."

"I liked your songs," he said, but it felt like lying. The statement was so inadequate. "I loved them. When I love something, this is what I do." He gestured at the notes. "Books. Poems. Like I did earlier when we were reading Langston Hughes?" She nodded, and he said, "I heard it, so I had to write it down."

He was talking too much. He stopped to give her a chance to speak, but she only stared at him, her face soft and open, like he'd never seen before. She flipped through the journal again. "I wish I could hear it."

Luke glanced at his truck. "My guitar is—" He stopped when he saw Jessica walking toward them. She was dressed in a volleyball T-shirt and shorts with her game shoes slung over one shoulder. He looked at August and choked out "Sorry" before Jessica reached them.

"There you are," Jessica said. Her eyes skidded to August but quickly refocused on Luke. "I was waiting."

Luke had forgotten he was giving her a ride home. "Sorry."

"You say that a lot." August's voice was colder. There was no trace of the vulnerability from earlier.

Jessica frowned and whispered, "Okay, bitch."

Luke looked back and forth between the two, mentally hovering above the situation and trying to figure out the best way to disrupt the tension. The truth would only make things worse. *Hey, Jess, this thing with August is a pathetic one-sided crush with no hope of reciprocation. And, August, Jess and I had terrible sex. But we also said I love you, so if we break up over that, it means we're terrible people.*

"We should go," Jessica said to Luke. "My parents said there was traffic on the way to 30-A, so I don't know when they'll get to the beach house. They always call to check in."

Luke hated how she spoke to him, as though they were the only two people in the conversation. He looked pointedly at August. "She's having a birthday party tonight," he said. "Everyone'll be there. You should come."

Jessica stiffened at his side. She'd be furious with him later. "Yeah," she said, eyes full of daggers. "Please. Come. *Everyone* will be there."

August smirked and said, "I have plans. But enjoy your birthday." She looked at Luke and added, "I hope you get everything you want."

Luke watched August gather her things and leave. He wanted to say something, signal that this guy he became around Jessica wasn't him. But whatever August had dislodged inside him earlier was wedged firmly back in place.

Jessica patted his back as they walked to his car. "Niceness is wasted on that girl. At least you tried."

Luke nodded, even though he hadn't.

———◊———

August had considered accepting that invitation to Jessica's party just to see what her face would do. During the brief conversation, her expression had shifted from mild irritation at Luke to a sour snarl when she spotted August, to a bland smile that was supposed to hide her anger but only made her look like a demonic American Girl doll. If August had said "I'd love to" in response to Luke's offer, Jessica probably would have sprung a leak somewhere.

Despite how misguided Luke's invitation had been, it had come from a place of genuine kindness, which was his default. If Luke Randall could be himself, he'd slide into goodness with little friction. But he had Friends, the capital *F* kind that tainted your instincts by deeming anything genuine a social sin. That was the good thing about being a pariah; the only person August had to please was herself.

Still, it would have been nice to have real Thursday night plans, something illicit and chaotic, like normal seventeen-year-olds. Instead, she sat in her room with a cordless phone cradled in her lap, editing the list of notes she'd made to navigate a phone call with her mother.

Meticulously planning her interactions with Jojo was part of the weirdness that came with having a famous parent. There were rules for keeping her mother's undivided attention. The first was no rambling. The conversation had to be interesting enough to feel like it wasn't a waste of her time. August tried to be sharp and funny, even when she wasn't in the mood to be. That was rule number two—no sad talk. No whining about your day, which was tiny and insignificant compared to Jojo's big, important life. August's goal during every call was to make sure the conversation didn't become a chore.

She dialed Jojo's number. Her mother's assistant answered the phone. "Is this Miss August? Hi, sweetie, how are you? She's putting her face on, so it'll be a second."

"Thanks, Patty," August said. "How are your kids?"

Patty launched into a story about her little Caleb's first steps, and August pretended to be impressed because it was the least she could do for the woman who picked out her birthday gifts each year.

"Here she is," Patty announced. There was a short period of fumbling with the receiver and distant voices before Jojo said "Hi!" with too much enthusiasm. She answered everyone's call with the same warmth, even telemarketers, like she'd been secretly hoping to hear from them.

"Hi," August said, staring at her notes. Jojo was in Kansas City at a folk music festival. She'd mailed August a flyer with her name in a small font, buried in a sea of other musicians. "Excited about the show?"

Rule number three. Start with her. Always. Never you.

"Oh, I guess so. It's a little thing, opening for someone I never heard of. The usual." There was a muffled sound, like she was covering the receiver. "Sorry, people keep asking me questions I don't know the answer to. What was I saying?"

"That you're opening for someone who's overrated."

Jojo laughed. Pleasure pooled in August's stomach. She was doing well.

"Yep, exactly. So, how are you? How's school? Your friends?"

In her efforts to reassure Jojo that it was safe to call on a regular basis, August had embellished her teenage life with imagery stolen from John Hughes movies. There were best friends who invited her to sleepovers. There were science fairs. There were plays in which she sang in a large chorus, and that explained the lack of pictures. The boys were nice to her but standoffish because they were intimidated by her famous mother.

She wasn't sure what Jojo would say if she knew the truth: that August hadn't had a real friend since fifth grade, before everyone decided it was embarrassing to have a Black mother who wore cowboy hats and used to yodel in beauty pageants. She couldn't tell her mother how badly she'd fumbled her chance to reinvent herself at a new school by sleeping with the first guy who offered her an Arcadia Eagles welcome pack of M&M's.

"School is fine. It's great. Homecoming is next month." August was only slightly confident this was true. She'd thrown the event calendar in the trash seconds after it was handed to her.

"Oh Lord, homecoming. I remember that. Is there a dance? Are you going?"

Jojo had a habit of stringing multiple questions together, probably because it saved time. August picked the easiest one to answer. "Yes, there's a dance. I think it's a Motown theme. Everyone's supposed to look like the Temptations or Supremes."

"I like that. What are you gonna do?"

"I haven't decided." She wasn't going, but she couldn't help thinking about it. She loved Motown. "Maybe Aretha."

"Good choice. Let me know if you need help with a costume."

The idea of Jojo taking time out of her busy schedule to style her wig and wing her eyeliner made a lump form in August's throat. The worst lies were those you wished were true. "I will," August said.

There was a silent beat, a lull too long for comfort. August asked

"When are you coming down?" just as Jojo said "Sounds like you're keeping out of trouble."

Trouble in the Lane house was shorthand for a sprawling list of sins. Failed classes. Drugs. Sex. Are your skirts too short? Are your legs too open? Are you like me in all the ways everyone hates?

August was nothing like her mother, but sometimes it was hard to remember that. Physically, they were opposites. Jojo was all long, skinny angles, with chestnut skin and green eyes that no one could pinpoint the source of. August was kinkier and curvier, with big dark eyes that made her look sleepy or startled, nothing in between. In third grade, a boy once told her that staring at them felt like being pulled into a tar pit.

But the story of Jojo and August always started with how alike they were. Jojo was born at midnight after a thunderstorm, and so was August, even though the seasons were different. They both took exactly eight hours and thirty-five minutes to enter the world, which was always mentioned with reverence, like the number was a spell someone had cast over their lives.

To August, it felt like a curse. When she hit puberty, everyone had waited with bated breath for the trouble to start, just like it had with Jojo.

"No trouble here," August reassured her. "I'm boring these days. Birdie's teaching me how to knit, so be on the lookout for an ugly scarf in the mail, which you're legally required to wear at least once where other people can see it."

She expected Jojo to laugh. But her mother fell silent, then said, "How is she?" in a tone that had plummeted several degrees.

"Birdie? She's fine. Busy. Good." August bit her lip so she'd stop stringing adjectives together. All these years, you'd think she'd be better at avoiding this source of tension. Jojo only spoke to her mother when it couldn't be avoided, usually about the money she sent each month. Birdie was just as reluctant to interact with her daughter and constantly tried to manage August's expectations regarding Jojo. "That girl may love you, but she'll never do it well."

August took a deep breath and dove into a different topic. "I'm starting a new job next week."

"Are you?" Jojo's question was forcefully cheerful. She was equally determined to turn the conversation around. "Where?"

"King's. It's part-time."

"Silas do that for you?" Her mother's voice changed again—the careful, crisp vowels stretching into her real accent. It happened when she was annoyed or angry.

"I don't know. I just walked in and applied." August tried to make it sound nonchalant, an audible shrug. Jojo always ate at King's when she was home, so August thought the topic was safe. But Silas was Theo King's brother. Jojo could barely say either name without spitting. "It's the only place you can earn tips."

"What do you need money for?" Jojo asked. "What are you doing with what I send you?"

August had to be careful. She'd been saving the money her mother sent to pay for the move to Nashville. There was enough to cover the deposit and two months' rent at the cheap apartment complex she'd found online. Paying for studio time and a demo was another story. She wasn't sure how much it would cost, and the one person who could tell her refused to entertain the idea that her daughter would become a singer. "You don't want this," Jojo had said when August hinted at being interested in music. "This business is factory work. You're not built for it."

When August questioned Jojo's reasoning, her mother shut her down. "The only thing I'm paying for is college. You do anything else, you're on your own." So for the last two years, August had saved every cent she could from her monthly allowance, hoping it would be enough.

"The job is just something to do," August said quickly. "It'll be spending money."

There was a soft tapping sound at her window. August looked up and saw Mavis outside, motioning for her to open it. August pointed at the phone, mouthed Jojo's name, and lifted a finger, indicating she should wait. Mavis shook her head, eyes wide, and mouthed, *"Now."*

"Are you listening to me?" Jojo asked.

"Sorry, I got distracted."

"I need to go anyway."

She felt a familiar panic. Each time Jojo left, whether it be a visit or phone call, August wondered if it would be the last time they ever spoke. "Okay. Good luck. I mean, I hope it goes well."

"Be good, Augustina," Jojo said, then hung up.

Mavis's climb through August's window was slower and clumsier than in the past. She was out of practice. Her cousin hadn't appeared unannounced like this since junior high. Mavis wore AHS volleyball gear identical to what Jessica had been wearing earlier. Her hair was even pulled back into a matching braid.

"Before you say anything, yes, this is rude of me and no, my parents don't know I'm here. No one does."

"Okay." August wasn't sure whether to keep standing or sit. She walked to her dresser and leaned against it, splitting the difference. "Glad we're on the same page."

"I have to tell you something."

"Okay."

"Don't interrupt me."

"I hadn't planned to, but fine."

"And no jokes. Not even the kind you just did."

"That wasn't funny enough to be a joke."

"August. Stop! I can't do this if you—" She gulped down air. "I'm pregnant," she said, then covered her face and cried.

CHAPTER SEVEN

2023

August took the long way home from work so she could stop at the fairgrounds. It felt silly, but after her encounter with Luke the day before, she wanted to see where the festival would happen, maybe even stand on the stage where he'd perform the new song. After their argument, she'd gone home shaken, convinced she'd made a mistake by blackmailing him into working with her. She hadn't written new lyrics in years. But the next morning, she woke up calmer and clear-headed about her plan. This would be like the Writers' Round in Nashville she'd heard about, where people performed their music on a shared stage hoping to find a collaborator or convince some A&R rep to offer them a publishing deal. Instead of pitching to a small crowd, she'd be doing it to the entire industry at once, courtesy of Luke's "fairy-tale comeback," as they were already calling it on the MusicRow website.

Things were about to change for her. Exactly how, she wasn't sure, but people said luck was preparation meeting opportunity, didn't they? She'd been preparing for this her whole life.

The grounds were on the sparsely inhabited south side of town. When August turned onto the dusty road that led to the even dustier parking lot, she was greeted by a billboard advertising her mother's show. Jojo cradled a carbon microphone, her face hidden by a teal cowboy hat that matched her boots. Her first name was written in novelty Western font dotted with reflective lights that made the letters shimmer in the sun. The other performers were listed in smaller, less shimmery letters beneath it. Luke was one of Jojo's five opening acts, a roster of mostly white men with progressive reputations and multiple top-ten hits. It made Luke's inclusion even more of a Cinderella story guaranteed to revive his career.

The grounds were already crowded, which was unexpected. In past years, most of the setup wouldn't happen until a few weeks before the event. A white tent advertised festival jobs. Sweaty applicants stretched in front of two women August recognized from church. Both looked tired and overwhelmed. One of them, a choir member named Fiona who occasionally chatted with her during practice, spotted August and waved. Her older companion leaned over and whispered in her ear. Fiona's tentative smile vanished.

Luke's return had made August forget it wasn't safe to be out in public. Her social media feed was filled with people sharing Shirley Dixon's posts. Terry's wife had posted a barrage of Bible memes and old wedding photos she claimed to have found while cleaning out her phone. The commenters encouraged her to "keep going high" because "some folks only want what they can't have."

Meanwhile, Terry kept sending August text messages, begging to talk. She'd finally blocked his number but screenshot everything in case she was accused of trying to wreck his marriage again. She'd have to be careful around Luke, too. His wife had a doxx-friendly fan base that reveled in rumors of Luke's infidelity. August didn't want to be their next target. Her sidepiece era was officially over.

She moved past the employment tent, wandered a bit, then stopped short at the sight of a massive steel stage she'd never seen at prior festivals. It looked like something from CMA Fest. The logo of a brewing company was on a banner waiting to be hung. Silas used to complain about how hard it was to convince major beverage companies to sponsor the festival. "It's a visibility issue," he'd told her. "They called our audience niche."

Mavis stood near the stage, speaking rapidly to a man in dirty coveralls. She wore a navy-blue suit, another relic from her law firm days. The man stared at her blankly, fidgeting like he wanted to escape. He looked relieved when August approached them.

"What you've done is going to set us back two days," Mavis told him. "Tell your crew to pay closer attention to their instructions. Can you do that?"

The man drawled, "Yes, ma'am," in a robotic tone that said we've done this dance before. August touched Mavis's shoulder. Her cousin spun around, irritated by the interruption.

"Oh. Hi." Mavis turned to face the man, but he'd vanished. She flung her hands up and sighed. "Thanks for that."

"It was an act of mercy. How long have you been chewing him out?"

"Not long enough." She hitched up her chin. "This was his second mistake, and we're already behind schedule."

"Whose schedule? My mother's?"

Mavis tensed, which confirmed August's suspicions.

"Don't let her stress you out," August told her. "Award or no award, she's just your auntie."

"It's not Jojo," Mavis insisted. "Or I don't think it is. It's the sponsors. They've given us money, but we're still footing most of the bill. They've threatened to pull out and take the concert somewhere else if we can't meet their expectations."

"Then let them," August said. "This isn't Coachella. We barely have enough people to run this thing most years."

"We've already invested more than we can afford to lose. And the festival needs this after so much time away. The *town* needs this." She looked around. "All our businesses are closing. We're losing our people."

Mavis was right. Just last week, August heard rumors that Kroger, the only grocery store within city limits, would shut down next year. That meant people would have to drive to Walmart, thirty minutes away, to buy a loaf of bread. What was the point of living in a town that couldn't sustain you?

Still, hitching their hopes to Jojo's career was foolish. A single concert wasn't a new factory offering livable wages. And August knew firsthand how risky it was to depend on her mother for anything. That's why Luke needed to trade his duet for a solo that would stand out in a sea of flashier opening acts.

"Is this where the money for Silas's showcase went?" August gestured at the stage. Mavis grimaced and nodded.

"We'll do modular for everyone else," she said. "They're cheaper. But the streaming service insisted on steel for Jojo's concert because of how it looks on camera."

"Streaming service?"

Mavis named one of the few streaming apps August spent money to access. "They're going to debut it in theaters first. Then make it available everywhere. Even internationally."

No wonder Luke was so determined to appease her mother. All he had to do was perform the same song he'd been singing for years and millions of new fans would be born, all of them with Spotify accounts and YouTube playlists.

She didn't feel guilty about threatening him. But the amount of power she was taking for herself was frightening. She wasn't sure what to do with it.

"Okay, so I get that this is a big deal," August said. Mavis looked annoyed, so to appease her, she added, "A *huge* deal. But neglecting the rest of the festival is a mistake. This is one concert for one woman. The showcase is so much more than that."

Mavis gave her a long look. "Is there something going on with you and Jojo? This award is major, and you're not remotely interested. I know you two have your differences, but it's almost like you don't want to see her."

That was because August didn't. Not like this. Not during Jojo's big moment, cheering her on from the audience like some starry-eyed fan. That's what Jojo would expect from her daughter: unwavering support and loyalty. August couldn't give that to her after their last argument.

It had been about Birdie's funeral. In hindsight, they'd both probably been too emotional to think rationally, but burying a body wasn't something that could wait on the stages of grief. People kept asking when Jojo was coming home, and August had been tired of making excuses. Or maybe she'd just been tired of being expected to.

Jojo had answered the phone with a smile in her voice, like always. August recited a laundry list of decisions that had to be made in twenty-four hours. Jojo responded with variations of "That sounds fine" and "You choose" and "You care more about those things than I do" until August finally snapped.

"You're not listening to me."

"I am. I just don't care."

August had stopped breathing. Something sharp pricked her lungs. "What?"

"She's dead, baby. Doubt she'll be able to smell those lilies."

"Why would you say that?"

"Because it's true," Jojo tossed back. "I'm paying a lot of money so everyone who claimed to love her can cry in public. But that's all they're getting from me. I'm not stressing over woodgrain options for a box that's going in the damn ground." She paused. "You know what I think."

"Birdie didn't want to be cremated."

"And I don't want the image of her dead body haunting me the rest of my life."

"You mean like me? I'm the one who found her."

Jojo swore under her breath. "Sweetie, I didn't know."

"You didn't ask. Ever since she died, you've made it all about you. Which isn't surprising, just more irritating than usual. I need you to think about Birdie for two seconds, Jojo. What she would want."

"I did that already," Jojo snapped. "She still called me a whore. Sacrificing yourself on someone's altar won't make you worthy, little girl. They're going to die thinking the worst of you."

"You're wrong. Last thing she said was how grateful she was for a daughter to take care of her. She died thinking I was you."

Jojo made a sound, a hitch of air that could have been tears. "You're trying to hurt me."

"Yes, I am. Crying would be something, at least. Effort on your part."

"I'm not coming to that funeral."

The pain in her lungs seized, replaced with stillness. A chilly nothing. "You're a terrible person."

"Yeah. Well, you get it from me."

August disconnected. They hadn't spoken to each other since.

"We're not talking right now," August admitted to Mavis, hoping it would make her drop the subject.

It worked. Mavis nodded curtly, aware of their history. While she admired her aunt, she'd always been the first to point out when Jojo was being selfish or unreasonable, probably because she'd been both while facing motherhood before she was ready. "It's like, you're not the problem," Mavis had told her once after too many margaritas. "But you also are."

August had agreed. She still did, which was why being angry with Jojo had never changed how much she loved her. But love had limits.

"Oh no." Mavis stared past August, then tried to hide behind her, which was ridiculous. August wasn't short, but Mavis was a glamazonian giant. "Did he see me?"

"Who?" August tried to look, but Mavis hissed a warning to be still.

"David Henry. Your mother's manager. Or handler. Or... Who's the right-hand man in mafia movies?"

"The consigliere?" August turned to study David. Despite the heat, he wore shirtsleeves and a tie. His dark hair was streaked with gray and slicked into a side part with pomade. He cut his eyes at everyone he passed, as if they were all trespassers in his executive suite. August nodded. "Okay, yes, I see it."

"I hate that guy," Mavis grumbled. "I don't work for him, but he always acts like he's seconds away from firing me."

"He's like that with everyone."

Mavis's eyes widened. "Of course you know him." She grabbed August's arms. "Deal with him for me. Please? I'll owe you."

It had been years since August had seen David, not since she was little. There was no way he remembered her. But she wasn't about to pass up the chance to extract a favor from Mavis, who, unlike Paul Cleebus, the man they called "ghost mayor" because no one ever saw him, was one of the most influential people in Arcadia.

"Move that money back to the showcase."

Mavis's shoulders slumped. "I can't. It's already spent."

"Well, do something. Find another sponsor. Make sure Silas doesn't cancel it."

She took a deep breath. "Okay. I can't promise anything, but I'll see what I can do."

Before August could thank her, she pivoted and escaped with a brisk walk. David reached August minutes later and eyed the divots left by Mavis's heels.

"Probably something I said." He stuffed his hands in his pockets.

Again, August was struck by how unbothered he seemed by the heat. The beads of sweat on his brow were the only sign he was standing in the same ninety-eight-degree hell as everyone else. "I have that effect on women." He focused on August. "The stage is wrong."

"I know. So does Mavis."

"Is it being fixed?"

"Yes, in two days."

"Perfect." He clasped his hands together. "See? She didn't have to run away. I can be reasonable."

"Pass that along to your demanding client." She pointed at the billboard. "That thing is tacky. She looks like the star of a Black *Hee Haw* revival."

David gazed up at Jojo's image, his expression unreadable. "Be nicer to your mother, August."

"You remember me?"

"I gave you a doll once." He finally looked at her. "The kind that pees. Do you remember what you said?"

"No. But if I was older than ten, blame the hormones."

His mouth twitched, fighting a smile. "*You don't have kids, do you?* That's what you said to me. Then you tucked that expensive doll under your arm like a football and went to your room."

"Was that Christmas?"

"Only one I ever spent here." He looked around. "Nothing's changed except you."

She ran a hand over her hair, suddenly conscious of her appearance. He was probably used to being around women who considered makeup and hairstyles a hobby. Or, as in her mother's case, part of their job description. "Kids grow up."

"Which makes them harder to parent, or so I'm told."

"Good thing she never tried."

"See? That's what I mean. I don't want you poking at her like that when she gets here. She's already dealing with people questioning whether she's earned this award."

"Will she actually show up, though? I mean, the woman couldn't be bothered to come back for her mother's funeral. It's hard to believe she'll show up to sing with Luke Randall, of all people. Why would she bother?"

David pulled out his phone and opened his Spotify account. August watched him search for "Another Love Song" with her heart hammering at her ribs. She didn't want to hear it.

"Look at this." He started scrolling, showing her a list of covers by other artists. "What do you see?"

"Questionable choices."

"Fair. But what else?"

She stared at the tiny icons, then focused on the names attached to them. "They're all white. More famous than him."

"Why do you think that is?" He stuffed the phone into his pocket. "None are better singers. Half of them don't even record anymore. Just a bunch of no ones with silly hats and lots of airplay. And the more of them that cover Luke's song, the deeper they bury the guy who wrote it. Pretty soon, no one will remember it was him."

She forced a shrug. "Happens all the time."

"Yeah, well, it shouldn't. Not when everyone's claiming that today's a new, more inclusive day. He should be the face of his own music. Every artist deserves that."

He couldn't know. No one knew. But it still felt like a well-placed dagger. "You're right," August said, focusing on the billboard again. There was a streak of bird shit on Jojo's hat. It made her smile. "Too bad he won't be singing it."

――•―○―◦―•―

Four hours later, August could tell by the rapid cop knock on her apartment door that Luke knew what she'd done. She ignored him. Telling David that Luke planned to pitch new music had been risky, but she didn't regret it. Luke was a Band-Aid picker who would have inched toward breaking the news until the very last second, then claimed it was too late to change the set list. August ripped her bandages off as soon as possible, sometimes before the wound had time to heal. With the show less than two months away, it was better to face the fallout now.

"Open the door!" Luke pounded again. She touched the doorknob, took a deep breath, and yanked it open. His eyes seemed darker than usual, like his pupils were devouring the irises. Her body reacted instantly, a hot quickening she tried to ignore. She was always that way with beautiful men. Hungry for poison. Ready to wreck herself for a taste.

"What did you do?" Luke shouldered his way inside before she could answer. She closed the door and immediately regretted it. He was big and warm, while her apartment, with its sputtering window air conditioner, was uncomfortably small.

"Hi, August," she said in a singsong voice. "May I come in? Why, sure, Luke. But keep your dirty shoes off my carpet." She gave his feet a pointed look. He shuffled, wavering, and she knew it took all his strength not to comply. Even when he was mad, the man was polite to his core.

"Don't change the subject." He was stubborn for thirty seconds before muttering "Goddammit" and bending down to yank at his laces. August watched him take his shoes off with a tight throat. This would be easier if he weren't still himself.

"I know you're mad—"

"You think!" He straightened and pulled out his phone. "David accused me of sabotage. He thinks I'm working with Charlotte on some elaborate revenge scheme." He showed her his screen. Instead of reading the texts, she stared at his bare fingers. She'd never thought of him as the type of husband who wouldn't wear a ring.

August forced herself to focus on his phone. Besides threatening legal action, David accused Luke of lying about having new material. *There are better ways to impress a pretty girl. Signed divorce papers would be a start.*

August laughed, which made Luke's eye twitch. "None of this is funny."

She pointed to the text. "That's a little funny."

"This is serious. David never wanted to hire me. He's itching to replace my duet with one of the other openers."

"No, he isn't. He was curious when I told him you were working on something new. I could tell." She waved away the phone. "All of that is because I wouldn't give him any details."

"Because there aren't any. You can't bullshit a man like this, August."

"You did. You should have heard him going on about you getting credit for *your* song. 'Jojo wants to uplift Black voices.' Made my teeth ache."

He studied her long enough to make her squirm. "Is that why you did this? To get back at Jojo?"

Of course he'd think that. Easier to brush off a petty revenge plot instead of taking responsibility for his actions. "This isn't about her."

Luke shook his head. "I don't understand you. Why would you try to get me fired? I thought you wanted this."

His words felt like a jab to the throat. He'd been gone for nearly half their lives. He didn't know her anymore. "I think I want it more than you," she said.

He blinked. "What does that mean?"

"You're terrified." She let her worst suspicions bubble to the surface. "Is it because you know people will see the real you? They're already writing think pieces about Luke Randall embracing his roots by working with Jojo. It'll only get worse if you sing something I wrote."

Luke's eyes went dark again. "What the fuck are you asking me?"

Hurt lined his voice, a slight quaver that revealed his insecurities. It made her wonder if he'd ever talked about this before, how closely his popularity was tied to colorblindness. It made him indistinguishable from other voices on the radio. Jojo used to say that fitting in was how you got an invitation to the party, but taking risks kept them coming. Luke had sat in the corner, playing it safe for so long his career had gone to rot. "I'm asking if you're brave enough to be honest this time."

"So now I'm a coward because I busted my ass to make music some redneck DJ wouldn't toss in the garbage? You don't think I had enough doors slammed in my face?"

"Maybe not. Look where it got you. Standing in this shitty apartment, yelling at me for telling that man the truth."

"I'm not yelling!" Luke shouted. He closed his eyes and took a breath. "You don't know half of what you think you know."

"I know enough."

His eyes flew open. "Really? So, you're an expert in copyrights? You understand fee splits and what kind of legal clusterfuck it'll cause if word gets out that a huge commercial hit has an uncredited songwriter? You understand all that?"

"I didn't cause that problem."

"Naw, you just want to make it worse. Why is that? You could have spoken up years ago about writing that song, but you didn't. Never said a word."

"At least I'm not a liar."

"No, you're just a coward," Luke snapped. "I made mistakes, but at least I did something. I tried. It was ugly and messy." He slapped his chest. "But it's *my* ugly. *My* mess. You want to pick at that, go ahead. But we both know it's because you're too afraid to pick at yours."

August hated arguing. It wasn't safe. There was always a chance she would say or do something she couldn't take back, like the other day with Shirley. And now, with Luke, she could already feel herself turning vicious. Mainly because he'd picked *this* fight while she was standing in the apartment she'd rented to know what it felt like to have something of her own.

She'd spent years in Birdie's house, doing instead of living, never acknowledging her wants because there was nowhere to put them. Jojo used to stand outside and yell when she got bored. August tried it once. She stood in the yard and screamed until it hurt, but the sound evaporated, like it had never been there at all.

Giving up was how she'd survived. If he'd stayed, he would have known that. He would have seen how little of her life belonged to her anymore. If he'd called, she might have forgiven him for lying. That's how desperate she was to have a best friend again.

"If I never faced my mistakes, you wouldn't be standing here." She grabbed her shoes from a rack near the front door.

"What are you doing?"

"You're stalling," she said, relieved at how calm she sounded. Lacing up her Nikes gave her time to focus. Luke was a means to an end, and she needed to treat him that way. This wasn't the boy she knew. This was a stranger who wanted to manipulate her. "You're trying to bully me into keeping my mouth shut. Well, joke's on you. I've been bullied my whole life. I'm bully-proof."

She yanked her laces tighter and grumbled under her breath. "Dumb little August doesn't understand the music industry, so I'll scare her into letting me off the hook for being a thieving fraud. Then I can shuck and jive for her mama like the good little clown I am."

"If that's what you think I'm doing, you don't—"

"Know you at all?" She straightened to glare at him. "You're wrong. I know you better than anyone. You're afraid of me. And you'll do anything to avoid saying my name on that stage."

Luke flinched and swallowed hard, as if she'd fed him something scalding. "You're right." His eyes roamed over her, taking in all of her at once. "You're terrifying. But not the way you think."

She hadn't noticed how close they were standing. He could reach for her if he wanted, something she'd usually consider inevitable if a different man was eyeing her like he was. Instead, he balled his hands into fists. August opened the door and let in the blistering humid air.

Sweat coated her skin almost instantly. She could hear Luke calling after her, telling her to stop, but lagging behind because of his bare feet. She headed for his truck. A guitar case was visible in the passenger seat. That was how she'd end this fight: by dumping it into his hands and saying shut up and sing, or she'd tell the world his dirty secret.

August yanked at the driver's-side door and was surprised to find it locked. No one locked their cars in Arcadia. She looked through the window. There was a rolled-up blanket on the floorboard. A toothbrush sat in a red Solo cup. Dozens of empty water bottles were in the passenger's seat, too many for the fast-food bag he'd converted into a trash container. His duffel bag was propped against the guitar, overflowing with clothes.

She could sense Luke behind her, but he wasn't yelling anymore. She'd already seen what he was trying to hide. August turned around, but he wouldn't look at her. He stared at the space above her head, like the clouds were more likely to answer his question. "Why are you so stubborn?"

Luke unzipped his guitar with more care than necessary. He was stalling. August seemed fine with letting him do it, hovering quietly instead of asking questions. What she'd seen told an ugly story, one he'd never wanted her to know.

He should have thrown away those water bottles. She probably thought he was using them to piss in.

"Look at me," August said, then touched his shoulder, which meant they weren't fighting anymore. Touch was how she cared for people. She used to do it without thinking—rub his back, rest her head on his shoulder. He could never summon adequate words to tell her how it made him feel. It was an agonizing joy, the kind only someone raised in a violent house could understand.

Luke finally looked at August and immediately regretted it. Her anger was better. Anger was what he deserved. Now anxious fear lined her face, the kind that precipitated her attempts to fix someone's problems. He used to love that about her, the way her walls would crumble in the face of suffering.

No. Not used to. Still. Maybe always.

"You can't sleep in a car," she said. "It's dangerous."

"It's not that hot at night."

"You could get robbed. Or arrested."

"Who's gonna rob me out here? Walt Jenkins?" He thought about the thin man with rheumy eyes who used to trade stolen lawn ornaments for weed. "No way that dude's still around."

August sat on the couch. "Please talk to me."

Her hands were bunched inside the skirt of her sundress. The thin cotton, with its tiny pink floral pattern, had distracted him since he'd arrived. When had that started? The girl in his memories lived in T-shirts and jeans. He wanted to know the exact date and time she'd shed that skin and put on this one.

"I'm broke," he said, sitting across from her on a barstool. The choice was purposeful. The lack of a seat back forced him upright, allowing him to face her with squared shoulders instead of letting a chair do the heavy lifting. "Spent all my extra money coming down here. Haven't gotten my performance fee, so I can't afford a hotel room right now."

"How? You had a hit song. I still hear it all the time."

"That's just your algorithm. It'll probably pop up if you played something similar or searched for Black country artists." He hesitated. "Earlier, when I mentioned all that stuff about rights and royalties?"

She nodded, and he watched the memory of their argument cool her expression. Good. Maybe she'd stop looking like she was two seconds from pulling him into her arms.

"They didn't teach us any of that on *Country Star*," he said. "It was all voice lessons and branding. How to be a guy who looks good on TV." He dipped his head and pushed the memory of the stage away, how bright and blinding it was. That was how they wanted him. Shiny, bright, and blinded. "I signed everything they put in front of me. Didn't read a lick of it."

"You were only seventeen."

"Eighteen by the time the show was over," Luke corrected her. "Old enough to enter a contract. They could get away with things back then that they can't now." He hadn't realized how much he'd signed away until Charlotte's girlfriend broke the news during their first conversation about a divorce settlement. The record company owned nearly everything. The rest he'd signed away to his manager.

"Delilah Simmons, a show producer, offered to manage me after I got eliminated. She knew I was desperate to stay." He glanced at August and quickly added, "It was Ava I was avoiding."

"This woman took advantage of you?"

Luke wasn't sure how much he wanted to tell her. Delilah had been the first person in Nashville to believe in him, which had made him loyal even when she'd lied to his face. She'd negotiated large fees for herself and flat-out stolen money when he was too drunk to pay attention. She'd booked him at venues filled with dixie chintz and rebel flags. There was one time, early on, that she'd dropped him off for drinks with a popular DJ, and Luke spent the entire night keeping the man's hands off his ass.

Delilah had called him later, furious. "He called you an uppity asshole."

"Fuck that racist piece of shit," Luke had said, or slurred more accurately, because he'd kept drinking long after the man had left. "He just wanted to fuck me."

"Of course he did. They all do. That's how you survive this business, with some power broker's limp dick in your hand." Her voice softened. "These guys are gross, but they also gatekeep the one hundred. You're not a kid anymore, Luke. Grow up before they stop wanting to fuck you. That's when your career is over."

Luke didn't have sex with that DJ. But he'd slept with enough women who ultimately helped his career to make the line between liking someone and using them blurry enough to hate the person he saw in the mirror.

"She was shady from the jump, but I pretended not to notice because money was coming in. Or I thought it was. Seven years later, I woke up one day and realized I didn't have an ATM card. Like, if I wanted to walk up to a bank and get cash, I wouldn't be able to." He looked at August. "When I finally found someone willing to show me financial statements, I learned I was broke. Nothing was there, just piles of debt from running around, pretending to be a baller."

He cleared his throat, summoning more courage to admit the part he'd never forgive himself for. "I don't own the masters of my music. The royalties I get barely cover rent. I do the bar circuit, yard work, whatever I can find. That's the money I used to come down here." He didn't add that he'd also arrived early because he couldn't wait eight more weeks to face her after a decade of hiding.

August gazed at the floor, deep in thought. He liked these silent moments, when she was too distracted to notice him staring. He could study her. Get reacquainted with his favorite parts. A faint indention on her chin made Luke accuse her of having a dimple once, something she'd flat-out rejected. "Don't you dare call me cute," she'd responded.

August cupped her chin, and the divot disappeared. She looked resolute, like she'd settled on something and was deciding how to break it to him. "You're not sleeping in that truck."

Luke sighed. "I won't let you pay for—"

"I'm not paying for anything. If I could afford a hotel, you think I'd be here?"

Luke looked around. Her place was small, similar to the sterile studio he rented in Memphis, but with an extra door, which meant it probably had a real bedroom. There were unopened U-Haul boxes in one corner. The move must be recent.

"Are you offering your couch?" The sagging cushions would wreck his back, but so would the truck cab.

August straightened. "No. I can't—" Her eyes swept over him. "You'd take up too much room."

He wasn't sure if she meant physically or something else. But he didn't hate how she looked at him. Like a mountain he'd dared her to climb.

"I don't know many people in town. Not well enough to be a houseguest." He went down a mental list and came up with a bunch of teenage faces that probably didn't live in Arcadia anymore. "Is Silas still around? I could crash at Delta Blue for a few days."

"You can stay at Birdie's," August said. "The house is empty. There's no one around for miles." She twisted her hands in her skirt again. "No one will know you're there."

"I can't do that," Luke said, but struggled to articulate why. It was a feeling. A lack of worth. "The cost of keeping the lights on alone—"

"Jojo pays for it. If she bothers to look at a utility bill, she'll assume it is me."

Luke wanted to ask why she and Jojo weren't speaking, but it felt too invasive. Despite their current softer mood, they still weren't close. Far from it. "Why do you live here?"

August scanned the room. "I know it's a waste of money. But I needed a break from that house." She rubbed her face, scrubbing away the melancholy. "A lot of family members have died there. Might want to sage it before you move in."

"It's not a good idea."

"The walls are too thin to play music here. It's perfect."

"Sounds like being out there is hard for you. I don't want to put you through that."

"I'll be fine," she said. Fine, as in mind your business. There was no hint of awareness that she wasn't following her own advice. "Besides, if you owe me, maybe you won't disappear again."

Luke realized how his protests sounded to her. He'd literally slept with a foot near the gas pedal last night. "All right. I'll stay there if that's what you want."

"It is." She looked him up and down. "You should take a shower first."

Luke lifted the neck of his T-shirt and sniffed. He smelled like outside and sweat. Nothing horrible, but nothing to brag about, either. "Did my best with limited resources."

"Like a public restroom sink?" Guilt must have shown on his face because she burst out laughing.

"Where's the bathroom?" Luke stood and eyed the identical doors on his right. August cut him off.

"Stop. Don't move." She slipped through a door and positioned it to obscure what was happening inside. Drawers opened and closed. The shower curtain rustled.

"I don't care about your bathroom secrets," he shouted, trying to ensure she heard him over her chaotic cleaning. "We all got soap scum and squeeze toothpaste from the middle."

August jerked the door open and brandished a black silicone stick with a large bulb on the top. "This is a back massager."

Luke eyed the thick black column. "Is it?"

"*Yes.* There isn't enough room to store it in that tiny vanity."

"Ah. So this is a preemptive explanation." Luke reached for it, and she moved it behind her back.

"What are you doing?"

"I like a massage in the shower, too."

She bit back a smile and said, "Get your own." She returned to her task. He listened to her movements and the mundane sound was comforting. It gave him hope. Made him feel like they could be okay.

CHAPTER EIGHT

2009

Luke wouldn't have gotten drunk at Jessica's birthday party if August had been there. Or at least, he wouldn't have done it the way his friends did, gulping beer so fast it shot straight into their bloodstream. He didn't want her to lump him into that group more than she already did. He wanted to be different. Worthy of her attention.

But she wasn't there. It was just him, his angry girlfriend, and a gang of classmates he barely recognized watching every move he made. The party was so packed that walking through Jessica's living room felt like wading in damp breath.

Despite being surrounded by people, Luke was alone. Even when Jessica stroked his arm or Shane shouted his name, Luke felt invisible, which was what he usually wanted. Hiding behind a smile was survival. But the minute he arrived at Jessica's house, he'd questioned whether that should be the goal. Was tiptoeing around a minefield the best version of living he'd ever have?

He couldn't think like that. At a party, he shouldn't be thinking at all. Not with people watching. Not surrounded by mines.

Luke knew how to handle unwelcome thoughts because he'd been doing it since he was twelve. Start with vodka, the good kind from someone's liquor cabinet, not the cheap stuff that tastes like rubbing alcohol. Don't sip it, though. This ain't a dinner party. Throw it past your taste buds like the medicine it is.

"Are you drunk already?" Jessica glared at him, which was confusing because she was the one who'd been pouring his drinks. Luke smiled and threw his arm around her neck to prove he was the version of her boyfriend who knew how to have a good time.

"You look good." He eyed her pale pink top. "I like this color on you."

"You've seen this a million times." She paused. "Why were you talking to August Lane earlier?"

Luke pulled his arm away and looked for the keg. "Why wouldn't I? Something wrong with her?"

"No." Jessica searched his face. "I mean, she's a complete slut, but that's not a personality flaw."

"Really, Jess?" Luke stared at her. "Why would you say something like that?"

"I don't know." She shrugged. "Because I'm a bitch. Which you know. Or you would if you ever paid attention to me anymore."

"You're not a bitch," Luke said, but it sounded like a question. Jessica's face hardened. Before she could speak, Luke pointed to the keg and said, "I'll be right back." Then he walked away to escape her wrath.

"Hustle in the House" started playing, and someone cranked the music up loud enough to make liquor bottles near the speaker vibrate. Luke poured a beer and watched everyone clump around a picnic table. Richard climbed on top, red-faced and sweaty, shouting the lyrics while motioning for them to join in.

Luke was only half paying attention. Lately, he couldn't stomach the sound of Richard's voice. He kept feeling August's hand in his, how it trembled when she told him about the rumors.

Richard shouted Luke's name and stared at him with bloodshot eyes. He had a familiar look on his face, something he usually reserved for the field but occasionally wielded in public. A quarterback stare that demanded fealty.

People liked Luke. But Richard was respected. Team captain. Class president. He was a leader in ways that sounded good in college essays. If football were an orchestra, Luke would be the flashy talent, wowing the audience with flawless solos while Richard conducted from the podium and received credit for the discipline of everyone's performance. Luke was liked because Richard allowed it, which meant he could take it away at any time.

"Let's go!" Richard punched the air. The people around him shouted back, waving their hands and dancing under his thrall. Richard was in the zone, swaying with open arms like he owned the room. They'd crowned him king of everything.

Everything except Luke. Even in his drunken state, Luke knew that whatever spell the guy had cast over him had been broken. Listening to Richard shout about wearing durags and gold on his neck made something knot in Luke's stomach. He felt hands on his back, shoving him forward, and people chanting "Go Luke!" like he was still in a game, their only hope for a touchdown. Luke stumbled forward, nearly falling before he reached the table.

Richard grabbed his arm and yanked him up to stand beside him. He leaned into Luke's ear and shouted, "Sing with me!" He was so close that Luke felt the spittle against his neck. Then Richard leaned back and shouted a "*young nigga*" lyric at the top of his lungs.

Luke froze. He checked for similar discomfort in the crowd, but they all seemed oblivious. He looked at Richard, who grinned at first but stopped when Luke didn't smile back. Then it hit him, what he'd said and who he was standing next to. In that moment, Richard saw Luke more clearly than he ever had. But he kept singing, refusing to let go of the moment.

"You know this song," Richard said, then slapped Luke's back hard. Luke remained silent. Richard leaned in again and said, "Sing it, asshole." Then he reared back to shout the next line, another "*nigga*" thrown carelessly to the crowd.

That knot in Luke's stomach wasn't just a feeling; it was a beast in a cage. Later, he'd blame that last beer. And August. And hearing that word in Richard's quarterback voice, being wielded like a boot on his neck.

Luke swung hard, aiming for Richard's jaw. There was a cracking sound, and Richard fell back onto the ground. The crowd gasped, but Luke ignored it and followed him down. That guy they liked was gone. There was only the beast now.

The story of Luke's fight with Richard spawned like a living thing. It started after Jessica wedged herself between them, narrowly escaping their fists. Some partygoers saw one friend attacking the other unprovoked. Others remembered a tense conversation between the golden couple before the first punch was thrown. It was a love triangle! A secret romance between the white quarterback and the Black volleyball captain, like in that Sanaa Lathan movie, *Something New*. Luke was Blair Underwood, only violent. "There's something off about him. Did you hear about his dad? Shit is *dark*. Jessica should have dumped him a long time ago."

Luke's memory of that night was just as hazy as everyone else's, but he did remember Richard's swollen face and the way he'd groaned when someone lifted him to his feet. What Luke had done was a crime. He'd spent the weekend hovering at the living room window, waiting for the blue lights of a squad car that never came.

Ava only acknowledged him when he started dry heaving in the living room. She brought him a mop bucket and closed the blinds. "I don't care how good you are at sports. You can't run around beating up white boys."

Luke stared at her. "You heard what happened?"

She handed him a glass of Alka-Seltzer. "Bill called. He convinced Richard's parents not to press charges. Both of y'all were underage drinking. They didn't want the hassle." Her voice was flat when she said it. Bill Parnell used to be one of his father's best friends, something Ava only admitted when Luke asked why they didn't like each other. "That cop is the only self-appointed judge in the county," she'd said. "I don't like people looking down at me."

Now she patted Luke's arm with a relieved sigh and said, "Thank God he's got a soft spot for you."

Luke made it through one class on Monday. He could barely hold a pencil with his bruised hand and turned in a blank test he couldn't afford to fail. As he walked the halls, no one would make eye contact with him. His name floated through the air in hostile waves.

When the second-period bell rang, Luke ducked into the theater, praying no one had spotted him. Thanks to the drama class he was required to take last year, he knew there was a dressing room with a broken lock the teachers used for storage. He ducked inside and pushed a pile of musty costumes from a velvet settee. Exhaustion gripped him as soon as he sat down. The last two nights, all he'd done was dodge phantom fists in his dreams. He fell asleep almost instantly.

Luke woke with a jerk, sensing he wasn't alone. August sat across from him, holding a half-eaten sandwich. He looked up at the clock. Two hours had passed.

"Never seen anyone sleep that hard before," she said. "You looked dead."

Luke sat up. "How'd you find me?"

"I eat lunch in here." She took a deliberate bite for emphasis. "One of the few places I can be alone."

"Sorry to ruin it for you." Luke's stomach growled. He usually grabbed lunch in the cafeteria because his mother barely bought enough groceries to feed them once a day.

August offered him the other half of her sandwich. He didn't take it. "I'm good."

"No, you aren't." She refused to lower her hand. Her eyes said the sandwich wasn't just a sandwich. It was commiseration. He was in her territory now, on the bad side of rumors with staying power.

He accepted it and took a large bite. It was gooey white bread slathered with more mustard than cheese or bologna. He gulped it down and prayed he didn't choke. "You make this yourself?"

"Don't be an asshole." She bit her apple, and a piece of hair nearly caught in her mouth. Her loose ponytail was gradually working its way free of whatever she'd used to hold it back. He wanted to fix it for her, smooth the runaway strand back into the rest.

"I'm surprised you didn't go home," she said.

Luke took another bite to put off answering. He'd been looking for a safe place; home was never that. "I usually give Jessica a ride."

Her expression shuttered slightly. "Why were you fighting over her?"

She eyed her apple like the exposed core was more interesting than his answer. "Did she cheat on you with Richard?"

"No." The second question was easier to answer than the first. He'd been fighting over a girl, yes, but not the one everyone assumed. Luke had finally admitted that to himself last night. He'd thrown that punch for August. Because Richard had tricked her into having sex. The scariest part was how good it'd felt. Like he was made for that kind of destruction.

Jessica had screamed at him later. Her dining room had been a fishbowl with people watching them behind glass doors. Luke hadn't said a word. He'd absorbed every accusation like a sponge. Eventually Jessica lowered her voice and asked, "Is this about August Lane?"

The guilt he'd been ignoring surged forward, and he rocked back in his seat, trying to escape it. "Why do you keep bringing her up?"

"I saw how you looked at her." Her voice was tight, poised to shout again. "You're fucking her, aren't you."

"No!" Luke tried to wave off the accusation with his good hand, but his movements felt slow and unconvincing. The county fair, the notebook, the music he'd written her. Strung together, it was obvious what he'd been doing. "I'm not sleeping with August."

"You want to," she said. "She's not Jojo, you know. Her pussy won't get you closer to fame."

"Why would you say that?" Luke tried to reconcile the girl he cared about with the bitter person looming over him. He never thought she saw him clearly, but maybe it was mutual. Maybe they'd both been dating someone else. "You think we're all like Richard? Using people for clout?"

Her glare was acid. "You're not better than me."

"I never said that's what you—"

"You don't say anything, Luke. And I'm sick of waiting for you to."

It was an official dumping, "I quit" via a weekend-long ghosting paired with the silent treatment during class that morning. Their only interaction had been her eye flick in his direction when someone mentioned sending Richard a care package. Jessica flipped her braid back and volunteered to help.

"I ruined her birthday," Luke admitted to August. It felt like one of his more egregious offenses. Jessica had been talking about the party all month, eyes glittering with joy that made him jealous. Luke dreaded his birthdays. Ava made them feel like a chore. "She didn't deserve that."

"Richard did," August said, with a devilish grin that made her even cuter. Luke barely suppressed his own smile. He didn't want to joke about hitting someone, but August's moods were infectious. She made wallowing in guilt feel like a wasted effort.

"Coach suspended me from three games," he said, which had seemed like a big deal when it happened. Now it sounded silly. No football for a month. Some punishment.

"You hate playing anyway."

"No, I don't," Luke lied, but then remembered what he'd admitted at the fair. "Okay, I do, but I hate being suspended from anything. Everyone will know why I'm not out there."

"And they'll talk about it," August said quietly. "Behind your back."

He realized how he must have sounded to her, whining about the same thing she dealt with every day. "I didn't mean to—"

"You can't hide in here forever." She started gathering her things. "The fall play is coming up. And the toilet's broken, so unless you plan to shit in a bucket, you'll have to show your face in public again."

He watched her toss her trash with growing panic. "Don't go."

"You'll be fine." She was talking to herself now, eyes on anything in the room except him. "Just make another touchdown, and everyone will get amnesia. Or write her a song. Girls love hot guys with guitars."

"August, stop." She ignored him. He stood, heart pounding, and grabbed her hand. "Don't leave." She jerked away. Luke's face caught fire, and he stepped back. "I'm sorry. I shouldn't have grabbed you. But I want you to stay."

"Why?" She rubbed her palm where he'd touched it. "We're not..." She trailed off, unwilling to finish the rest of that thought. "I don't know what we are."

"It doesn't matter," Luke said. He could feel something loosening inside him, that same unraveling he'd experienced when they'd met in total darkness. "I've never written music for someone before. Not like I did for you. It felt—" He stopped because, as usual, the words weren't coming. "I want to do it again."

August fidgeted. "I was joking earlier. I don't know if a love song will fix your relationship."

"It's not about that." He knew he needed to fix his reputation and make things right with Jessica. But he also knew that sitting with those lyrics, putting melodies on paper, had been more intoxicating than the vodka that had caused him so much trouble the other night. "I think I'm meant to write music. Like you."

August went still for a second, and he glimpsed that raw hunger behind her eyes. But then she was smirking and shrugging, and it was like he'd imagined it. "I'm pretty sure real people don't have destinies."

"I've seen your writing," Luke said, ignoring her sarcasm. He was starting to recognize her defense mechanisms. "You were born for this. I hope you believe me."

She looked away like she didn't want to. "If you want to write songs, then write songs. You don't need me for that."

"I can't."

"It's not that hard."

"Not for *you*." He paused. "Would you help me? Teach me how?"

She huffed a laugh. "Like a tutor?"

Luke realized he'd been reading the conversation wrong. He'd been so caught up in daydreams about songwriting with August that he'd forgotten they weren't that close. Just two people with similar interests who'd stumbled into knowing more about each other than they should.

"Yeah, like a tutor," he said, cleaning it up. The moment immediately felt smaller. "I could pay you."

August took her time responding. "How much?"

He was relieved but also disappointed. A small part of him hoped she'd say working together would be enough. That she was just as excited about it as he was. "How much do you want?"

"Three hundred dollars. I had it before, but my cousin needed help. I have to put it back."

He remembered what she said about moving to Nashville, how she was saving money for an apartment and demo. "Three hundred is fine." There was money in the bank from his father's life insurance payout. It was supposed to help pay for college, but something about using it to make music felt right. Like his dad would have approved.

PART FOUR

THE CHORUS

This Is Our Country: Podcast Transcript

Episode 12—"Jojo Lane"
August 21, 2024

[*cont.*]
Emma: Let's talk about songwriting.
Jojo: Hate it. I hate writing songs.
Emma: Really? Wow.
Jojo: I know, I know. We're all supposed to love it. I used to lie when people asked me because it was easier. It's like admitting you don't like dogs.
Emma: [*laughter*] You don't like dogs?
Jojo: I plead the fifth. [*laughter*]
Emma: Why don't you enjoy songwriting?
Jojo: It's thankless. Writing is easy, but writing something good is so, *so* hard. You spend hours agonizing over every word. And you're pouring pieces of yourself into it because everyone knows that's where the good stuff is. Your life, your trauma, your insecurities. You use them to make this thing that feels like your child. I've had a kid, so I can say this. It feels like handing your newborn to a bunch of executives who plop it in a crib and say *Thanks, you can go now! We'll package it any old way. What you think is irrelevant.* But it's about me! How can I be irrelevant when it's my song? And don't even get me started on what happens once it hits the radio.
Emma: Is that worse?
Jojo: No one listens to podcasts anymore, right? How many subscribers do you have?
Emma: People listen to this podcast.
Jojo: [*sigh*] Whatever, let 'em drag me. I hate putting songs in the world because no one listens. Not the way they should.

Emma: Do you think the way we consume music has changed?

Jojo: We've always been this way. If someone says who they are or what's important to them, we take it as criticism, like they're saying this is who you should be. Or you get accused of writing some stereotype because they've heard your story before. But it's still your story. Only now, because it's playing during their carpool, it's cliché.

Emma: Is this why you collaborate so much? Because you don't enjoy the process?

Jojo: Honestly, yes. It's not their face on the album, so I figure it's easier for them. I don't know. I should ask Ellis.

Emma: Ellis Jackson? You've worked with him a lot.

Jojo: I love Ellis. He gets me. His songs feel like something I would have come up with if I was one of those perfect country girls people love.

Emma: Okay, you have to explain that.

Jojo: Well, there are themes, you know? You've got to sing about going home or how you regret leaving in the first place. And it's always some small town that sounds like something out of a movie. The way we wish small towns still were. Idyllic and slow, with cozy restaurants. Real small-town folks do a lot of riding around and drinking. That part country gets right, 'cause ain't shit else to do on the weekend. I don't drink, but I've got three tracks with whiskey in the title.

Emma: Are you saying it's fake? That's interesting because there's this constant authenticity debate, right? Kind of like hip-hop and street cred. Whose country enough to be taken seriously.

Jojo: You'd think people obsessed with authenticity would want us to be honest when we're singing. But no one wants to hear my version of things. My hometown is Black and dying in ways people pretend not to see. There's no main street anymore. No farms. Just people getting by and sometimes failing. But that's not a radio hit. I'll never write about my life anymore.

Emma: What about love? Or romance? Would you write about that?

Jojo: Well, I don't do that anymore, either. [*laughs*] I'm kidding. Falling in love is so messy. And embarrassing. You'd have to be the bravest person alive to talk about how you love in a song.

CHAPTER NINE

2023

August hadn't heard from Luke in two days. She had assumed he'd reach out once he was settled at Birdie's, but he was avoiding her. It made her view their last argument differently. She thought they'd reached a truce. But Luke never committed to keeping his end of the bargain; he'd only listed all the reasons he shouldn't.

Once the breakfast rush at King's was over, August drove to her childhood home. There were two parts of the Eastside neighborhood: the newer area closer to town filled with apartments and duplexes, and the older part, hand-built houses passed down through generations with murky titles that would never stand up in court. Birdie's house was on five acres her father bought during the Great Depression. According to Birdie, neither of her parents wanted to live in the middle of nowhere, but Eastside was one of the few neighborhoods the government would approve for Black mortgage applications in the county.

As she approached the house, August noticed the siding had recently been patched with fresh paint. A rusted toolbox sat on the porch. Luke's truck was parked in the driveway, dotted with earth from the surrounding dirt roads. The Chevy looked like it belonged there.

Bill Withers was playing and August followed the music until she found the source. Luke was in the side yard removing a dead rosebush beneath her old bedroom window. He wore work shorts and a sweat-soaked T-shirt. His skin was darker than when she last saw him, burnished copper, which meant he'd been outdoors for a while.

She watched him move the spade back and forth, pull it out, and then push it back in again. It was obvious he'd done this before, often enough to sing "Use Me" in perfect pitch while his muscles strained and flexed with the rhythmic motion. August cupped her hands around her mouth and shouted, "Thought you had my number!"

Luke used his phone to turn off the music, then squinted through the sweat sliding into his eyes. "To the phone in this house," he said. "Not your cell."

She folded her arms but immediately uncrossed them because it was too hot to touch herself. "If I share it, you can only text me for work purposes."

"Is that what they call blackmail these days?" He frowned at her sundress as if he didn't approve. It was white linen with pockets. Cool and functional. Undeserving of his attitude.

"Don't be dramatic. It's a business arrangement."

"Where's the contract?" He wiped his face with the bottom of his shirt and gave her an eyeful of the fitness magazine ad hiding beneath it. A sculptor couldn't carve more perfect ridges. She hadn't expected that. In high school he'd been strong but lean, two skipped meals from skinny.

"What's the split on rights?" Luke asked. "Fifty-fifty? Or do you plan to take everything to get even with me?"

He was testing her, focusing on the business side of her scheme to see if she'd cave. But he was also fidgeting, moving his hands from his pockets to his sides and back again. He had every right to be nervous. Based on what he'd told her about his career, holding his comeback hostage probably triggered bad memories.

"I don't know," August admitted. While she didn't owe him comfort, lying wouldn't get either of them what they wanted. And she did want more for him. At least, more than what she'd seen in that truck. She could hate Luke and hurt for him, too. Jojo taught her that. Feelings didn't have a straight path. They were riddled with forks and ditches, blocked by rivers too strong to wade through. "I'm being impulsive, which shouldn't surprise you. People don't change much."

She looked at her old bedroom window. The flowers taped to the glass had been there since her tenth birthday. It had been a good one, predictable the way special days should be when someone cared enough to plan them. "I want to build a time machine," she'd told Birdie, because the sun insisted on setting no matter how closely she watched it. Everyone knew that was the quickest way to slow a thing, keeping your eyes on it. Birdie picked wildflowers from the yard and pressed them inside a book. Once they were dry, August had hung them next to the worn chair she used for writing and dreaming.

"Everyone changes." Luke followed her gaze to the window. "The boy you see when you look at me is gone. Just like the girl who hung those flowers." He met her eyes. "Who do you want to be now?"

She understood his point, but he was being naive if he thought they weren't still carting those damaged kids around. The high set of his shoulders proved he was still bracing for impact. His hands still twitched when they were empty, always grasping and striving. And here she was, still aching for someone who'd hurt her, tempted to fill those restless hands with her own.

Those kids weren't gone. He'd just forgotten that ghosts were real.

"I want to do this together, like before," she said, because if there was a different way to write with Luke, one that didn't end with him leaving and her gutted, she couldn't see it. But what was one more heartbreak when you'd survived dozens? She'd heal like always. The music was all that mattered. "I'll take my fair share of any money because that's how it should have been before."

His jaw flexed like he was about to say another hard thing. That was all they did now. Exchange truths that had been sharpened into weapons. But instead he looked down at himself and took stock of the grime coating his body. "I'll get cleaned up so we can start."

August eyed the pile of dead rosebushes he'd collected next to the house. Pots of red Knock Outs were lined up, ready to replace them. "Where did you get these?"

Luke took his time answering, staring at the flowers like they might jump in and do it for him. "One of your neighbors needed help with his yard yesterday. I took his leftovers instead of cash."

"But you need the money. Why would you do that?"

Luke pointed to the dead roses. "These were yours. First thing you ever planted. I think you were nine—"

"Eight." She didn't want to think about Birdie anymore. But trying to resist the memory felt like pushing fog. "I'd been begging her for roses since I was six."

He smiled. "Right. You planted them together."

August pictured her grandmother crouched in the dirt, waving around a gardening spade while swearing never to touch them again. "They're your responsibility," Birdie had claimed. But she couldn't help herself. August would grab a watering can, determined to keep her promise, but often find Birdie outside, tending to the flowers.

Luke passing up cash to get her roses was one of those small things that felt big. Like making a stranger laugh in the dark. "You don't have to do this," she said. "Or paint or fix anything. I offered you the house, free and clear."

"Like I said, that's not why I did it." He peeled off his work gloves and threw them on the ground. "The roses are yours. So is the house. I want to give them back to you."

He tried to make eye contact, but August refused. His gaze was too earnest and open, the kind she used to fall into. Luke would offer some sweet gesture and she'd gorge herself sick, convinced it was enough to live on. It wasn't. Kindness didn't make you trustworthy.

But dear God, she loved his sweetness.

Once the screen door slammed behind him, August let out a shaky breath. She rubbed her eyes, grinding sweat into them as punishment for her thoughts. Luke was a married man. Everyone already thought she'd wrecked one home. She'd never live down wrecking another a few weeks later.

Someone said her name, and she ignored the familiar voice, sure it had been conjured by her guilty conscience. But then she heard it again, louder and more insistent. August opened her eyes to see Terry Dixon glaring at her with a bouquet of red roses in his fist. He kicked up dirt around the flower bed. "Didn't take long to replace me, did it?"

Luke rushed through his shower. He was eager to return to August now that he knew she was serious about working with him. When she'd first suggested it, he could only focus on the risk of getting fired for refusing to sing "Another Love Song." But last night, he'd thought up a different plan, one that would get them both what they wanted.

He was going to pitch the new song to Jojo herself.

Despite her denials, August wanted her mother's approval more than anything. A new song from him might go viral for a few days, but Jojo releasing a single written by her daughter would earn a different level of attention. Maybe get August a publishing deal. It might even heal the mysterious rift between the two women, which was worth more than fame, money, or rosebushes. Facilitating their reunion was the closest thing to atonement he could offer.

In his rush to get back to her, Luke pulled his T-shirt and jeans on over damp skin and didn't bother tying his sneakers before walking out to the porch. But August wasn't alone. She was standing next to a stocky Black man holding a bouquet of roses that looked so similar to the ones Luke hadn't planted yet that, for a second, he thought she'd caught a thief. Then he noticed the even cut stems bound by grocery store tissue paper. August said, "It's not what you think," and Luke knew he'd stumbled into an argument between two people with history.

Or maybe they were still together. He'd never asked if she was seeing anyone because he didn't want to know.

Luke stepped back, intending to retreat without being noticed, but the guy set furious eyes on him. August followed his gaze and winced. She gave Luke a tired look that said his timing was terrible. Luke answered with a shrug that told her he was aware.

"There he is," the guy said. "Flavor of the week."

August blocked his view of Luke. "Go home, Terry. You're drunk."

"Shirley threw me out again. I don't have a home, thanks to you." Terry glared at her. Once Luke saw the bloodshot glitter in the man's eyes, he moved closer so he could jump in if necessary.

Terry noticed Luke sizing him up and chuckled. "Chill, Country Drake. I ain't here to fight you. Not over her."

His tone implied there were better prizes. Better women.

"Then maybe you should leave, like she said." Luke glanced at Terry's flowers. "Take those with you. She's got plenty."

Terry eyed the unplanted bushes. "Hope she made digging all them holes worth your while, at least."

Luke knew his temper intimately. It flared as faint needles along his spine that would cluster and steamroll over everything in its path. He could barely restrain it when he was drinking, but he typically won that battle now that he was sober. It'd been years since he'd brawled over dumb shit he could barely remember the next day. But he'd never learned to restrain himself when it came to August. Watching her now, how she shrank from Terry's insults, erased every anger management strategy his therapist taught him.

He wanted to break this man. Grind him to dust.

Luke's hands were in fists before his brain registered the movement. August touched his arm and said, "I can handle this." She stepped to Terry. Luke wanted to snatch her back. She shouldn't have to deal with guys like this. Richard Green in high school. Now this asshole. She deserved someone who knew how to love her.

"You're hurt," August said to Terry. "But picking a fight won't help."

"Who's trying to fight?" Terry forced another laugh. "I'm just stating facts. Dude, ain't you married? She likes 'em unavailable."

Luke started to speak, but August touched him again, asking for patience. "You're hurt," she repeated, in a louder, stronger voice. "Birdie died and I used you to make me feel better. I should have told you that from the beginning instead of letting you think this was something it wasn't. I was careless and I'm sorry. But regret is all I owe you. And it's the last thing you'll get from me."

Instead of responding, Terry looked at Luke. "You in love with her?"

Luke was grateful that August was focused on Terry. He knew the answer was clear on his face. Terry grunted and hurled the roses into the yard. They all watched them fall into the grass, a red heap in a sea of green. Terry gave August one last dirty look before he walked away.

August didn't speak until Terry's car became tiny brake lights in the distance. "Were you about to fight for me, Country Drake?"

Luke grimaced. "I don't look like that dude."

She laughed—and, holy hell, how he'd missed it. The sound hummed in his stomach. "I'm getting divorced," he said, because Terry's taunts had bothered him. He didn't want the news to get out before Charlotte was ready, but that had nothing to do with August. He needed her to see him clearly.

"Isn't everybody?" She looked pointedly at Terry's abandoned bouquet.

"Charlotte and I have been separated for ten years," he told her. "She finally signed the papers a few weeks ago." Knowing she had every reason not to trust him, he pulled out his phone and showed her the signed settlement Darla had sent that morning. The email from Charlotte's future wife was riddled with exclamation points. She was excited about starting the next phase of their lives.

August read it, flicked her eyes up, then refocused on the screen and whispered, "Oh." Her mouth puckered over the word longer than necessary. The woman was painfully kissable. Resisting the urge was going to give him migraines.

"How do you feel about that?" she asked.

"Good. Relieved. For her more than me. I'm heavy baggage."

"No shit."

Luke laughed. She watched him, smiling, and then said, "Terry told me he was getting divorced, too. Then I found out he was lying, so I dumped him and picked a fight with his wife."

He raised his brows. "A *fight*, fight?"

"Hair was pulled."

"Did you win?"

"I can't believe you just asked me that."

"It's a fair question." He stepped back and looked her over, using the moment to admire how that thin sundress hugged her curves. "Trying to picture you scrappin' on the ground."

Her skin flushed—deep umber brushed with red. If things were different, if they weren't who they were, he'd grab that little knotted belt beneath her breasts and tug her closer to get a better look.

August wiped away the sweat on her neck. "None of that bothers you? Me being with Terry?"

"Only if you love him."

It was basically a confession. *Please don't*, is what he was saying. *Hate me all you want, just don't love him where I can see.* Luke was stronger in a lot of ways: Physically. Mentally. But not when it came to her, his favorite weakness.

August seemed confused at first, then seconds from laughing, but finally settled on irritation. "Why do you care?" she asked, but then immediately shrugged. "Forget it. Doesn't matter."

"You deserve better. Mistakes are one thing, but loving a guy like that—" He gathered his thoughts. Thinking about how Terry had spoken to her made him angry again. "It would mean you don't believe in it anymore. Not the way you used to."

August folded her arms like she needed protection from him. Maybe she did. He couldn't be trusted when she was like this, all teasing smiles and sweaty skin devouring light. He'd slip up at some point, admit to having feelings she didn't want to know about, and their fragile truce would be over.

"Those were just songs," August said.

"They were your stories." She tried to move past him, but Luke blocked her path. "Don't you remember?"

CHAPTER TEN

2009

Birdie stood at the kitchen counter with a line of baking ingredients in front of her, frowning at an open cabinet. There was no cookbook or recipe card. She made everything from memory, even the complicated desserts she was known for. Every major event in Arcadia had been blessed with one of her triple-layer cakes.

"What are you making?" August plopped her strategically heavy book bag on the kitchen table. It was filled with thick textbooks she hadn't opened in months. "Is that for Aunt Carrie's birthday?"

Birdie's eyes cleared. She snatched a can of evaporated milk from the shelf. "Yes. Caramel is her favorite." Birdie looked August over, noting her new outfit. "Why'd you change clothes? Didn't you just get home?"

"I'm going to the library with Mavis."

Birdie's suspicion faded just as August knew it would. No one thought her cousin would lie or make mistakes. Once, when August had brought home a first-place ribbon from the third-grade spelling bee, she'd been accused of stealing it from Mavis, who was in the same class. "How could I have known?" was all Birdie said when Mavis confirmed August had beaten her that year. To drive home her point, Birdie had hung the ribbon on the bottom corner of the refrigerator surrounded by coupons and old Polaroids, confident that it would be August's lone academic award.

She'd been right. But still.

If Birdie knew where August was actually taking Mavis that afternoon, it would break her heart. The women's clinic was an hour away, and Mavis needed someone to drive her home after the procedure. August had offered to stay with her, but Mavis refused. "Everyone knows we don't hang out anymore," she'd said, looking mildly ashamed of that fact for the first time in years. "I'd never be able to explain it to my mom."

Caroline shared Birdie's views about abortion and would guilt her into canceling the appointment. "Plus, Chris is Catholic," Mavis added. Her boyfriend was a sweet but restless six-foot-four center with dreams of playing in the NBA. "He'd be ring shopping by the end of the week."

"I'll pay for it," August told her, offering her Nashville money. "I'll drive you, too. Whatever you need."

Mavis had started crying again. "Why would you do this for me? I feel like I've been neglecting you."

"Jojo," August said, which told Mavis everything she needed to know. This wasn't just for Mavis, even though part of her hoped it would bring them closer, make her cousin less ashamed of her. It was for her mother. It was for every teenage girl forced to become a woman after making a childish mistake. It was for all the unwanted kids who never stopped paying for it.

Today, as August watched Birdie retrieve a tub of sour cream from the refrigerator, she felt a lot less panicked about the situation. No one knew she was helping Mavis. All she had to do was get out the door without making her grandmother suspicious.

"Why are you all dressed up to study with your cousin?"

It was a fair question, one that August had asked herself when she'd burned her neck with a curling iron. The new hairstyle and cute clothes weren't for Mavis's benefit. Later that night, she had her first songwriting lesson with Luke. Even though she'd sworn to stay single until she could legally buy enough whiskey to face dating again, there was nothing wrong with wanting the hottest social pariah in school to find you pretty. She was aiming for that moment in the movies when the mousy girl took off her glasses and became more than anyone imagined. She wanted his earth to shift a little.

"Mavis always dresses like this," August said. She wore a ruffled top and bootcut jeans. "I'm trying to bond."

"By copying her clothes?"

"She's not that deep, Grandma."

Birdie pursed her lips. "Watch your mouth while you're over there."

Her plan was working. Birdie wasn't suspicious anymore, just irritated by August's attitude, as usual. "I will," August said. "That was a joke. Mavis is smart. We're just different."

"Oh, I know," Birdie said. She grabbed a measuring cup and scooped out cake flour. "You're more like your mother."

August glanced at the clock. She didn't have time to be pulled into one of Birdie's anti-Jojo rants. If she didn't leave now, she'd be late. "Well, I should—"

"Love was always a test with that girl. She'd figure out the worst thing you could imagine, hand it to you on a silver platter, and resent you for not gulping it down." She blinked at the mixing bowl. "Always testing my tolerance for pain."

Birdie's eyes shifted to August and then hurried away. She knew her grandmother didn't consider her one of Jojo's painful tests. But she also knew that Birdie blamed Jojo for bringing Theo King into their lives. If Jojo had been Birdie's version of a better, obedient daughter, August wouldn't exist.

When Birdie got like this, August usually apologized on her mother's behalf. *I'm sorry Jojo left the way she did. I'm sorry she never speaks to you. I'm sorry she didn't love me enough to stay.* But today was different. Maybe it was the thrill of finally wearing clothes that fit. Or that Mavis had chosen her of all people as a savior. Maybe it was Luke Randall looking at her like he'd stumbled across a diamond. August faced Birdie with all those possibilities lengthening her spine and said, "I don't want to talk about Jojo anymore."

Birdie whirled around, ready to argue, but saw something in August that changed her mind. She straightened her apron and said, "No point in complaining, is there?" Then she returned to the cake bowl and started measuring.

Luke sat in his truck, wishing he owned a smaller vehicle. The minute he'd parked his F-150 at Delta Blue, a man glowered at him through the window, daring him to get out of it. It had to be Silas King, someone Luke only knew through stories, most of which began with his rap sheet. Silas was rumored to greet unwelcome strangers with a double-barrel shotgun. Luke wouldn't be surprised if it was trained on his windshield.

August was forty minutes late, which meant she probably wasn't coming. Luke glanced at his guitar, the dreadnought taunting him with its large size, which took up the entire passenger seat. He closed his eyes and leaned his head back. If August didn't show, that meant this was over—whatever *this* was.

Someone tapped on his window, and Luke's eyes flew open. The man who had been watching him earlier motioned for him to roll it down. Luke briefly considered driving away, but the man's hands were hidden. His old Ford couldn't outrun a bullet.

"I'm Silas. Are you Jason's boy?"

"Yes, sir. Luke. Lucas. I'm waiting for August. She told me to meet her here."

"Why? You not welcome at Birdie's house?"

Luke pictured August's grandmother, the formidable woman who always seemed to be wielding a cake knife. "I don't know. Sir."

Silas leaned back, the bottom of his jaw jutting with chew. "Mmmm. Sounds about right. August is hard to read sometimes."

Luke thought about his interactions with her. How easy she was to talk to. "Not to me."

Silas raised his eyebrows. He glanced at the guitar. "What do you play? Blues? R&B?"

"Sometimes." Luke hesitated, then said, "Country." He braced himself for ridicule.

"Country?" Silas's eyebrows shot higher. "What do you know about country? Ain't no trap beats or Lil John shoutin' in the microphone."

Luke smiled. "Been listening to it all my life. Hank. Johnny. It's what I was raised on."

"Johnny's good." Silas leaned an arm against the truck. "I can't hang with Hank, though. Something about his voice. You listen to Patsy?"

"Cline? Yeah, I . . ." Luke spotted August's blue Focus kicking dirt up at high speed. She turned into the lot with too much gas and nearly spun out before she parked.

Silas watched it all, unconcerned. He tapped the roof of Luke's truck. "Your date's here."

"She's my tutor," Luke said quickly. He was paying her. There were too many gross implications to calling it a date.

"Tutor?" Silas frowned. "Are we talking about the same girl?"

Luke tried to open the door, but Silas pushed it shut again. "Where do you think you're going?"

Luke realized the music conversation was a test he hadn't passed yet. Failing meant he'd never step foot on this man's property. "I don't want to greet her sitting down like this," Luke said. "It's disrespectful."

Silas stared, silently assessing him, before a wide grin spread over his face. He stepped back, pulled Luke's door open, and waved his permission to exit.

Even though it wasn't a date, Luke had put more effort into his appearance than usual. He wore a blue button-down and the newest pair of jeans he owned, but he had resisted aftershave because something about altering his scent felt like shouting, "I'd like to fuck you!" Which was fine, if that was your goal, but it wasn't his with August. After what happened with Richard, he wanted to prove he could be her friend without an ulterior motive.

The minute Luke got a good look at her, he saw the flaw in his logic. He could act like some pious monk all day long, but in reality, he was just a boring sinner. August wore a frilly red top with a lower neckline than usual. She'd curled her hair, and it spilled over her shoulders, framing the most magnificent pair of breasts he'd never see.

Good Lord, he thought he'd wanted something before. He thought he knew what it felt like.

"I'm late," August announced, in a matter-of-fact tone that told him to get used to it.

Luke said, "You're fine," in a way he hoped didn't reveal the rest. That he'd wait all day if she asked.

Silas looked back and forth between them. "Lucas here says you're his tutor. Is he lying?"

August laughed. It was big and loose in a way he'd never heard before. Maybe it was being in this place with her uncle, so far from town. "We're writing lyrics," she said. "He's paying me to help him write a love song for his girlfriend."

Silas's expression darkened. "Is that right?"

"No." Luke looked at August. "The song is for me."

"A love song," she said. "They're what you like, right? They're what everyone likes."

Luke couldn't argue with her. If he ran down a list of his favorite songs, they'd probably all be about soulmates and heartbreak. It was probably why he couldn't look at her without that fluttering in his chest. "Yeah. I want to write a love song."

She made eye contact with him, and they were briefly in sync, caught up in the same moment. But then her lips tilted into a smirk that made it all a big joke. "It's okay to be predictable, Lucas. Embrace cliché. It'll make this easier." She looked at Silas. "How long can we use the studio?"

"Long as you want," Silas said. "Just finished working on the demo with that jazz trio. It's all yours."

Silas's face softened when he looked at her, his affection clear in his voice. Luke never had that kind of relationship with his family. His mother's parents refused to meet him. His father's family hated his mother for inheriting their family's land, so they also pretended he didn't exist. Sometimes his little brother's love felt like a burden because they were all each other had.

He wanted to ask her what it felt like. To be loved for existing. To reach for someone and find them already reaching back. How did it feel when someone held on to you?

Luke retrieved his guitar, and they made their way inside. He had only seen nightclubs in movies, and Delta Blue was a mix of those images and things he didn't expect. There was the typical long mirror over the bar and round tables clustered near an empty stage. But there was also an art installation covering an entire wall, a collage of vintage album sleeves, handwritten song lyrics, CD covers, and photographs.

Luke spotted a picture of Jojo Lane standing onstage. She smiled at the unseen photographer with one hand on a microphone, her face damp and gleaming as if she'd just finished performing. Luke stared, searching for August in her features.

Silas pointed to a photograph of a Black man in a bowler hat holding a harmonica. "You know who that is?"

"No," Luke said. "Is he famous?"

"That's DeFord Bailey. First Black man Nashville ever recorded. Got inducted into the Country Hall of Fame a few years ago."

"He played here?"

"Lots of people did, back when they were just getting started. Delta Blue is part of Black music history. Folks don't realize that."

August made an impatient sound. "He'll talk your ear off if you let him."

"I don't mind," Luke said quickly. The only Black country singers he knew were Charley Pride and Darius Rucker. But apparently there was an entire history he wasn't aware of. "Are these people country singers?"

"A lot of them. Cleve Francis. The Pointer Sisters. Bill Withers—I know what you're thinking, but that man is country, don't let anybody tell you different. In fact, did you know Tina Turner has a country album? I've got a first edition copy in my—"

August groaned, cutting him off. "Not the *record collection*."

Silas cut his eyes at her. "Go on, then." He looked at Luke. "Come by sometime and I'll tell you more about it."

Luke left the conversation dazzled. Country legends had performed in the same building where he would write his first song. It was inspiring. But then he walked into Silas's studio and it became intimidating. The walls had been soundproofed with foam panels. There was a small analog mixer, microphones, and a computer on an L-shaped desk against the wall. Tall speakers were set up on either side. It was a room built for the real work of real singers, not his timid attempts to mimic Garth Brooks.

Luke propped his guitar on the wall but immediately regretted emptying his hands. They flapped at his sides while he watched August deposit a stack of notebooks and pencils on the couch.

Neither of them spoke at first. Luke said, "You look different," because he was too nervous to focus on anything besides how beautiful she was. "You curled your hair."

She ran her hand through the strands, which conjured an image of him doing the same, only slower and with proper reverence.

"I . . ." She tucked her hair behind her ears. "I have a date. After this."

"Oh. Oh! Yeah, that's good!" He was being too loud and saying too many fucking words. But the clown act was necessary for survival, since he was pretty sure being rejected by August Lane would kill him. "Do I know him?" he asked and prayed he didn't. He prayed God would spare him the indignity of rubbing shoulders with this guy in the cafeteria.

"No," August said. "He's a freshman. In college." She paused. "Philander Smith."

Luke pictured some pretty boy Kappa with brains and ambition, then decided he'd heard enough. "We should get started." He pulled three hundred-dollar bills from his pocket and offered them to her. August stared at the money but didn't take it.

"Can I be honest with you?"

He lowered his hand. "Of course."

She smiled at him, and his mood brightened a little. College boyfriend or not, he could have these moments. Her tiny slants of light.

"I don't know what I'm doing," she said. "I've never taught anyone how to write before, and I'm afraid you'll be disappointed."

"I won't be."

"You might," she said firmly. "Keep your money until I deliver on what I promised."

Luke wanted to argue further, but she looked determined. He returned the cash to his pocket. "Fine. I'll wait. But you're going to take this money, regardless. Okay?"

She hesitated but nodded. There was another awkward beat of silence, so Luke gestured toward her notebooks. "Should I grab one of those?"

She looked at his guitar. "I'd like to hear you play first."

A fresh bout of anxiety gripped him. "Play what?"

August picked up the notebook he'd returned to her. She flipped to the music he'd written for "My Jagged Pieces" and handed it to him.

"You want me to sing, too?" He'd played in public plenty of times but only sang alone. "I'm not as good as you."

"Good thing it's not a competition."

Her jokes eased his stress. She was right. They were in this together. He put the notebook on a table and dragged it close to keep it in his line of sight. Once the guitar was in his hands, his body transformed, adjusting to what felt like its natural state. This was why he'd roped her into helping him. Aside from when he spoke to her, Luke only felt like himself when his fingers were on the frets, his feelings buried beneath a C chord.

August watched him closely, but he wasn't nervous anymore—just poised to tap into something bigger than himself. The music. There was something holy in those first few notes.

Luke played the verse. While his music was solid, his voice was halting and unsure because he knew that his interpretation may not be what she'd intended. But he relaxed at the chorus because it was his favorite part. "*Sometimes it's bitter / Sometimes it's sweet / But I think / since you left / it's forgotten how to beat / So don't send your sorrys / thinking they can fix us / I won't live like this*—"

August waved to get his attention. "Stop. Stop singing."

Luke stilled. "I messed it up, didn't I?"

"No! No, that was *beautiful*. You sound like—" She blinked and rubbed her face. "You were perfect."

Luke shifted in his chair, happily exploding inside. Nothing compared to this feeling. He'd be chasing it the rest of his life. "Thank you."

"I'm the one who messed up. The story is wrong. It's too angry." She grabbed the notebook and went at it furiously with a pencil. "Don't send your sorrys," she mumbled. "Thinking they can fix us. I don't…" She trailed off, searching his face. "Can't. I can't love like this."

"In jagged pieces," Luke finished.

"Yes!"

He played the music again and sang the revised chorus, changing the tempo to make it more vulnerable, the way she wanted. August sang along and Luke let his voice fade. He watched her while he played, too caught up in the melody to notice he was tumbling into something vast and endless.

CHAPTER ELEVEN

2023

August never struggled with writer's block. Even when the words weren't there, the ideas would be. She'd map out themes and imagery and wait to be inspired, which always happened eventually. But the minute she sat across from Luke, her mind went blank. She had nothing. Or nothing she could share with him, anyway.

She kept thinking about his divorce. How long were they really together? Did he still love her? Charlotte had found someone else, but what about Luke? Had he dated other women in secret? She had a million questions about his life, all centered on the realization that they'd both spent much of the last decade alone.

One of her favorite songs was "Help Me Make It Through the Night" by Kris Kristofferson. It had been covered by different people: Tammy Wynette, Johnny Cash, Elvis Presley, but she'd never cried until she'd heard Tina Turner's version, with its sleep-thick delivery, like she'd recorded it while lying on one side of an empty bed. That song was a story of desperation, the kind that whispered in your ear at your lowest. It said take something. Anything. You won't last much longer if you don't.

Was that what Luke had been doing too? All those years. They could have been reaching for each other.

"I'm too distracted," August told him, because she had to come up with an excuse. She was getting mad about things that only mattered if *he* mattered, which he did not. He was her golden ticket. An on-ramp. No one pondered their ladder's feelings about being stepped on. They just used it.

Luke nodded and said, "Terry." Although it was true that her ex's appearance had been objectively messy, August didn't correct him. She gathered her things and lied about needing to go back to work.

That night, she unpacked a box of old notebooks she'd brought to her new apartment. The rest were still at Birdie's house. Those were older and filled with naive optimism about her relationship with her mother. The journals August had packed were more recent, when she was old enough to translate the true meaning of Jojo's words. "I'm too busy" meant this isn't a priority. "Arcadia is out of the way" meant I hate that place, so stop calling it home. "I love you" meant this is all I'll give you, and I don't understand why it isn't enough.

August never learned to translate Luke's words accurately. The truth was skewed by what she wanted. He'd said "You're amazing," and she'd heard I see you. He'd said "I need your voice," and she'd heard I'll never leave you, which had proved laughably untrue.

Luke was playing guitar when she arrived at the house the following morning. She let herself in and followed the sound to the kitchen, but stopped to listen when he started singing.

There was a reason August had always hated the way Luke sounded on "Another Love Song." The production was too hopeful. Too smooth. You just knew the man in that song would ride off into the sunset with the girl at the end. But Luke's real voice was smoke and pain, lost love, and the realization that a broken heart will never beat the same.

> *"When I say I'm fine / it means I need you / If I say go / please stay / I need you / When you see me lying, close your eyes / Listen to the space between / 'cause Lord, I need you."*

When the song ended, he hugged his guitar to his chest and stared at the wall. She thought he'd smile at least, take some sort of pride in his performance, but he looked distant, like he'd gone to a place where things like pride didn't matter.

"That was really good," August told him, because it felt wrong not to. Her chest was heavy. The song refused to let her go.

Luke looked embarrassed. He lowered the guitar to his lap. "Sorry. Should have been listening for the door."

August sat across from him. "I've never heard that one before."

"It was on my debut. Most people quit listening after track three."

"Wait." August frowned. "Was it the last one? The weird honky-tonk thing with a keyboard in the background?"

"Yep."

"It sounds different when you play it." She thought about the rest of the album and its unrelenting optimism from start to finish. "I was so mad when I heard them layer all that noise over your guitar. It's gorgeous by itself." She shrugged. "That's why I stopped trying to learn. I would never be as good as you."

Luke grinned. "So I should stop singing, then. Next to you, I sound like a frog choking on a lily pad."

"No. You sound like heartbreak." He tried to meet her eyes, but she focused on his guitar. "You always did, no matter what you were singing. Rainbows only came at the end of a storm. Every love song was about how you lost it." She reached over and strummed the first chords of "Another Love Song" but made it their version, slower and sadder. "People take a sweet thing for granted. But no one forgets what makes them cry."

Luke touched the guitar, his fingers inches from hers. "I don't want to make you cry, August."

There was a scar on one of his fingers, barely visible beneath the letters tattooed on his knuckles. She knew where it came from, what it had looked like fresh and bleeding. She wanted to ask whether all his body art was camouflage, a way to hide his trauma.

August stood and grabbed her journal. "Maybe we could work on some of my false starts." She flipped the pages and leaned back in her chair. "Tell me what you think."

He read the page she showed him with a furrowed brow, which made her nervous. It had been years since anyone critiqued her work.

"Is this about Jojo?"

August glanced at the pages. The working title was "Bitter," and the song opened with a poison metaphor. *If I die tomorrow / blame the lies you fed me.*

"I don't know," she said. "Maybe?"

"Were y'all fighting when you wrote this?"

She tried to remember. She knew it had been after Birdie's second nurse quit, and Jojo had been slow about hiring a replacement. Their texts had grown progressively hostile until August said Birdie would probably die before Jojo wrote another check. They didn't speak for months.

"That's what we do. Argue over bills. Avoid each other." Only with Birdie gone, there was no reason to make peace anymore.

"Is that all she did to help you? Send money?"

"Yes."

"No wonder you got so mad when I offered it to you." Luke skimmed the lyrics again and said, "This is good."

"Thank you."

"Angry."

"Good art often is."

He flipped the pages, scanning different songs. "Anything else in here?"

She snatched the journal back. "If you don't like it, just say so."

"It feels unfocused. I don't think you should launch your career with an improvised dis track."

She read through it again, noting incoherent themes and structure. The song was a stream-of-consciousness rant. "Fine, you're right. But don't go digging around in my journal. Some of it's personal."

"Everything's personal," Luke said. "Trust me, being up onstage with thousands of people judging every word that comes out of your mouth is as personal as it gets. The real question is what you're willing to give them. Because once you do, it's gone. You don't own it anymore."

"Like 'Another Love Song'?" She couldn't help herself. Anytime he brought up ownership, she remembered what he stole.

He nodded curtly and leaned away from her. "Yeah. Exactly like that. I gave it up the minute I sang it on *Country Star*." He rubbed his palms against his jeans. "Gave up a lot of things."

August was hit with a sudden, bone-deep weariness of the topic. Rehashing what he'd done wouldn't help her write anything new. Based on her lack of progress, it was doing the opposite.

"I'm out of ideas," she admitted. "I stayed up all night trying to think of something, but I think it's been too long since I've done this."

Luke leaned in, hands dangling between his knees. "Tell me a story."

"That's my trick."

"It's a good one. Never forgot it. No one wants to hear mine, but you?" He gazed at her. "I know you've got stories to tell."

"I'm not writing about Terry."

He laughed. "No one's asking you to. Start with emotion." His face grew serious. "When's the last time someone broke your heart?"

"You really want to know?"

She could swear he was about to say no, but then he swallowed hard and nodded. August crossed her legs, making herself comfortable. "Too bad. I'm not giving that story to anybody."

He looked relieved. "All right, then. What will you give me?"

"One-night stands," she said. "Adventures in stress fucking."

He rubbed his hands over his jeans again. The room was chilly from the air conditioner, so the heat wasn't causing him to sweat. "I don't know if—" He frowned. "What's stress fucking?"

"Rough. Sweaty. All bodies, no kissing."

"No kissing?"

He seemed annoyed by the thought. August stared at his mouth and decided it was a stupid rule to keep. His lips looked big and soft, a nice contrast to the roughness of his beard. Or it could be the opposite—hard, hungry kisses with pillow-soft hair against her cheek. "No one polices that sort of thing," she said. "Feel free to improvise."

Her voice was husky enough to make the joke an invitation. Luke's body seemed to tense and slack simultaneously. "Good to know," he said.

She cleared her throat. "Anyway, that's my love life. Probably too smutty for Jojo's wholesome homecoming."

"I wouldn't call that a love life."

"Okay, sex life. Either way, no one's come close to breaking my heart. They'd have to get to know me first." She bobbed her leg and played with her hair to prove how little she cared. "I don't make it easy."

"Maybe they weren't paying attention."

"Or they were focused on the wrong things. Like marriage and babies."

"You don't want to get married? Have a baby?"

Sirens were screeching in her head, warning her not to answer. "I don't know," she admitted, because warning bells were wasted on her. Might as well put up a sign that said come hither. "I come with so much baggage. Who'd want to take all that on?"

"When you love someone, it's worth it."

They weren't talking about her hypothetical boyfriend anymore. "Love shouldn't be hard."

"If it's easy, how do you know it's real?"

Four days later, August had written and rejected twenty song titles for reasons she struggled to articulate. Her muse kept saying, no, this is wrong. You don't care about what you're writing. Come back when you do.

At first she thought it was nerves, but during their last failed co-writing session, when she spent five minutes watching Luke's fingers dance over his guitar, she realized he was the problem. Specifically, what happened when she forgot to hate him. Letting go of her anger made her defenseless against what replaced it.

She genuinely liked him. Luke was thoughtful and generous in ways she could never anticipate. Besides the work he'd done outside the house, he'd taken on other small projects, like fixing broken chairs in the dining room and removing stains from the hardwood. He'd also cleaned the cloudy glass in Birdie's family photographs, a collection of frames that covered an entire wall. One day she arrived to discover that he'd pulled out a sewing machine and started mending the ancient living room drapes.

"You sew?" She tried to imagine Luke's large frame hunched over the yellow Singer.

"Yeah," he'd answered, with a tone that asked, *Don't you?* "It's a good hobby. Saves money and keeps my hands busy." He flexed his fingers, and the simple motion wreaked havoc on her insides.

That was her second problem. In addition to lapping up his sweet gestures like a delirious cat, she couldn't stop picturing those fingers "keeping busy" between her legs. It was her own fault. She'd poked a very horny bear with that stress-fucking nonsense. It had felt too much like tutoring him again, only this time on how to self-medicate with dirty sex. That was one of *her* favorite hobbies, stacking orgasms with a big, beautiful man who could toss her around like a sack of potatoes. Luke was a people pleaser who showed affection through acts of service. He probably wouldn't question what she wanted. He'd merely ask when, where, and how hard.

Unresolved sexual tension had an obvious solution. But that was dangerous thinking with Luke. He could see through her defenses. Enthrall her with a melody. When she arrived for their fourth session, determined to stay on task, the sight of him stirring a pot of greens while wearing a paisley apron crumbled her resolve like it was tissue paper.

"You're *cooking* now?" Meat was roasting in the oven. Yeast rolls were being kept warm by one of Birdie's blue-and-white tea towels.

Luke wiped his hands and motioned for her to try one. "Surprised I'm a grown man who can feed himself?"

She pinched off some bread. "I thought those were extinct." She took a bite. "Are these from scratch?"

He nodded, smugger than she'd ever seen him. "What do you think?"

"You should sell these at King's. They're that good." She scanned the kitchen. "Where did you get all this food?"

August immediately regretted the question. They hadn't discussed his finances since she'd offered to let him stay there.

"You mean, where did I get the money?" He poked at the greens again, tasted them, then grabbed a bottle of hot sauce. "One of Ava's neighbors is a contractor. Been helping him out with a few jobs."

"Ava?" She kept her voice flat to hide her irritation. The only way he would have met this person was if he was still visiting his mother. "Do you think seeing her is a good idea?"

Luke opened the oven and pulled out a pot roast. She sat down at the kitchen table as he piled her plate high with meat, greens, and rolls. He took his time fixing another plate before answering her question. "I don't know. But she's not doing well and I'm the only one around to help her."

She considered asking about his brother, Ethan, but decided against it. Luke was fighting the same battle she'd repeatedly lost with Jojo, so she wasn't qualified to offer advice. No one ever won those, though, wars waged on mothers. You can't change who carried you. Sift through the skeletons in your closet and you'll find their bones.

Once both plates were on the table, Luke sat down and waited for her to eat. August picked up her fork. "We're supposed to be writing."

"That wasn't happening. Figured I'd try something else."

She prodded the food. "Did you put something in this?" He laughed. She took a bite of the roast, and it tasted like heaven. "Oh. Just your foot."

"All right, smart ass. Finish your dinner so we can talk about what's going on with you and this song."

Her appetite vanished. Luke ate for a while before he noticed she'd stopped. "What's wrong?"

"Not hungry anymore." She stood with her plate. He stood, too, blocking her path to the kitchen.

"Don't do that."

"What?"

"That." He flung a hand at her. "Shut down and pretend you're not upset. We both know you're struggling. I thought we could work on a solution together—"

"I know what the problem is. And you making the best meal I've had in weeks wearing"—she flicked her hand at his chest—"an apron, of all things, isn't helping."

He ripped it off, revealing a formfitting black T-shirt that made her want to bare her teeth like a wild animal. "Better?"

"Fuck you." She tried to move past him. He grabbed her arm, and all the food on her plate slid to the ground. They stared at the mess until August looked at him and said, "I was going to eat that later."

Luke squeezed her arm. "If being around me is this hard, maybe we should stop. I'll think of another way to get your song out there. We don't have to do it this way."

August gripped the plate tighter, pressing the edge into her stomach. Another insult was on the tip of her tongue, waiting for deployment.

But she was tired of arguing. Sick of hiding. "I don't think I hate you," she said. "And I should. Right?"

His grip slackened, and he took a deep breath. "Yeah. Probably."

She looked at his mouth. "What does that say about me? After everything. That I don't want to do this without you."

He bit his lip. "Don't look at me like that, August."

"Like what?"

"Like..." He swallowed hard, his fingers tight on her arm. "Just don't put the plate down."

August stared at the only thing separating their bodies. "They're ugly anyway."

She let it fall, and his mouth was on hers before it shattered.

Touching her was a mistake. He thought he was long past those with August, but she made it so damn easy to keep turning left when all his instincts said turn right. Left was the road of no return. That's how it felt when he kissed her, like there was no turning back from this. No waking from the dream that was her lips parting to welcome him, her tongue slow dancing with his.

He leaned back to get his head straight, but then her hands were on him, sliding under his shirt, while she kissed his neck and chin. He started trembling, fucking *shaking*—that's how good it felt. But he needed to stop. His brain knew this was a bad idea for so many reasons, but his hands didn't care. They'd been waiting years for this moment, so he let them roam. He gifted his palms with her hips, his fingers with the dip of her spine.

"What are you doing to me?" was all he could ask, because he'd never felt so out of control before. Not high. Not drunk. He nudged her back to the table, knowing he shouldn't. He fisted her hair and tugged, opening her wider, fully aware it was a mistake. He kissed her again and again, damning himself thoroughly because a man like him, who'd done the things he had, could only have something this good if he stole it.

He stepped back to do what he'd been dying to ever since he saw her in one of those little sundresses. He pulled the skirt up, baring her thighs and a strip of cotton. He traced the edge, watching her face. She looked ready to catch fire. One good spark and she'd be ashes.

He licked two fingers, and August made a strangled sound that raked through his body. He pulled her panties to one side and massaged her clit. She grabbed his neck, whispering, "That's good. You're so good Luke." Her praise poured into him, weighing him down, filling all the empty gaps. He wanted more of it. He wanted to be so heavy and full that if he waded into water, he'd sink like a stone.

She was writhing, quaking with tight little shivers. One strap of her sundress had collapsed, and he leaned over, kissed her bare shoulder, her collarbone, the swell of her breast. He pushed his fingers inside her, and she cried out, clenching over them. Feeling that, owning it, triggered some primitive part of his brain that wanted to know how much she could take.

He started stretching her. She moaned, then whispered, "Don't stop." The words echoed and fractured in his mind. Don't stop. Don't *stop*.

Don't.

Stop.

What the hell was he doing?

Luke straightened and pulled his hand away. "August, I'm—"

"Shhh." She tugged him closer. "Don't say whatever you're about to say."

He felt her thigh press against his damp hand, her skin soft as silk. "We need to talk."

"You're right. I'm on birth control. Condoms are in my purse. I've been tested recently. All negative. What about you?"

That wasn't what he meant, but he answered anyway. "I've been tested. Plus, it's been over a year, so..."

Her eyes widened. "A year?"

Yes, a year. Because people in recovery weren't supposed to date. Or at least they should be slow about it. Luke had been glacial. He didn't want to inflict himself on anyone ever again. But August didn't know that. She didn't know he was defective in ways he'd never told her.

Luke took a step back. "We shouldn't be doing this."

August looked confused. "What?"

"This was a mistake, and I'm sorry. I shouldn't have...I took advantage, and I'm—"

"Are you being serious right now?" She yanked her skirt down and righted the strap that had fallen. "Don't apologize to me. And don't ever call me a mistake. I'm not a fucking mistake."

"No, of course not! I meant me." He touched his chest. *"I'm* the mistake. What we just did...it's too fast—"

"It's been thirteen years!" She was breathing hard, blinking through damp eyes. "Which I don't want to talk about anymore. It hurts!"

"I know," Luke said. "But you're still angry with me. I can't sleep with you and not—" He stopped because the confession was too big. She would never forgive him. She shouldn't. Which meant if he had her, he couldn't keep her. And he'd never survive that. "I don't want it to be another thing you regret."

Her faced flattened into an expression he couldn't read. And that hurt more than anything—how quickly she closed herself off to him. "What do you think I regret, Luke?"

He'd turned it over in his mind so many times, rewound every choice that led to this: lost moments, misspoken words, every chance he had to love her the way she deserved, but saved himself instead. He gathered it all in his mind, held it there, and said, "You never should have met me."

She smiled the worst smile he'd ever seen. Like a gaping wound. "You're wrong. I never should have lost you."

Luke was too stunned to respond. She used his paralysis as an opportunity to gather her things. There was so much to say. But none of it mattered. "You didn't" was all he could manage as she slipped out the door.

PART FIVE

THE SECOND VERSE

This Is Our Country: Podcast Transcript

Episode 12—"Jojo Lane"
August 21, 2024

[*cont.*]

Emma: How old were you when you entered your first pageant?

Jojo: Oh Lord. A baby? I don't remember.

Emma: Did you enjoy them?

Jojo: Sometimes. I liked singing in the talent competition. Birdie made me one of those sparkly cowgirl costumes and the judges ate it up. Little five-year-old Black girl belting out "Jolene" like she's got a man to steal. [*laughs*] I also enjoyed being told I was pretty, particularly during those awkward years when no one felt pretty.

Emma: I had plenty of those. Did you know about the racial history of the Delta Teen competition when you entered?

Jojo: Not completely. I knew what everyone knew. The pageant was white. Very bottle blond and blue eyeliner. And entering those pageants was expensive, so all the Black girls had to be smart about which ones they spent money on.

Emma: So why did you do it?

Jojo: Well, at that point, I was sixteen and had been doing pageants for years. I was a pro. So when my mother got the invitation—they sent those to everyone in the county back then—she said, "Maybe we should skip it." I told her no. I'd won all the Black pageants, and I wanted a challenge. I wanted white people to tell me I was pretty, I guess. It was silly.

Emma: Silly is a strong word. I mean, you won. The first Black Miss Delta Teen.

Jojo: And that was fun for a hot minute. Then the death threats started coming.

Emma: You received death threats?

Jojo: Of course. They tried to hide them from me, but people approached me in the street. I remember this boy, one of the few little white boys in my class, shoving me into a locker. He was spitting mad. Literal spit flying everywhere, and he called me... I can't say it on here, can I? The N-word. And it sounded strange coming out of him, like he wasn't used to saying it. Or maybe he just wasn't used to shouting it in someone's face. Either way, he got suspended. His little friends were mad at me. Like I was the one who put that nastiness in his mouth.

Emma: Were you bullied at school?

Jojo: A little. When I won something, girls would start rumors.

Emma: We can talk about it if you want.

Jojo: No, you asked about Delta. Let's get that out of the way. I don't want people to think I was ungrateful for it. I know it meant a lot to people to see me wear that crown. I think it still does, even with how it ended. That wasn't intentional. I wasn't hiding that I had August; I just didn't read the rules.

Emma: Can we talk about that now? Becoming a teen mother?

Jojo: Sure. It was a hard year, so I may need to take a break now and then.

Emma: That's fine. And start wherever you'd like.

Jojo: I should talk about Theo.

Emma: Theo King? Your daughter's father?

Jojo: Don't call him that. He never wanted to be called that, so let's not do it here.

Emma: My apologies.

Jojo: It's okay. People are supposed to want their children. It's a natural assumption to make.

Emma: I know that's not always the case.

Jojo: It's not. And that's the real damage, isn't it? When they know you don't. When they can look in your eyes and tell?

CHAPTER TWELVE

2009

"Pick a story, Luke." August took a bite of her sandwich. She'd made two that morning and was more attentive to the ratio of meat to mustard this time. Luke's included lettuce, which August never ate because it had no taste. Adding it to bologna felt performative. But Luke seemed like the type who'd be comforted by familiar sandwich structures.

He took his time crumbling the foil into a tiny ball and stuffing it into the paper sack they were using as a trash bag. He did that a lot, drew out basic movements while gathering his thoughts. "You mean like a topic?"

"No, a story. Something with a beginning, middle, and end. You don't have to tell the whole thing, but it helps to keep it in mind as you write."

"Okay." He nodded, but still looked confused. "Is that my homework assignment?"

He'd been doing that since they started, trying to apply a rigid structure to their lessons as if he were still learning formulas in second-period trigonometry. After three days of meeting during their lunch period and at Delta Blue, the only thing he'd written for her was a playlist of his favorite R&B songs titled "Slow Jams for Augustina" with a rose doodle attached.

She needed to shake him loose somehow if this was going to work.

"It shouldn't feel like an assignment," August said. "It should feel like pulling something out of yourself that's already there. Excavating an emotion."

Luke rubbed his neck, then ran his hand over his hair. It was getting longer, forming cute little spirals. "The way you talk makes me wonder if I ever had an actual emotion at all. How do you come up with this stuff?"

"Don't overthink it," she said, pulling her knees up to her chest. "Start with something personal. A moment that's meaningful to you."

Luke stiffened. "Personal how?"

"Like your relationship with Jessica." She'd thought about this last night. Despite the minor crush she had on Luke, talking about the girl he actually wanted would be the quickest way to get something useful out of him. "Think about the day you met. Or when you kissed her for the first time."

Luke looked pained. Like everything she'd listed was the last thing he wanted to talk about. "I don't..." He grabbed a broken cat mask and crushed the ears in his fist. "There isn't much of a story there."

"I bet there is."

"You'd lose that bet."

"You're being difficult."

"I'm being honest." He shrugged. "Everyone doesn't have some grand love story. Sometimes you're just—"

"Down to fuck?"

He paused. "That's not what I was gonna say."

"Sorry." She lifted both hands. "Please continue. Sometimes you're just what?"

"Some things just happen. Like...a door that's left open, and it looks cool, so you...walk through."

August stared at him. "Do you know how lazy that sounds?"

"I told you. There's no story there."

"There is! There always is. If something elicits a feeling, it's a story. That's how our brains work." She cut off his protests with a silencing hand. "Let me give you an example."

August grabbed her notebook, flipped to the front page, and handed it to him. "This is about my first kiss."

Luke read it eagerly. "Fireflies?"

"I was only nine, so it was a completely innocent cheek peck. But it still counts. His name was Lawrence, and he was obsessed with bugs."

The memory had faded in parts. She couldn't remember his last name. His face was a mishmash of features that may have been pulled from other boys she grew up with. She did remember that he was staying with an aunt who lived in the duplexes filled with people who never stuck around for long.

"I didn't have friends back then," August said, but kept her eyes averted because Luke knew that had never changed. "And Lawrence was only visiting for the summer. He was so nice to me, and I wanted to keep that. I wanted to keep him. But it felt like trying to stop sand from escaping my hands. I was so lonely and—" August stopped because that felt like too much. Irrelevant to the lesson. Instead she said, "At night, we'd chase lightning bugs."

Lawrence had asked her which bugs were her favorite. She told him she liked lightning bugs because they only showed up during the summer. "The day he left for good, he asked his aunt to stop by our house so he could say goodbye. But I didn't want to watch him leave. I could hear him crying, begging his aunt to wait a little longer, but I knew that if I came out, I'd cry, too. It scared me. That kind of sadness still does. Makes me afraid I'll never stop."

The terrible choice still weighed on her. The instant regret. "Later that night, I found a jar of fireflies outside my window. I knew it was his way of saying don't forget me. And so I wrote a song to make sure I didn't." She looked at the journal in Luke's hand. "*When the fireflies return / that's when he finds her / Calling him home with a flickering light / She only gives to the summer.*"

Luke didn't speak. She still couldn't look at him, and the silence was stifling. "Did you know fireflies only live a few weeks after they become adults?" She flipped the notebook pages, disrupting the moment with rustling paper. "Their lights are mating calls. So, they spend their entire adult life looking for someone to love before they—"

He grabbed her hand. "You're amazing. Do you know that? Has anyone told you?"

This wasn't how it was supposed to go. She was supposed to give him an example, and he'd think about whichever girl was lucky enough to be his first. He wasn't supposed to listen so closely.

"Stop distracting me with compliments," she said, pulling her hand away. "You still need to write something."

"I wasn't doing that," Luke said. "I mean, I was complimenting you, but it wasn't a tactic. I honestly don't think I can turn a moment into lyrics like that." He reached for his guitar. "But I can do this."

Luke started playing, and the notes floated into the air like those flickering bits of light she'd written about. He paused, pointed to the first verse, and played it again, singing along this time. His voice was hesitant, asking if this was what she meant.

August answered. She started singing, matching his key, but added all the feeling that had inspired the lyrics. Her voice grew louder, grittier at the chorus, which always happened when she set it free. It rolled over Luke's baritone, and the unified sound rewired her senses. It was sweet in her mouth. It was plunging into cool water on the hottest day.

When they finished, she was trembling. Sometimes a good thing was too good, and what it revealed was terrifying. She'd always thought her voice was her voice, flaws and all, the end. But the universe doesn't work that way. She could see it in Luke's stunned, shaken expression. When stars collide, they're irrevocably changed.

The next morning, Luke thought of a story. He wrote it down, then immediately erased it and tried to pretend it never existed. The idea was, for lack of a better word (which was at the root of his problems) stupid. Boring at minimum. After yesterday, he was pretty sure August liked him, so he didn't want to ruin it by plopping some underbaked idea that made him look lazy in her lap. Digging through his past had always been risky, so he wasn't very good at it. Simple things like his first day of kindergarten triggered an avalanche of bad memories: a spilled bowl of cereal, Ava screaming, Ethan crying. She'd forced Luke to wear the milk-soaked pants all day and ordered his teachers not to let him change.

"Don't think about it" was his mantra, his entire approach to life. Now August wanted him to rummage through those mental trash heaps and find something that would make a good love song.

"You thought of something, didn't you" was the first thing she said to him at Delta Blue. Instead of answering no like a normal person with self-preservation instincts, he said, "Yeah. It's about my first love. But not the kind you think."

Her eyes rounded, more doe-like than usual. "Sounds mysterious."

"It's not a person." His skin caught fire the minute he said it. This was the stupid part.

"Congratulations. I'm both confused and intrigued." She sat on the couch and patted the cushion next to her. His eyes were drawn to her bare legs. She wore jean shorts with a red T-shirt that said THERE'S NO APP FOR THIS. Their knees touched when he sat down.

"I'm not sure where to start," he said, waiting for her to move away. She didn't.

"With a feeling. How did whatever this is make you feel?"

"Happy."

"Okay. Reckless choice for a country song, but let's go with it. What made you happy?"

"Holding the guitar pick right. I would sneak and watch Pete play—"

"Who's Pete?"

"My little brother's father. Pete was a banjo player in a folk band. Taught me about roots music. I wanted to learn how to play but was afraid to ask."

"How old were you?"

"Five or six. My mom would tell me not to bother him. He was kind to me. Nicer than I thought adults could be at that point."

"Nicer than your mother?"

He hated when he slipped up like that. Ava wasn't a safe topic. "Yeah. So anyway, I used to watch him. Then, when he was gone, I would sneak into the garage, where he stored all his instruments, and try to play his guitar. One day he caught me. I thought for sure that was it. I'm going in the closet for days. But he asked me if I wanted to learn. The first thing he taught me was okay."

Her lips quirked. "Okay?"

Luke retrieved a pick from his bag. "You make an okay sign like this. And slide the pick here..." He pointed to his thumb and forefinger. "So that it's facing the strings when you turn your wrist."

She watched him closely. "Let me try." She took the pick from him and tried to mimic his hand position.

"No, that's wrong."

She moved one finger lower. "Like this?"

He cupped her hand and gently put her fingers into position. "Like this."

August met his eyes. "Your hands are warm."

"Sorry." He pulled them back.

"No, it's okay. Mine are cold, that's why I..." She waved away the rest of her sentence. "I think I got it."

"Good. Yeah, good." He wiped his hands on his jeans so he wouldn't grab her again. "How does it make you feel?"

"Vaguely competent. But six-year-old Luke was thrilled, wasn't he?"

"Felt like I'd cracked the world open."

She smiled. "I love that. Write that down."

He did as he was told. August studied it for a while, then added *Boys like me / never find the right road / until we hitch a ride on someone else's dream.*

"That's really good," he whispered.

They locked eyes. She was close enough that he could lean over and kiss her. He was about to ask if it was okay when she said, "What was that stuff about the closet?"

He blinked. "Stuff about what?"

"You said something about going into the closet if you got in trouble."

The closet was in the hallway near his mother's bedroom. It locked on the outside and there was only one key. He'd had nightmares about Ava misplacing it when she was high. "Oh, nothing. It's a joke me and my brother used to tell about being sent to our rooms. They're tiny."

She scooted back until they weren't touching anymore. "Do you miss Jessica?"

"I uh... hadn't thought about it." He was barely listening, too busy beating himself up for lying about the closet. But he couldn't tell her everything, could he? No one would stick around after learning all that.

She crossed her legs, swinging the top one lazily. "What's it like to be in love?"

It felt like she was testing him. If passing meant lying again, he'd rather fail. "I don't know," he said. "I only told her I loved her because she wanted me to."

"But you don't."

"No." Admitting it out loud made him feel worse. Plus, Jessica had seemed to resent him for saying it. Now it would always be the first time he said those words, as weak appeasement for a girl who barely knew him.

"Why would you—"

"Because I do dumb shit to make people like me." He rubbed his neck and closed his eyes. "I don't like talking about it."

The couch sank lower, and she pressed against his side. He opened his eyes, and she leaned her head against his shoulder. "Sorry if all that love talk gave you heartburn."

He exhaled slowly, relieved the truth didn't make her hate him. "Did you know your voice gets softer when you say *love*? *Love*, just like that. Is it your favorite word?"

She shrugged. "I don't know. Never thought about it."

"I think it is." He touched the hem of her T-shirt and rubbed it between his fingers. "I also think your favorite color is red because you have a different energy when you wear it."

Her smile nudged his arm. "Good energy?"

"Yeah. Augustina Rose with no thorns."

She lifted her head. "I have thorns."

He snorted. "Fake thorns. If *love* is your favorite word, they're not hurting anybody."

"I never said it was my favorite." She leaned against him again. He'd give anything if she never moved another muscle. "Do you *want* to fall in love?"

"There it is again. *Love*. So soft."

She prodded his arm. "Answer me."

He looked down at her. She caught his eyes, and he brushed a strand of hair back from her cheek. "I just want to write a love song."

Crushing on Luke didn't make August special. If anything, pining after the perma-prom king made her basic and boring, the kind of character she'd roll her eyes at in a movie. She wouldn't even watch this one. The ending was predictable, the lessons trite: There are more important things than being chosen. You're enough as you are. A real hero won't wait for some makeover to notice you.

But that meant her hero was Luke. He'd liked her before he ever saw her, when they'd been two nameless strangers in the dark. He spoke to her, laughed with her, knowing she was social kryptonite, which made him braver than he'd ever give himself credit for. Over the last three days, August had written so many variations of his answer to her love question that she couldn't remember exactly what he'd said anymore. "I want a love song" became "I'll write a love song," and then it was "I want love" followed by her tiny, scribbled "Me too." Then she threw the journal at her closet like it had tried to bite her.

Not loving Jessica didn't change who he was. Each day the tides were slowly turning in his favor. The first step was collective amnesia about his fight with Richard, a topic everyone had become bored with. Next, because Luke was Luke, he would eventually do something kind for someone who mattered and the people who never wanted to hate him anyway would be relieved they could publicly wave his flag again. Once his football suspension was over, his redemption arc would be complete. They'd have their golden boy back and August would be left with a bunch of unfinished songs. Another jar of dead fireflies to keep her company.

Or she could end things now. They had dozens of verses with titles that could easily become choruses. That's what she planned to tell him once he arrived at Delta Blue that night. She'd taught him what she knew about song writing and he could do the rest on his own.

That's what she would have said—if he wasn't two hours late.

It was 9:00 p.m. on a Thursday and Delta Blue had come alive. Each time August left the studio to check the parking lot for Luke's truck, the club was louder, filled with more voices and bodies. Silas kept checking his watch and shooting her grumpy looks that signaled it was past time for her to leave his adult-only business. August was too worried about Luke to pay him any attention. This wasn't like him. Luke was usually so punctual that Silas had started inviting him in early to talk music while they waited for her to arrive.

She had his phone number, but something about the way he spoke about his mother had always made her reluctant to use it. Today she was more afraid of what might happen to him if she didn't. August was reaching for the phone when she heard Silas order someone to leave. A familiar voice answered. She rushed out, pushed her way through the crowd until she spotted Luke. He was at the front door, frantically gesturing inside.

"Can't let you in," Silas said. "People will think I served you here, and I can't risk it."

"Let me talk to her, please! I won't stay, I swear."

"Find her at school tomorrow."

She touched Silas's back. His voice softened when he focused on her. "He's drunk, baby."

August stared at Luke. His eyes were glassy. A red mark on his cheek would probably become a bruise. The fingers clinging to his guitar case strap were covered in fresh scabs. "I'm not drunk," Luke insisted, stubborn in his delusion. "I mean, I was, but I'm fine now."

"What happened to you?" August pushed past Silas.

"I'm so sorry I'm late," Luke said. "You believe me, don't you?"

"I do. But Luke, what happened to your—"

"This melody came to me when I was thinking about... well... you and fake thorns, and... *shit!*" He took a deep breath. "I can't say it right. I need to play it." He looked at Silas. "Please let me in."

"It's past your bedtime," Silas said, then glanced at August. "He shouldn't be driving in this condition."

"I'll take him home."

Silas didn't seem to like the idea, but then glanced at the crowd. He couldn't leave when it was that busy. "You sure?"

She didn't answer. The car keys were already in her hand. "Let's go."

August knew Luke lived on a farm, but it was far enough outside Arcadia city limits that she'd never seen it. The property was huge, with miles of land dotted with rolled hay for grazing cattle. It took a while before she saw his house, a brick rectangle in the distance. Luke twisted in his seat, angling himself away from it, and said, "I can't go home right now." She could tell he was trying to sound less panicked than he was.

"Where do you want to go?" She couldn't take him to her house. Birdie thought she was with Mavis, studying.

His eyes darted around and landed on a line of trees in front of them. "Turn there," he said, pointing at a dirt road. "No one knows about this place but me."

August followed his directions, letting the woods swallow them until they reached a pond in a small clearing. She parked on the flattest patch of grass and cut the engine.

"Do you swim in that water?" The night was windless, which made the surface eerily still, like it was trying to trick you into thinking it was a mirror.

"Sometimes."

"Is it dirty?"

"Filled with nature."

"So that's a yes."

"We won't be swimming. Just follow me."

They got out of the car and walked closer to the water. Grasshoppers chirped and cicadas buzzed. The pond was alive, playing its music.

August sat, drew up her legs, and watched him do the same. "What happened to you?"

Luke rubbed his forehead, flashing his ruined hand. It had to hurt, but he didn't show it. Maybe he was used to pain because of football. "I lost track of time."

His expression begged her not to ask again. But she had to. He was her friend. "What happened to your face? And your hands?"

Denial must have been the only thing keeping him upright. His whole body went limp—arms, spine, and shoulders caving under the weight of what he didn't want to tell her. "There's this loose front step on our porch, and I ... I went down face-first on the concrete."

"That's it? You got drunk and fell?"

He shook his head. "My mother took something from me, and I spent most of the night trying to find it. That's why I was late. She came home from work and told me she threw it away."

Luke's voice was bloodless. She'd never heard anyone sound so tired. "What was it?"

He didn't answer right away, which wasn't surprising. Luke felt things first and tried to make sense of them later. It was part of their rhythm. August would ask, and Luke would answer, but there would always be a beat in between.

"It was a book," he finally told her. "My dad's poetry. It's out of print." He started picking at his nails, digging viciously into the cuticles.

"Is that the one you wrote music in?"

He looked startled. "You remember that? Of course, you do. You're a good person." He smiled, but it never came close to his eyes. "Yes, it was that one. With my notes."

"Why would she do that?"

"I wasn't supposed to have it. She threw out all his stuff when he died. Said it was too painful to keep." He paused. "I look like him."

He made it sound like an admission of guilt. August studied his face—the coffee eyes, sharp jaw, and lush mouth—trying to reconcile its poetic symmetry with the shame she heard in his voice. Something so beautiful could never be a burden.

"You look like your dad, too, right?" he asked.

"Yes," she admitted, even though she wasn't supposed to know. Silas kept a picture of Theo in his office but had never shown it to her. She'd found it while snooping around his desk when she was ten. The minute she saw the man leaning against an old Cutlass, she knew it was her father. She'd seen the shape of herself in his frame. "I think that's why Jojo stays away."

Luke nodded. "Ava would avoid me too if it weren't for Ethan. She loves him a lot." He spoke with pride, like it was an accomplishment. She wondered if he knew what it implied, that Ava didn't feel the same way about him. That had to be wrong. Love was the bare minimum for a parent, the part that took the least amount of effort.

"You think she would abandon you?"

"Not abandon." He fidgeted, uncomfortable with the question. "I can take care of myself."

August was suddenly very sure that he couldn't. Years of being punished for existing had stripped him of boundaries or gut instincts. None of it was his fault. Life was different for kids like them. They were never wanted, which made them obsessed with being chosen.

"Do you remember any of your dad's poems?" August asked him. "Or the music you wrote?"

Luke nodded. "Some of it, yeah."

"Wait here." August went to her car. She rummaged through her backpack and pulled out her journal and a pen. When she returned, she offered both to him. "Write it down."

"I only remember parts."

"Then write those. Before you forget."

He flipped it open to the first page. *For Luke* was written at the top, followed by her attempts to turn his desire to write a love song into lyrics. *I'd rip up the pages / Try to find someone new / But every chord spells your name in different keys.*

His scarred fingers fanned over the words. He stared at the lyrics long enough to startle her when he finally looked up. For the first time that night, he seemed completely sober. Sharp-eyed and aware. Then he started writing.

Luke's notes were chaotic, alternating between lines of poetry and chord progressions positioned randomly on different pages. He occasionally rubbed his head, deep in thought, until his curls were ruffled into spikes she was tempted to smooth back into place. August could picture doing it clearly. His muscles slack and still. Her fingers threading through his hair. His entire world calmed by her hands.

CHAPTER THIRTEEN

2023

Luke called his addiction "the Snake." He used to call it "that Asshole" but eventually realized that he was letting it off the hook. There was power in a name; it was a sign of respect. That's why it took him so long to admit drinking was a problem. He didn't respect its power. He thought it was just that asshole, a buddy who tagged along when he partied. Assholes may be annoying and cause trouble, but no one drops a friend because he screws up now and then. Only then, he starts tagging along to your shows and business lunches. Then one day he's pouring gin down your throat at six a.m. and you wonder what the hell is going on. Why's the asshole here? It's fucking breakfast. Who told him he was invited?

Snakes were sly, secretive predators. Tricksters that slept with their eyes open, waiting to strike. Five years sober, and Luke still had mornings like this one where he woke up hating himself for ruining things with August. He cleaned the kitchen, wondering if she'd ever speak to him again. Then he remembered how she'd gotten drunk over Terry, which made him wonder whether Birdie used to drink, which made him realize he hadn't checked the house for liquor before he moved in. That's when the Snake woke up and said, *It's been five years. Love is hard. A little nip won't hurt anything.*

Luke immediately searched for the closest twelve-step meeting. He wasn't surprised that it was being held at Arcadia Baptist. It was the biggest church in town and rumored to be responsible for all the failed attempts to allow liquor sales in Arcadia. The surprising part was seeing Silas King, owner of the most notorious bar in spitting distance from the city limits, leaning against the lectern while the group trickled in.

He caught Luke's eye and nodded in acknowledgment, almost like he knew this was where they'd reunite after all these years. Silas had met the Snake years ago.

Once they'd all settled into pews, Silas cleared his throat and said, "Name's Silas, and I'm an addict." The group acknowledged him, and then he led them through the serenity prayer. It was comforting, and he was sinking into the words when the door to the sanctuary opened again. Silas paused midsentence to shoot an annoyed look at the newcomer. "We start on time here."

"Sorry." David Henry glanced at Luke and shrugged. "There are nine churches in this town, and they all look alike."

Luke was tempted to leave. David must have followed him there, looking for an excuse to fire him. They locked eyes, and Luke raised an eyebrow that said, "See? I'm being good."

David sat in the same pew but far enough away that no one would suspect they knew each other.

"All right," Silas said, then clapped his hands to regain their attention. "It's been a while since we've had new faces, so, gentleman, please introduce yourselves. First names only."

David glanced at Luke. "Guess he means us."

Luke didn't acknowledge him. "I'm Lucas."

A chorus of hellos greeted him. David cleared his throat and said, "I'm Dave—Jesus Christ, this place is getting to me. *David.*"

Silas introduced the topic for that day, which was making amends. A few people gave examples of their attempts to apologize to aging parents they'd neglected and young children they'd traumatized. One guy broke down after admitting he'd finally gone back to his sister's house after slamming his car into their garage last year. "I couldn't ring the doorbell," the man confessed. His name was Frank. He wore a Pearl Jam T-shirt and his arms were covered in hives.

Once they reached the end of the meeting, Silas asked if anyone else wanted to share what was on their mind. He looked at Luke when he said it. David's presence made it tempting to remain silent, pretend this was all just maintenance. But again, that was the Snake talking.

"I didn't want to come here," Luke admitted. "To Arcadia. I didn't want to come back to this town." He glanced at David, whose expression was unreadable. "Bad things happened to me here. And it'd be a lot easier to forget that if I was drunk. That always made it easier to pretend that nothing bothered me. No one could touch me because I was floating. Chasing clouds." He shook his head. "But you can't hold on to those, can you?"

Luke took a deep breath and tried to focus. He needed to talk about August. "You were discussing amends earlier, and I sat here listening, knowing that's my problem. Amends are holding me back because I'm still figuring it out. You're supposed to apologize, but only if it doesn't hurt them more than you did before. But how are we supposed to know? What heals and what hurts? Especially when she looks at you like—" He pictured her face when he played for her. "Like this thing you do, the *only* thing you do well, is what she's been waiting for. Like it could save her."

He looked down at his hands, at the tattoos covering his old scars. "I want to make things right, give her what she asked for. But I still love her. So, it feels selfish. Like I'm taking something else I don't deserve."

He thought of her first song, the one about fireflies. That was August in his mind. A girl who loved so hard she had to put the feeling in a jar and wait for someone to find it. "She used to love me," he said. "And it's getting hard to remember that it was one of the worst things that ever happened to her."

No one spoke. Luke could feel Silas staring at him, asking questions Luke wasn't ready to answer. Eventually Silas focused on David, who seemed to chafe under the attention.

"I'm supposed to follow that?"

"Speak your mind," Silas said. It sounded like a demand. People were never forced to talk at meetings, but this small, close-knit group wasn't used to strangers. Silas knew Luke, but David was being tested.

"Okay." David straightened and yanked at his shirt, smoothing the creases. "I'm no poet, so I'll make it brief and boring. I'm an alcoholic. Never said that out loud before. Never done this, either..." He waved at the room. "Never thought my drinking was a problem because it wasn't. I'm what they call *high functioning*." He made air quotes. "Which means I can hold a meeting while blackout drunk and no one can tell."

When they'd met in Memphis, David had been clear-eyed and steady. It was hard to believe what he was saying was true.

"So, what brought you here?" Silas asked.

"Boylan Heritage." David looked at Luke when he said it. "It's good stuff. Makes it easier to say no when someone offers you a cocktail." He paused. "And I met this guy, this singer, who I'd written off as a talentless hack years ago. Listened to him play the most lackluster set of covers I'd ever heard." He lifted a finger. "Except for Patsy Cline. 'I Fall to Pieces.'"

Frank grunted his appreciation. "Love that song."

"Yeah, me too," David said. "But this guy broke it open. He took something I loved, something I thought I knew inside and out, and told me I was wrong. There were emotions I hadn't felt yet. Son of a bitch nearly made me cry." He leaned back in the pew. "I don't cry. And I'm never wrong. But I didn't notice what I usually see in people who become stars. My career is based on knowing who's special." He shrugged. "I blame the booze. So now I'm here."

Silas glanced at his watch. "All right, we're out of time. Luke. David. Thank you both for sharing."

Luke approached David as people slowly filed out of the room. "Was any of that true?"

"All of it. My lies are more interesting." David shoved his hands in his pockets and rocked back on his heels. "So that's why you're here before rehearsals? A forgiveness tour? Groveling to some woman you cheated on?"

"I didn't cheat on her. And I don't expect her forgiveness. A good thing now won't erase the bad from before."

"Where was all this lyricism on your albums? A chipmunk could have written your singles." Luke laughed. David's lips hitched upward like he was trying to resist the urge. He rubbed his face and sighed instead. "Promise me that whatever happened with this girl isn't a bomb about to go off in the middle of Jojo's concert."

"It's not," Luke said, because it wasn't. It was a bomb he was quietly diffusing to repurpose for something better. Something Jojo would thank him for. "Despite what you heard earlier, I've got it handled."

David nodded and looked at Silas, who watched their conversation while tapping a pack of cigarettes against his palm. "This guy scares me."

"I know him."

"Good for you. I'm out of here." He pivoted but paused. "We should talk once this is over. About your career."

Luke nodded. "I'd like that."

Once David was gone, Silas sat down, lit the cigarette, and smoked with relish. "Don't tell anyone I did this in here," he mumbled. He puffed while Luke grabbed a matching chair and pulled it up to him. "Heard you were back."

"For a few weeks now." Luke took in Silas's older, grayer appearance. "I should have called."

"I heard those pitiful albums you put out. Probably better you didn't."

Luke laughed. "All right. Lay it on me."

"Nah, you already know. My question is what are you doing now? Or what do you want to do?"

Luke hadn't asked himself that question in years. When he was recording, he did what his producers told him, changing his pitch and diction, playing up his drawl, all to increase his chances of being played by country radio. After two weeks of working with August, he'd fallen back into old habits, playing blue notes when he felt like it and adding more grit to his voice. "I want to play like I used to. Back when no one knew me."

"I can make it happen," Silas said, and put out his cigarette. "Come by the club tonight. Bring a hat." He narrowed his eyes. "You staying with August?"

"No sir," Luke said quickly. Silas cared about him, but the man loved August like his only daughter. "She's got her own apartment. I'm at Birdie's."

He sighed. "Has she talked to you about it? Taking care of her grannie at the end?"

"Some. But not really."

"She needs to talk to someone," Silas said. "With Jojo coming back, it's hitting her hard. She's reckless when she's hurting."

"I know." Luke pictured her that first day at King's, drop dead gorgeous and mad enough to scald him. She'd used that blackmail scheme to wake him up, remind him how to make music. "I love her reckless, though. She's brave."

Silas raised his eyebrows and lit another cigarette. "Y'all talk about *that*?"

"I'm less brave."

"Son." He touched Luke's shoulder. "You're not a coward. That's your mother talking. That's the addiction. But you're here, upright and sober. And it sounds like you're trying to help that girl through all this, even though I bet she's fighting you pretty hard."

"Sometimes." Lately he'd been fighting with himself. "I haven't told her everything. Why I stayed away."

"Sounds like you two need to have a real conversation."

Last night flashed in his mind, her begging him not to rehash things. "What if it hurts like I said earlier?"

"Pain is a sign of life. If it hurts, that means there's something worth saving."

Mavis gave her stock answer when August asked for legal help. "I don't work with family."

"It's one little contract," August replied, even though she suspected there was nothing little about a document that could change your life. Luke had ruined his career thanks to a contract he'd signed as a baby adult. "Don't you owe me a favor for some kind and generous thing I did? Because that sounds like me."

Mavis fell silent, and August was belatedly reminded of the kind, generous favor they never talked about anymore. The pastor's wife's teenage abortion was the kind of secret that could ruin lives—both Mavis's and her husband's. Their congregation could forgive a lot of things, but their leader's marriage to a mortal sinner wasn't one of them.

"You used that favor," Mavis said eventually. "For the showcase, remember?"

August had been so wrapped up in Luke that she'd forgotten about Silas's predicament. She'd lost sight of a lot of things, including the reason she'd blackmailed him in the first place. Luke wasn't auditioning for the role of loser boyfriend number eighty-five. He was a means to an end. She couldn't risk losing what could be her last chance at a career because some hot guy with a guitar made her yeast rolls.

"Yes, the showcase. Any new developments?"

Mavis sighed. "Fine, I'll write your little contract. Email me the details and meet me at the fairgrounds tomorrow."

When August arrived at the fairgrounds the next morning, she had to park on the street because of the equipment trucks and construction crews covering most of the parking lot. There were also news vans near a cluster of people who were holding signs. A white man with rolled-up shirtsleeves and sweaty hair gestured at the group as he spoke to a camera.

"It's too early to call this an organized movement, but emotions are high, and protests like this one are increasing as we get closer to Jojo Lane's induction into the Country Music Hall of Fame. Industry insiders credit the backlash to multiple factors, namely Jojo's relatively recent radio dominance that critics claim was manufactured by the new 'woke agenda' in Nashville. Add the controversy over Charlotte Turner's cover of 'Invisible' to the mix, and you have a heated debate over who gets to sing what and what the real face of country music looks like. With Jojo Lane's new single battling Charlotte Turner's latest hit on the Hot Country 100, I predict we'll be hearing more on this topic in the days to come. Back to you, Anne."

A man carrying a HALL OF SHAME sign shouted, "Fuck critical race theory!" The people behind him yelled more clumsy insults before they landed on a unified chant. "What country? *Real* country! What country? *Real* country!"

August understood their passion. When she sang along with Allison Russell about being both a wounded bird and a hawk in "Nightflyer," the song felt like her personal anthem, a reminder that, despite her reductive reputation, she contained multitudes. But no one could take that feeling. It didn't matter how many rants people wrote about the death of real country; they couldn't steal the joy she felt while listening to the music she'd always loved. These protesters, with their fear-fueled outrage, thought they were preventing a robbery when all they'd lost was the lie that the genre belonged to them.

Mavis approached her, grabbed her arm, and eyed the crowd. "Don't make eye contact. Some of these people look like they haven't eaten in weeks."

Mavis walked August to the card table she was using as a desk. Legal pads, pens, and a container of Delta Music Festival stress balls were neatly arranged around her laptop. A fan blew hot air toward the chair. Her cousin looked overheated and exhausted.

"How long has this been going on?" August waved at the protesters. One of them narrowed his eyes and spat on the ground.

"All week," Mavis said. "More keep coming. Plus, my festival hashtag is being taken over by racist trolls."

"Has Jojo said anything?"

"Not yet." Mavis's eyes brightened. "Could you ask her to make a statement? I mentioned it to her henchman, but he brushed me off."

"David is probably working on it," August said quickly. She didn't want to derail the conversation with more talk about her mother. When Jojo wanted to speak to her, she would. "Anyway, isn't this normal for high-profile events like this?"

"Yeah, I guess." Mavis eyed the group with a creased brow that said she wasn't convinced. "Anyway, please explain why you're running around with Luke Randall again."

"I'm thirty-one years old. I don't *run around* with people. It's a business arrangement." She could see her contract on the table. It looked official, with numbered paragraphs and signature lines. A perfect reminder to stay on task.

"I've seen the man. That beefy, roughneck, *just stole your debit card* vibe is completely your type. He's also married, which—"

"He's getting divorced," August interrupted. "They haven't made it public yet."

Mavis raised her eyebrows. "Where have I heard this before?" She meant her fling with Terry, the gift that kept giving.

"Okay, but Luke and I aren't together. There's no reason for him to lie."

"So, what *are* you doing? That contract looks like the same tragic dance you two did in high school. The one that ended with him on TV and you crying your eyes out for months."

Mavis had only seen part of it. While it was true she'd cried some, she'd mostly become numb in ways that frightened her. There were days when she woke up and didn't remember going to bed the night before. She ate sporadically, sometimes only when Birdie forced her to because she'd lost so much weight. But the worst part was avoiding music. She'd shared so many of her favorites with Luke that nearly a year passed before playing them didn't feel like losing him again.

"That was a long time ago," August told her. "We've both changed."

Mavis slid the contract over. "If you need this, then he hasn't changed that much, has he?"

August didn't answer. Her attention had been captured by a group of people on the stage built for Jojo. Most were fiddling with microphones and moving speakers around with headphones slung around their necks. Luke was at the center of the activity, playing warm-ups on his guitar.

"First rehearsal," Mavis said.

"Oh" was all August managed, because Luke hadn't mentioned any rehearsals, which seemed like a huge omission since the song they were working on wasn't finished yet. "Have you seen his set list?"

"They don't share those with me," Mavis said. "Is that what this contract is about? I'm not sure you should—"

"Shhh." August silenced her when Luke started playing. It took only a single chord for her to recognize "Another Love Song."

August knew her limitations. She used to make lists about them with the goal of improving as a person: Be less impulsive. Get more hobbies. No one wants to talk about the origins of outlaw country all day. Read a book besides *White Teeth* and *The Hunger Games*. She'd made progress on all those things. She'd grown.

But there was one bullet point she could never cross off because deep down, it was a lesson she didn't want to learn. Turn the other cheek. It was great in theory, but not when a man played games *directly* in your face.

August grabbed the first thing within reach, one of Mavis's stress balls. She squeezed it so hard it might never bounce back.

"Are you okay?" Mavis pried it from her fingers.

August stalked to the stage but was blocked at the stairs by a tall Black man with mirrored sunglasses.

"Hey, ho!" He raised his palms. "No fans."

"She's with me." Mavis showed him the contract. "Special delivery."

August snatched it from her and shouldered past security. Luke had started the first verse, playing that God-awful arrangement that made him sound like the cheesy ghost of country past. She stopped a few feet away, put her fingers in her mouth, and blew a piercing whistle.

"What the fuck?" One of the sound guys glared at her. "We're trying to work here."

Luke ripped the guitar off his chest and marched over with the same ferocious warning in his eyes that made her drop her dinner plate the other night. Something inside her, one of those weak parts that was still a work in progress, whispered, *Stop pretending you don't like it. He tastes better this way.*

"It's just a sound check." Luke gestured behind them at the stage. "David called and—"

"Sign this." August handed him the contract.

Luke glanced at it. "Not until we talk."

"Okay, fine. Deal's off." She went to the microphone. A crowd of festival volunteers and journalists had gathered with their phones and cameras pointed at the stage. She grabbed the mic and heard a burst of laughter from the crowd. "Hell yeah!" someone shouted. "Give us a show, August!"

People she knew, people she'd spent the last decade trying to convince that she was past her reckless, messy stage, stared up at her with knowing smiles. They'd been right all along. This angry disaster was all she'd ever be.

She couldn't move. Could barely breathe. Luke's arm slid around her waist and she leaned into his warmth. His lips were at her ear, telling her she was fine. She'd be okay. August closed her eyes and let his words wash over her. She wanted to believe him.

Luke led her to the large trailer the performers used as a greenroom. He tried to make her sit, but August refused, still clutching the contract like a lifeline.

"What was that out there?" he finally asked.

"I was angry."

"No, I mean—" He stared at her. "Do you have stage fright?"

Her chest tightened again, air scraping through her lungs. "I don't know what you're talking about."

"Is that why you stopped singing?" He moved closer, searching for something in her expression. "Because you haven't mentioned it since I came back."

"Why do you care if I sing or not?"

"Because I care about you. I don't need some contract to want what's best for you. And I'm starting to think that's not me singing another song you wrote." He took a deep breath. "Look, I'm sorry about earlier, but I had to—"

"There's your favorite Band-Aid." Her voice was hard but fraying, the threads holding her together snapping one by one. He was quitting. Trying to call her bluff. And she'd just let him win, hadn't she? Where was her courage when it counted? *Sorry.* Do you even know what you should be sorry for? Maybe you should ask me instead of tossing out clichés and platitudes. Write a better song, Luke."

He was quiet for a long moment. Then he grabbed a folding chair and sat in front of her. "Tell me. What should I be sorry for? Don't hold back."

Those three words unlatched a door she'd vowed never to open for anyone again. It was too painful. But Luke still had a key she'd given him years ago, which meant he'd find a way in, eventually.

"You should apologize for lying," she said.

"I didn't lie to you."

"Don't interrupt. I won't be able to do this if you keep interrupting."

Luke pressed back into the small chair and folded his arms.

"You said you believed in me. But you didn't. If you did, you would have come back." She could tell he still wanted to argue. His body was rigid and his eyes were shouting she was wrong. "You should apologize for being my only friend. For making me need you."

"I needed you t—" He grunted and rubbed his face. "Go on."

"Apologize for making me think I could keep you." Her volume rose with each demand. They were flowing out of her now, faster than she could think, a jumble of words in free fall. "You let me take us for granted. I loved you like breathing. But then you left and stole my air."

Luke lurched forward, reaching for her. But she backed away. "Apologize for making me invisible. For erasing me from your life."

"I didn't—"

"Apologize for offering me money."

He stood. "August—"

"Say you're sorry for making me hate you. For making me hate our song."

"I love you."

"*Don't.*" That was how she'd always been loved. In absentia. As a dwindling shape in someone's rearview. "You *destroyed* me. No note. No phone call. I thought you were dead, Luke. And when I saw you lying about us on national TV, I wished you were. Because then all of it would have meant something. *I* would have meant something. Do you know what that feels like? Carving yourself open for someone who flinches and runs away?" She clenched her teeth, ground them until her jaw ached. These weren't memories gripping her. It was fear with its strong monstrous hands, yanking her back to a time when all she did was fall. When there was nothing to hold on to.

"I know I'm not perfect," she said. "I know I can be a lot. And I tried to do better. For Jojo. For you." She held her breath, despising the question, but unable to stop it from spilling out. "Could you tell me why? Why am I so easy to walk away from?"

Luke grabbed both of her arms. She tried to pull away, but he held on tight. "Do you know why I keep singing that song? The real reason?"

"Because it's all you have."

"Right," Luke said, nodding slowly. "All anyone wants from me. That's what I say, but it's not true. That's the biggest lie I ever told."

He took a breath, eyes red and glittering. "I don't have to sing it," he said. "I could have stopped a long time ago. But I didn't. Deep down, I knew that if I wrote something people liked, they wouldn't want to hear 'Another Love Song' anymore. And I need it. Because you're right, that song is *all* I have left. It's the only way to keep you with me."

She felt dizzy. Her heart slammed against her rib cage like it was desperate to escape. He cupped her cheek and she could feel his pulse racing.

"I use it to go back to you," he said. "To us. Each time I sing it, I get to fall in love with you again." His lips twitched into a brief smile. "Hurts like hell when it's over, but it's worth it. I want to hurt that way for the rest of my life."

Tears spilled down her cheeks. Luke kissed one, then the other, and touched his forehead to hers. "I didn't walk away from you, August. I never even tried."

She closed her eyes. Luke wrapped his arms around her, and they stayed that way, wrecked and raw, vibrating from too much truth spilled all at once.

"Is this the part where I forgive you?" August whispered. "You've always loved me, so we kiss and forget?"

He stroked her face again. "I don't think forgiveness works that way."

The flash of a photo being taken startled them both into jerking apart. David Henry stood at the door, staring at his phone. "This is definitely going on Insta." He strolled into the room and showed them the photo, which made it look like they were seconds from kissing. "After that little stunt you both pulled out there, it'll probably go viral." He started typing. "Hashtag, Luke should have told David that Jojo's daughter is his fucking mistress."

PART SIX

THE BRIDGE

This Is Our Country: Podcast Transcript

Episode 12—"Jojo Lane"
August 21, 2024

[*cont.*]

Jojo: Have you seen that Maya Angelou quote about believing people when they show you who they are?

Emma: Yes, I have.

Jojo: I wish I'd read it before I met Theo. I was only fourteen, so maybe I would have ignored it, but maybe I wouldn't have. You never know.

Emma: Did you meet at school?

Jojo: Honestly, I'm not sure. He was in and out of school, always getting suspended. All of us kids thought it was funny. But the adults knew. Birdie used to say the King family was cursed. That one of his ancestors died in a way they shouldn't, and it ruined the bloodline. But I didn't believe in curses back then.

Emma: Do you believe in them now?

Jojo: Sometimes. Sometimes I think people just weren't raised right.

Emma: Maybe what people call curses is intergenerational trauma.

Jojo: Young people call everything trauma these days.

Emma: Okay, fair. But that doesn't mean it's not true.

Jojo: All I know is there was only one decent boy in the King family, and Silas still ended up in jail.

Emma: That's a common risk for Black men in—

Jojo: Okay, yes. Put your little sociology degree away. I know all about that. We watched our men taken when no one cared enough to put it on social media. Do you know how many funerals I've been to? All young bodies.

Emma: I'm sorry if I came across as disrespectful. It wasn't my intention.

Jojo: No, it's fine. What I'm saying is we treated it like a joke. Cops are coming for another King. We made it into a song. Theo cornered me a dozen times before I agreed to go out with him, saying I was already his. He was seventeen. Almost a man. I was a little thing. But instead of thinking this near-man is blocking the door, or he's so big and tall no one can see it's me he's talking to, I thought, this is hot. This is sexy, like in the movies. He showed me who he was, and I made him into something else. But later, when he held me down? When he proved what he said was true, that I didn't belong to myself, that's when I believed what he'd already showed me. That he was a wolf.

Emma: He [*redacted*]

Jojo: I can't answer that. Legally.

Emma: I'm sorry. Yes, I understand. Does anyone know what happened?

Jojo: Everyone knew. I went to the hospital bleeding. Forty weeks later, I had August.

Emma: That must have been a hard decision.

Jojo: There was no decision. I was a wild child living in a godly house with a godly mother. She never gave me a choice.

CHAPTER FOURTEEN

2009

August sat on the floor of the theater dressing room, chin resting on her hands, her eyes fixed on the lopsided Hostess cupcake wilting under the heat of a single birthday candle. Luke sat across from her, waiting for her to blow it out. Half their lunch period was gone, but August didn't care. If the day ended at this particular moment, she'd be fine. It'd be perfect.

Luke finally broke the spell by asking, "Are you going to make a wish?"

"You haven't sung to me yet."

Luke looped his arms around his knees. "That's for tomorrow, the actual day of your birth. This is birthday eve."

She took her eyes off the snack cake to grin at him. "Are you one of those monthlong birthday celebration people?"

"No, I just get excited about other people's special day. Especially my friends."

August tried not to be disappointed by the category he'd lumped her into. A month ago, she'd have been thrilled to be included in that group. Now she wanted to be something else. Someone special. "What are these mysterious tomorrow plans?"

"It's a surprise." He suddenly looked serious. "Unless you don't like those."

She normally didn't, but only because they weren't usually the good kind. "They're fine," she said. "But you don't have to do anything else. Today was plenty."

"Today was me stopping by the vending machine on the way here. What kind of birthdays are you used to?"

August swiped a bit of melted frosting and licked it from her fingers. "Nothing at school. I never tell anyone."

"Why not?" She gave him a *Really?* look, and he lifted his hands. "Never mind. What about your grandmother? Does she do anything?"

"Breakfast cake," August said. "It's a tradition. She makes my favorite and lets me eat it for breakfast." She thought about waking up to the smell of buttery sugar and coffee wafting from the kitchen. Birdie would leave a note on her nightstand that read *Remember, you are fearfully and wonderfully made.*

"Breakfast cake," Luke repeated, and it sounded decadent when he said it. Like she was rich and famous. "What's your favorite?"

"Devil's food. She does this chocolate cream cheese frosting you could eat with a spoon."

"That sounds so good."

"I'll bring you some," August said. "Unless that'll ruin your surprise."

"I can't bake," Luke said. "We're meeting at Delta Blue, so I'm sure Silas has forks."

Luke had apologized repeatedly to Silas for showing up drunk last week. Her uncle had mentioned it in passing, along with a warning to be careful with him. "Luke's struggling with something, and I don't want it blowing back on you." But when Luke arrived for their last tutoring session, Silas greeted him with more affection than usual, feeding him dinner and offering use of the pullout sofa in the studio if he ever needed it.

"What time are we meeting tomorrow?" Birdie was taking her out to dinner that evening. She wanted plenty of time to enjoy Luke's gift.

"How about one? Will that work?"

August nodded and resumed staring at her snack cake again. The icing had dribbled down the sides. She blew out the candle. "I wished for a bicycle."

"No, you didn't. But you're not supposed to tell me anyway." He paused. "Does Jojo do anything for your birthday?"

August took a bite before answering. "She'll call me later. Send a present." She took another bite. It helped to multitask while she talked about her mother—no room for self-pity when you were trying not to choke. "It's a hard day for her."

"For her?" Luke looked skeptical.

"She didn't want to have me," August said, and was proud of how normal she sounded. Nothing to see here. Only facts. "Birdie made her. Jojo was only fifteen, so I don't think there was any expectation that she'd raise me, but she still had to carry me. Give birth." August paused and added, "She hates my father."

"I heard stories about him."

"Me too." She had trouble swallowing. A lump had formed in her throat too quickly for her to stop it. "Anyway, I don't blame her for not wanting to celebrate that day."

Luke retreated into his thoughts. The bell would ring soon, but she'd ignore it, if needed. They'd both been so good recently, letting things like school bells and curfews dictate their time together. They deserved to be selfish.

"I do," he said eventually. "I blame her for not wanting to celebrate with you."

"It's not—"

"It's okay if you don't. I get it. You love her, so..." He trailed off, looked away, and then focused on her again. "You need to make it okay. But I don't. I can want more for you."

The bell rang. Luke didn't move. They watched each other, mutually deciding that today, of all days, they could break the rules.

"She tries to love me," August said, because she didn't want Luke to hate Jojo. She didn't want to choose. "I don't make it easy," she continued, but looking at him while she said it was hard. Her fake thorns were gone. He'd plucked them one by one. "For people to love me, I mean. I can be a lot."

"You're the easiest person to love I've ever met." The words slid so quickly from his mouth that it was like he'd been possessed. No halting half sentences. No long stretches of gathering his thoughts. He nodded at her journal. "It's right there on paper. You see the world in colors I never knew existed. The rain plays you symphonies. You are so special, August Lane, and I can't imagine anyone not seeing it."

Sometimes kindness could be cruel. There was a difference between lacking something and losing it. August had never been sure which would hurt more, but now she knew. Losing it would be worse. She covered her face with both hands so he wouldn't see how much the thought scared her.

"Hey. Are you okay?" He knelt at her feet, trying to make eye contact. August launched into his arms. He hugged her, squeezing until her ribs ached and whispered, "Hey." But it wasn't a question this time. It was *I'm right here. Hold on tight.*

Two hours later, August arrived home so giddy from her lunch with Luke, she nearly overlooked the sleek black sedan parked out front. She hadn't wished for anything when she blew out the candle, but when Jojo greeted her with a dazzling smile and said, "Happy birthday, Augustina!" it felt as if there had been some other magic in that moment. There was no other explanation. No one knew that this, her mother's welcoming arms, was the only birthday gift she'd ever wished for.

August woke to the smell of birthday cake and coffee. But there was also another scent in the kitchen, the spicy bloom of Jojo's designer perfume. It filled her nose when her mother kissed her forehead before sitting across from her at the kitchen table.

Jojo had gone to bed early, complaining of jet lag. She'd just returned from Japan, where her albums were so popular people shouted her name on the street. After ten hours of sleep, she looked rested and attentive, her face stripped of the heavy makeup she usually wore. Her silk blouse and trousers had been replaced with jeans and a cotton top covered with embroidered daisies.

"Is this Folgers, Mama?" Jojo made a face as she sipped her coffee. "What happened to the good stuff I sent you?"

"Too strong," Birdie said, and put a piece of cake in front of Jojo.

"I can't eat sugar this early," Jojo said. She looked at August's plate. "But you eat up, birthday girl."

"It's a tradition," August told her, poking at her slice.

"One that's older than you," Jojo said. "Carrie and I both had our favorites. Mine was a dream cake. It's yellow cake, whipped cream, pudding. Every dessert you could want layered into a waking dream."

"Carrie hated that cake," Birdie said with a sigh. "She liked strawberry. But not the real kind, the radioactive pink one from a box. I'll never understand that girl."

"It's the predictability," Jojo said. "Same reason she loves cozy mysteries and wants to move to Florida when Mavis graduates. Killer's always caught. Weather's always sunny."

"Florida has hurricanes," August pointed out.

"That part's predictable, too," Jojo said. "Knowing your storms will have a season is comforting." She tapped her nails against the table. "I'm sorry to visit unannounced. You probably have plans."

August thought about Luke's surprise and said, "I do, but it's this afternoon. I'm free otherwise." The moment the words escaped her mouth, she realized she'd forgotten about her dinner with Birdie. She looked at her grandmother, who started wiping down the counter she'd already cleaned.

"If you want to take her out, that's fine," Birdie said, and draped the damp towel over the sink to dry. "It'll be good for y'all to spend some time together."

"We can all do something," Jojo said, then looked at August. "What are these afternoon plans?"

"A friend of mine planned a surprise."

Jojo's eyebrows arched. "Boyfriend?"

"August doesn't do that," Birdie said. She picked up the rag again, wiping over the same spot she'd already cleaned twice.

"Do what?" Jojo stared at her mother's back. "What is it that August doesn't do?"

"You know what I mean," Birdie said. She scrubbed harder, fighting a war against invisible crumbs. "Don't encourage it."

"All I did was ask a question." Jojo moved to Birdie and snatched the rag from her hand. "Could you at least look at me?"

Birdie propped a hand on her hip and glared. "Okay. I'm looking at you. Now what?"

"Mom, it's fine." August pushed her half-eaten cake away and tried to capture their attention. "She means dating. I'm not allowed to date." She looked at Birdie. "It's not a date."

"Better not be," Birdie grumbled. She gave Jojo her back and made a wiping motion. It took her a second to realize her hand was empty. "Where'd I put that cloth?"

Jojo tossed it on the counter and turned to August. "Come to my room. I want to give you something."

August followed Jojo into Birdie's sewing room, which now contained the roll-away bed they used for company. Seeing the cheap white sheets next to Jojo's flashy luggage was jarring. August tried to view the room through her mother's eyes and failed. Jojo stayed in luxury suites in cities August didn't know existed. Her imagination could only reach so far outside the Arcadia city limits.

"Found this in Kyoko," Jojo said, handing her a slim velvet box. August sat on the bed and pried it open. It was a gold pendant with a diamond-studded constellation etched inside. "I got it at the Star Festival," Jojo explained. She took out the necklace and motioned for August to turn around. She put it on her neck and took a moment to admire it. "Looks good on you."

"What's the Star Festival?"

"Oh, something about star-crossed lovers," Jojo said. "Separated by the Milky Way. They angered some powerful god, and now they can only see each other once a year." Jojo looked at the clothes spilling from her luggage. "I don't know why I packed so much stuff."

"Thank you," August said. She cradled the pendant in her palm. "I love it."

Jojo smiled, but it seemed tired, her brief burst of energy already spent. "So, were you telling the truth in there? This afternoon surprise isn't a date?"

August hesitated. "He didn't call it that." But Luke had hugged her yesterday. He thought she was easy to love. "It could be something, though."

"Well, I'm excited for your something," Jojo said. "Don't listen to Birdie. She's still not over me running around and talking back when I was your age." She paused. "Younger than you. My God, you're eighteen. When did that happen?"

She touched August's face like that would help her understand it. Then she flashed a retail smile and pointed to the old record player in the corner. "You ever use that? It was Daddy's. He used to drive Mama crazy playing Muddy Waters on Sunday." Jojo laughed. "Bet she kept those records. That woman throws nothing away." She flipped her hair back. "I'm leaving again. Europe. For a year."

For a second, August thought Jojo was about to invite her to come along. Instead of going to Nashville, August would roam the streets of Paris or Berlin with her mother. But she should have known better. Later, she'd blame Luke's little cupcake for that pointless burst of hope.

"You won't hear from me for a while," Jojo said. "International rates are expensive. And I'll have to miss your graduation."

August could feel herself shrinking. Hardening. "Right," she said. "I get it."

"I knew you'd understand." Jojo patted her shoulder. "Now tell me about this boyfriend. Is he cute? He better be if you're running around behind Birdie's back."

"He's not my boyfriend," August said. "He's a musician." She wanted to add that they both were, that her words were his inspiration and the music they made together was better than anything Jojo put on her CDs.

"But is he cute?"

"Yes. And really nice."

"Oof. Watch out for nice musicians. They'll treat you well, but we all love the stage more than anything. Nothing else comes close." She gave August a pointed look. "I don't want that for you."

Jojo always said that, but she never explained it, never added anything she did want for August. She never said I want you to be happy, or I want you to achieve your dreams, or I want to slay the beasts that scare you.

"He's not like that," August said, and then looked at the clock. It was almost eleven. "I should probably see if Birdie needs help cleaning up."

Jojo's lips thinned. "I'm sure she'll appreciate it." She stood. "I'll straighten this up so she doesn't complain about the mess."

August watched her snatch up a bra and throw it at her suitcase. It immediately fell to the floor. "We usually go to dinner," August told her. "I pick a new restaurant at random. It's another tradition."

"That sounds fun," Jojo said, but didn't offer to join them. August walked out and closed the door behind her. She leaned against the wall, looked down at the necklace, and had the urge to rip it off. The chain was loose and fragile enough to snap with one hand.

Nashville, TN (August 28, 2023)—Charlotte Turner released the following statement today through her personal attorney and business manager, Daphne Ficus, in light of inquiries regarding her marriage to Luke Randall.

"I'm stunned and devastated by the stories being reported by the press about my husband and our marriage. Jojo Lane's induction into the Country Music Hall of Fame should be a historic celebration of a music legend. Instead, it's become a political talking point for divisive politicians and fodder for more salacious gossip about my private life. Marriage is hard and gets even harder when you're in the public eye. Luke and I are working through our issues together and request that our privacy be respected at this time."

CHAPTER FIFTEEN

2023

Charlotte blamed her publicity team for her statement. "I didn't see it before they sent it out. They had this elaborate plan for announcing our amicable divorce. The photos made them panic."

Luke believed her. It was easy to outsource your life when you were famous. Charlotte's pristine reputation was worth billions. No one trusted her, a mere human with flaws, to make decisions about her personal life. "I'll do an interview to clear things up," she said. "One of the big morning shows."

Luke pulled his truck into the Arcadia Inn parking lot and cut the engine. "Ken won't let you do that."

"I'm firing him. He's a shitty publicist anyway."

"He was doing his job. Trying to protect you."

"That's everyone's excuse. It was your excuse, too. We should have ended this years ago."

Luke didn't respond to that. He remembered those conversations differently—with her posing it as a question and ignoring his tentative agreement. The cowardice was mutual. "When were the divorce papers filed?"

There was silence on the other line. Luke closed his eyes. "Come on, Charlie."

"This morning. Daphne held off to avoid all the Jojo drama. She thought people would assume I was divorcing you for performing with her. But God, you sleeping with her daughter is so much worse."

"I'm not sleeping with her."

She laughed. "Okay, Luke. Pictures don't lie. I don't blame you. She's gorgeous."

He knew what she was talking about. Those pictures told a whole story, one he'd been hiding for years. They started with August standing at the microphone with windswept curls and midnight eyes, looking like a sea siren in need of rescue. Then his arms were around her, his mouth at her temple, in a pose so intimate he could barely look at it. Thanks to the protest coverage, every local news outlet in the region had captured it on camera. The Delta Festival hashtag had been flooded with amateur photos and eyewitness accounts the minute they'd left the stage.

The timing was terrible. He'd just poured his heart out to August, confessed what he'd been afraid to admit to himself, that his career had stalled because he wanted it to. Moving on from his one hit would have meant moving on from her, something he could never do. There was no chance to talk to her about it once David walked in. Luke had been ordered to leave the fairgrounds and not show his face until he was summoned. August slipped out while he and David were arguing and was ignoring his texts and calls.

"I've known her a long time," Luke told Charlotte. "She's a songwriter." He paused, remembering how she'd frozen onstage. "A *singer-*songwriter. We reconnected, and it's been... intense. This didn't help."

"I'm sorry. I thought I was helping by waiting to file. Jojo's furious, right?"

Luke had no idea. David wouldn't return his calls, either. "Don't know," he admitted. "But I'm about to find out."

Luke knocked on room 105A three times before hearing movement inside. David opened the door and grimaced. "Right. Saw you left a voice message like a goddamn psychopath. Didn't listen. What do you want?"

Luke was expecting the insult but figured it would be paired with a swift firing. But David stared at him like a pizza guy at the wrong address. "An update would be nice."

"Oh, those are all over the internet," David said. There was a sheen to his eyes that hadn't been there the last time they spoke. He'd been drinking. "You two already have a nickname. LukeLane. Could get dicey since her mother has the same last name."

"Have you heard from Jojo?"

David rubbed his face. "It's hot. Come in and have a drink. Water, of course."

Luke followed him inside, surveying the room for signs of a bender. It was aggressively tidy. The only evidence of occupation was a black suitcase near the bathroom and an open laptop on the bed. David grabbed a glass and removed the plastic covering. "Tap okay?"

"Not thirsty," Luke said. "Just impatient."

David snorted. "Want information, do you? That's ironic. You've been keeping a lot from me."

"August and I aren't together," Luke said. "We have history, but it's not an affair like everyone's saying."

"Cry that river, Lucas. Get snotty with it. Still won't change what's in those pictures."

"I'm not married anymore."

"Mmmmm." David went to his computer and typed in silence. He scanned his screen and then looked at Luke. "Not according to Google."

"So fire me," Luke snapped. "Then we can end this bullshit conversation."

David sat on the bed with his computer in his lap. "You were not invited here. You were told to find a deep hole and hide in it until someone came looking for you."

"Don't talk to me like that," Luke said. "I don't give a fuck who you work for. You talk down to me again, and we'll have a different problem."

They eyed each other silently. David broke eye contact to bring up another website. "Jojo seems to think this is all August's fault. Her daughter is angry with her for something she refuses to share and is lashing out by seducing, and I quote 'the prettiest dark meat in my lineup.'"

Luke waited for more. The recriminations. The firing. David picked up his glass and took a drink. "That's it?" Luke asked. "That's all she said?"

"Yes. Your job is safe because of familial strife. And also because a lot of people hate your ex-wife. I mean, *a lot*. Black X/Twitter thinks Jojo rescued you from the sunken place." He showed Luke an online marketplace people used to resell concert tickets. "General admission is going for a grand online."

What David was saying shouldn't have been a surprise. Everyone knew that bad press could have a weird bounce that became a net positive for brand awareness. The messy tangle of Luke, Charlotte, and Jojo had ensnared August, too, only not as a burgeoning songwriter the way she'd planned. Instead, she'd been cast as the other woman again, only this time, in front of the entire world.

"I don't want to sing that song."

David rolled his eyes. "This again?"

"August and I are working on something new. Something Jojo will love." Once August pushed past her writer's block, whatever she wrote would blow everyone away. "She should sing it with her daughter. That's the story everyone needs to hear."

"August wants to sing now?" David flung a hand at Luke. "And what do you plan to do? Play backup?"

"If they want," Luke said. "I could..." He trailed, thinking about his recent shows. The thought of recycling the same old covers made him nauseous. He'd been working on a new setlist with Silas, something he'd planned to try out at Delta Blue. But he wasn't ready to talk about it yet. "I could do something else."

David leaned forward. "Listen to me. Some singers are artists. Others, like you, are entertainers. Entertainers give people what they want, and right now, that's you onstage with Jojo, singing a song they forgot they knew all the words to." He steepled his hands together. "These are thousand-dollar tickets, son. We owe them their expectations."

Luke had heard this pitch before, and it always felt like being offered riches from the devil. "Cut off your wings, and I'll hand you the world" was only tempting if your soul was worthless. Maybe his was. But he'd only sell it again for August.

"Ask Jojo what she thinks. She might disagree."

"She won't," David said. "The woman's ruthless about her career. She's worked hard for this award and won't risk it for anything. Singing with you is the safe choice."

"Not even if it helps her daughter?"

David slowly shook his head. "Not even for August."

August was the most famous home-wrecker in the world. She could feel it in the air when she arrived for her shift at King's Kitchen. The cooks barely made eye contact with her when she put in orders. Gemma, who usually insisted on splitting her tips, claimed she couldn't afford it tonight and accidentally called her Charlotte three times. The few customers in her section whispered to each other behind their hands and typed rapidly on their phones while food congealed on their plates.

Being judged at church was one thing. Those people put odds on each other's damnation like they were placing bets in Vegas. But hostile strangers were dangerous. One woman wrote *Bitch* instead of a tip on her receipt.

August had nearly finished the dinner shift when two white men carrying bulky cameras sat at one of her tables. The older one read her name tag out loud and asked, "Did Jojo tell you to fuck Luke Randall?"

The question paralyzed her. But then, just like with Shirley's slap, she had the urge to lash out, smash their equipment to the floor. Instead, she opened the camera on her phone and aimed it at them. "What did you just ask me?"

The younger one recoiled. The older one, who'd probably chased OJ's Bronco in the nineties, smirked and said, "You trying to get us canceled? Make us the villains of the week?"

"I'm not making you anything," she said, switching to landscape to capture both of them. "You're doing fine by yourselves."

His smirk curdled. "Can we at least get a quote?"

"Order something or leave." August saw the door open in the corner of her eye. Bill Parnell walked inside and immediately focused on the men. He was behind them, so they didn't notice.

The older one tsked his disapproval. "You're not a very nice girl, August."

"Leave, or deal with Bill."

He frowned. "Who's Bill?"

"I'm Bill." He puffed his chest to show off his badge. Then he tipped his hat to August. "Go on to the back. I'll take it from here."

August fled to the kitchen. She pressed her back to the wall and took slow, square-shaped breaths like she'd learned in the only grief counseling session she'd attended. She should have gone back. At the time, it had felt excessive, like a lazy way to deal with vanilla grief. That kind of comfort should be earned by surviving some big tragedy. She hadn't realized losses could accumulate over the years, gathering mass like snowballs. The women from the grief counseling session probably knew that. If she walked into that room today, they'd probably take one look at her and say "Oh no. You made choices, didn't you? Bad idea before you clean up the slush."

She took out the trash and bused tables until closing. Once everyone left, she sat in a booth and scrolled through her messages. Mavis had texted twice. Silas left a voicemail. Nothing from Jojo, who was probably waiting for an apology for embarrassing her. But August wasn't in the mood. If Jojo was content to let the news cycle churn, so was she. There were more important things to deal with.

Luke had called numerous times but didn't leave a message. He'd sent one text. I'm here when you're ready, and then went silent. She was grateful for the space. His confession had changed things, tilted the past enough to make her look at it differently. It was like he'd found a broken clock she'd thrown out years ago and said "Try changing the batteries." Yes, that might work. But after sitting in the trash for so long, was there any point in trying?

August opened her YouTube app and typed his name. One of the first results was a 2013 performance at a small state college titled "Another Love Song Live." She played the video and the crowd's rhythmic chants burst through the speaker: "Love Song! Love Song!"

Luke's hair was longer, his beard thick and messy. His head was bowed, and he seemed to ignore the crowd. He grabbed a red Solo cup from a stool and gulped the contents.

"What about 'Tennessee Whiskey'?" he slurred into the microphone. He scanned the room and shouted, "George Jones. Y'all know him?"

The chants continued like he hadn't spoken. Luke plucked at his guitar strings. "All right," he drawled, smiling the worst smile August had ever seen on a man, grim gratitude for the gallows. "Let's sing a love song."

The chants became screams. Instead of playing the intro, Luke set his guitar down. He grabbed the microphone with both hands and sang the first lines. *"I'm frozen in place / My heart's gone numb / But you keep breaking the part that still feels something."*

Screams continued to fill the room, but Luke didn't acknowledge them. He turned inward, closing his eyes and pulling the words from a place so deep it looked painful. Every muscle popped and strained, like it took effort not to burst from his skin.

The song was nearly unrecognizable without the music: a haunting plea in a rough baritone that made it soulful and timeless. August remembered what Luke said about conjuring her during his performances. She pulled a pen from her pocket, grabbed a napkin, and wrote, *You look like every moment that could have been better.*

Someone knocked on the door. August stood, peering through the glass, and locked eyes with Ava Randall. It had been a long time since she'd seen Luke's mother. The woman kept to herself, rarely leaving the farm. She looked thin and sallow. Undyed roots framed her face with dingy gray. Her eyes were the same, honey gold when the streetlights hit them. Beauty that masked her ugly. That was why Luke never told anyone how she abused him. "No one sees her that way," he'd said. "They wouldn't believe it."

August unlocked the door and cracked it just wide enough to say, "We're closed."

"Five minutes." Ava's pupils were blown. Words dripped from her, like she was speaking in slow motion. "I need to talk to you about Luke."

"Did you drive here?" August looked past her to the parking lot and spotted Luke's old truck, rusted and peeling from neglect. Seeing it again triggered memories that made her want to slam the door in Ava's face. "You shouldn't be on the road like this."

"I'm not—" Ava faltered, realizing that whatever story she told herself about her medication wasn't fooling anyone. "I can make it home all right."

August shoved the door open. "Come inside. I need to do a few more things, and then I'll drive you home."

Ava followed her and seemed to shrink now that she'd gotten her way. She watched August grab a broom and start sweeping. "I didn't realize you still worked here." She waved at the parking lot. "Noticed your car out front, so I stopped."

August kept her eyes on the broom. "Is there something you want to say to me?"

Ava looked like a woman facing a short jump into a deep hole. "You love him," she finally declared, and seemed irritated by it. "Don't lie, I could tell from the pictures."

"That's none of your business."

"I love him, too." She swallowed hard once she said it, like she wasn't used to the taste. "I don't care if you believe me. It doesn't look the same on everyone. But I know my heart, and I know his. He's been coming to the farm out of obligation, but you know it's not good for him. It's not good for either of us."

They locked eyes. Despite spending most of her life despising this woman, August suddenly understood her perfectly. "What should I tell him?"

Tears coated Ava's eyes, turning them into liquid gold. "To forgive me. Or stay away."

CHAPTER SIXTEEN

2009

Luke always left the keys to his truck in the living room next to the television. He'd done it so many times that when he went to retrieve them, and they weren't there, he stared at the empty spot for a moment, waiting for them to materialize. Then he started looking everywhere—under the couch, between the couch cushions, inside drawers, with no success.

It was ten minutes till one. August would probably be late for his birthday surprise at Delta Blue, but he needed time to set everything up for her arrival. He'd bought her a stack of expensive journals with the kind of thick, grainy paper that made every word more important. He'd also bought her a copy of his favorite Ray Charles album, which he'd planned to present to her, wrapped and bowed, before revealing her last present, the reason they were celebrating at Delta Blue.

August wanted to be onstage. At the club, she'd stare at the black riser with obvious yearning, but brush Luke off when he suggested she sing at the open mic night. "People will recognize me" was all she'd say, which never made sense to Luke because she sang at church all the time.

Luke had a plan, though. Today, the club would be empty. He'd play "Proud Mary," a song she could never resist belting at the top of her lungs. He'd offer his hand and lead her to the microphone. Once she got started, her nerves would vanish. She'd be eager to do it again.

The longer Luke searched for his keys, the more frantic he became. He started looking in random, unlikely places out of desperation. Ava walked into the kitchen and saw him sliding his hand beneath the refrigerator.

"It's nasty under there," she said, reaching for her purse. She retrieved a lipstick tube and moved to a mirror. "You lose something?"

"My keys. They're not where I usually put them."

"I have them." She showed him the loop of his key ring on her finger. "Don is having my car detailed, so I'm using it for errands."

Luke snapped, "I need it," without thinking. Letting Ava know she had something you wanted only made her more possessive.

"For what?" She dismissed him with a flick of her hand before he could answer. "Doesn't matter. I'm not sitting in this dirty house so you can run around town chasing pussy. Should be doing homework anyway. Your grades are shitty."

She moved to the door. Luke followed, trying to think of ways to make her listen. "It's my friend's birthday."

She pushed the screen door open, and humid air rushed in. The high temperatures had risen steadily all week, still clinging to summer even though it was technically fall. Ava paused on the porch to slip on shades. "Goddamn, this weather."

"Ava." Luke hovered in the doorway behind her. "Mom, wait. I need to be somewhere at one."

She gave him a look he'd never seen before. Pained, but not the usual kind. Somewhere other than her body. "Why do you only call me Mom when you want something?"

Luke opened his mouth, but nothing came out. She was right. In his mind, she was always Ava, the ruler of their house. His tyrannical queen, not his caretaker.

"Can you drop me off?" Luke asked out of desperation. He glanced at his watch. He was already five minutes late. "Delta Blue isn't far from here."

"Delta Blue?" She snatched her shades away and stared at him. "You seriously think I'm going to drop my son off at some bar?"

"It's the middle of the day!" Luke could feel his temper rising, his control slipping, but he couldn't stop it. Ava was ruining August's birthday. And while he was fine with her trashing his life on a whim, August didn't deserve it. She deserved the wrapped gifts he'd left sitting in the passenger seat. She deserved the roses he'd planned to buy from Kroger on the way. She deserved to hear him butcher "Happy Birthday" before he dragged her onstage to pretend she was already in Nashville, realizing her dream. It had become his dream, too. That's what he'd planned to tell her. "Wait for me," he'd say. "Once Ethan's at college, I'll come find you. We'll dig out our old songs and be us again."

Ava's eyes were glassy with rage. His temper was a beast, but hers was a dragon. "Who do you think you're talking to?"

"I'm sorry." Luke lifted his hands in surrender. "I really need the truck. Someone will be disappointed if I don't show up."

She stared at him hard. "Not Jessica?"

Lying was pointless. "No."

"Then who?" When Luke didn't answer, her eyes became slits. "Whatever. Keep your secrets. And tell that bitch I said good luck. If she's messing around with you, best get used to disappointment."

Ava stalked to the front door, slammed it closed, and locked it. Luke thought for a moment she'd changed her mind about dropping him off, but then she waltzed to the truck without a word. He tried to follow her, but she stopped him. "Wait here."

"What?"

She pointed to the stoop. "Sit on that porch and wait for me to get back."

Luke shook his head. "Why?"

She yanked open the driver's-side door. "So I don't throw you out of my house."

He moved, but the look on her face stopped him. It was eager. This was something she'd been waiting for, an excuse to do what she was too impatient to let happen on its own. No more Luke down the hall. No more fighting. No more reminders of what she'd lost.

He stepped back. Ava's eyes shuttered, and she started the ignition. He watched her pull away with August's gifts still in the passenger's seat, only he didn't sit like she'd told him. He stood, staring at the road until the truck disappeared.

She'd taken his house key. Both doors to the house were locked with a deadbolt. Ethan was at band practice and wouldn't be back for hours. The sun was blazing, so Luke moved to the porch. The shade wasn't much relief from the heat. He wore an undershirt under his button-down and took off the top layer. Only ten minutes had passed since she drove away.

Thirty minutes later, his T-shirt was soaked to the skin. He ripped it off and blotted the sweat streaming down his face. He thought about cooling off with the water hose but remembered that Ava had cut it off last year, complaining about the water bill. There was nothing to drink. Realizing it made him thirsty, and his mind spiraled from one panicked thought to the next. She may not come back. No water in ninety-degree heat was dangerous.

He thought about his freshman year when one of his teammates had collapsed during practice. They were all struggling, so when the guy complained about being dizzy, everyone ignored him. The sight of his body crumpled on the field ran like a film reel through Luke's mind. They'd had to call an ambulance. The paramedics had asked for his name, and no one remembered. New Kid. That's what they called him. New Kid can't take the heat. New Kid nearly died.

Luke's chest was being squeezed slowly, choking off his airway. He had to get inside. That's what his lungs were telling him. Get inside that house, or you'll never breathe again. But the doors were locked. So were the windows. Even outside his home was a prison.

He stared at the locked door, then ran into it, shoulder first, but it didn't budge. He screamed, "Fuck it! Fuck you! Fuck *you*!" until his throat was raw.

There was a rock beside the stairs. He picked it up and hurled it at a window. It flew through the glass, made a collage of webbed cracks bursting from a hole the size of a baseball.

He stared at it, blinking through sweat. Then smashed the glass with his fist.

Luke dreamed about August. She hovered over him, backlit by the sun, singing the lines she'd written the last time they were together. *"You can take this part / Keep it close / There's no space in my heart / But don't worry baby / I'll slide you over / if there's room."*

In his dream, she kept repeating *don't worry, baby* on a loop. *Don't worry, don't worry, don't worry* over and over until the sun dimmed, and the singing became sobbing, and Luke tried to blink away her image because he didn't want to dream anymore.

August cupped his face and leaned in close. "Luke. Can you hear me?"

She smelled like lavender and buttery lotion. Her hair haloed her face in huge curls. He tried to touch one but stopped when pain knifed through his arm. His hand was covered with cuts. A bloody T-shirt was wrapped around his forearm and held in place with rubber bands.

Luke realized he was lying on the ground. He tried to sit up, but August stopped him with both hands on his shoulders. "Don't move. Tell me where the phone is so I can call an ambulance."

The cordless phone was in Ava's bedroom, which they were forbidden to enter without permission. "Don't do that," Luke managed. His words slurred and his mouth tasted like sour cotton. "Don't call anyone. I'm fine."

"No, you're not." Her eyes were swollen from crying. Blood streaked her hands and clothes. "I got worried when you didn't show up, so I came here. You were passed out." She gestured at the floor next to the couch. An empty Jim Beam bottle lay on top of bloodstains on the carpet. Luke remembered thinking he could pour it over his wounds like he'd seen in movies. Then he'd thought of August waiting for him, how he'd ruined her birthday, and he'd poured whiskey on that, too.

"You're still bleeding." She probed his arm. "I think you need stitches."

Luke moved his fingers and was relieved that, aside from the pain, they were still functioning. He hadn't done any permanent damage. "I can take care of this," he said, even though he wasn't exactly sure how. "You should leave before she gets back."

"She who? Your mother? I'm not leaving you with her."

"I can handle it."

"Well, I'm here now. So you don't have to."

Her panicked expression had changed to stubborn resolve. It cleaved him in two—half giddy she wanted to stay, half terrified she actually would and be trapped in this prison with him. Luke touched her cheek with his left hand, which was still clean and good and useful.

A key rattled in the front door. Luke tried to angle his body in front of her to protect her from Ava's wrath. But it was Ethan. His little brother stepped inside and took in the blood and the broken glass with wide eyes. "Luke?"

"I'm fine." Luke tried to make it more convincing by standing, only he used the wrong arm to push off with. He cried out. The pain was agony.

August wrapped her arms around him and he used her for leverage. "Ethan, this is August."

"I know." Ethan moved closer, eyes bouncing between them. "What happened to my brother?"

"She wasn't here," Luke said before August could respond. "I got locked out and..." Got wasted. Why the fuck did he do that? "...did something stupid. August found me and stopped the bleeding, so I'm fine." He didn't know if that was true, but he needed to cool what was burning in Ethan's eyes. He knew exactly what his brother was thinking. Ava had done this. Someone should make her pay.

"We should call Bill," Ethan declared.

"No." Luke untangled himself from August. "No police. Nothing happened. Because if something did, people would ask questions about other things, and neither of us is that good a liar." He glanced toward Ava's room, and Ethan followed his gaze. Luke could tell when the reality of their situation hit him: the liquor bottles, the pills, the fake names on her prescriptions. If the cops saw all that, they'd take Ethan away.

"You're wrong," Ethan said. He disappeared into his bedroom, then returned with a baseball bat and a bag of balls. "You're the bad liar." He dumped them by the broken window and looked at August. "Take care of him. I'll clean this up."

She stared at the blood. "It's a lot."

"I'll handle it." Ethan's voice sounded like Luke's on a bad day. Bitter but resigned. Resentful that he had to be. Then he said, "Ava won't believe I did it, but she won't argue." That's when Luke knew he had to leave. He couldn't let Ethan become collateral damage in his war with their mother. Luke had stayed to keep Ethan safe, but *he* was the real threat to his brother's safety.

"My bedroom is the first door on the right," Luke told August. "There's a packed duffel under my bed."

She didn't ask why he kept a go bag in his room, and he was grateful. Once she left, Luke told Ethan, "I'm not coming back, but I won't be far." He didn't know where he was going, but Ethan didn't need to know that. He just needed to know that he wasn't being abandoned. "I'll send money. Hide it where she can't find it."

Luke hugged his brother with his good arm as tight as he could. Ethan clung to him. Luke mumbled more reassurances, emptier than he'd like because he didn't have much else to give. *I want to keep you* was all he could offer anyone. *I want to keep you, even though I shouldn't.*

⊱⋅⊰

Her hands were shaking. Luke waited patiently while August fumbled with the car door, even though she knew he was in pain. He looked terrible. Once in the passenger seat, he closed his eyes and slumped against the window, as if looking at things took too much effort.

She stayed quiet as she drove, partly because any sounds she made wouldn't be rational or human. Her nails were caked in dried blood. Black flakes floated to her dress like snow.

Silas met them in the Delta Blue parking lot. He assessed things quickly and retrieved Luke from the passenger side. Once inside, he cut away Luke's shirt, revealing the damage he'd done climbing through the broken window. His upper body was covered in tiny, vicious cuts. A large bruise covered his shoulder. Silas's hands hovered over the blood-soaked T-shirt on Luke's forearm before he gently pried it loose. It was the most unsure she'd ever seen her uncle.

Luke tried to smile at her as the shirt was peeled away. Silas barked at August to get water and soap from the bathroom, but she didn't move. She couldn't stop staring at the deep cut with its cruel jagged edges.

"He needs a doctor," she said.

"No doctors." Luke was frantic. "They'll call the police."

Silas said, "He's right." He pulled out his flip phone. "Calling a friend of mine. He knows how to treat a wound."

The man Silas referred to as Ghost was tall and slender, with a large afro and stern expression. After examining the cut, he looked at Luke and said, "This gon' hurt."

Luke glanced at August. "Can we do it somewhere else?"

It took her a moment to realize what was happening. "No! I'm not leaving you alone."

"Where can we set up?" Ghost asked Silas, ignoring her protests.

Silas pointed to the studio. "It's soundproofed."

August shouted, "No!" again, but they kept ignoring her. Silas talked Luke through what was about to happen in slow, simple terms. They were being treated like children who needed protection. It was too late for that. Someone should have protected them a long time ago.

Silas held her back when she tried to follow Ghost and Luke into the studio. His grip was iron, and she couldn't shake it off. "Look at me," he demanded. August finally stilled and stared up at her uncle, blinking back tears. "Tell me what happened."

"I don't know," August said. "I think... his mother locked him out of the house. He broke a window to get back in and then..." She pictured the empty liquor bottle. Silas had to know that Luke was drunk based on smell alone.

"In this heat," Silas grumbled. "Did Ava come back while you were there?"

"No."

Silas glanced at the clock. "You need to call Birdie."

August hadn't realized how late it was. They were supposed to have dinner two hours ago. "I can't. She'll make me come home. I can't leave him."

"Then tell her that." Silas gave her his phone. "She deserves to know the truth."

August took the phone and dialed. Birdie picked up on the first ring. Her hello was trembling, braced for bad news.

"Grandma?"

"August! August, baby, where are you? What happened?"

"I thought he was dead." That was the scream she'd been suppressing in the car. The horror of it. The gruesome image of Luke's bloody body slumped on the floor.

"Who? What happened?"

"My friend. He was hurt, and I found him."

"Are you at the hospital? I'm coming to get you."

"I'm with Silas. He's taking care of us. Luke's mother is abusive, and I didn't know. I didn't realize how bad it was. I can't leave him alone."

Birdie didn't speak for a long time. "Are you in any danger?"

"She doesn't know I was there."

"Put Silas on the phone."

"Please don't tell Jojo—"

"August. Put him on the phone *now*."

August offered the phone to Silas, pleading for his help with her eyes. He took the phone and said, "Hello, Mrs. Lane."

August watched him listening, her grandmother's voice too faint for her to hear. Silas said, "Yes, ma'am. Jason's boy." He paused and said, "No, nothing like that. You know I don't abide foolishness." He glanced at August. "I hear you. Them folks mean well, but they hurt more than they help sometimes." He turned his back to August. "Yes. Yes ma'am, I'll tell her."

August waited until he disconnected. "What did she say?"

"You can stay awhile. Then you need to go home."

"How long—"

"August." Her name was a warning. This was what he'd negotiated. "There's a shower in my office. I'll bring you something to change into."

August looked down at herself. There was blood smeared on her clothes. She hadn't worn a dress since that humiliating day at school, but she'd wanted to wear something special for Luke's surprise.

She'd been right before, though. Surprises were never good.

"How could she do this?" August asked Silas. "Do you know her? Was she always a bad person?"

Silas sighed. "No one's all good or bad." He pointed to a photo on the wall. "That's Luke's dad. Found it last night and put it up there so I could show it to him today."

August stared at the tall, handsome man grinning at the camera. The smile was identical to Luke's: lips askew, a shallow indention on his right cheek that became a dimple when he laughed.

"How did he die?"

"In a bar fight, trying to protect somebody. Doubt he knew their name. That's the kind of man he was. Someone was being bullied and he took it personally."

August smiled. "Luke got it from him, then? He's so kind to people."

"Maybe." Silas gave her a pointed look. "But did you hear me? Jason was in a *bar fight*. On a Wednesday afternoon."

Ghost walked into the room before August could ask Silas what he meant. She jumped to her feet. "How is he?"

"Doped up and loopy as fuck. Cut looked worse than it was. He'll be okay." He looked at Silas. "Took them sutures like infantry, though."

Something flowed between the two men that August couldn't decipher. Instead of trying, she rushed past them to get to the studio. Luke was sleeping on the couch, his arm covered in bandages.

August sat beside him. His eyes fluttered open, glazed and unfocused. He smiled and whispered, "You," then he fell asleep again.

"That's right. Me." She kissed his forehead. "I'm sorry I wasn't there. But I'll never let anyone hurt you again."

CHAPTER SEVENTEEN

2023

What Luke loved most about the pond on his family's farm was how hidden it was. He'd found it by getting lost one day like a little boy in a fantasy novel, and that's what it became for him: his own secret garden. His rabbit hole. Sitting beside the water under a full moon was still comforting, even though his most vivid memory of the place was scribbling pieces of his father's lost poems in August's journal with his brain still swimming in beer.

What he'd told her that night was true. He'd tripped and fallen while trying to leave the house. But he'd left out details, like Ava calling him useless and shoving him on his way out the door. He'd been afraid August would judge him for it, that she'd wonder what kind of man he was or why he'd let a woman do that to him, even if Ava was his mother. Looking at him back then, the big, tall football player, it would have been natural to assume that *he* was the threat, something his mother had implied more than once. Ava used to call him scary if he looked at her sideways during one of her rants. "Oh, so you're a man now? Big and scary? What kind of real man threatens his mother?"

That question had always plagued him. What kind of man was he? He knew kindness and loyalty were the goal. He knew he didn't want to be "big and scary," even though sometimes those assumptions could be a shield. But he didn't want to be a safe choice either, some easy-listening earworm everyone loved until the song was over. Good art should be dangerous. Those songwriting lessons from August had ruined him in ways that saved his life.

The music industry, however, was a game. He'd made a mistake thinking he could win it with an August-Jojo reunion. But the business was cyclical, a constant rotation of bad and worse choices. Winning implied an ending.

Luke texted Ethan but skipped the greeting because he was tired of pretending they were being read. I'm not good at being honest. It was never safe for us. I always told people what they wanted to hear, including you. I think that's why you stopped listening. So, here's the truth. I don't regret leaving you. But I should have told you why I stayed away.

The pond was suddenly doused in headlights. Luke shaded his eyes and stared until he could make out August's car. She climbed out holding a can of bug spray. "You've been in the city for a while, so I figured you forgot we bathe in DEET this time of year."

He lifted his hand. She tossed the canister to him and watched as he covered his skin with the smelly spray. "What are you doing here?" he asked.

August didn't answer right away. She was dressed in khaki shorts and tank top, which was only slightly less distracting than those sundresses she preferred. He preferred them, too. Each time she wore one, it felt targeted, like a problem she was daring him to solve.

"Your mother showed up at King's."

Luke stilled. "Was she on something?"

"Yes. I drove her home."

An image of her wrestling Ava into her little Nissan made his stomach churn. "You shouldn't have to deal with that."

"Neither should you." She gestured at his truck. "So go home. I'll check on her before I leave."

Luke didn't normally let people do things for him. It made him feel lazy, like he couldn't be trusted to clean up his own mess. But help from August felt like a gift. *You're not alone*, tied with a bow. He moved closer, just shy of arm's reach. "You still mad at me for stopping the other night?"

Her eyes dipped to his mouth. "Yes."

"Me too." He'd thought about it so much that his reasons for pushing her away had become blurry. His only sharp memories of that night were the sounds she'd made, staccato bursts of pleasure.

But he couldn't reach for her right now, even though he wanted to. Thirteen years still needed to be accounted for. He was running out of time.

"Come talk to me." Luke moved to a spot near the water. She followed him, and they sat in the grass.

"Ava wants you to forgive her."

He dangled his arms over his knees. "Is that all?"

"Right now, it's all that matters. You know you don't owe her anything, right?"

"I know, but..." He pictured his mother the last few times he'd seen her. There had been no sign of the volatile woman who'd raised him. Instead she was deeply fearful, resistant to the slightest deviation from her routine. The scared little boy inside him was smug because now she knew what it felt like, how exhausting her chaos had been. But now he was also a man who'd destroyed things, thoroughly and permanently. "I understand her more than I used to."

"She hasn't earned that, either."

"It's not about that. Earning things. We can't cancel out bad with good. People are both."

August shoved impatiently at her hair like it was arguing with her, too. "But it's also okay to avoid people who hurt you."

"You mean like me?"

Luke studied her closely, trying to gauge her reaction. They both knew she should stay away from him, that any rational person would tell her to do exactly that. The past ruled them like gravity, pinning them to a place where he'd never stop running, and she'd always be left behind.

"I meant it when I said I didn't come here for forgiveness," he said. "That's not something I expect from anyone, but especially you. I'll always be the guy who left, who lied."

"Luke—"

"I can answer questions, though. Explain things. But only if you need that."

She drew her knees to her chest, made herself into a hard little ball. Luke braced for what was coming because the truth would be embarrassing no matter what she asked. He couldn't think of a single story about his life he'd be proud to share.

Lying about her song was the big one. Why hadn't he said her name when the *Country Star* producers asked for writing credits? The truth was that he had. That first day when they threw so much information at him it was hard to remember his own birthday, Delilah Simmons, his future manager, had asked him who wrote it.

"A friend of mine."

"Girlfriend?"

"No. Well, maybe. It's complicated."

She'd huffed and mumbled, "Not good," which made Luke feel like he'd already lost the competition.

"She wrote the lyrics," he'd offered, trying to recover. "I wrote the music."

"So you did write it."

"The music."

"Songs are music."

He was confused by her irritation. "Yeah, but they're also words."

"Luke, I need you to focus. When someone asks you who wrote it, tell them what you told me. That you wrote the music."

Delilah had rewritten his story with a sleight of hand that he never saw coming. "Luke wrote the music" became "Luke wrote this" when he was too distracted by all the attention to correct anyone. Once he realized what was happening, revealing the truth meant being a liar. Liars didn't win reality shows or sign production deals. They were sent packing, dumped at the bus stop with a ticket back to their shitty farm and their shitty mother, and that shitty future they were trying to escape.

"I want to know why," August said, finally. "If you loved me, why did you stay away?"

He should have known she'd get to the heart of things. It's what made her a good writer. His reasons for lying about the song were obvious.

But not coming back, never calling, made her question everything else he'd said.

"Because I was a drunk who wanted to keep drinking. And I couldn't be that with you."

She closed her eyes like it hurt to look at him. This was his worst fear. This was her in all his nightmares. "I wouldn't have—"

"I never wanted to be like her," Luke interrupted. "But that's exactly what happened." August's eyes flew open, and he knew she understood him. She'd just poured his mother into her car.

"That's not true."

"I've been sober five years, but I'll always have a disorder. I'm still tempted to drink when things get hard. But accepting that changed my life." He took her hand in his. Her fingers were long, tapered, and delicate. He ran a thumb over her knuckles, pausing at each bone. "I'd never put my hands on you," he said softly. "I'd die first. But there's lots of ways to break a person. I couldn't risk it."

She stared at their hands. "I would have helped you."

"I didn't want help. Drinking was the only thing that made my life bearable, and I chose it over you every time. Once I was in recovery, I'd been gone so long I figured it was best to stay away."

She pulled her hand back. "You were wrong."

"I know that now. And I'm so sorry."

A long moment passed before she spoke again. "What made you decide to get sober?"

He had stories. Everyone in recovery had them, things the average person would find horrifying. They always underestimated someone's rock bottom because they couldn't see down that far. They had reasonable limits. But the Snake wasn't reasonable. It only cared about the next drink.

"I was at this bar in Memphis, and this guy recognized me. Big dude, way bigger than me. He started hassling me, asking where I'd been all these years." Luke had ordered a beer in the middle of the guy's verbal assault. He'd been on autopilot, dodging the sight of an empty glass. "Something he said set me off, and to this day, I don't remember what it was, but I hit him. Then I was on the floor getting the shit kicked out of me."

Luke remembered staring at the ceiling, thinking, *I can take it. I've lived through worse.* But for the first time, he also thought, *What if I don't?* "Dying like my father was comforting to me—that's how fucked up I was. It felt like I was following in his footsteps."

Luke had kept his eyes lowered as he spoke, but now he looked at her, drank her in just in case this was the last time they were close like this. If she ran from him after tonight, he wouldn't blame her. "Then I thought about you. Because I always think about you, even when I shouldn't. I didn't want it to be all you knew about me. His death. Your song. None of it mine. I shoved that guy off me and got out of there. Checked into rehab the next day."

She didn't speak for a while. The pond was quiet, too, no croaking frogs or buzzing insects. Everything held its breath.

"I'm sorry," she finally said. "I knew you had a problem, and I never said anything. I never got you help."

Luke was stunned. "We were teenagers," he said, even though it felt impossible they were ever that young.

"Still. I promised to take care of you."

At that moment, Luke realized something that made him want to hold her so badly that he had to lock his muscles to remain still. This woman, fierce and loyal with the biggest heart he'd ever seen, would never reveal his lie. She'd throw her future away to keep a thirteen-year-old promise because the only way she knew how to love was through sacrifice.

But no one had ever sacrificed anything for her.

August dug something out of her pocket and offered it to him. "I wrote it at work. Thought it might be the start of something."

She didn't wait for him to read it. He watched her climb into her car and didn't look at the note until she was gone.

Summer nights were the coldest / I'll regret those forever / 'Cause now you look like every moment / that could have been better

Luke reread the words. Then he texted Charlotte's publicity manager, asking for a phone number. It didn't take long to get a response: **Bitch nearly ruined Charlotte's career, but you do you.**

Luke made the phone call with his stomach in knots.

"This is Emma Fisher."

"Ms. Fisher? Luke Randall. I want to pitch you a story about August Lane."

She laughed. "I think everyone else beat me to it."

"Not this one." He placed August's note on the ground to keep her words in front of him. "It's about who really wrote 'Another Love Song.'"

File Name: Luke Randall
Audio Length: 0:46:23
Transcriber: Emma Fisher
Date transcribed: August 28, 2023
Luke Randall:

[*Excerpt*] I never went on vacations growing up. We took a trip to see my mother's family once, but that didn't go well, so we never tried again. Used to go to the lake with friends, but that was less than an hour from home. I was still tethered during those trips. This is a terrible metaphor, but we used to have cows on the farm that had to be tethered sometimes to keep 'em from grazing outside a certain area. That's what lake days were. Safe grazing. I could look at the skyline and it would be the same sky I'd seen my whole life. I'm telling you this so you'll understand how different it was for me in Nashville. I was alone. No one knew I was there. And that city was big. Arcadia barely had four thousand people when I left. The Nashville bus stop was the size of my high school.

Country Star was doing auditions, but that's not why I went there. Never thought I could make it onto a TV show. I went because of August. She was always talking about moving to Nashville after graduation, and I wanted to be there when she did. *If* she did. There was no set date or way to get in touch with her, but I was trying to increase the odds, I guess. Sounds silly now, but I was in a bad place. Made sense at the time.

But back to the tether. I get off the bus and it's gone. I'm standing on some street I can't name, surrounded by strangers staring at me like I've never been stared at my whole life. Blank, empty eyes. "Hello, nobody." When people say they want to be someone, they're usually talking about fame, but this was different. This was I'm a tree falling in the woods. If someone shoved me into traffic, I'd bleed out and disappear.

My brother had given me a *Country Star* flyer and I showed it to people, asking them to point me toward the Ryman. I walked there. Probably could have taken a cab, but I'd never done that before, either. Got lost three times before I found it. There was a line of musicians camping out early, so I lined up, too. People stared at me, asked what I played and did I know what kind of show this was, all so polite, like they wanted to point me in the right direction. First, I'm nobody. Now I'm this odd thing that doesn't belong, even though we're all sitting there with guitars and drawls, playing shitty Bob Dylan covers. Those white city kids were singing about missing a simple, small-town life they never had. Meanwhile, I'm so fresh off the bus you could still smell the country on me. But I'm the one they think is lost.

If they didn't let me audition, I had no place else to go. So I smiled a lot. Made jokes. Laughed at their confusion because it reassured them it wasn't racist to question my presence. I played Johnny Cash and Hank Williams because everyone loves them, and it worked. I made it to the quarterfinals. Then a producer asked for the title of my original song—not whether I planned to write one, but where is it, like "Hand it over, dummy." And if you've ever been the person who knows nothing while being surrounded by people acting like they know everything, you'll understand why I didn't speak up, why I didn't say, *Hey, I've never actually written a song on my own* or *What do you mean by "original"* or *What the fuck's a copyright?* I just kept smiling. Kept laughing. Then I pulled out August's notebook to remind myself of what we'd written and the first thing I saw was "Luke's Song." My name was literally on the thing. So, I played it for them, the real version, not the way it sounds now. I had written some of the music before I left, but the rest...I don't know where it came from. Good melodies are like that. All gut and feeling. Like you didn't write it, you found it waiting for you. That's what I should have told them. I didn't write this. Someone left it for me.

They came up with the title. Made it faster. I hated the changes, but when I played "Another Love Song" in front of all those people, I didn't get blank stares anymore. They were screaming my name. Thousands of people at home were voting for me, saying yes, keep him. We love this guy. And that was it for me. I was hooked on the worst drug in the industry. It convinced me that as long as I gave people what they wanted, I'd never be that lost country boy again.

But that wasn't true. Standing up there, serving bold-faced lies with a smile, that would never be my tether. August is. She always finds me.

PART SEVEN

THE CHORUS

CHAPTER EIGHTEEN

2009

August finally had the house to herself. Birdie and Jojo had gone to the church picnic, and she'd volunteered to do chores while they were gone. She played *Rumours* at high volume as she cleaned, starting with "Dreams" because it had the strongest hook on the album. She'd been studying song structure and had learned that a hook could be anything: a line, a riff, an instrument, whatever made you stop and listen. In "Dreams," she'd initially assumed it was the repeated lyric about losing love. But after replaying it a few times, she decided it was the warning about loneliness.

August was singing along to the second verse when Jojo's voice joined in with a dramatic flourish. Her mother danced into the room, waving her arms in a way that evoked Stevie Nicks's witchy persona. She motioned for August to keep going.

They had sung together before. Birthday songs. Church hymns. All situations where pitch was irrelevant, and an off-key clash matched the moment. This was different. Jojo's voice shimmered, her soprano soaring in a crisp, deliberate key. August couldn't match that, so she sang beneath it, harmonizing with Jojo by using a smoother version of her real voice, the one she'd only shared with Luke. At the end, August closed her eyes, lost herself in the music, and it wasn't until the last line that she realized Jojo had stopped singing and was now watching her with a dazed expression, as if she'd driven the wrong way down a one-way street.

"Do you always sound like that?"

August said "Yes" even though it wasn't true. Sometimes she sounded better. "I was copying you, though. Trying to harmonize."

"At first, maybe. The last bit was something else."

August turned down the volume on the CD player. "You sounded different," she said. "Is it the new voice coach?"

"Hell no. Voice lessons make me radio friendly. Sand down all the edges." Jojo tapped her nails on the table while she spoke, a nervous habit. The sound was more muffled than usual. She'd gotten a manicure, and they'd been filed into blunt, red squares. "I don't think anyone could do that with you. Take that away. Wouldn't be much left."

August hadn't thought about that before. Songwriting was her main focus. But what if Jojo was right? What if her voice wasn't "radio friendly" enough for anyone to want to hear them?

"I should have stayed with you instead of going to that picnic." Jojo propped her feet up on another chair. "It's too hot to be outside. And I never ate those damn fish sandwiches when I was little. Sure don't want 'em now."

August pictured the buffalo fish served with mustard and a single slice of Wonder Bread. "Why are they called sandwiches? The fish has bones in it."

Jojo sighed. "You've always been like this. My little why-child. Never accepting things at face value."

"Is that bad?"

"No. But sometimes it's easier." Jojo stared at her for a beat. "Where do you go after school?"

August had answered this question enough times that her response was robotic. "The library. With Mavis."

"What are you studying?"

"Math?"

"Are you asking or telling me?"

"It's a good excuse to get out of the house."

Jojo tapped her nails again. "Are you sneaking off with that boy Birdie doesn't know about?"

Not sneaking off *with* but sneaking off *to*. Luke had been recovering from his injuries at Delta Blue for a week now. Birdie knew where August was going but had kept her promise not to tell Jojo. "Your mama can't handle any kind of violence. Just hearing about it will send her running out the door."

There'd been no sign of Ava. Luke refused to talk about her, so August avoided the subject. Between songwriting sessions, they talked about everything but what happened to him—worst books, best movies, which cafeteria worker composed the most balanced lunch trays. After school, she brought him takeout from King's Kitchen, and they'd eat salty catfish baskets with Silas's records playing in the background. Luke seemed happy, more content than he'd ever been. And August slowly realized why he couldn't write a love song on his own.

No one is born knowing how to love. You learn from parents, grandparents, friends. If all they taught you was how dangerous loving was, or the ways it could hurt, you'd never learn how to do it properly. So how could he write about it? He didn't have the vocabulary. All he had was emotion, big feelings he captured in melodies. August was his transcriptionist, trying to craft verses strong enough to contain them.

"I'm failing chemistry," August told Jojo. "Mavis tutors me at the library, that's all."

Jojo's phone rang, rescuing August from the interrogation. She started to stand, but Jojo motioned for her to stay. "I'm talking to my daughter," she said, instead of her usual cheerful greeting. "Stop worrying, David. If a half hour is all we've got, then we'll kill 'em for thirty minutes. Let it go."

She hung up and said, "He's in love with me. I pretend not to know, but it's obvious." She gestured toward August. "Look at me telling the truth. See how easy that was?"

August pictured David Henry's slick smile and flint-colored eyes. She couldn't imagine her mother's manager pining for anyone. "Do you love him, too?"

"He's married. Plus, he's a drinker. They'll slap you around when they can't get hard. Not worth the hassle." Jojo stood and straightened her shirt. "You hungry? Let's make waffles."

August nodded, but then, with her feelings for Luke burning bright in her mind, she asked, "What do you think he'd do if you told him?"

"Told him what?"

"How you felt?"

"I never said—" She stopped when August rolled her eyes. "Fine. He'd be happy. Probably file for divorce. Then he'd make a bunch of promises and break every single one."

Luke used up all his unexcused absences. On his first day back at school, he wore long sleeves to hide most of his bandage, even though it was still hot enough for shorts. His cheeks were leaner, and his eyes were bloodshot from lack of sleep. Everything he'd hidden for years—his messed-up family, the abuse—was clear on his face.

Silas had let him borrow a car and Luke drove into town slowly, with his stomach cramping in protest. He parked in the back of the school lot so no one would see him. The stomach cramps became dry heaves the minute he opened the door.

The second tardy bell rang before he made it to class. His teacher looked irritated by his lateness, but softened when she noticed his arm. "Take a seat," she whispered, with enough pity to smother him. Shane, who he hadn't heard from since being suspended from football, raised a brow and mumbled, "Where the hell you been?"

It hadn't occurred to Luke to come up with a good lie. He didn't want people making up wild stories that reached some teacher or administrator who would then immediately call his mother. The image of Ava barreling through the doors in an oxy-fueled rage had him eyeing the exits and plotting an escape.

He skipped his next class. Instead, he went to the theater dressing room and left the lights off. The darkness was soothing, and he focused on slowing his breath.

A few minutes later, the door swung open and filled the room with light. He blinked until Jessica's face came into focus. It had been a month since they'd spoken. Everything about her was softer. Her shirt was pale pink, her hair a cloud of spirals, and she smelled like an apple orchard.

"Knew I'd find you here." She sat in a chair. "Tell August that rehearsals for the fall play are starting soon. She'll have to say goodbye to your sex den."

"We eat lunch here. That's it."

"Someone's definitely eating something." She eyed a pile of velvet pillows. "I don't see the appeal."

"How did you know? Did you see us walk in, or..." All that time they thought they were hiding. Did the entire school think they were having quickies during lunch?

"Calm down. I knew this was August's hideout a long time ago. When you disappeared from our lunch table and she started bringing two brown bags every day, I figured it out." She tilted her head. "That's really sweet. Her feeding you."

"Knock it off."

She rolled her eyes. "You're always so uptight. Like a hot Quaker. I kind of miss it." She pointed to his arm. "Did Ava do that?"

Luke was thrown by the question. Ava loved Jessica and had fawned over her the few times he'd brought her home. "Why would you ask?"

Jessica gave him an impatient look, like this was a race and he needed to catch up. "She called my dad and told him you were running around with Silas King."

It never occurred to Luke that staying at Delta Blue would put Silas in Ava's crosshairs. She was probably afraid he knew what she'd done. Luke could imagine her spinning some sob story about her troubled son in case there was a police report. "What did your dad say?"

"He asked if I had seen you. I said yes, you were fine." She picked a loose thread in her jeans. "I also said Ava was paranoid, and that you were probably staying at Shane's to get away from her." She paused. "Have you really been hanging out with Silas King?"

Luke thought of Silas's Cadillac, currently sitting in the parking lot. It was damning evidence. "I'm staying with him," he admitted. "Ava and I got into it. I can't go back."

She looked at his arm again. "I knew she was awful. Even though she was nice to me, with some people, you can tell."

Luke didn't respond. Despite everything, agreeing with Jessica felt like a betrayal. Ava was his mother. Nothing would change that. "Thank you for covering for me. Especially with how we left things."

"You're welcome. But you'll ruin all my efforts if you keep freaking out and disappearing. People are noticing. You can't hide forever, Luke."

She was right. Jessica's lies would be easy for her father to verify, starting with the football suspension. Next he'd speak to Luke's teachers, who would probably get the district involved if they looked too closely at his poor attendance records. Then came his worst nightmares: Ava's drugs being discovered. Her getting dragged away in handcuffs. Ethan being sent to some group home. Luke would be powerless to stop it all from happening.

Every box he'd worked so hard to fit inside was collapsing. His reputation used to protect him, make people see him the way he wanted. It was naive to believe he didn't need that anymore. "It's hard being back," he admitted. "Everyone wants me to be some guy I don't even know anymore."

Jessica slumped in her chair. "My mom walked in on me making out with Shirley last week."

Luke stared with wide eyes. "The girl that's obsessed with horses?"

She nodded. "It's not serious. We were just fooling around, but Mom freaked out. Started crying." She tried to sound flippant, like it wasn't a big deal, but he knew it was. Jessica referred to her mother as her first best friend. "When I reminded her that homecoming was this weekend, she said she didn't trust me to make good decisions."

Luke thought of Ethan, and how long he'd had to hide who he was from their mother. Jessica had been forced into the exact situation his brother was desperate to avoid. He didn't know how that felt. But Jessica looked like she was slowly drowning. "Your parents trust me, right? What if I took you?"

"To homecoming?"

"Yeah. I mean, it'll help us both. People will see me out having fun like normal, and your parents will think you're..." He trailed because he wasn't sure how to phrase it.

"Still having fun like normal?" She smiled. "Let's do it."

The door opened again. This time it was August. Luke stood so quickly he nearly stumbled while trying to distance himself from Jessica. August kept her hand on the door, as if she didn't plan to stay. "Sorry to interrupt."

Luke wanted to laugh because the idea was ridiculous. He'd been waiting for her. But he knew how bad this looked. Jessica, the interloper, lounging in August's chair like she planned to stay awhile. Luke felt like he'd been caught at the scene of a crime.

"You should go," he told Jessica.

She ignored him and focused on August. "What's for lunch?"

"*Jess.*" His voice was harsh enough to capture her attention. "I'll see you Saturday."

A tense silence followed. Jessica took her time sliding her backpack over her shoulder. When she finally left, August shoved a bagged lunch into Luke's hands and sat in a wobbly chair to avoid the one Jessica had just abandoned. She started eating like nothing had happened.

Luke sat on the couch. "That wasn't—"

"Whatever you're about to say, don't. You and I are *friends*. That's all." The way she said *friends* implied the opposite, that they were so much more. "Don't do that whole, this isn't what it looks like thing, because it'll be embarrassing." She glanced at him. "For you. Not me."

Luke remained silent. All the feelings he was hiding had gummed up his brain. If he tried to speak, he'd say I love you, which was the last thing she'd want to hear, especially once she knew what he was doing for Jessica.

August stared at him, her expression growing colder the longer he remained silent. "You know she's a terrible person, right? Please tell me you know that." It sounded like she was begging him to prove he wasn't a complete idiot.

"People are complicated."

"Not her. She wants you back."

"No, she doesn't. And even if she did, I don't want her."

"But you're going out with her Saturday."

"It's homecoming. I'm doing her a favor." He wanted to tell August the whole story, but he didn't want to betray Jessica's trust. "I owe it to her" was all he said.

August balled her trash up and stood. "Why do you care so much what people think of you?"

Luke remembered what Jessica had said, how he needed to convince everyone he was fine. "Because I have to."

"No, you don't."

"You don't understand, August."

"Explain it to me."

"I don't think I can."

"Try!"

"Because I should!" Luke shouted. "Because it matters. Who are we if no one gives a shit about us?"

August pushed past him, rushing to the door. Luke grabbed her arm. "I was four when Ava started locking me in a closet as punishment. She'd spank me raw and then shove me inside to cry myself sick."

August looked horrified. He clung to her as the story spilled out of him. He'd never told anyone. Not even Ethan. "After a while, I realized it was the only time she didn't put her hands on me. So I started liking it. I'd seek out that dark when I knew she was mad about something. I still do, like that night you found me at the fair." He looked around the dressing room. "You like this place for the same reason. Because it feels safer than what's out there. But this is the closet you let those people put you in. It's your prison."

August stopped speaking to him. He tried confronting her in the hallway, but she would dance around him, avoiding his eyes. In English class, she sat on the opposite side of the room. As the week went on, he grew more desperate, writing sloppy, rambling apologies and stuffing them in her locker. She stopped coming to the dressing room, which hurt more than being ignored to his face. She'd found a new place to hide and he wasn't invited.

By Saturday, he was a wreck. The homecoming theme was Motown, and he was supposed to be Smokey Robinson, but the bridal shop had only two suits left. One was too big, and the other was too small. He'd chosen the big one, and the result was clownish and childlike.

Jessica's corsage was white carnations, flowers that screamed lazy and last minute.

Shane rented a limo with a fully stocked bar. His parents were so hands off they'd probably handed him a credit card and looked the other way. Once inside, Luke grabbed a bottle of something and poured a shot without reading the label.

An hour later, he was gone. His body was a shell, and his mind was liquid, flowing toward the barrage of energy that greeted him at the gym. The dance was voices, bodies, and heat, and Luke was into it for real, not just pretending. He danced with Jessica, bumping and grinding, but didn't actually see her because clarity was unnecessary. They were all just existing inside a sweaty, feverish realization that all this was fleeting. They got drunk and high. Jessica made out with her teammate in the bathroom. Shane got rejected by the homecoming queen and cried about it on the dance floor. Luke climbed onstage with the band and sing-shouted nineties covers until he was hoarse.

They'd been immortal these last four years. Tonight, they partied like they were dying.

Luke fell asleep when they returned to the limo. He was shaken awake by Jessica, who coaxed him toward the lobby of a Holiday Inn. "Why are we here?" he asked her.

"Because everyone else is," she said, which was always enough for her. Jessica would miss the rapture if all her friends were going to hell.

"Oh," Luke said. He needed a bathroom, and checking into a hotel room was one step closer to relief.

Thankfully their room was a double. Jessica laid on the bed in a cloud of purple taffeta. Luke shucked off his shoes. He groaned when his head hit the pillow.

"We could fuck if you want." Jessica sounded bored by the idea, annoyed that she had to offer.

"I don't want."

"Because of August?"

He ignored the question. "You still have that Hennessy?"

"You drank it all. You drink too much."

"You should mind your own business."

Jessica sat up and stared at him. Luke started to apologize, but she cut him off before he could finish and said, "I like it when you're mean. It's hot."

He sat with what she said, thinking about how hard he'd worked to be liked. To be accepted. Then he thought about August and how eager she was for kindness. How little of it they'd both had in their lives. "I think you're spoiled," he told Jessica. "I think you're surrounded by people who love you, and you take it for granted."

She was quiet for a while. "Does *she* love you?"

He closed his eyes. "I don't know," he said, even though he did. He'd realized it when he called her haven a prison. He had seen it on her face, an agonized breaking before she pulled away so hard and fast, he couldn't stop her.

Being entrusted with something so powerful and fragile was scary. It was the same way he thought of August, with her gorgeous fire and poetic mind. She was his mountain on the verge of erupting.

"Are you in love with her?"

"Why do you care?"

"Because I worry about you." Jessica propped herself up on one arm. "You're too trusting."

"I trusted you."

"Exactly. I cheated on you with Richard. Multiple times."

"Shit, Jess..."

"Like you care," she said with a hand wave. "You don't even like sex."

"That's not true."

"Oh. So, you don't like it with me. I take it back. You're an ugly asshole."

"Can we sleep?" He gave her his back and pressed his head into the pillow. "I'm tired."

"Did you get her pregnant?"

Luke shot up. "What?"

"Lisa Strayer's mom works in the office across from that women's clinic in West Memphis. She said she saw Mavis taking August there a few months ago. It's where they give abortions."

"That's not true," he said quickly, then realized he wasn't sure. A few months ago, he barely knew her. A few months ago, she'd just broken up with Richard. But then a memory surfaced, the three hundred dollars she'd used to help a friend, and he was so relieved that it spilled from his lips. "No, if anyone had an abortion, it was her cousin. August just paid for it."

"Saint Mavis Reed was pregnant?" Jessica laughed. "You expect me to believe that?"

"Believe what you want," Luke said, lying back down. He closed his eyes and let a drunken sleep take him.

This Is Our Country: Podcast Transcript

Episode 12—"Jojo Lane"
August 21, 2024

[*cont.*]

Emma: You had to be shocked.

Jojo: Hell yeah, I was shocked. We were all shocked because it came out of nowhere. Big lies like that usually leave breadcrumbs, like whispers or blind items, stuff like that. But it was like he woke up one day and remembered he took credit for something he didn't do.

Emma: That's exactly what that phone call felt like. He was so calm when he told me, though. He must have been thinking about it for a long time.

Jojo: Weighing on his soul, most likely.

Emma: Do things like this happen a lot? People taking credit for someone else's work?

Jojo: Sure, but it's usually behind the scenes, wrapped in legalese to help them get away with it. Luke's problem was that he'd gone on that reality show and lied to the world before he had a record deal. *Country Star* made that song part of his story, the Black teenager who cobbled together a massive country hit in his bedroom.

Emma: Like Lil Nas X.

Jojo: You know, I didn't think about that, but yes. Oh, the industry loves that, don't they? Magical musical negroes. It excuses them from actually nurturing talent and supporting our careers. Anyway, turns out none of it happened.

Emma: Some of it did, right? He wrote the music.

Jojo: Maybe. Memories can be kinder to us than we deserve.

Emma: Did you know your daughter was a songwriter?

Jojo: No. And you're probably wondering how that's possible, but she wasn't living with me when all this happened. Never said a word. Probably because she knew I wouldn't approve. I just wanted something else for her, something easier. But my girl doesn't do easy, and I respect that. She knew how good she was. Have you heard the original version? It's on YouTube. What was Luke thinking, letting them ruin her work like that? Probably that he didn't care because it wasn't his to begin with.

Emma: It sounds like you don't think he wrote any of it.

Jojo: I'm saying men lie for one of two reasons. To get out of trouble they should be in or to get their hands on something they don't deserve.

Emma: Pivoting a little, why do you think this emboldened the people protesting your award? You're not the one who lied.

Jojo: Emma, you're a smart woman. If I didn't believe that I wouldn't be here. But I'm about to hurt your feelings a little.

Emma: [*laughs*] Okay, I guess I asked for it.

Jojo: [*laughs*] You kind of did. Asking why I got blamed for Luke's lie means you think there's something logical in their argument, that those people are really concerned with the integrity of that institution. If you can't see the mental laziness of their bigotry, how they'll grab any excuse to hate? Maybe you weren't the best person to write that article.

CHAPTER NINETEEN

2023

August had learned that Silas was in recovery for opioid addiction when she was twelve. A kid in her class had called him a junkie, and she'd defended her uncle's honor so vehemently that she'd been sent to detention for disrupting the lesson. After school, Silas sat her down and explained that he'd used heroin to cope with being incarcerated and couldn't stop once he got out. "That was a long time ago," he'd said. "But it's still something I live with."

She'd bombarded him with questions, afraid that the sickness he called a use disorder would eventually take him from her. He answered them all honestly, including how staying sober meant changing his entire approach to life. "I hated being a King. Hated my father. My brother. They were monsters, so I thought I'd become a monster, too. But that hate was the only monstrous thing about me, so I let it go. Started doing good things, making the world better 'cause I'm in it." That was why he held the Delta Blue Showcase. To help young musicians. He also started the only local twelve-step program and volunteered as a sponsor.

Luke fixed things. Birdie's house was freshly painted. Scarlet roses were planted along one side. The grass was cut. The walkway was weed free. Inside, every room had been deep cleaned to a level of spotlessness it hadn't seen in decades.

He was focused on rebuilding, not tearing things down like she'd been lately. Last night, August had done some soul searching, questioning whether her plan was worth putting his comeback in jeopardy. There were other ways to start a career—slower, more ethical paths used by others who ultimately made it. But those had eluded Black country artists for years. Most likely, she'd end up waiting for a chance that would never come.

August couldn't wait anymore. She'd been waiting her whole life.

Sacrificing Luke on that altar wasn't the answer, either. She'd landed on a solution that wasn't perfect, but it was better than the scorched-earth approach she'd used before. Now she had to get Luke on board. They had five weeks, enough time to iron things out with Jojo and convince her to allow Luke to debut his new single during her show.

Cool air spiced with sandalwood incense greeted August when she walked inside Birdie's house. Luke was playing the latest War and Treaty album and singing along while he cleaned the living room. He didn't mimic their vocals. Instead he harmonized in a key that slid perfectly inside theirs. He used to do the same with August, use that immaculate ear to hook into her chaotic runs, as if he could see them coming.

The music cut off abruptly. The smile he gave her was quick and easy, unlike anything she'd seen since he returned. Luke unburdened was a sensory assault. It turned his eyes to bronzed light, his skin to amber honey. He even moved differently, with the grace of a lion who'd captured his prey.

August sat down. "I've been thinking."

He joined her at the table. "All right."

"Forbidding you from singing with Jojo was shortsighted. I hate the idea of that duet, but it's a means to an end."

He was quiet for a moment. "What end is that?"

"Launching your new album. We'll announce that we're working together, maybe ask David to help with a press release. It's a good opportunity to clear up the rumors about our affair—"

"August—"

"—but not make it *too* clear. We want to make everyone curious, right? Enough to watch the show once it's streaming and then—"

"I have a different idea." He raised his voice to speak over her. "But I need you to answer a question first. And be honest with me."

That made her nervous. What did he think she would lie about? "Okay."

Luke leaned in and seemed to look past her eyes, to where her secrets were buried. "Why'd you stop singing?"

He was right. She didn't want to answer that. "I sing in the choir every Sunday."

"You know that's not what I mean."

"I'm not a performer. Writing is what I'm good at."

"You're not being honest."

"That's the most honest I've ever been with myself." She swallowed whatever was welling in her throat. Those dreams were too old to flare up now. "I don't have a voice for radio. It's too distracting."

"That don't make a lick of sense."

"Why are we even talking about this?" She stood, intent on ending the conversation. Luke rose quickly and blocked her path to freedom.

"Do you have stage fright?"

She tried to glare him into retracting the question. But this new, purposeful Luke was stubborn. He didn't even bother folding his arms. He just stood there, velvet-eyed and patient.

"No," she said, but then remembered what happened last week, how her jaw had locked the minute she touched a microphone. "Maybe. Who cares?"

"I do." He adjusted his stance and spoke with his hands, like a coach pitching a new play. "You're fighting for the wrong thing. None of these plans will give you what you want. What you deserve."

"And what's that?"

"To be a star."

A laugh burst from her throat. "Might as well throw unicorn princess in there, too. I'm not a kid anymore."

His eyes lowered briefly to her lips. "I'm well aware of that, sweetheart."

August pointed the conversation in a much more interesting direction. "Call me that again."

His breath hitched, then stopped completely. "What? Sweetheart?"

She wrapped the hem of his T-shirt around her finger. "Aren't you tired of talking?"

He watched her pull his shirt up with lust-glazed eyes, but then pried her fingers away. "Stay here. I'll be right back."

Luke left the room, and August did what she was told, mainly out of curiosity. His preoccupation with her singing was a sweet waste of time. They both knew he was the talent. Why was he suddenly obsessed with her performing?

Luke returned with his guitar and a worn notebook. "Do you recognize this?"

She did. It contained "Luke's Song," along with everything else they'd written together. "You kept that?"

"Of course I did." He grabbed his guitar. "Those lyrics you gave me last night reminded me of something I wrote in there a while ago." He started playing, a slow bluesy progression that fit seamlessly with what she'd written. Then he stopped and said, "Can you hear it?"

"Of course I can."

"No, listen..." He played some of it again. "It sounds like you, doesn't it? Southern sexy. A face full of smoke. Go on and sing it."

"I told you, I'm not—"

He grabbed her hand and squeezed. "You are. You're just scared to want it. Because then everyone will know you do."

He was right. Deep down, she was still that little girl, desperate for acceptance. She didn't want to be alone onstage, with everything she lacked on display. "What if they hate me?"

Luke hugged his guitar and leaned closer. "What if they don't?"

The front door burst open. Mavis barged inside, a large iced coffee in one hand and her phone in the other. She stopped short at the sight of Luke, and her lips curved into a snarl. She reared back and hurled her cup at his chest. It exploded on impact, drenching him in ice and foam. "You *stole* her *fucking* song?"

⋆

Luke had dropped a bomb on country music. The media covered every aspect of his confession: the lie. The racist *Country Star* auditions. The exploitive record contract. His firing from Jojo's show was swift and public. Every major sponsor swore never to work with him again. August, formally the internet's favorite villain was now its favorite victim. "He made her his sidepiece *and* stole her music? Girl, blink twice if you need help."

August didn't speak to anyone for days. There was no point. Luke had ruined their future with that phone call. When she'd asked why he did it, all he'd said was "I love you. And there's a right way to do that."

It was too much. She couldn't handle declarations of love while being cut off at the knees.

A text from Silas ended her self-imposed exile. **Luke's singing tonight. Thought you'd want to know.** The protests had doubled in size since the story broke. Performing so soon after his confession would make it worse. Provoking an angry mob was out of character for him. Maybe it was a cry for help. Luke had been facing a mountain of backlash alone, while she'd been hiding, wallowing in slipper socks and a supersize jug of cheese puffs.

The customers were sparse for a Delta Blue open mic night. Silas spotted her immediately when she walked inside. He hugged her, which he rarely did anymore, and said "Good to see you" in a way that made her feel pathetic. Silas usually took bad news with his chin out, daring it to do real damage. Today he looked defeated. "He's warming up in the back."

"Oh. Okay."

Silas fidgeted. "Why didn't you tell me?"

"Because you love him."

"I love you both." He rubbed her back. "Y'all still fighting?"

She answered honestly. "I don't know." Mavis was the only one who'd yelled at Luke. August had asked for space so she could disintegrate privately. Meanwhile, their fragile relationship had been left in limbo.

The lights flickered a five-minute warning. Silas led her to a table in the corner. She sat down as Luke walked onstage. He wore a T-shirt and jeans, with a black cap pulled low, obscuring the top of his face. Paired with his beard, which was fuller than when she last saw him, he was nearly unrecognizable.

"He's been practicing for weeks," Silas said. "Signed up with a fake name so he could sing what he wants."

That explained the small crowd. Only a few of the audience members were paying attention. Most were chatting over food and drinks.

"He asked me about a job," Silas said.

"Here?" August gaped at him. "He lives in Memphis."

"I know. I was just as surprised as you. He offered to book talent. Clean the place. Even said he would serve drinks, like he has any business—" He glanced at her. "Did he talk to you about that?"

"Being in recovery? He told me."

"Well, I'm looking after him, just so you know. He's been going to meetings. Working the program."

"That's good to hear." Luke had seemed confident about his sobriety, but that was before everyone knew he'd been lying for years. She was grateful he had help.

Silas left her to emcee the show. He called Luke "Jason," as in Jason Randall. His father's name. Luke started singing "If I Could Only Fly," the first song he'd learned to play on his own. It was perfect for the distracted crowd, the solemn simplicity demanding stillness to be heard. Slowly, he drew everyone's attention to the stage.

Luke's voice was deep and melancholic, with only a hint of the drawl he overused on his albums. It grew louder during the chorus but also felt quieter somehow. The wish to fly was a prayer he was afraid to utter, a held breath he wouldn't release because he knew it was foolish to want things when you're broken. By the time he moved into the second verse, August was fighting tears.

"Doesn't this piss you off?"

David Henry stood behind her, cradling a highball glass. He raised it to his lips and frowned when he realized it was empty. "Why does club soda go so fast?"

"Could you stand somewhere else? I'm trying to listen."

"Why don't I sit instead?" He sat across from her, folded his arms, and settled in.

"What are you—"

He shushed her but focused on the crowd instead of Luke. The applause began before the song ended. A few people whistled. David grumbled under his breath, "Talented little shit." He glanced at August. "Heard there was an open mic night and got nostalgic for my scouting days." He looked around. "It's more depressing than I remembered. How do places like this stay in business?"

"It's not usually this empty."

"And why did Luke use a fake name? People pay good money to watch natural disasters."

"Because this isn't a publicity stunt." She gestured to the stage, where Luke had started singing Rissi Palmer's "Seeds." "He wants to sing in peace."

"He's still got a few die-hard fans," David said. "More than this sad little showing."

"They only want one thing. A live performance of their favorite song."

He snorted. "That shitty song isn't anyone's favorite. Their favorite karaoke train wreck, maybe. Or their favorite alternative to the dentist's chair."

"Stop calling it shitty," August snapped. He knew she'd written it. It felt like being accused of setting Luke up for failure.

"All due respect, the song *is* shitty. The whole album's terrible. Except 'If You See Me Lying.' That one's just boring."

"You know that wasn't him."

David leaned forward. "I don't know that at all. I know the man refuses to talk seriously about his music. If I ask who his influences are, I get canned, bullshit answers his publicity team wrote back in 2010. I know he's so obsessed with setting *you* up with a record deal that he tanked what was left of his career. Meanwhile, he's squatting on a voice that sounds like Marvin Gaye and Hozier made a country-fried baby who can play the hell out of a guitar lick. And I don't respect it. I can't respect a man who was gifted with that kind of talent and buried it in auto-tune for money."

August understood his frustration. She'd assumed for years that Luke had sold his dignity for fame. But he'd really traded it for different chains. That was why he'd looked so much happier the morning that article had been published. He'd finally unlocked those shackles. Telling the world had been the key.

No. That wasn't the part of David's rant that infuriated her.

"You're nothing like Jojo said you were," she told him quietly. "It's disappointing."

David didn't speak at first. He blinked and sat up in his chair. "What did she say about me?"

"That you were serious. The real deal. She said she never met a man with an ear like yours. That you were all about the music." She let her gaze slide over him. "I think you're the least serious person I've ever met."

"Are we on the playground now? I poke him, you knee my balls?"

"You're the only one playing games. This is his life. Our lives. All you do is throw peanuts. She *pays* you for that?"

"You don't know what I've done for your mother *and* you. I came here to offer you—"

"I don't want it."

He clenched his teeth. "Listen. Jojo's record deal is with—"

"Do you know the real reason this place is empty?" She waved at the room. "Because of people like you, with the power and connections to make someone's career with a phone call, sitting on your ass until you're convinced to give a damn about someone. We have to prove ourselves, over and over again, before you see us. Do you know how exhausting that is? A heart can only break so many times before it quits."

She looked at the stage, where Luke was chatting with an older man sitting in front. He was smiling. Living. She hadn't realized how lifeless he'd been until now. "Look at that wall over there," she said. David followed her gaze to Silas's photo collage, filled with decades of performers at Delta Blue. "We are blues. We are rock. We are country. And all those things are us. *We've* always known that. Jojo said you knew it, too." She shook her head. "But I don't think so. I think everyone looks the same to you. Which makes you useless to someone like me."

She pushed back from the table, but David grabbed her arm. "Wait." She jerked away, and he lifted his hands in surrender. "I'm sorry," he said. "I uh…" He cleared his throat. "I'm an asshole who's used to dealing with other assholes. Good people confuse me, but I'm learning. Give me five minutes. *Please.*"

Something about David's tone made her curious enough to settle back into her seat. Once she did, he relaxed and attempted an appeasing smile. It made him look like a prisoner trying to convince the parole board he'd been rehabilitated.

"I used to be a lawyer. Litigator. Someone accused me of loving to argue once, and I thought it meant I should go to law school. That's how shallow my emotional well was. Someone points out a flaw, and I build a career around it instead of trying to be a better person." His lips twitched into something more genuine. "Made me miserable. It made me drink, not that I needed much of an excuse. The only solace I had was music. I probably went to every live venue in the city at least twice before I was twenty-five."

"The city?" She rolled her eyes. "Oh, you mean New York."

"So, one night, I go to this dive advertising folk music, and there's this Black woman onstage, singing 'Folsom Prison Blues,' and I think, what the fuck? This isn't folk. So I ask the guy managing the place about it, and he looks at me like I'm stupid. 'It's just a song, man' is what he said to me. And it made me angry." David's voice was tight at the memory. "I got so angry at how small this guy's world was that I quit my job the next day and researched talent scouting."

Silas appeared onstage and announced the next act. David waited until he was finished. "So that's my origin story. Dave got mad. But then I lost sight of what I was so angry about, and it took some washed-up one-hit wonder to remind me." He stared at August. "I think I get it now. Why he threw it all away for you."

"He didn't," she said. "He could still—"

"He can't. Emma's article inspired sympathy, but no one will touch him. They've got no reason to. It's you they want."

August frowned. "What?"

"That's what I was trying to tell you. You've got all of Nashville wanting to sign you because they heard this." He pulled out his phone and opened a voice note. It was a recording she'd sent Luke weeks ago, a piece of a song she'd ultimately rejected. "I got this the day the story broke with instructions to stop playing it safe. That was a reference to something I said to him, which he apparently took offense to and proved me wrong." He put the phone down. "I like the guy. But I also hate him a little."

"I don't understand. It's not a whole song. There's no music."

"Didn't need it. I said your name, and people put everything aside to listen. That's currency, August. That's cash in hand. But it's temporary. You have to use it now."

"How?"

"I chatted with a few of those assholes I mentioned earlier. Luke is out. You're in. Same deal we offered him, a duet with Jojo during the show. I'll try to work in more, but they're focused on leveraging the controversy of 'Another Love Song.' You'd perform it publicly for the first time. Reclaim your words in front of the world."

August couldn't speak. There was a strange stillness inside her. She was so used to wrestling with the different parts of herself, trying to parse through what she should and shouldn't feel, that the sudden quiet confused her. But then a ripple of something new trembled low in her chest and spread until it danced along her skin. Joy. It'd been so long since she'd felt it. David just offered her every dream she'd ever had, including one she hadn't shared with anyone: singing with her mother.

But the second she named it, the feeling slipped away as the reality of what he was saying sank in. She was a replacement. Damage control. The stripped recording was good, but it wasn't the best she could do. They'd only heard her searching for the voice she'd lost. They hadn't heard her find it with Luke.

August scanned the room, searching. Luke's set had ended a while ago, and she'd assumed he'd join the crowd. "I need to talk to him."

"About that," David said. "Give the songwriting a rest for now. They want you focused on performing."

He didn't say the rest, but she knew what he meant. Luke or Jojo. Cling to the past or embrace the future. It was an obvious choice, wasn't it?

She should have seen it coming.

This Is Our Country: Podcast Transcript

Episode 12—"Jojo Lane"
August 21, 2024

[*cont.*]

Jojo: Birdie got saved when I was twelve and I hated her for it for a long time.

Emma: Saved as in...

Jojo: Became a born-again Christian. It felt like I'd been tricked into believing that the person who raised me was who she would always be. Kids like patterns and routines. That's what love is to them. Something invisible that makes them feel safe. If they can see the effort, they can see all the ways it can be taken away.

My mother started reading the Bible after my father died. Really reading it, not just flipping to the scripture when a pastor told her to. I'd been doing pageants and shows for a while and something in those pages convinced her it put my soul in jeopardy. I mean, I wasn't driving myself to these things. I wasn't buying the costumes.

Emma: Did she stop taking you?

Jojo: There was money coming in, so no. But she started giving me these warnings about how I should act around the men in the building. It was mostly women who worked directly with us, but men ran everything, the pageants, the concerts. The whole ride over, I had to listen to all the ways these men could hurt me. How they could damn me to hell before I became a woman? It messed with my head. All these folks smiling in my face were secret demons? And I was just a little girl, so how was I supposed to protect myself? How do you fight a demon?

Emma: That sounds horrible.

Jojo: I didn't know any better. It's probably why I liked Theo. He never hid what he was. And when you're scared of the unknown, a known danger feels safer, even when it isn't.

Emma: Have you ever talked to your mother about this?

Jojo: I tried. It never went well. Eventually I had to let it go. Birdie had early-onset dementia. Barely recognized anyone when she died.

Emma: I'm sorry to hear that.

Jojo: I found this nurse who grew up in the next town over to help take care of her. Birdie always remembered her. Never forgot her name. But she confused me with August all the time.

CHAPTER TWENTY

2009

August rode to church with Jojo. The Mercedes had more room inside than she'd pictured. The seats sank like pillows when she sat on them, and the air smelled artificial, like expensive plastic.

"You seem sad," Jojo said, easing the car down Main Street. She slowed even more after spotting a man selling peaches on the side of the road. "Remind me to stop there on the way back."

August smoothed a wrinkle from her dress. It was a knee-length cotton navy that Birdie had embroidered with white flowers at the hem. Those handmade touches were always comforting, like nothing could harm her while cloaked in her grandmother's love.

"Someone hurt my feelings," she said. "I'll get over it."

"Should you?"

August had lost count of Luke's apologies. By Friday, while everyone else obsessed over homecoming, he was slipping notes into her locker, begging her to talk to him. She'd ignored them, but over the weekend she'd started to regret giving him the silent treatment. He was right about her hiding in that dressing room. If Richard Green's opinion didn't matter, why was she avoiding him? Why did a smirk from Jessica Ryder turn her inside out?

"He didn't hurt me on purpose," August said. "He tries to make everyone happy, even when he can't."

"Except you." Jojo's voice was steeped in judgment.

"He makes me happy," August said, though it sounded inadequate. Before Luke, she'd been starved for feelings she didn't know existed. *He feeds me* would have been more accurate. *Loving him is water.*

They arrived late, but Jojo had never cared about that. She enjoyed making an entrance. It used to thrill August when she was younger, walking down the aisle at her glamorous mother's hip. But now, August avoided being the center of attention. People rarely stared at her for a good reason.

Birdie spotted them from the choir stand and motioned for August to join her.

"Not today," Jojo said, and grabbed August's arm. She stared at Birdie as she spoke. "They can live without you for one week. I want my daughter beside me."

These were the trickiest parts of her mother's visits, knowing who to side with when they disagreed. Birdie was the everyday authority August obeyed by default. Jojo was the wildcard that had to be handled cautiously. When August took her mother's side, it was in situations like this one, when Jojo seemed eager to fight about something that seemed insignificant on the surface. Her mother had fault lines. August often saw them too late, when the ground was already shaking.

Jojo looked around, gifting her glossy pink smile to dazzled faces. Service was delayed because people refused to settle into the pews before greeting her. August received more smiles than usual. She whispered in Jojo's ear, "They're never this nice to me."

"I know," Jojo whispered back. "Hypocrites are always first in line when you have something they want."

August nodded, even though she couldn't imagine having anything they'd consider valuable. But then a little girl said, "You look like her," and it clicked. Today, she wasn't Theo's orphan or Birdie's burden. She was the daughter of Jojo Lane. Exceptional through proximity.

"They're gonna ask me to sing," Jojo said halfway through the service. August agreed. Their pastor had spent ten minutes of their praise and worship time praising and worshipping Jojo for returning to her church home, which he'd somehow connected to the virtues of tithing. August tried to exchange an exasperated look with Mavis, who sat directly behind him in the choir stand. Mavis didn't smother a smile like she usually did. Instead, she glared and looked away.

"Is that little May?" Jojo asked. "That girl got big and beautiful. When did that happen?"

August stared at her cousin, silently willing her to make eye contact again. "She hates that nickname."

Pastor Reed invited Jojo to the microphone. The room stirred as Jojo walked to the front and asked the band to play "God Is Trying to Tell You Something."

Everyone got excited. The song was popular, but that wasn't why Jojo had picked it. Years ago, while August was watching *The Color Purple* with her, crying during the reunion of Shug Avery and her pastor father, Jojo had said, "She doesn't need that man's forgiveness. Look how she owns that church. Sailing on a sea of sinners and ministering to saints."

Now as Jojo sang, the same people who constantly gossiped about her mother's past raised their hands and shouted "Amen!" Jojo put on an impromptu concert, mixing hymns with songs from her album. Three hours later, August was tired and starving, seconds away from recommitting herself to God if it would close the open call for prayer.

When they were finally dismissed, August found Mavis and tapped her shoulder. "Is everything okay?"

The look Mavis gave her was worse than the earlier glare. It was fury skinned alive. She grabbed August's arm and pulled her into an empty hallway. "Who did you tell?"

August immediately knew what she meant. "No one."

"Jessica Ryder called last night and asked if I had an abortion."

"*Jessica?* I would never . . ." August trailed. She would have never told Jessica about Mavis's pregnancy. But she had told Luke that she needed money to help a friend. She'd been trying to impress him, make him think she was a good person. "I told Luke I was helping you. That's all."

"Luke Randall? He took her to homecoming Saturday!" She groaned. "Why do boys make you so stupid?"

You should talk, August thought, but she didn't say it. She didn't want to sink that low. "He paid me to teach him how to write a song. I don't know how he figured out—"

"It doesn't matter." Mavis's face was stone, but tears spilled down her cheeks. "I told her it wasn't true. That I was the one helping *you*."

It took August a second to realize what she was implying. "You said what?"

Mavis covered her face and started crying. "It slipped out!"

August yanked Mavis's hands down so she could see her eyes. "What did you tell Jessica?"

"That it was you. You had the abortion."

Someone gasped. August turned to find Birdie staring at them, horrified. Jojo stood a few steps behind her, but she wasn't looking at August. She kept her eyes on her mother.

Birdie yanked open the closet door and started shoving August's clothes around, like there were more secrets in the coats and jeans pockets. "What am I gonna find?"

"Nothing," August said. She sat on the bed, watching her grandmother unravel. Jojo hovered in the doorway, arms folded, with an expression August had never seen before. Her mother seemed angry, but also a little scared.

Birdie faced August. "How long has Mavis been lying for you?"

August took her time answering. They'd only heard the end of the conversation, but Mavis had been terrified, seconds from confessing. She wasn't built for this kind of trouble. The fallout would crush her.

"Just this once," August said quietly. She glanced at Jojo. "There's nothing else."

"I don't believe you." Birdie whirled around and yanked more clothes onto the floor. "You've been sleeping with that boy. That *Luke*. You killed his baby!"

"It wasn't a baby," Jojo said.

Birdie glared at her. "You be quiet."

"Don't get mad at her," August said. "I did this."

Birdie squeezed her eyes shut. "That man lied to me. Silas said he was looking after you."

"Silas?" Jojo rounded on August. "What does he have to do with this?"

August recoiled at first, but then straightened her spine. Silas wasn't Theo. He was family and he loved her. "Silas didn't do anything wrong. He helped me when I needed it."

"Helped you get in trouble, sounds like."

"Well, at least he's *here*," August snapped. Jojo stilled. They had a standoff, until August lowered her eyes and mumbled, "Sorry. I didn't mean that."

"Yes, you did." Jojo looked at Birdie. "You knew about this? That she's been going to Delta Blue?"

Birdie stared at August, her eyes red and shimmering. "Why didn't you tell me?"

The truth was right there, ready to come out and heal things. August could tell them she'd never been pregnant and had lied to protect her cousin. But Mavis didn't cause this. None of it would have happened if August hadn't said what she did to Luke.

"You would have tried to make me keep it," August said, which was true. If she'd come home pregnant, Birdie would have emptied August's bank account, put padlocks on the windows, done whatever she could to save her immortal soul. "No one should be forced to—"

"Leave her alone, Mama," Jojo interrupted. Her arms were still folded, but now her nails clawed into her biceps, rippling the skin. "You're making it worse."

"Don't tell me how to discipline a ch—" Birdie stopped, startled, as if she'd just realized the word *child* didn't apply to August anymore. "I raised her."

"But *she's* my mother," August countered.

"*She* tried to kill you! I saved your life!"

Jojo stalked out of the room. August stared at the spot she had abandoned before shoving off the bed and rushing after her. Birdie didn't move.

"Mom! Jojo! I'm sorry."

"Don't apologize to me." Jojo went to her room and grabbed her suitcase. She started packing, throwing linen and silk into a messy pile. "Don't ever apologize for being right. I'm never here. I don't belong and I should stop pretending to."

"Yes, you do." August dug deep, trying to find the version of herself that her mother liked. The funny, interesting girl on the phone calls. "Birdie's just—she didn't mean what she said. You know how she gets about this stuff."

"I do know." Jojo clicked the suitcase shut. "Better than you. She'll never forgive me for any of it. Theo. Having a baby." She looked past August, at the wall. Her voice had changed, anger smoothing into detachment. "I was supposed to die here with her. Now she's got you."

This was like a nightmare August used to have. She was standing next to a tiny crate, and Jojo tried to shove her inside, claiming it was a game. "You'll like it" her mother cooed with a nail and hammer in her hands. August tried to protest, explain what games she actually liked, but she couldn't speak. Silent bubbles floated from her mouth, hovering before they burst in the air.

"I'm not staying here," August told Jojo, because she'd stopped having that dream a long time ago, once she started writing. "Graduation is in a few months, and then...I..."

Jojo raised an eyebrow. "Then what?"

August touched her throat, fingered the necklace Jojo had given her. "I can come with you."

If rejection had a sound, it was the tortured gasp that escaped her mother's lips. "That's your career plan? Freeloading? Taking vacations on my dime?"

"I'm a singer," August told her, because Luke was in her head egging her on, saying she was born for it. "I thought I could...shadow you or something. Meet your people."

Jojo gripped her suitcase with both hands. "I'm gonna tell you what I wish someone had told me before I let them put that crown on my head. This is *your* life. It's happening right now and it's the only one you'll ever have. Stop asking permission. Don't wait to be saved. Fight hard and fight dirty until they're afraid to take anything from you."

Jojo hugged her on the way out. August hugged her back even though she wanted to shove her mother away and rip the necklace from her throat like the spoiled child Jojo had reduced her to. The front door opened and closed. The house was silent. Eventually, August returned to her bedroom and was surprised to find Birdie still there. She sat on the bed, hands folded, calmer than before.

"There you are." She looked past August, into the hallway. "Alone?"

"She's gone," August said. "Re-abandoned me before she left."

Birdie furrowed her brow. "I'm sure it's not as bad as all that."

"She hates me," August said. She kept her eyes on the floor. The way she'd sided with her mother against Birdie made her burn with shame. "Maybe that's why I'm like this. Gullible. Trusting all the wrong people. I just want someone who can look at me and not hate me."

Birdie touched her back. "I don't hate you."

"You lost her because of me," August said, finally meeting her eyes. "I'm what she runs from."

Birdie clasped August's hand and closed her eyes. August jerked away. "Don't pray for me."

"I will *always* pray for you," Birdie said. "I will put a roof over your head, clothes on your back, and food in your body. I'll protect you no matter what." She grabbed August's hand again and pressed it to her chest. "Because you're mine. I love you because you're mine."

August hugged her, buried her face in Birdie's neck. Birdie rubbed her back, shushing and mumbling comfort. "I've got you, baby" she whispered. "My little Johanna."

Homecoming was a blur. Luke could only remember random moments, bits of conversations he couldn't be sure were accurate. He remembered talking to Jessica about August. He remembered waking up the next morning, feeling like he'd done the right thing, only to find out he'd done the opposite. Somehow defending her had put a fresh target on her back. By Monday morning, the entire senior class had lined up with darts.

"It was Richard" was the rumor during first period.

"Wasn't she messing with Luke?" someone asked at lunch.

"It's Coach Ramirez" everyone decided by the end of the day. "That's why he got fired last month."

Luke tried to argue with them. He did try. But it was like telling little kids that it was impossible for Santa to float down a chimney. *You just don't believe in magic* their faces told him. *Don't ruin our fun.*

An apology wouldn't fix things, but he still owed it to her. He tried to call, but no one answered, so he borrowed Silas's car and drove to her house. He didn't want to show up unannounced but there was a ticking clock inside him, counting down to something he didn't want to identify. He only knew it grew louder the longer they were apart.

The house was smaller than he'd imagined. All the Lane women had big personas, so he'd envisioned something sprawling and picturesque, not a skinny white shotgun that looked like something you'd find down in New Orleans. August's car was parked out front, but when the door opened it was Birdie Lane glaring down at him from the porch.

"Can I help you?"

"I'm Luke—Lucas Randall, ma'am. I'm here to see August."

"Jason's boy?"

"Yes. He was my father."

"You look like him." She came down the stairs. "Smell like him, too."

Luke took a step back, even though there was plenty of space between them. He resisted the urge to sniff himself. "I've been staying at Delta Blue," he explained, which sounded better than the truth, that he'd bathed in so much pilfered vodka Saturday night the scent might never wear off.

The door opened again, and August stepped out. She was dressed in jeans and a T-shirt, her typical uniform. Her hair was straight and loose, like it was most days. Seeing her again, looking exactly like herself, made him happy enough to explode. That's how much he missed her. His body was too small to contain it.

"I need to talk to him," she told Birdie.

"He smells like that bar." Birdie blocked his view of August. It was like that night at Delta Blue when Silas stopped him at the door. Another family member walling off the path to her forgiveness.

"We won't be long," August said. She held a journal, the one with "Luke's Song" inside. The sight of it calmed him a little. Birdie was trying to keep them apart because she didn't know. No one had heard their music yet. But they would. He was sure of it.

"Five minutes," Birdie said, before retreating into the house. August watched her with a somber expression that made him nervous. He didn't have a speech planned. The only way to stop a lie from spreading was to tell the truth, something he didn't think August wanted to do. All he had were reasons and explanations. A heart full of hope.

"I tried calling," Luke said once they were alone. "No one an—"

She grabbed his shirt, fisting the fabric at his neck, and pulled him down to her. Their eyes caught and then she kissed him, hard and deep. Luke didn't hesitate, or at least his body didn't. His thoughts were a confused jumble as he pressed closer and kissed her senseless. *Finally*. It was tongues and breath, hand seeking purchase, and bodies welded so tight they started sweating.

"Augustina Lane!"

Luke wrenched away so fast he nearly fell to the ground. Birdie had the screen door open and gaped at them wide eyed and fuming. August smoothed her hair and yelled, "Sorry! Won't happen again!"

"Three minutes," Birdie said, and motioned for them to separate.

Luke complied, but August stayed where she was, watching him through her lashes. Once Birdie left, she said, "I'm mad at you."

"Oh?" His stomach sank.

"But only because I love you. So it's okay."

He was already unsteady from her kiss. Now she'd split him open. "I love you too," he said, and his voice was gruff, coated with rust. That's what happened when you held something in for so long.

His answer made her happy. It was a brief shimmer, but definitely there. Then the somberness was back. "Birdie's sick," she said. Luke looked up at the house, at the place where her grandmother was just standing, and she added, "You can't tell. Mild cognitive impairment, they said. Rare at her age. They're running tests."

That internal clock started up again, counting down, warning him to get ready. Here it comes. "I'm so sorry."

"That's why I missed school. I'll probably have to do that a lot. Take her to appointments. Work. She's gotten lost a few times, nothing major, but now she's afraid to drive."

"I could help," Luke said quickly. "Drive her around. Take some of the load off you."

"It has to be me. If I'd been around more maybe…" She looked at the journal in her hands. Luke kept his eyes on her face, refusing to acknowledge what she was implying, that they should feel guilty about finding each other. There was nothing to regret.

"You couldn't stop it," he told her. "There's nothing you can do."

"We like to think that don't we? When it's hard? But there's always something." She offered him the notebook. He didn't take it. They stayed like that for a moment, then August said, "Could you hold on to it? I don't have time for music right now. Taking care of Birdie, plus school and graduation—"

"What are you saying to me?" She'd just kissed him. Said I love you. Now he was being dumped? What kind of story was that? They couldn't skip the part where they tried.

"She needs me right now. More than you."

Right. So that was his mistake, letting her think he was fine. That he'd come here standing upright instead of on his knees. "You need time," he said. "I get it. Take all the time you need."

She offered the journal again. "Luke—"

"*Do not* give that to me!" he snapped. "I never paid for it. It's not mine."

"I never wanted your money." August smiled. "I just wanted you to like me."

She pressed the journal into his hands. Giving him the notebook was a request for space. And he had to respect that, even if it meant he couldn't keep her.

Or at least, not all of her.

Luke took the journal. "It worked. I like you more than anyone, I think."

She kissed his cheek, destroyed him one more time, then returned to the house.

Luke got into his truck and sat for a while. He couldn't feel the clock ticking anymore, probably because there never was one. That was just his heart breaking.

CHAPTER TWENTY-ONE

2023

Luke stayed late to help Silas close Delta Blue after open mic night, so he was surprised to see August's car when he returned to Birdie's house. It was nearly two in the morning. The lights were on and music greeted him when he walked inside. She sat on the couch, reading the album sleeve for *Color Me Country*. Linda Martell's cover of "I Almost Called Your Name" flowed from the speakers.

"I blame her," August said. She moved to the record player and stopped the music. "Linda was the reason Jojo became a country singer, even though everyone kept telling her not to." She glanced at Luke. "Have you ever heard of her?"

"Of course." Luke picked up the album and flipped it over to study the track list. "Is this an original copy?"

"Silas gave it to me." She looked at an open box of albums near the record player. "These are mine. I put them away because it hurt to look at them."

"I'm sorry. I got bored and started rifling through closets."

"It's okay." She stared at the album sleeve. "Linda performed at the Opry twelve times. *Twelve*. Then everyone forgot about her. Like she was never there."

"Like *we* were never there," Luke added. Like most country fans, he'd grown up listening to superstars like Dolly Parton and Willie Nelson, white singers he heard on the radio. Although he enjoyed their music, hearing it had never inspired him to follow in their footsteps. Listening to Jojo's albums did that. Silas's Black history lessons made him question every assumption he'd made about what country was supposed to sound like. Working with August made him want to write his own.

"That's one of the reasons I couldn't stop thinking about you," August said. "After that night at the fair. I couldn't get over it being *you* gushing about 'Island's in the Stream.' It made me feel..."

"Seen? Me too."

She removed the Linda Martell record and flipped through her albums, slowly walking her fingers over each one. Luke watched her with a growing uneasiness. August wasn't a patient person. When she did anything this slowly, it was to avoid what came next.

Eventually she settled on Ray Charles and used the tonearm to find "I Love You So Much It Hurts."

Goddamn. Was it that bad? "Is something wrong?"

She let the intro play, waiting until Ray finished crooning about his blues before she answered. "David offered me your spot. Same duet and everything."

Luke kept his face stoic but shoved his hands into his pockets. They were his worst tell. His fingers were already twitching, eager to grab hold of something. Like he could stop her from slipping away.

"Same publicity, too," he said, with a light chuckle that felt more like ripping himself open and pretending it tickled. "Same shot at a record deal."

"Same, same," she singsonged, but it sounded bitter. "It's what I always wanted."

"I know."

"But I have to stay away from you."

He swallowed a surge of hurt. "Figured."

Earlier that day, Luke had received a voicemail from his old record label that forbade him from speaking to August directly. Shut your mouth while we handle this was the gist, which meant they planned to use strong-arm tactics to discourage her from suing. Luke had deleted it and ordered David to get her an attorney and publicist. It made sense that whatever team David put together considered him the enemy.

"You knew this would happen, didn't you? When you sent that recording."

Luke looked out the window at the sky. It was sprinkled with stars. He'd missed that, living in the city. Once she left, he'd have to focus on the little things to keep going. Cold comfort was still comfort. He may have lost her, but he still had the stars.

"David knows talent when he hears it. Glad he was smart enough to listen."

August paced a little, her brow wrinkled like she was thinking hard about something. Luke was done with all that. He was in sensory mode now, focused only on what he could see, smell, and hear. Like the mysterious creamy scent beneath her floral perfume. Or how that yellow dress gave her skin a subtle glow. He didn't want to miss any of it worrying about things he couldn't control.

"I said I never wanted to see you again once this was over. But I didn't mean it."

He could tell she was rewinding that first day, reliving all the anger flowing between them. Whenever he pictured it, they were different people. Some liar with his face spouted nonsense about money and copyrights. The woman threatening him was too cruel to have ever written a love song. "You were mad at me."

"Only because I love you. I never stopped. I don't think I ever will." She folded her arms as if she were holding herself together. Good for her, because he was in pieces. Maybe if he'd let himself think about it, hope for a miracle, it would have occurred to him that all that hate August had spewed wasn't hate at all. It was her love inside out—battered, bloody, and unrecognizable. It was her saying *See what you did? How you left me?*

"I'll always love you too." He moved closer, ready to hold her, but she shook her head. Her eyes were liquid, filled with tears she held back with stubbornness.

"I was horrible to you. I called you a coward and you gave me roses."

"Everything you said about me was true."

"No, it wasn't. I read that article. Sharing all that with the world? That's the bravest thing I've ever seen."

Luke didn't want the compliment. Showing up was the bare minimum, wasn't it? She'd always been the brave one—the warrior. It had taken him more than a decade to figure out what to fight for. "I'm not—"

"I saw you perform tonight," she said. "You were gorgeous up there. So peaceful. I stole that from you."

"No, you didn't. I can play anytime I want, just not..." His voice trailed as the reality of his situation slammed home. His career was over. No one in their right mind would book him to sing a stolen song. Once the lawyers got involved, he'd be bankrupt, too. "What I lost wasn't mine."

"I never would have told anyone you lied."

"I know," he said. "That's why I had to."

Tears slid down her cheeks. "I'm sorry for threatening you. It was so pointless and...shitty."

He smiled. "Good people do shitty things sometimes." He pulled her closer and smoothed her hair back behind her ear. "Especially when they're lonely."

"Is that why I did it? Because I'm lonely?"

"Yeah." He stroked her cheek. "But I'm here now."

Luke kissed her. And it wasn't like the first time all those years ago, which had gone so fast it was a memory longer than a moment. It wasn't even like last week, when it was hard to tell whether they were kissing or fighting. This was the kiss in his daydreams. The patient, thorough exploration of a man with all the time in the world.

He licked deep and slow, drinking her in. She moaned into his mouth, and the sound reverberated at his core. He tugged her head back, devouring everything, even her gasps. That was how empty he'd been. He'd never get enough.

She put her hands on his chest and leaned back. "Are we doing this? Or will you change your mind again, remember to be good and noble?"

This was how she dealt with tension, by cutting it with a joke. He couldn't let her do that. Not tonight. So he let go of his guilt, his *good and noble* compulsion to do the right thing, because fuck it, this might be the *only* thing they could ever have.

"I'll be what you want." He pulled her against him so she could feel how much he meant it. "You want me weak? I'll be that. You want to hurt a little?" He tightened his grip, and she shivered. "I can do that, too." He brushed his lips along her neck. "Use me. I'll be anything you need."

She grabbed his nape and let her head loll to one side. He pressed kisses to her shoulder, her collarbone, her jaw. When they finally locked eyes, hers were slick pools of moonlight. "This is going to sound strange."

"Tell me."

She suddenly looked younger. Like whatever she was struggling with had stripped away her confidence. "I've never been with someone who loves me before," she said. "I've never been...touched that way. I don't know what it feels like."

Luke took her hand. "Let me show you."

August was never nervous about sex, not since she'd been a teenager struggling to articulate her needs during backseat groping sessions in high school. You can't tell a guy how to please you if you don't know yourself. Now she was an expert communicator. Condoms and lube required. No socks, please. Touch me there and it'll ruin the mood. And most men, the confident ones anyway, appreciated the clear guidance. She'd hand over her body but never her heart and disappear inside her own pleasure long enough to make life bearable.

That felt good. Safe. Nothing like the frenzy she felt with Luke. No one kissed her the way he did, like a lost man in the dark chasing light. His lust was a big, yawning thing that wanted to swallow her whole and she welcomed it, was seconds from begging to be his possession. The idea of belonging to someone used to be scary, something she would run from.

"What made you start wearing dresses?" Luke kept his eyes on her while he closed the blinds. August hovered near the door, so unsure of herself that she couldn't fully commit to being inside the bedroom. It had been being used for storage before he'd moved in. Luke had cleared out the boxes and covered the queen-size bed with a white quilt. A copy of *The Fire Next Time* was on the nightstand, his place kept with a skinny silver bookmark.

"I've always liked them," August said, running her hand down the front of her cotton minidress. The marigold empire waist showed more cleavage than usual, which had felt appropriate for a night at Delta Blue. Now as Luke's eyes raked over her, she was more aware of how much skin it exposed. "I didn't wear them in high school because—"

"Boys are idiots?" He dimmed the lamp, still watching her. "And you in a dress made them dumber than they were on a good day?"

She fidgeted, rubbed her neck, and shoved hair off her shoulder. Luke made a low sound in the back of his throat. "This is gonna be harder than I thought."

"What is?"

"Being patient. Waiting to have you."

"You don't have to wait," she said quickly. He could grab her, pin her to the wall. Thinking about it lit her skin on fire.

"Uh-uh," he said, with a half grin that tried to yank her heart out. "Not tonight. You asked to learn something, so come here and let me teach you."

She sat on the edge of the bed and was surprised when he didn't join her. Instead, he knelt on the floor. He was tall enough that it brought them face to face. "I really like your dresses," he said, fingering her skirt. She watched, mesmerized, as he stroked it with reverence, as if it were an extension of her skin. "So soft. Like you." He met her eyes. "But not fragile."

She thought of his earlier offer to make it hurt. The good kind that scrambled your senses. "Not fragile," she said, answering the implied question. He was big all over. Strong. But their encounter last week had showed her the delicious potential of his contradictions. Luke would be cautious with his strength. He'd never leave a bruise if he held her in place.

He hooked his hand behind her knees and pulled until her thighs were at his waist. She lifted her hips so she could feel him, but he stayed out of reach. He ran his palms slowly up and down her thighs, pushing her dress up a little higher each time until her legs were bare. "Where'd you get this skin?" he asked, but it wasn't a real question. It was bearing witness. He hunched low and pressed kisses against her thighs. His beard grazed her, prickly through her thin underwear, and she wanted more.

She wanted to grab his neck and put his mouth on her, but instead she fisted the fitted sheet. It popped free from the mattress. Luke kissed her knee, then straightened to look at her. "You okay, sweetheart?"

"Call me that again and I'm pinning you to the ground."

He laughed, deep and rumbling. She leaned forward and kissed his neck and felt the vibrations dancing on her tongue. Luke's voice had always worked magic inside her. Laughing. Singing. It cast her favorite spell.

He untied the straps around her neck. The dress collapsed, revealing her strapless bra. He nudged the fabric farther down until it bunched at her waist, then leaned back and hissed "Jesus" in a way that sounded more like a prayer than a curse. She looked down at herself, trying to see her body through his eyes. The bra was sheer lace but lined with industrial-strength under wire to hold her breasts in place. She hated how difficult it was to find pretty, delicate lingerie in her size. "I can take it off."

"Don't touch it." He traced the wire at the top, the shallow indention it made on her skin. "You're fucking beautiful," he muttered. "Do you even see it?"

She tried to, but all she could see was how her flesh puckered and rolled in places it never used to. It made her self-conscious. Luke must have noticed because his lips thinned, and he sat beside her on the bed. He pointed to the dresser mirror and said, "Look."

August was startled by her reflection. Arousal made her skin luminous in the lamplight. The sheer bra was lurid next to the guileless cheer of her yellow dress.

Luke moved behind her, one hand splayed over her stomach. He pulled her hair back and kissed her shoulder, mimicking her gentle nips and licks from earlier. The cool air pumping through the vents made her shiver. Luke noticed and rubbed her arms until the gooseflesh disappeared.

"Why are you so sweet?" she muttered, then leaned back to kiss him. "So good."

"Is that right?" He put his hand between her legs, inside her panties, and strummed a rhythm that had to be a direct path to damnation. "Is that good, too?"

August moaned and let her head fall back against his chest. "*Yes.* But it's not—" He stole her sentence with a gentle tug that made her gasp, then soothed her with more gentle stroking. "*Yes.* More of that."

Luke took her at her word. Soon she was splayed over his lap, sweating and squirming while he fingered her, his other hand exploring her breasts. But he wouldn't let her come. She pleaded, begged for relief. "Not yet" was all he'd say each time he brought her to the brink.

Eventually he nudged her back onto the mattress and finished removing her clothes. He took his time, caressing and kissing each part he exposed. Then his mouth was between her legs and there was no way she could stop what came next. She couldn't revel in the hot sweep of his tongue, or the greedy sounds he made, like he'd found ambrosia. He was too good at this. Or she was too easy. Either way, Luke's mouth was her undoing, and she yelled in frustration, bucking against his chin as she came in record time.

"Do you feel it now?" He yanked his shirt over his head. His body was covered with tattoos that extended down his sides and stomach. "How much I love you?" He kissed her before she could answer. Their tongues twined and danced while he yanked at his jeans. "Do you feel it?"

She shoved his pants over his hips, and his hands trembled as he ripped open a condom. She loved seeing him so out of control, that she'd made him that way. August took it from him and rolled it on, cupping and stroking him once she was done. He took a hard breath, his back bowing as if the pleasure hurt. Like she'd broken him in all the right places.

He pushed inside her, and the slow stretch was torture, the friction bliss. Luke braced himself on his hands to watch her, rolling his hips in a measured, teasing grind. "Am I still good?"

"No. You're fucking evil."

He laughed, then hitched her knee up to his hip, and gave her exactly what she wanted: steady, deep strokes that pinned her to the mattress.

She grabbed his neck and propped herself up to whisper in his ear. "Yes, I feel it. I knew you'd feel like this."

He thrust faster, harder, reached between them to stroke her clit. She came without warning, a sudden pressure that burst into waves. Luke chased his release with rapid, shallow thrusts and watching him catch it was breathtaking. He groaned and shuddered, gasped her name like it was fire in his mouth, then collapsed on the bed. They lay together in silence, limbs entangled, until their breathing returned to a normal rhythm.

August lifted her head to look at him. His face was slack and sated, his eyes heavy slits. She wanted to keep this more than anything, more than the concert, the money, her name in lights. She rubbed his chin, sliding her fingers through his beard, and whispered, "Thank you for coming back to me."

"I had to." He took her hand and kissed her fingertips. "You're my home."

PART EIGHT

THE OUTRO

This Is Our Country: Podcast Transcript

Episode 12—"Jojo Lane"
August 21, 2024

[*cont.*]

Emma: Have you heard Charlotte Turner's version of "Invisible"?

Jojo: Of course. It was inescapable for a while. One journalist played it on his phone while he was interviewing me.

Emma: Okay, that's rude.

Jojo: He wanted a very specific reaction.

Emma: Which was?

Jojo: Oh, you know. Clickbait. A little Black rage to feed the news cycle.

Emma: Which you didn't give him.

Jojo: Didn't have any. She isn't the first white woman to cover one of my songs. She won't be the last.

Emma: That is true. I hear them all the time.

Jojo: They're all deep cuts, though. No lead singles.

Emma: Why do you think that is? The deep-cut thing. They never intended to release Charlotte's cover. It only got attention because—

Jojo: You wrote about it.

Emma: Right. She said the song had personal meaning. Maybe she was trying to keep it private in a way.

Jojo: I don't know. And to be honest with you, I don't care. There. You got the clickbait. Jojo Lane doesn't give a shit about why that girl sang her song.

Emma: We can move on if you like.

Jojo: Hold on. I want to tell you why. I don't care because it's not for me. I'm not her audience. And that's okay. Music isn't supposed to speak to everyone. You lose the point if you try.

Emma: The point?

Jojo: The message. The heart. If you're not speaking to a certain someone, you're speaking to no one. Charlotte wasn't talking to me when she sang about feeling invisible. She was talking to a girl dealing with things thirty-something white girls deal with these days.

Emma: Wow. Lots to unpack there. Don't you think some themes are universal?

Jojo: I'm not talking about themes. Themes grab your attention, but they don't hold it. Someone sings a revenge song, and your brain says, I know this story. I've listened to "Goodbye Earl" and "Before He Cheats." I like songs like these because they remind me of my no-good ex. This is gonna be worth my time. But then the song plays, and the story gets specific in a way that either pulls you closer because it feels like your truth or pushes you away because it feels like someone else's. Some people get angry when their experience is shoved to the margins.

Emma: As a queer woman, I've gotten used to being shoved into margins. I'm sure you have, too.

Jojo: No, we expect it. But we don't like it any more than they do. Black folks who have never heard me before get excited about the idea of a Black country singer. But then they put my song on and that pedal steel winds up the intro and I lose them. They decide it's not for them before two words come out of my mouth.

Emma: Does that bother you?

Jojo: No. Or... I don't know, sometimes. Like I wish more people heard "Invisible" the way I sing it first. Then they might have heard what I was saying. Who I was talking to.

CHAPTER TWENTY-TWO

2009

Luke went to the farm to see Ethan. But he drank whiskey before he left because he hadn't been there since he woke up bleeding on the floor. By the time he arrived, he felt good enough to saunter up the steps. It was Tuesday, a Bible study night for Ava and her sanctified boyfriend. Ethan opened the door, and when Luke saw his little brother's face, healthy and clear of visible injuries, it was a relief.

"Luke!" Ethan threw his arms around his waist. Luke held on tight and rocked a little before stepping back.

"How are things going?"

"I'm okay. I mean, as okay as possible. She's using more. I think she misses you."

Resentment and despair bubbled up together, but Luke easily choked them down thanks to the magic of Jim Beam. "I'll call her once I'm settled."

Ethan's face brightened. "Right. Hold on." He went to his bedroom. Luke remained standing, unwilling to sit on a couch with bloodstained cushions. Someone had tried to clean the floral fabric, but there were pink splotches between the pastel petals.

Ethan returned with an overstuffed backpack. "I wasn't sure when you'd come for me, so I figured it was good to be prepared." He gave Luke a flyer. It was an advertisement for *Country Star* auditions. Ethan had written notes on the back, lists of bus routes and Nashville hostels.

Coming back this soon had been a mistake. He should have given his brother more time to cool off after everything that had happened. Ethan still had that look in his eyes, like plan B was burning the house down.

"I know you said you didn't want to be on TV, but what if we tried together? Two Black kids has to be different enough to get some attention, right? I can do a cowbell and I've been working on spoons—"

"You're not going anywhere." Luke tried to give the flyer back, but Ethan refused to take it. Luke stuffed it into his jeans. "Not until you head off to college."

"I'm not staying here with her."

"You're too young." Ethan ignored him and grabbed his backpack. Luke snatched it from his hand. "They'd come after me for taking you. Accuse me of kidnapping."

"Show them her stash!" Ethan shouted. "Tell them about the closet she used to lock us in. Tell them there's never any fucking food in this house!"

"They'd still take you away." Luke kept his voice calm and even, hoping Ethan would listen. "You want to end up in foster care?"

"I want to be with you." Ethan's eyes filled with tears. "Please don't leave me, Luke."

There was a moth on the ceiling, and Luke fixed his eyes on it to keep from breaking down. Both of them bawling in the living room wouldn't fix anything. Only time could do that. A plan and some purpose. "It's not permanent," he told Ethan. "Just until you're done with school." Luke smiled, trying to get Ethan on board with his vision. It was as clear as a photograph. Him wiser. Ethan older. Their frictionless escape from this life. "I'll use my dad's money to pay for your college. It's not much, but it'll buy books and pizza. That stuff adds up."

Ethan didn't smile back. He twisted his hands and said, "She didn't tell you?"

"Tell me what?"

"That money's gone. She closed your account when you left."

Luke heard him, but only in fragments, like a faulty connection over the telephone. "She closed my account?"

Ethan looked nervous. "Yeah. Like I told you earlier, she's been using more. That's how she could afford it."

What Ethan was telling him finally registered just as the front door opened and Ava walked inside. Her boyfriend stood behind her. Don wore a white shirt and khaki pants, with a gold class ring that glinted on one hand. A set of car keys was held in daggers between his fingers.

"What are you doing here?" he asked Luke, with the keys half raised and ready to use as a weapon.

"Visiting my brother." Luke glanced at Ethan, who was focused on Ava. She hid behind her boyfriend's arm.

Don curled his upper lip. "Right. A friendly visit. Nothing to do with us clearing out that bank account, huh?"

Luke stared at him. "That was you?"

"We didn't steal it," Ava said quickly. "My name was on the account, so it's half mine."

"We're not keeping it all," Don said. "Just the half that belongs to your mama. The rest'll go to your college fund."

"What fund?" Luke flung a hand at Ava. "She spends everything on fucking pills!"

"I'm sick!" Ava shouted. "You know I'm sick."

Ethan snorted and rolled his eyes. Don glared at him, but Luke sidestepped to block his view. "Knock it off," he whispered to Ethan.

"Don't tell me what to do."

"Both of you boys need to learn some manners." Don pointed to the hallway. "Ethan, go to your room."

"Fuck off."

Don reached for his belt. Ava's eyes flew to Luke, and whatever she saw on his face made her touch Don's arm. "Not right now."

"Discipline needs to be swift to be effective." Don yanked his belt from the loops. He folded it in half and slapped his palm. The sound flipped a switch in Luke's head.

"You touch him, and I'll kill you."

Don went still. "Don't threaten me."

Ava stepped between them. "Luke, you should leave."

"Give me back my money," Luke said to Ava. "Dad left it for me."

"He left it for *us*," she snapped. "You didn't even know him. And thank God, he died before you—"

Luke grabbed her arms and held her still. He was trembling, fighting the urge to shake her. "Stop," he said, his voice cracking. "Please, Mom. Stop."

"Get your hands off her!" Luke's back caught fire as Don hit him with his belt buckle. Luke spun around as the man wound up to hit him again. He grabbed Don's wrist and twisted, then slammed his fist into his face.

Ava screamed. Don stumbled back, arms flailing, and crashed into Ethan. Luke watched helplessly as his little brother fell into the coffee table.

"Call the police," Don groaned, crouched on the floor. His nose was gushing blood. When Ava didn't move, he screamed at her. "Call them now!"

She jumped to action, rushing into her bedroom to retrieve the cordless. Luke crouched beside Ethan, checking him for injuries.

"Get out of here," Ethan said, while staring past him to where Ava crouched next to Don. Don jerked the phone from her hand and jabbed at the numbers, dialing 911. Ava looked at Luke, flicked her eyes at the open front door, and mouthed, "*Go.*"

Luke kissed Ethan's forehead and mumbled "I'm sorry" before he ran out the door.

Delta Blue was crowded, so no one noticed when Luke slipped into the studio and started packing. He had to leave town, get far enough away from Arcadia to figure out what to do next. Don wasn't like Richard, who was too embarrassed about losing a fight to press charges. Ava's boyfriend was righteous, a terrible trait for a man who viewed the world with the compassion of a debt collector. He only cared about what it owed him.

Someone knocked at the door. Luke remained silent, hoping they'd think the room was empty. But then Silas said "Bill's here" and Luke's shoulders collapsed. There was no window to crawl through. Nowhere to hide. He had to open the door.

"I need to call August," he told Silas, who immediately shook his head.

"No time for that." Silas grabbed his duffel. "Come on."

They walked into the club, weaving through oblivious customers to where Bill Parnell stood in full uniform near the entrance. A few people looked their way, but they were used to cops hovering around their good time, so Bill's presence was met with a collective shrug. Silas locked eyes with Bill, who then gave Luke a stern nod of acknowledgment. "You ready?" Luke shook his head, and Bill sighed. "Yeah. Stupid question. Let's go."

Silas clapped a hand on Luke's shoulder and walked him outside. They stopped in front of the cruiser. Bill stuffed Luke's bag in the trunk. "Don't look back," Silas said. "Eyes forward, you hear me?"

Luke stared at him, realizing that Silas had been here before, on his way to a jail cell. "Is that how you handled it?"

"No. So I know what I'm talking about." He stood between Luke and the police car. "Some of this is your fault. But most of it isn't. Try to remember that."

Silas hugged him. Luke's throat tightened as they parted. He could feel himself reverting to the guy he was before he met August. The one who could never find the right words. "I'll call you when I can."

Luke climbed into the back seat. The door slammed, shrouding him in darkness. It was hard to breathe. "Can you roll the windows down?" Bill glanced over his shoulder through the grid now separating them. Luke added "Please, sir?" because it felt appropriate. They weren't neighbors anymore. They weren't friends.

"I can crack it," Bill said. "Can't let anyone see you, though."

The drive was longer than he expected. When Bill finally let him out, Luke was surprised to see they were at a bus stop. "What are we doing here?"

Bill didn't answer. He moved to the trunk, then pulled out Luke's bag and his guitar. "Here you go."

"I thought you were arresting me."

"So did Don. We went to school together. He's always been a whiny bitch." Bill pulled out a bus ticket and an envelope of money. "This'll get you to Little Rock. Not sure how much money Silas sent, but it'll pay for a place to stay."

Luke took the ticket and the money. "Why are you doing this?"

"Because your dad was my best friend. I loved him, which means I love you too." He tugged his hat down over his ears. "And there's a right way to do that."

He climbed into the car and drove away.

The bus was leaving in half an hour. Luke pulled out the cell phone he'd recently purchased. He flipped it open and dialed August's number. Birdie answered on the second ring.

"Hello?"

Nothing came out when he opened his mouth. She must have heard him breathing.

"Lucas Randall, is that you?"

"Yes, ma'am." He swallowed hard. "Can I speak to August, please?"

Birdie was quiet for a long time. "What do you think will happen if you do that?"

She knew what he'd done. Silas must have told her or maybe it was on the news, some all-points bulletin labeling him a fugitive. "She'd find me," he said, which is what he wanted. He wanted August to run away with him, share whatever terrible life was at the end of this bus route so he wouldn't be alone.

"I can't let her do that. Do you understand?"

"Yes." He blinked, blinded by tears. "Yes, ma'am, but could you… could you tell her I lo—"

The phone clicked and he heard a dial tone.

Mavis and August sat across from each other with barely touched dinner plates as Birdie wiped down the counter, pretending she wasn't eavesdropping. August wasn't eager to talk, but Mavis kept tossing her anxious looks while picking at her spaghetti.

"Are y'all hungry? I can fix you something," Birdie said.

Mavis's eyes darted to her plate and then to Birdie's back. "No, ma'am?" It was a confused question, and August waved her hand, signaling that she should ignore it.

"Not good for young girls to skip…" Birdie's voice trailed off when she spotted their full plates. She rubbed her face and walked past them, out of the kitchen. "Let me know if you need anything."

They were silent until she was gone. Mavis stared after her. "Did she forget making us dinner?"

August didn't want to talk about Birdie's memory issues. Not until they had a diagnosis. "She's distracted."

"Does that happen a lot? She's only fifty-seven."

"Things have been stressful lately."

They fell silent again. Mavis cleared her throat and said, "We should talk about it."

August picked up her fork and stabbed a green bean. "Why?"

"Because that's what normal people do."

"I shouldn't have told Luke anything. I'm sorry I did that."

Mavis's face crumpled. Tears started flowing. "Jessica threw it in my face. She sounded so happy when she said it, like she'd caught me being evil. I would have said anything to make her stop."

"It's okay."

"You've always been tougher than me, so I thought—"

"It's okay." August raised her voice to stop her. "I forgive you."

Mavis's mouth fell open. "What? Why?"

"Because it feels worse not to. You're the only person in this family that gets me."

"I don't understand you at all."

"I don't understand you, either. But see how we both get that? That's more precious than a grudge."

Mavis burst out laughing. "You're so weird. But you're also amazing." She sighed. "I don't get what you see in Luke."

August ran her hands over the table. "It's a long story."

"Have you spoken to him since it happened?"

"Since what happened?"

Mavis looked surprised. "He got arrested."

August stilled. "What?"

Mavis told her what she'd heard from friends. Luke had attacked his family and run away. "I heard they're charging him with assault. Maybe attempted murder."

August remembered what she said to him, all that stuff about needing time and space. What did that even mean? She was sitting here eating Ragú, for fuck's sake. He was out there, dealing with this alone.

"I have to find him."

"Don't!" Mavis grabbed her arm. "He could be dangerous. This isn't the first time he's hurt someone."

August ignored her. She grabbed her keys and rushed out the door. Ten minutes later, she pulled into Delta Blue at high speed. It was late, and the club was still crowded, but Silas stood outside, like he was waiting for her.

"Where is he?"

"Gone," Silas said. "Bill put him on a bus a while ago."

"To where?" Silas didn't answer. They faced off until her control snapped, and she shouted, "Tell me!"

"I gave him some money," Silas said. "I don't know what he did with it."

She looked at the empty road as if it could tell her what her uncle wouldn't. "Did he leave a message for me? A letter or... a notebook? Something with songs in it?" There would be new music notes alongside a city and date. He would have drawn her a map.

Silas sighed. "August..."

"Anything?" Her voice was rising again. If it was possible for someone to rip themselves apart, she'd do it. It'd feel better than this. "Did he mention me at all?"

Silas looked away, which answered her question. Luke had taken the money and run. "He would have left you something if he had time," he said. "That boy loves you."

"No, he doesn't." A sob clogged her throat, and she choked it down. She'd never cry over Luke Randall again. "If he did, he would have waited. He would have stayed."

CHAPTER TWENTY-THREE

2023

Luke prided himself on being a good cook, but desserts had never been his strong suit. No matter what he did, the three layers of devil's food cake remained lopsided. He thought adding the icing would help, but the glossy chocolate cream cheese only highlighted his mistakes.

He should get used to that. According to the internet, he was the biggest fraud since Milli Vanilli. There was a petition to add a worst songwriter of the year category to the Golden Raspberry Awards, even though he hadn't released anything new this year. That was how bad his career was going. They wanted to change the rules to memorialize his fuck up.

"Do I smell cake?"

August walked into the kitchen just as he added the candle. It was a red-and-white thirty-two that he'd planned to light before waking her. She stopped when she saw it, her expression unreadable, and for the first time since he found Birdie's recipe card, he doubted his decision to surprise her. It didn't go so well the last time he'd tried.

"It's my birthday," she said, in a way that sounded like both a statement and a question.

He gestured at the brown monstrosity he'd created. "It looks worse than it tastes. I used your grandmother's recipe, so—"

"This is Birdie's devil's food?" She studied the cake more closely. She was wearing his T-shirt and nothing else. Her hair was a fluffy, wiry mess. She looked so sated and thoroughly loved-on that a rush of pride flowed through him, swiftly followed by the desire to do it again.

"Yeah." He tried to focus on the cake. "It's all the ingredients, anyway." He grabbed the recipe card and showed it to her. "She didn't leave any instructions on how to decorate it, though."

August held the card carefully, as if it could crumble in her hands. "Everyone loved her cakes," she said softly. "After a while, she couldn't make them without help. I tried." She shook her head. "But it wasn't the same. She'd get so frustrated because they were never right."

Luke put his arms around her, pulled her into him. "I didn't mean to make you sad."

"You didn't," she said. "I miss her. I always will." She leaned back to look at him. "But I'm also grateful. I always tried to ignore this day. But she never let me." She glanced at the table. "It's the perfect gift."

Luke kissed her temple. "Don't thank me until you taste it."

They sat next to each other with plates of cake. Luke grabbed his fork but waited until she took the first bite. She made a soft, pleased sound. "Perfection."

He ate some and agreed. Ugly or not, it was damn good. "I'll make some eggs and bacon before you head to rehearsal."

August stopped chewing. "What?"

"A message came through on your phone. I wasn't spying. Just saw it when I was cleaning up." Her notifications were flooded with people trying to reach her. David, in particular, had resorted to all caps, demanding confirmation that she would perform with Jojo.

August put her fork down. "What if I say no?"

Luke paused, but then took another bite of cake. He couldn't feed her fear with his pining. They weren't children anymore. "Not an option."

"It's not your decision."

"This is what you've always wanted. You're about to perform with your mother."

She slumped in her chair like a sullen child. For August, any mention of Jojo would always rewind time a little. "It wasn't her idea," she said. "This was David doing damage control. Pulling strings behind the scenes."

"That's how this stuff works."

"I hate it," she said. "All of it. They told me I couldn't work with you. What kind of dream is worth having if it breaks your heart?"

Luke grabbed her hand. "Let me tell you a story."

She rolled her eyes. "Don't."

"Once upon a time, there was this beautiful, talented, but stubborn little girl—"

"Enough. I get it."

"Who couldn't take a compliment," he continued. "Because she didn't hear them enough. So even though the girl was all those things, she hid them from the world because she didn't feel entitled to them. And everyone around her, whether or not they meant to, constantly confirmed that. She had a thunderclap of a voice, and all they knew about storms was that they were dangerous. Something to be avoided."

She propped her cheek on her fist and gave him soft eyes. "So, who are you in this story?"

"Oh, I'm the cautionary tale. I'm the boy who bumbles around, not even knowing storms exist until I'm standing in the eye of the most beautiful hurricane in creation. But I don't know what to do with it. I try to hold it in my arms, but that's not what hurricanes are made for. You can't keep a force of nature."

Luke leaned over to brush cake crumbs from her lips. "Everyone gets it now. They're offering you what you're owed. A record deal. Maybe a tour—"

"They haven't offered me anything."

"They will," he said. "And when they do, it'll be your happy ending."

She bit her lip. He could tell she was softening, bowing to his logic. "But is it yours?"

When Luke thought of August, there was always a whispered hope he'd refused to listen to, fearing it would overwhelm him. Now he let it surge forward, painting images he'd avoided for years. Her in a white wedding dress. The house they chose together. Rooms filled with photos and trinkets, evidence of their shared life. He saw her laughing and happy, nursing babies that had her big, dark eyes. Their life sprawled before him, years of learning each other until there was nothing frantic in how they touched. Just quiet knowing.

That ending, the selfish joy of letting her throw everything away for him, squeezed him so tight he couldn't breathe. But he didn't tell her any of that. He touched her face and asked, "Do you love me?"

August didn't hesitate. "Yes."

"Do you trust me?"

Again, there was barely a beat before her answer. "Yes."

"Then yeah. It's also mine."

When Luke left to help Silas with the club, August was alone long enough to give in to the temptation to search her name online. Aside from a few caustic social media posts, most of it was positive. A major news outlet ran an article with a candid picture of her at the fairgrounds. It was the day she'd confronted Luke onstage and everything exploded. She was in profile, steps from the microphone. Beside it was a picture of Jojo performing at her last concert. Her mother's arms were outstretched, her long hair lifted by a wind machine.

The article summarized the controversy surrounding Jojo's award and included a link to another piece about Luke's confession. August didn't click on it. Those articles all read the same, as snide jabs at his integrity along with a cursory nod to his youth and subsequent battle with addiction. Instead, August focused on the effusive praise the media was giving Jojo for adding August to the lineup. "Bringing her daughter onstage will be a pivotal moment for the genre. It's a nod to the erasure of Black artists the industry has yet to answer for. What was stolen will be reclaimed when the Lane women sing *their* version of 'Another Love Song.' Jojo Lane is a visionary. A pioneer. But most important to her talented daughter, a devoted mother."

August closed the article and switched to her messages. Still nothing from Jojo. She opened her contacts and stared at her mother's number, trying to will her fingers to do the work for her. But she kept hearing their last fight in her head, the apathy in Jojo's voice when she announced she was skipping Birdie's funeral. Why would this be any different? Her mother would probably show up the day of the show and saunter onstage to play the devoted mother like this had been her plan all along.

August switched to the King's Kitchen GroupMe and read through the rants that used to annoy her. Now it felt comforting to see Rodrigo's intense opinions about the grease catcher. "You have to heat the grease first! THEN you clean it. Cold grease just gets smeared everywhere!"

It was nearly closing time, which meant they'd be doing clean up. August drove to the restaurant, intent on being useful. When she arrived, there were more cars out front than she'd expected. Mavis's sparkling Land Rover was parked near the entrance.

The door was locked. August knocked and a young woman she'd never seen before walked to the door and yelled, "The kitchen is closed!"

"I work here," August yelled back, and the woman stared blankly, unmoved.

"Let her in," Mavis shouted. The new employee sighed and finally unlocked the door. August was stunned to see her cousin wearing brown dungarees and plastic gloves. Her hair was covered with a scarf.

"What are you doing here?" Mavis asked.

August tried to walk inside but the new girl, Anita, based on her temporary name tag, blocked her path. August tried to stare her down, but Anita stared back, unintimidated.

"I will pay you to move," August said.

"That's my boss," Anita countered, gesturing over her shoulder. "She pays me once a week."

"*She's* your boss?" August met Mavis's eyes. Her cousin sighed and told Anita it was okay to step aside.

"I knew you'd do this," Mavis said. "I told Silas the minute they added you to the lineup that you'd run off and bury your hands in dirty dishwater like it's a better use of your time."

"They want me to sing a song I've known for years. Might as well be useful while I wait." She looked Mavis up and down. "Why are you here?"

Mavis peeled the gloves from her hands. "Cleaning the grease catcher."

"Seriously?"

"Yes. Or I was about to before you interrupted."

"You mean before I saved you?" She pointed to Mavis's scrub brush. "This isn't the right equipment. You need a face mask, nose plugs, and a bag of edibles."

Mavis sat at a table. "I'm avoiding my husband."

August sat across from her. "Why?"

"He wants kids. I don't."

"Does he know about..."

Mavis nodded. "I told him. He claims it's okay, but I don't think it is. He was fine with it just being us before he knew, now he acts like having a baby will cleanse me of sin or something."

"Oh God," August whispered. "You know that's not true."

"Yes. But it means I'd rather clean a grease catcher than face him." She stared at her hands. Her wedding ring was missing. "I don't want a divorce. But I'm tired of arguing. And I think if I hadn't given up my career that I wouldn't feel guilty about not wanting to be a mother. It'd be easier for him to love me if I loved myself."

August grabbed her hand. "I love you. I always have."

Mavis squeezed her fingers. "You don't count. It's in your nature." August tried to pull back, but Mavis held on. "Which is a good thing. But you never made us work for it. You give and you give, and we all take without acknowledging it." August tried to interrupt, but Mavis spoke over her. "I should have helped with Birdie. I should have defended you to Phillip when he banned you from the choir. Telling Jessica Ryder that you had an abortion instead of me was the worst thing I've ever done. I have to do better by you."

August immediately wanted to reassure Mavis that none of it was necessary. But then she thought about what the last decade of her life might have been like with someone to share such a heavy load. She might have started writing again. Maybe she would have been brave enough to call Luke and they could have reconnected sooner. Maybe there'd be an album out there with her name on it because someone offered help instead of pretending not to notice she needed it.

"You're right," August said. "I needed you."

The tears in Mavis's eyes spilled down her cheeks. She looked relieved, like being held accountable had set her free. "You have me," she said. "Starting with me taking over this place, so you don't have an excuse to avoid launching your career."

"You're not seriously working here."

"I'm buying it. Silas agreed to sell it to me last week. I want something of my own."

August looked her cousin up and down. "So, what you're telling me is that you're secretly rich."

"I'm a smart investor with good credit. Oh, and you're fired." She wiggled her fingers toward the door. "Go be famous."

Mavis was just like Luke, convinced that the concert was the key to her future. Everyone was acting like her fate had been sealed when they placed her name on Jojo's billboard. But just last week, it had been Luke's name. His fate. Which meant it wasn't destiny at all, just a publicity stunt that people were paying thousands to witness in person. That duet had become a glorified audition to be crowned the new Black voice of country.

Mavis started to stand, but August stopped her with a question. "What you said before about people taking and never giving? Do you think my mother does that?"

Mavis sat back down. "I think she survived terrible things and did the best she could." She paused. "I also think people can only give what they have. Some of us don't have much."

Over the next week, Luke settled into a comfortable routine. Mornings were for taking care of August, ensuring she had plenty of coffee and a good breakfast before she went to rehearsals. Once she was gone, he'd get a workout in and tackle one of his projects around the house. Late afternoon, he'd go to Delta Blue and pitch in wherever Silas needed him. At night, when August returned, they'd have dinner, make music, and then tangle up in each other until their bodies gave out from exhaustion. Then he'd wake up the next morning and do it all again.

He was surprised at how easy it was. In Memphis, he'd had to drag himself out of bed to face the day. Now he was up at sunrise, devouring every minute like crumbs of the best meal he'd ever tasted. He had love. Sobriety. Work that made him feel like he'd accomplished something. If someone told him this was it, this was his peak and the rest was a downhill slide, he'd be okay with that. How steep could it be? Ava Randall had raised him. He'd cut his teeth on ravines.

Right now, it was Silas's downhill slide that had him worried. Although selling King's Kitchen to Mavis Reed provided some needed cash flow, most of it would go to unpaid bills. If things kept going the way they were, Delta Blue would be gone by the end of the year.

"How's it looking?" Silas joined him in his office and deposited a ream of printer paper on the floor.

Luke gestured at the Excel sheet he'd created against Silas's will. "About as you'd expect. Sales would normally be up this close to the festival. The protests are killing us."

Silas rubbed his neck. "Maybe I should call it. Sell this place to them boys in Shreveport looking to expand."

"August would kill you."

Silas raised an eyebrow. "She may not be around to have a say."

Luke grabbed another bill and ripped it open with more force than necessary. Silas watched him and said, "You okay over there?"

"You should call the electric company and ask for an extension."

"You could go with her."

"As her groupie?"

"As whatever she wants you to be."

Luke had already thought about what Silas was proposing. Even if they could make it work for a while, being useless would get to him. And he knew exactly where that road ended. On the floor of some bar.

"I'd rather stay here," Luke said. "She'll come home when she's not on the road."

Silas sucked his teeth. "Cause you two being apart worked so well before?"

He had a brief silent standoff with Silas that ended when Bill Parnell walked through the door. It was the first time Luke had seen him since the night he left town. Bill's eyes still sparkled like he'd just heard a funny story and was dying to share it with you. He still stood bowlegged, with his hands on his hips, like an old-school cowboy. Like all of them, Bill was older and grayer, but he wore it like a costume. Underneath, he was the same.

"Mornin'," Bill said, smiling at Luke. "Little Jason. Always forget how much you look like him until I set eyes on you. Been a while."

Luke approached him and extended a hand. Bill held on longer than necessary, staring into his eyes, like he was greeting the friend he had lost as well.

"I should have reached out," Luke said.

Bill laughed. "Nobody round here reaches out to me unless there's trouble."

"No, I mean, I never thanked you for what you did." A memory of Don's face as he called the cops rose in Luke's mind. Ava's boyfriend had thrived on spite and vengeance. "You probably saved my life."

"Jason did the same for me," Bill said. "Always meant to tell you that story, but it's kind of long and embarrassing, so I try to keep the details to myself. Never streak for a political cause, son. Won't change a single vote. Everyone'll just point and laugh at your little ding-a-ling. Ain't worth it."

Silas snorted. "Not gonna rest until we're all traumatized by that image, are you?"

"The *moral* of the story is that most mistakes, not all mind you, but most, are like footprints. That's what your daddy told me when he brought me my pants. We all make them. But they're not permanent. They don't have to define who we are." Bill smiled. "That man was a damn good poet."

"He was," Luke said, thinking of the book Ava threw out. He could never find another copy in print.

"That's how he convinced Ava to—" Bill snapped his fingers. "That's why I came looking for you. Something's going on at your mama's house. Got a call about a big truck parked out front and some strange man taking all her things. I would have gone out there, but she still hates me. Don't wanna make it worse. Figured I'd tell you and tag along if you want."

Luke pictured the late mortgage bills he'd spotted a few days ago. He knew Ava was struggling to pay them but didn't realize it had gotten so bad. "No, I'll handle it. Thanks for letting me know."

Thirty minutes later, Luke pulled into Ava's driveway and parked behind a white moving truck. A silver SUV was parked in the driveway. Luke climbed out of his truck just as the front door opened, and a tall Black man dressed in ripped jeans and a B.B. King T-shirt walked outside. The stranger moved closer, and the sun illuminated his face. Luke's breath caught when he recognized him. "Ethan?"

His brother took a few more steps, then stopped, looking uncertain. His arms dangled at his sides as if he didn't know what to do with them. "Hey, Luke."

The ground dissolved beneath Luke's feet. He felt suspended, waiting for someone to tell him that this wasn't happening, that his daydreams were getting crueler. Elation and fear warred inside him and rendered him mute.

"She's selling it." Ethan pointed to a Realtor's sign lying in the grass. "Got her checked into a recovery center in Little Rock yesterday." He cleared his throat. "Probably should have called you."

"Recovery," Luke repeated. He couldn't wrap his mind around it. All he could think about was getting his face slapped when he was twelve after she caught him sipping her cheap wine. She'd looked terrified, like she'd caught him loading a gun. "Was that her idea?"

Ethan nodded. "Yeah. I think seeing you like this." He motioned at Luke. "Healthy. Sober. That had something to do with it. Made her realize it was possible." He searched Luke's face with cautious eyes, looking for something he didn't want to find. "You've really been helping her out all this time?"

"Yeah. Wasn't easy. But things are different now." He thought about what Bill had just told him about mistakes. "I'm different."

Ethan nodded, still staring like he was trying to let it soak in. Luke didn't mind the awkward pauses. He was thrilled to be standing this close to his brother after so long. And he *had* changed because the old version of himself wouldn't have admitted that. The old Luke would have switched to a safer subject, like where the fresh mulch came from or whether Ethan planned to power wash the driveway. New Luke didn't have that kind of time. He took a step forward, extended his arms and said, "Can I hug you?"

Surprised flashed across Ethan's face, then crumbled into something raw and tender. He shuffled forward, and their arms flew around each other, aimlessly grasping until they settled into a rocking embrace. Luke cried into his brother's shoulder. Ethan cried, too, and when they parted, they were both soaked and sweaty, with goofy grins on their faces.

"It was that article," Ethan said, rubbing his nose. It was cherry red. His brother's entire face was a splotchy flush, and it felt good to know that some things would never change. "The part where you talked about going to Nashville. That was because of me, wasn't it? That flyer I gave you."

"Partially," Luke said. "You and August. It was silly, but I thought y'all would find me there. But when things got bad...well, I guess I didn't want you to."

Ethan sniffed, still rubbing his face. "I don't know why I thought cutting you off would help. Like if I hurt you enough, I'd hurt less? I was so fucking wrong. Demetrius would bring it up in marriage counseling all the time. How it never felt like I was arguing with him. He'd do something innocent, like turn his phone on silent and I'd be convinced he was leaving me." Ethan took a deep breath. "Your messages helped. I always felt better when I got one. He noticed that, too."

"Demetrius sounds like a good guy."

"He's wonderful. Patient with me, which I needed after..." His eyes slid to the house. Luke followed his gaze and cleared his throat.

"Need some help packing up?"

Ethan nodded. "She kept everything. Even stuff she claimed to throw away." His expression darkened. "There's something you should see."

Luke followed Ethan inside. The living room was covered in moving boxes, which he expected. But Ethan had also opened the attic, one of the many places Ava had forbidden them to go. He'd pulled down a mountain of black trash bags filled with old clothes, plastic bins of toys, and pots and pans scorched to uselessness. Ethan sifted through all of it to reveal a large box with JASON written on the side. He offered it to Luke and said, "I didn't open it."

It was sealed with old duct tape that had cracked in places. After so many years of owning nothing of his father's, Luke couldn't bring himself to touch the box. Whatever was inside probably wasn't much. Just enough to devastate him. "I don't think I can."

Ethan pulled a box cutter from his pocket and swiped it over the tape. They both stared at the contents like the man himself had been stowed inside. Luke spotted a photo album and grabbed it first.

There were baby pictures and class photos. Luke took in the slow evolution of his father, captured in snapshots and family portraits. Instead of being a story, his father became a person. A child who'd become a man. There were pictures of him with Ava, who looked young and beautiful and so vibrantly in love it could have leaked into his hands.

"Look." Ethan pointed to something else in the box. A book. Luke's breath caught when he realized it was Jason's poems, the copy Ava had taken from him all those years ago. He opened it and saw his old notes on the pages, music he thought he'd lost forever.

Discovering Ava's lie should have made him angry. But it didn't. He didn't think of her at all. Miracles were supposed to be more than just an old book in a dusty box, but he'd leave the big ones for other people. He'd take this feeling, this gentle realignment of his heart every time.

There were more books in the box. Luke pulled out the slim volumes, one by one, reading the familiar titles of his father's work with his heart pounding. There was one he didn't recognize, *The Bones of Us*, that had been published before he was born. He flipped it open and read the dedication. *For Lucas. I will hear you laugh. I will hear you cry. Your blood calls my bones, always.*

Luke closed it, bowed his head, and whispered, "Why would she do this?" Taking one book out of spite, he understood. But Jason had written this for him. Obviously wanted him to have it. "Why would she keep this from me?"

"You know why," Ethan said quietly.

Because she was in pain. Because she loved his father so much that looking at his son, his mirror image, was another ache without a cure. And she couldn't pretend. She couldn't watch Luke flip through photographs and read Jason's writings and pretend to be fine. She never forgave his father for dying and it kept her trapped in that single moment in time. If she was still angry that he'd gone to the bar, that he'd lost a fight, she'd never have to grieve.

"She dumped Don after you left," Ethan said. "Told him not to come around anymore. Then she just gave up being a parent. Barely noticed when I left for college."

"Can you forgive her?" Luke asked Ethan. "For everything?"

"I don't know," Ethan said, looking a lot like the trusting little kid who'd turned to Luke for guidance. "Should we?"

Luke looked at the box. Then he scanned the living room, which was filled with old junk and bad memories. "We can let go," he told Ethan. "Sell the house. Finally stop living here if you know what I mean. Whatever happens next with Ava is up to her. But this part's done."

This Is Our Country: Podcast Transcript

Episode 12—"Jojo Lane"
August 21, 2024

[*cont.*]

Emma: How did you find out about the Hall of Fame?
Jojo: David told me.
Emma: David Henry?
Jojo: Yes. He knows everything before I do. He knew I was allergic to dairy before my doctor did.
Emma: You've been together a long time.
Jojo: Together. That sounds so intimate.
Emma: I wasn't implying anything.
Jojo: Others have. He's a handsome white man who stuck by me when everyone thought he should have cut his losses. Everyone assumed we were together. That's what all the old suits thought. I was his Black mistress.
Emma: I'm honestly not sure what to say to that. It had to be frustrating.
Jojo: For David, yes. He had a wife at the time, and she did her best not to resent me, but she's only human. He really should've dropped me, but the man is arrogant and stubborn. If he gave up on me, he'd have to admit he was wrong to sign me. And he never admits to being wrong.
Emma: You almost sound sad when you say that.
Jojo: You can't get that time back. He's so good at what he does, but grinding for me took a toll. Sometimes we hang on to things long after we should have let them go.
Emma: After all that work, he had to be thrilled about the award.
Jojo: He was. Maybe more than me.
Emma: Really?

Jojo: I mean, you saw the protests. I've been doing this for years, and they're accusing me of not paying my dues. *Me.* I haven't bled enough, I guess. I changed what I sang. How I sounded. I did everything I could to please those folks. But all I heard was no. Not now, not you, not ever. Finally I get one yes, and it's a big enough yes for people to care about and suddenly I'm not qualified. I'm a gimmick.

That's why I never wanted August to do this. I never wanted her with me, seeing what I had to do to keep going. I never wanted to teach her those lessons. But that meant I was always gone, so I didn't teach her anything. And I don't know how to feel about that.

Emma: If you could go back, what would you teach her?

Jojo: I'd say... I'd tell her not to look at me. And don't look at anyone else. Turn off the radio and sing.

CHAPTER TWENTY-FOUR

2023

August wasn't awake when Jojo's text came. She was dreaming about Birdie's funeral. Only it wasn't her grandmother in the coffin. It was August. She was staring at herself, lying peacefully with her arms folded, and thinking of how well everything had turned out. How perfect. Then suddenly, she was dressed in satin, surrounded by roses, and she thought, *I know this song.* She had just looked up, searching for rainbows, when the vibration of her phone startled her awake.

Happy belated birthday was the first message, followed by, **I'm sorry.**

She could hear Luke in the kitchen, making breakfast, and August was tempted to show the text to him. Get his take on what it meant. But she couldn't move. Jojo had never apologized after one of their arguments, not spontaneously and unprompted. The concert was in less than two weeks. Most likely, David had convinced her to extend a strategic olive branch to ensure things went smoothly.

Or maybe it was genuine. Perhaps for once, Jojo was experiencing sincere regret.

August texted her back. **Can we talk? I'm sorry, too.** Then she waited for a response.

Nothing.

She tried calling, but there was no answer. "I got your message," August told her mother's voicemail. "I'd like to talk before you get here." She hesitated, tempted to end it there, but added, "Looking forward to seeing you."

The seed of curiosity grew into anxiety as she went through her day. It got worse when she went to the fairgrounds and saw the biggest crowd yet standing behind police caution tape. The people protesting Jojo's award exchanged insults with her fans while reporters narrated the chaos in front of large cameras. Bill and two other deputies stood beside cruisers, flashing silent blue lights. The scene felt ominous, like everyone involved was gearing up for a showdown.

Bill spotted her and waved her over. His cattleman sat farther back on his head than usual, which meant the situation was serious. "I'm gonna walk you in through the back," he told her.

She followed him silently, keeping the crowd in the corner of her eye. The messages on their signs had devolved into veiled threats, with LEAVE WELL ENOUGH ALONE on one side and THIS IS WHAT YOU OWE on the other.

"Is this even about Jojo anymore?" August asked Bill.

He shrugged. "Was it ever?"

The mood was lighter backstage, but most of it was forced. Everyone was eager to focus on the show instead of what was happening outside. August was invited to film a dance for social media three times. The audio engineer kept complimenting her dress during the sound check. Luke's name was whispered multiple times, in tones that reeked of judgment. David's directive to stay away from Luke had made August do the opposite. Everyone knew they were together and apparently had strong opinions about her fraternizing with the guy who nearly derailed their show.

David had vouched for her. Luke had ruined his reputation to give her an opportunity. August owed them this performance, but nothing else. She loved Luke, but this was *her* future, *her* career. She wasn't sure what it would look like, but she knew it would be on her own terms.

The longer August stood onstage, the more nervous she became. There were more festival volunteers milling around than usual, and she kept wondering what they were saying about her, what they'd think of her voice. It probably looked ridiculous to them, August Lane playing country star, pretending she belonged.

When it was time for August to sing, she grabbed the microphone head without thinking and feedback ricocheted through the speakers. Then she missed her cue, forcing them to start over. The last straw was her singing too close to the microphone, resulting in muffled, muddy vocals that made Jojo's stand-in grimace.

August didn't wait for the stage manager to stop her. She stepped away from the mic and signaled to the musicians. "I need a break."

Everyone exchanged *this was a mistake* looks. She left them there, retreating to the greenroom, but stopped short when she saw David Henry sitting inside.

"That was interesting," he said.

"I can't deal with you right now."

He splayed his hands to prove he was unarmed. "Nerves are normal."

"Mine aren't." She sat heavily beside him. "I can't do this. People look at me and I freeze." She glanced at him. "I should have said something sooner."

Instead of berating her for keeping secrets, David looked confused. "What are you afraid of?"

"It's garden variety stage fright. I'm not reinventing any wheels."

He laughed. "Specifically. What are you thinking about when you're up there? First thing that springs to mind."

August pictured herself three minutes ago. Her mind had gone blank and then flooded with one loud, persistent fear. "They know I don't belong," she said. "That I shouldn't be here."

"So, garden variety impostor syndrome?"

She cut her eyes at him. "Don't get insightful all of a sudden."

"This is my job. I am occasionally good at it." He threw his arm behind the couch, looking smug. "Want to hear the solution?"

"Please."

"Stop asking permission."

August immediately remembered Jojo telling her the same thing years ago. *Stop asking permission. Don't wait to be saved.* David must have given her that advice.

"You're looking out instead of in," David continued. "External validation is an old trap that's easy for artists to fall into. Ask your boyfriend. But it's only meaningful if you let it be." He pointed to her chest. "Why do you want to do this? Not the concert. Forget that. Why do you want to make music? What's the point?"

The answer came to her immediately. "I love it," she said. "It's who I am. And I think hiding it was slowly killing me."

He nodded. "So do that onstage then. Love it. *Live*. And fuck everything else."

It was so simple. So true. "Okay, maybe you could be slightly useful to me."

He threw back his head and laughed. Then he reached into his suit jacket and handed her a flyer. "Consider this a job application."

It was for the Delta Blue Showcase. The simple flyer was covered with names and booking fees written in blue ink. "What is this?"

"Me getting angry about the right things." He tapped the flyer. "There's a Black touring revue down in Biloxi. Noir Root. They do a little of everything. Country. Blues. Folk. These are the acts they could confirm. They're working on adding more."

She recognized a few names, but most she hadn't heard of, which was exactly what the showcase was for. Introducing new voices to the festival audience. "We can't pay them," she said, pointing to the fees. "All the money was used for Jojo's concert."

"I also lined up a sponsor," he said. "A patron eager to make amends for her role in some of your bad press."

August drew a blank. "I don't know anyone with that kind of money." Then it hit her. Bad press. "Charlotte Turner?"

"Luke's ex," David said. "She's looking to invest more. Fund an indie label. Maybe a publishing company. All more inclusive than what's on mainstream radio."

August stared at the list of performers, more than the showcase had featured in years. Delta Blue would reap the benefits, maybe even turn a profit this year. Even David looked eager, more optimistic than she'd ever seen him. "Indie? You?"

"I know. It's less money. But working with you is a much bigger reward."

The door swung open, and Mavis rushed in, breathless. "David, we need you," she sputtered. "Something is going on with Jojo's flight. I got this email from the driver we sent that she never boarded. I'm afraid there's been some mix-up with the airline."

David pulled out his phone and started texting. "That doesn't make sense. I confirmed it myself."

"She won't answer anyone's calls. I'm afraid something's happened to her."

Panic snaked through August. She retrieved her phone and opened her messages. Still no response. Just the original apology with no explanation.

"Pick up, Johanna," David barked at her voicemail. "Everyone's worried about you."

I'm sorry. For missing her birthday? No. For something else.

Oh.

Of course.

"Hang up," August said quietly. "David, hang up the phone. She's not coming."

He looked startled. Mavis tried to laugh. "Of course she is. We have a week of photo ops and school visits—"

"She won't come," August interrupted. "It's my fault. I know everyone put a lot of time and money into this, and I'm really sorry."

She could tell they didn't believe her. David left the room with his phone in his ear, shouting at someone. Mavis looked nauseous. "She wouldn't do that." She spun around, staring out at the expensive stage. "Not to all these people."

Sometimes it took hearing your despair in someone else's voice to recognize it for what it was. Before Mavis spoke, before her voice shattered over that final whisper, August had been cloaked in the usual numbness she felt when Jojo disappointed her. Fine, like always. Always fine. Only she wasn't. She was the girl it hurt to love. Jojo's trauma in the flesh. She never should have believed her mother could face all that in front of the world.

"You should go," August said. The voices outside were growing high-pitched and frantic. "They need you."

Mavis hesitated and then rushed out of the room. August closed the door, sat on the couch, and cried hard enough to lose her voice.

Luke thought David was calling to brag about saving the showcase again. He was slow to answer, prepared to be unimpressed. But then he heard

"August" and "You need to come now," and he ran out the door, ignoring everything the man was trying to tell him because he was too afraid to listen, too busy praying to a God he'd stopped talking to years ago.

It wasn't a good prayer—more like hysterical, empty threats. *Don't take her from me. Don't you dare.* He ran three stop signs on the way to the fairgrounds. There was a crowd out front, a sea of protesters and cameras. He would have punched his way through if Bill hadn't cut him off before he could reach them.

"Put your fists down," Bill said. "She's okay. Just real upset."

The story he was told on the way backstage wasn't true. He could tell by how consistent it was that everyone was reciting words from a press release: "Out of concern for everyone's safety, Jojo Lane decided to postpone the concert until further notice. The Hall of Fame induction will be held at a private, undisclosed location and streamed at a later date."

He didn't learn the real reason Jojo backed out until he reached August. Her eyes were swollen. She was slumped and lethargic, staring down at her hands. And he knew. This wasn't about security. It was Jojo, once again, abandoning her daughter.

Luke approached her, and she blinked as if she didn't believe he was there. He smoothed her hair from her face and tried to smile. "Hey, sweetheart."

She launched herself into his arms. He picked her up and she pressed her face to his neck to hide her tears. Everyone was watching. Musicians. Press. Volunteers. He ignored them all as he walked out slowly, whispering reassurances in her ear. "It's okay. I'm here. I'll always be here."

August had been through so much, part of him thought of her as invincible. Or maybe he'd thought that she'd mended so much of herself already, there was nothing left to break. It was hard being so wrong. She'd always fought her tears before, but these streamed in rivers down her face, formed pools on her neck. He couldn't do a damn thing about it. Nothing but hold her hand.

She claimed she was fine to walk once they got home. Luke hovered, because she still seemed unsteady. She spotted his guitar on the couch and sat beside it, then started randomly plucking strings.

"I was relieved," she finally said, her lost voice a whisper rubbed with sandpaper. "When they said she wasn't coming, it felt like I'd been set free. How can you want something your whole life and be happy when it's taken away?" She took a breath. "Does that mean I never wanted it? That I put you through hell for nothing?"

Luke thought about packing up his old house with Ethan. How good it felt each time he closed a box or took a trash bag out to the curb. "My little brother came home," he told her. August's eyes widened, and before she could bombard him with questions, he said, "We're selling the farm. Ava's gone, and I don't know if I'll ever speak to her again. And I'm thrilled. I'm happy."

It surprised him how easily the word slipped out. *Happy*. He finally was. "One thing I had to learn in therapy was that being abused wasn't my fault. I know how that sounds. I was just a kid. But I'm still a kid when those memories come for me. I'm in that closet convincing myself it's fine. I'm being slapped and spit on and taking it all instead of fighting back because I'm always the problem. Never her."

August nodded as he spoke. "That's how I feel when she leaves me. I'm eleven years old and shouldn't have asked for a bike at Christmas. I'm fourteen and kicking myself for a bad joke. I'm eighteen, singing to impress her, thinking it's the only thing she could like about me, then getting embarrassed and wishing I hadn't." She took a breath. "This whole week I've been waiting for another rejection. And when it came today, I thought *finally*, the wait is over. But I'm not a child who needs her approval. This is the only life I have. I don't want to waste it like this."

"Wait here." Luke retrieved some pens and paper, plus the copy of *The Bones of Us*. He returned and put it all in front of her. "Packing the house made all those memories start to feel like the past. Maybe it was because we were literally putting everything in boxes, but I felt sorry for that little boy I was for the first time in my life. I'm also proud of him, too, for surviving."

She flipped open the book and read the dedication. Fresh tears filled her eyes.

"You taught me to use memories to tell a story." He grabbed a pen and offered it to her. "I think it's time to tell ours."

"The Bones of Us"

Song by August Lane and Luke Randall

Verse 1: August
I hear she grabbed lightning from the sky
That's why thunder calls my name
But she don't tell that story and won't say why
That's fine
I don't want her eyes, anyway
Always staying where no one wants me
Don't sound country
I've given up trying
That venom tastes like how she raised me
Won't know it's poison 'til I'm dying

Chorus
Can I be more than just these bones
Your bones
Our bones
Your pretty words don't soften these blows
That break
My bones

Verse 2: Luke
Pain is what I'm made of
Blood that burns
Breaths that cut me
I sing about love with bruises
But listen closely
There's fire underneath
These bones don't break
Is that what scares you

A guy like me with this guitar
If three chords and the truth
Are these chords
Our truth
We'll finally see
What makes a real country star

Chorus
I can be more than just these bones
Your bones
Our bones
Your pretty words won't hide these blows
That take
My bones

The Bridge: August
More than bones
I'm flesh and blood
It's my forgiveness
That starts the flood

Chorus
We can be more than just these bones
Your bones
Our bones
Your pretty words don't soften these blows
That break
These bones

Two Weeks Later

The crowd was screaming. Camera phones dotted the dark. The cheers grew louder when she walked onstage, but August felt removed from it, like they were shouting at someone else. Then she heard David's voice in her mind, shutting down her doubts.

Love it. *Live.* And fuck everything else.

She grabbed the microphone and said, "I'm August Lane." Her voice flowed from the speakers surrounding the audience. She'd been resistant at first when Mavis suggested they move the showcase to the stage they'd built for Jojo. She thought it was too big. But Mavis was insistent. "You were right all along. We were thinking too small. This is what the festival should have been in the first place."

Charlotte Turner had introduced the first act wearing a sparkling BI Pride pin. The crowd grew larger with each performance, thanks to her viral videos on social media. Now it was August's turn. This was her stage. They were all just visiting.

"I'm gonna sing," she said, and there was more cheering. They thought they knew what was coming, a solo version of their favorite song. "But I have to tell a story first. You all know that, right? Every song has a story?"

The response was muted encouragement, with a tinge of impatience. August strolled across the stage. "I wrote 'Another Love Song' to impress a boy." There was laughter, followed by whoops and whistles. "Yeah, yeah," she said, "I know. But he was *really* cute. And kind. And played the most beautiful music. So, I wrote him a love song. Because I loved him. And he sang it for years because he loved me, too."

They were watching. Listening. Recording her with their phones. She let them in, moving to the front of the stage. A few people shouted their approval, and she was suddenly tethered to them, her head swimming with dopamine and joy.

This was what Luke meant. This high. She never wanted to come down from this.

"I've got a new song for you. But I need to fix the old one first."

She turned around and extended a hand. Luke walked onstage, dressed in black, with his guitar slung over his shoulder. The reaction was a loud, chaotic roar. Cheers, boos, whistles—it all rolled in their direction in a deafening wave.

Luke kept his eyes on her. He took her hand and his grip was warm and solid in every way she needed. He bowed to her, like he was greeting royalty, then positioned his fingers along his guitar frets.

They locked eyes again. Luke smiled her favorite smile and said, "I love this song," then leaned hard into the first chord.

The crowd was stunned. They took a collective breath. August let loose a loud, blazing note that lit up the sky. Not another Lane girl. Not a delicate country songbird. But something altogether different.

A sound of her own.

This Is Our Country: Podcast Transcript

Episode 12—"Jojo Lane"
August 21, 2024

[*cont.*]

Emma: Did you watch it?

Jojo: Everybody did. People that don't even like country watched that show. It was number one on that streaming platform for... how many weeks?

Emma: Twelve, I think. Maybe more.

Jojo: Set a record. I think it was curiosity at first. August singing "Another Love Song" with the man who stole it from her. Rubberneck viewing. But you can't tell me that anyone expected to hear it the way my girl sang it. I always liked that song because it was catchy. But it was also a little knuckle dragging, wasn't it? Giving some poor woman grief because she won't get over herself and let him write for her.

Emma: It had that vibe, didn't it?

Jojo: Sure did. So, if that's what you were expecting, the song you used to two-step to at the bar, that wasn't what you got. My girl is a soul singer. She's pulling something out of you up there. Anyone who's ever lost something, lost it all over again when they heard her.

Emma: I was never a fan of that song, or Luke Randall, until I watched that concert. I didn't realize he was a blues guitarist.

Jojo: Is he?

Emma: Right, I'm doing the thing—

Jojo: Roots, blues, Americana. Genres are stupid.

Emma: Critics say "The Bones of Us" defies categorization.

Jojo: Critics tend to listen with their eyes and not their ears.

Emma: Do you think it's just that? Those are classic blues guitar chords. August and Luke brought a choir onstage when they sang it at the showcase.

Jojo: There's also a banjo, a fiddle, a small-town country story...

Emma: Yes, you're right.

Jojo: They should have won that award last night at the CMAs. That's what I told August. You should have won that one.

Emma: Do you talk often? I know you attended her wedding.

Jojo: We're trying. You haven't asked me why I canceled the show, but I'm going to tell you anyway, because I know there's all kinds of rumors floating around. It wasn't death threats that made me cancel. It was the press about me being a good mother. I'm not. I never was. That was forced on me, by Theo and Birdie. August knew that, which made it hard to get close to her. I could never relax with that girl because she was always working so hard to prove she wasn't a mistake. But all she did was drag me back to that time where I had no control over my life. I didn't want the same thing to happen in front of a million people. I couldn't do it.

Yes, we're better now. She's happy and I'm happy for her, even though I'm keeping an eye on that husband of hers. That independent publishing company she founded, Firefly? That's all hers. Their group is called August Lane because she's the star of that band. I'll make sure he never forgets that.

Emma: After everything that happened, I'm sure he won't.

Jojo: [*laughs*] He's got a good heart, though. And they're making music out of love, regardless of what anyone calls it. I envy them. I wish I still loved it as much as I did when I started. I miss making music for the sake of it. Doesn't matter if people like it. They don't want to play you on redneck radio, that's fine. The music is still there. You sang it. You recorded it. This vision in your mind is something you can feel and hear, and that should be enough. That's what real love is. An act of worship. Something worthy of sacrifice because the mere doing sustains you. We all become foolish when we love, but that's what makes it special. Can you imagine life without it? No foolishness. Only a string of good choices and easy straight roads until the end.

There'd be nothing to look back on. No evidence of who you are.

"Another Love Song"

Lyrics by August Lane, Music by Luke Randall

Verse
I'm frozen in place
My heart's gone numb
But you keep breaking the part that still feels something
It's clear on my face
Can't lie while I strum
And folks always cry when I sing this one

Pre-Chorus
Tired of talking
Tired of standing still
Want the tempo to take me
And work its will

Chorus
I just want to write a love song
Just want to strum the chords
Write the perfect words
Been waiting here so long
Hoping maybe you will see
This is what we're meant to be
I just want to write a love song
Maybe we can write a love song

Verse
I'll love you forever
That old cliché
Is what happens when the guitar's thinking for me
I'd rip up the pages
Try to find someone new
But every chord spells your name in different keys

Pre-Chorus

We keep on talking
Always standing still
While the tempo's begging
To work its will

Chorus

You don't want another love song
You've heard it all before
You're tired of pretty words
Been doing this so long
You're starting to believe
We're never meant to be
You don't want another love song
You don't want to hear a love song

Bridge

I get it now
I've been listening
To all your won'ts
All your don'ts
I can't make you take this ring

Chorus

But if I wrote a different love song
Took your hand in mine
Threw out all the lines
And built a love so strong
If I promised to believe
Would you take this leap with me
And write a different love song
This is how you write a love song

ACKNOWLEDGMENTS

August Lane started with a love song. In 2010, Ben Folds released an album he cowrote with Nick Hornby called *Lonely Avenue*. The last song on the album, "Belinda," is about a singer whose only hit is about an ex-girlfriend he cheated on. No one wants to hear him sing anything else. The idea of being creatively trapped at that particular pain point sounded like torture. It also seemed like a cool idea for a romance. I pictured an aging pop star returning to her hometown to reunite with the grumpy cowriter she left behind. There would be a lesson about selling out for money and getting back to real music as they rediscovered their lost love.

I didn't immediately start working on it. Life happened—career changes, marriage, motherhood—and similar to my debut, *The Art of Scandal*, my musical second-chance romance sat neglected on the shelf. (By shelf, I mean the corner of my brain that houses stories I haven't fully committed to yet.)

Flash forward to 2021. Editors at publishing houses were reading *The Art of Scandal* and deciding whether to acquire it. I wanted to work on something very different from that book to distract myself. The "Belinda" second-chance romance idea was always at the back of my mind. I had also started listening to Rissi Palmer's Apple Music radio show *Color Me Country*, which features underrepresented voices in country music. Then I learned CMT had awarded Linda Martell, the first Black woman to perform at the Grand Ole Opry, the Equal Play Award. The premise for *August Lane* was born.

Like August, I grew up in a small central Arkansas town. My mother would turn the volume up when "Islands in the Stream" played on the radio. I memorized the lyrics to songs by Garth Brooks, Shania Twain, and The Chicks. I line danced to "Achy Breaky Heart" with my junior high drill team. But I never considered myself a country fan because it never occurred to me that I could be. When I put on boots and two-stepped at a pep rally, it felt like a costume.

But what if it had been Linda Martell my mother sang along to instead of Dolly? What if instead of considering Charlie Pride and Darius Rucker aberrations, I'd received an early history lesson on Black voices in the genre, and placed both men within the context of DeFord Bailey and Ray Charles? Would I have listened to "Stuck on You" by Lionel Richie and heard the Alabama in his voice? Would I have heard the West Virginia roots in "Grandma's Hands," and thought of Bill Withers's music as country instead of soul?

I honestly don't know. Maybe I still wouldn't have been a loud-and-proud country fan. But now we're living in the age of the Black Opry, Shaboozey, and *Cowboy Carter*. The name Lesley Riddle has become symbolic of our roots in country the same way Sister Rosetta Tharpe symbolizes our roots in rock. It feels a lot less lonely lately. Something special happens when one of your favorite songs plays and a stranger sings along with it, too. That moment of connection is what I wanted to capture in these pages. *August Lane* is me making eye contact with that other Black country fan in the room and saying, "Yes, this one's for you."

I'm so grateful to the wonderful people who helped bring this book to life. To my agent, Sharon Pelletier, thank you for being such an enthusiastic fan of August and Luke's love story from the start. Thank you to my editing dream team: Seema Mahanian, Rachael Kelly, and Karen Kosztolnyik. This book sings because of you. To the production, publicity, marketing, sales, and art teams at Grand Central Publishing, thank you for working so hard to get this book into the hands of readers.

Thank you, Roberta Lea, Serafia, and Stephanie Jacques, for sharing your experiences as Black women in country music with me. Listening to your stories was so inspiring and I can't wait for everyone to discover your beautiful music. To Dr. Francesca Royster, thank you for sharing your expertise and wisdom. Your research lit a fire under me while this book was coming together. You have a devoted fan for life.

To my dear friend Nikki Payne, thank you for listening to me pitch, brainstorm, and vent about this book for years. Your hype, love, and support mean the world to me. To Taj McCoy, our Sunday sprint sessions were my saving grace. To Angel, my twin and forever writing partner. Every book is for us. To James, thank you for loving me and supporting everything I do. To Finley, my heart, I never knew how powerful love could be until I had you.

Lastly, a huge thank you to all my readers. Time is a gift, and I'm honored to have been the recipient of yours.

ABOUT THE AUTHOR

Katie Childs

Regina Black is a former civil litigator, current law school administrator, and lifelong romance reader who has always been passionate about the depiction of Black women in popular culture. She currently resides in Little Rock, Arkansas, with her husband and daughter.

For more information you can visit:
    ReginaBlack.com
    Instagram @reginablackwrites
    Threads @reginablackwrites